F/F
125

(69380°

CLOSED CIRCLE

By the same author
A LONELY PLACE TO DIE
STORE UP THE ANGER
DIVIDE THE NIGHT
KLARA'S VISITORS

CLOSED CIRCLE

by

Wessel Ebersohn

LONDON
VICTOR GOLLANCZ LTD
1990

First published in Great Britain in 1990
by Victor Gollancz Limited
14 Henrietta Street London WC2E 8QJ

British Library Cataloguing in Publication Data
Ebersohn, Wessel *1940*–
    Closed circle.
    I. Title
    823 [F]
    ISBN 0 575 04848 4

Typeset at The Spartan Press Ltd,
Lymington, Hants
Printed in Great Britain by St Edmundsbury Press Ltd
Bury St Edmunds, Suffolk

To Thurza
For all the years, those
past and those still to come

"Towards the accomplishment of an aim which in wantonness of malignity would seem to partake of the insane, he will direct a cool judgment, sagacious and sound."
Herman Melville

Prologue

"Who is it?" From where the child lay on the narrow cot in her bedroom she could hear her father's voice and the soft sucking sounds made by his bare feet on the tiled floor. "Who is it?" She had been about to get up to answer the knocking when she heard him coming from the kitchen.

He mumbled to himself as he passed her bedroom door. "Damn people. Who the hell can it be this time of night?" They knocked again. "Wait a minute. I'm coming." His voice sounded tired and irritable.

The child heard the sound of his feet and the soft grunting noises he made when he was tired. She heard his voice again. "Just a second. I'm . . . "

Then, without warning, the sound of an explosion, amplified by the hard surfaces in the hall and the shattering of glass, consumed every other sound.

For a moment the child was unable to move or call to her father. The house had become silent again. There had been the explosion and then nothing. She had not heard him cry out or move away from the door or fall. She waited, for a sound, his voice, any contact that would tell her that he was alive, that the explosion she had heard had not brought death with it. Daddy. The cry was inside her, rising to the front of her being, but unuttered. Daddy.

She could hear him. He was coming away from the door, but the pattern of his footsteps on the sprung wooden floor was ragged and irregular. Daddy, her soul said, but she made no sound and there was no possibility that she might be able to go to him. Daddy.

She heard him take a few hurried steps. At any moment she must see him as he drew level with the study door. He moved again and, as she listened to the sound of his approach and before she could yet move, he tried to speak. It was little more than a groan with a strange bubbling element in it, the sound of liquid being blown away by the pressure of his breath.

And now she could move. She reached the study door as her father fell, face downward, at her feet. Already a stream of blood was flowing from him across the floor. Kneeling next to him, she lifted and turned his head towards her so that it would rest on her lap. The back of his shirt was bloodied and she saw the place from which the blood seemed to be spreading reddening the front of his shirt.

She cradled his head in one arm while trying to lift his shoulders with the other. "It's all right, Daddy. I'm here," she told him. His shirt front was almost completely red now and she could feel the warmth of his blood where it ran down his chest on to her thighs. I must lift his head higher, she thought. Perhaps that will stop the blood. "I'm here, Daddy," she said. "I'm here."

His face too was covered in blood. Where's it coming from? the child wondered. There's no wound on his face. "It's all right, Daddy. You don't have to worry. I'm here with you." She used her handkerchief to wipe away the blood, trying to clear his eyes so that he would be able to see her. But the lids were slightly parted and only a thin strip of the whites showed.

How much do you bleed before you die? she asked herself. How much blood must there be on the floor? "It's all right, Daddy." She thought he tried to turn his head towards her and that the eyelids flickered. He can hear me, she thought. He knows I'm here. "It's all right, Daddy. It's all right."

On the floor the pool of blood had spread right round her, soaking into her nightdress. His eyelids were completely still. Perhaps they had not moved at all. She drew his head against her bosom, still wiping his face, then trying to clear the congealing blood that filled his mouth. For the first time she was the strong one and he the weak. It seemed to her that she had become the mother and he the child.

Someone was running through the house from the back. She looked up as Joyce came into the passage, wearing her old faded dressing-gown, fastened by a cord at the waist. The child was thirteen years old and Joyce some ten years older. She stopped as soon as she saw the man and the girl, reaching out to the wall for support. "Aah, Lindiwe. Aah, God." Her voice rose to a full-throated wail, a powerful note of anguish, free of all inhibition.

"There's been a letter bomb or something. I don't know." The child's voice was sure and firm. She was the strong one now. Tomorrow she might die, just remembering, but for the moment she was strong.

"Aah, Fellows. Poor Fellows."

The child was still clearing the blood from her father's mouth and wiping it away where it spilled on to his chin. The brown of his face was overlaid with grey and she could feel no movement in his chest. "I don't think he's going to live, Joyce. In fact I think he's dead already." There was a great calmness inside her. She could feel it controlling her, steadying her voice, as if an outside force was imposed upon her.

"Poor Fellows." Joyce was still a few steps away, unable to come closer, her voice threatening to run away out of control, every time she tried to speak.

"It's not like in the movies," the child heard herself say, "when you know if someone is dead. It happens so slowly that you don't know." The force inside held and steadied her. "Listen, Joyce, I want you to phone."

"Lindiwe. My God, who . . . "

"Listen, I want you to phone the hospital first. The number's on the list at the phone. Then my mother and the police."

"I'll go. What about you?"

"I'll stay with him."

"Aah God." Joyce went into the lounge to phone, her eyes held by the father and daughter until she had almost reached the door. Once in the other room she could be heard fumbling through the directory, having forgotten Lindiwe's instructions, dropping it once, then starting to dial. Her voice came faintly from the other room. "Hullo, please help. There's been a murder."

Lindiwe looked down at her father's face, the broad strong face she had loved so well. She knew that whether or not his heart was beating and his lungs working, his life had ended and not a beating heart or lungs that were still pumping the air could save him. She stopped wiping the blood away and held his head hard against her. Already the skin of his face was cold to the touch. "It's all right, Daddy," she said. "It's all right. Don't worry, Daddy. I'm with you."

Guy Fawkes. Fucking arseholes, it's Guy Fawkes, Lionel Bensch's mind told him in the moment before he rose to full consciousness. Fucking arseholes.

The smell of the gunpowder was strong in the room, but it was the sound that overwhelmed the senses. He rolled out of bed and looked for Daisy. She was sitting upright against the pillows, her eyes wide and facing the window. Lunging forward, he grabbed her by the arm and pulled her to the floor next to him.

"What is it, Lionel?" she asked. "It smells like firecrackers."

In the faint light from the window he could see her face. It was a lovely face, often uncertain, and now it looked frightened. Lionel realized how badly he wanted to go on living, at least until they had fixed everything between them. "Stay on the floor," he shouted at her. Then he was crawling towards the door, still shouting. "Willie, Wendy, stay in your rooms. Don't come out."

The gun fire seemed to roll on and on as if it was never going to stop, each detonation merging with the next. He heard the front door shatter under the impact of the bullets. Fucking arseholes, he thought, as long as the kids stay in their rooms they'll be okay. "Kids, you don't come out."

The noise stopped abruptly, leaving the night quieter than had seemed possible, a stillness more complete than any he had ever heard. It was interrupted by the sound of a car moving off in the street outside, fading to join the more distant sounds of the city, sounds that Lionel could also hear now. "Willie, Wendy," he called. He was still down on his hands and knees.

14

"Can we come out, Lionel?" his son asked. The boy's voice was pitched higher than his normal treble.

"No. Stay in your room. Sit on the floor. Wendy?"

"It's all right, Lionel. I'm on the floor."

"Good. Stay there until I tell you." In a crouching run he crossed the room to the wardrobe. It took him only a few seconds to get the shotgun out of its cover and load it. The bastards, he was thinking. Twice in one year, the bastards. Please God, he prayed, let them still be outside.

From the place next to the bed where Lionel had left her, Daisy was watching him, her eyes wide with shock. "Are you going outside?" she asked.

"Stay here, I'm going to make sure . . ."

"Be careful, Lionel."

"Stay on the floor," he told her.

Lionel ran in a low crouch all the way to the back door, leapt the steps and reached the front of the house in the darkness of the sidepath. He stopped at the front corner for a few seconds before crossing the narrow lawn and going through the gate into the street. A man was coming towards him from the other side, rocking from side to side with a stiff-legged old-man stride. "Lionel". It was old Taljaart who had just had the open heart operation. "I heard them going," he was saying. "I heard their car. Did you see them?"

"If I'd seen one I would have plugged him," Lionel said.

"I heard them. Myrtle is phoning the cops."

Lionel turned back to the house. "I just want to tell Daisy and the kids they can come out. Fucking arseholes. Twice this year. The bastards."

The sky was light with the approaching dawn, but the streets were still in shadow and the few cars on the highway were all using their headlights. Dahlia drove slowly. Her body felt warm and lethargic, remnants of the previous evening's lovemaking and the interrupted early morning sleep.

She left the highway to pick up the suburban artery that wound slowly down the long hill towards the south of the city. Up ahead a police van came out of a side street and moved away from her, travelling in the same direction. She saw the van's brake lights come on as it slowed for a traffic light. It stopped only long enough to ensure that the road was clear before going through the red light to follow the route she would be taking. After that she saw them once more when they slowed at a corner, apparently searching for an address, before she stopped behind them in the drive of her own home.

One of the policemen, a young man with the body of an older one, his uniform straining across his bulging stomach, got out of the van and started towards her, blinking in the car's lights. She recognized him as one of those who had come to the house on past occasions. At the top of the stairs with one hand on the veranda rail and the other pressed to her throat Beryl was standing with her back to the lighted doorway.

Before Dahlia got out of the car she knew. She could not see Beryl's face, but it was there in the way she was standing and in the policeman's expression as he raised a hand to shield his eyes against the lights. She opened the car door and slipped her feet to the ground. Beryl shrieked from the top of the stairs, a sudden hysterical cry, almost a warning. "They kidnapped Ray. They took him."

The policeman turned to look at Beryl before stopping in front of Dahlia. "Mrs Baker . . . " His voice was formal and under strain, crackling slightly, a brittle sound. "Will you come? We found your husband. He's down by the old cycle track . . . " The policeman – she could not think of his name although she knew she had heard it – had not said that Ray was dead. He had stopped speaking and stepped back for her to pass, not knowing how to proceed. "Mrs Baker . . . " he tried again.

She came to his assistance. "I'll take my car. You drive ahead."

"I'm coming." It was Beryl's voice, breathless and agonized.

"No," Dahlia said. She had no need at this moment for Beryl's determined compassion. "I'll go alone."

As she got back into the car, Dahlia heard the other woman's voice again, the words coming in sharp staccato bursts. "I didn't know where you were. I couldn't phone."

The policeman drove slowly, making it easy for her to follow, down to the road that led into the top of Chatsworth, past the school and a thin unkempt banana grove, its ragged fronds gaunt in the gathering light, finally through a small suburban shopping centre, the pavements showing the day's first signs of life, and through the rusted wire gateway of the old cycle track. A second police van and a car, both empty, were parked at the foot of the overgrown mound on which the concrete track, now cracked and derelict, had been built.

The two policemen got out of the van and waited awkwardly for her to join them. "On the other side . . ." The same one spoke and again he seemed unable to finish what he had started to say. He walked ahead up a narrow footpath to the top of the mound with Dahlia following and the other man coming behind.

From the top she could see the long grey oval of the track and on the far side three men standing around Ray's body. The feet seemed to be neatly together, his arms at his sides, as if waiting to be inspected.

Why are they taking me to him? she wondered. Not for identification. They don't need me for identification.

She started over the gravel in the centre of the track and saw all three turn to face her. On either side and behind her she heard the two who had fetched her, their feet crunching the loose gravel surface. All warmth and lethargy had left her body now. Her skin felt cold and numb, her joints stiff.

Why do I feel nothing? she asked herself. Ray is lying there on the concrete and yet I feel nothing. It's not right, she thought. I should feel something.

Fellows Ngcube, Lionel Bensch and Ray Baker had all lived most of their lives in the same warm, outwardly placid seaside town. None of them had ever met the others. Each had ignored some of their society's most guarded precepts. And for that their names had come together on the same list, to be measured for the same punishment.

Part 1: THE CIRCLE

Johannesburg, Pretoria and Durban,
September 1984

One

Blythe Stevens disconnected the telephone, dropping the plug into the wastepaper basket. "You can't be too careful," he said. "But I suppose you know more about that than I do?" It was said as a question, his raised eyebrows giving his face a cunning appearance.

Coming down the passage from the lift, Yudel Gordon had passed a row of untidy offices, the walls covered by strident, often lurid, political posters. A number of equally untidy young men, both black and white, at a disparate collection of desks and tables, were either bent earnestly over sheaves of paper or just sitting and talking. "What sort of place is this?" he asked.

Stevens was only momentarily surprised by the question. "A publishing house. We are publishers." Yudel did not pursue the matter. He contrived only to look at the other man in what was intended to be a questioning way. "We publish a lot of black writing," Stevens continued. "Of course we have to do a lot to it, polish it up . . . " He paused, possibly feeling that he had already said too much. "Most of their writing is pretty good though, considering the inferior standard of their schools." None of his pronouncements were coming out well. He went on to other matters. "We heard about you. I have friends who know you, mutual friends . . . "

Yudel did not try to guess. He had many acquaintances in the academies, none whom he would have classified as friends.

"I've been assured that you are just the man for the job." He spoke in a hearty accepting manner that seemed to have as its purpose to show Yudel that he was trusted. Stevens was pressing himself back in his sprung chair by means of a denim-covered knee that stuck out above the surface of the desk. It was a practised posture, structured to look relaxed, bohemian and masculine. Yudel had little doubt that the impression created was often successful. The publisher was wearing a shirt that was open at the neck and a crinkled red neckerchief knotted at his throat. The clothing was as much a part of the careful production as the posture and the hearty tone of voice. "There's only one thing that my principals may find a problem, the fact that you work for the government." The eyebrows were raised again, suggesting that this was a difficulty Yudel needed to clear up. "That may be a problem." The doubt in his voice was deliberate. He looked at Yudel, waiting for a reply, and Yudel looked back at him curiously, without saying anything. Stevens's expression slowly changed to a frown. "You don't think it will be a problem then?"

"Mister Stevens . . . " Yudel started.

"Blythe. Please call me Blythe. And may I call you Yudel?" The question was followed by an expansive gesture of his hands that, in common with so much about the man, may have been practised before a mirror.

"By all means," Yudel said. "Blythe," he tried the name cautiously. He would have preferred Mister Stevens, but Blythe seemed to be unavoidable. "Blythe, I don't know what you want me to do. You didn't tell me much on the telephone . . . "

Stevens assumed his most doubtful expression. "Well, you know about the telephone . . . "

Yudel did know about the telephone. "I also don't know who your principals are."

"Ah." He got to his feet, crossed the small office in a few long strides and closed the door that led to the adjoining room. "As I said before, you can't be too careful."

Blythe Stevens was a tall man, almost a foot taller than Yudel's five and a half feet. He was broad in the shoulder and carried no excess weight. His face was strong, the cheekbones high and broad, the eyes deep-set and the chin square. Reinforced by the carefully chosen clothing and the practised gestures, Stevens's presence at a first meeting was impressive. He sat down again and rocked himself back into his original position, the denim-covered knee wedged against the desk as before. "My principals want to keep a very low profile, very low."

"Perhaps you should tell me what they want me to do then."

"Ah." He looked speculatively at Yudel, perhaps doubting that he should confide in him at all, or at least trying to make Yudel realize that such a doubt was possible. "As I said before, it could be that your working for the government might be a problem." When Yudel again did not respond he went on. "You are no doubt aware that a number of radical leaders have suffered attacks of various kinds in recent years. I am talking about politically motivated assaults and murders, the so-called Argentine option." The eyes had narrowed and he was looking at Yudel searchingly, apparently trying to read his reaction. Again the expression looked rehearsed. "Of course we know who is responsible, but we must have proof . . . "

For a moment Yudel's thoughts slipped away from Blythe Stevens and his careful posturing. He knew something of the world to which Stevens was referring, not very much, but enough to know that he would prefer to avoid it. Unbidden images returned momentarily to his mind, a bleeding unconscious priest in the dark highveld night, running for his life through burning maize lands . . . It was a world he would rather have left behind. "Finding proof is the responsibility of the CID," he found himself saying.

"Not in this case. In this case they're outranked." The cunning look was back, the eyebrows raised, waiting for Yudel's reaction. Eventually he found himself forced to continue. "We know that the security police are behind this. What we need is to be able to prove it."

Yudel did not want to hear this. He had experience of the security police and theirs was also a world he would rather have left behind. The memory of a woman struggling for breath in a dark cell was somewhere far in the back of his mind, as was the memory of the broken man in the cell next to hers.

"We have been led to believe that you have the talents that would be needed. We want you to get us the proof."

Yudel looked at the man seated on the other side of the desk.

His request had been put as if it was an ordinary thing to ask, something that would cause no special surprise. He was telling Yudel that he wanted him to find evidence with which to convict members of the security police on charges of murder and assault and, the way he had said it, it had seemed to be an entirely mundane matter.

Stevens misread Yudel's silence. "Of course we're willing to pay. My principals have mentioned a figure of twenty-five thousand rands."

Yudel put the security police behind him. He thought about the twenty-five thousand rands. He had payments on his car, the house, the washing-machine and his wife, Rosa's trip to the Seychelles a year before. To a prison psychologist, earning two thousand rands a month, this was more than a year's salary. He had never before been offered money for his work on murders. In most cases his assistance to the CID had been of an informal and fairly haphazard nature. And he was, after all, a civil servant. You did not pay employees of the state for doing their duty.

Money had always been a problem to Yudel. He had never managed it well, never earned very much of it and never anticipated possessing assets that amounted to much of it. Twenty-five thousand rands would solve a lot of problems, pay a lot of hire purchase agreements. It would also improve Rosa's disposition towards him. Compared to her many relatives, she and Yudel were poor. This was something that was never far from her mind. He knew that it was not so much that his earnings were lower than she would have liked, but that with his qualifications he could have done so well in private practice. Rosa had never understood his working for a government department. The money would solve problems of every sort.

"Of course there'll be far more in it for you than just money. You'd be protecting people, very fine people . . . " Stevens was still talking, but Yudel was not enthusiastic about the new direction of the conversation.

"What would I have to do to get this money?"

"We want proof that will lead to public exposure. We don't expect convictions. Naturally we'll only pay for results."

"Naturally," Yudel sighed. "What about expenses?"

"Oh yes, yes . . . " Stevens moved uncomfortably in his chair and tried to drop his voice still lower. "I'm sure we can arrange something."

Twenty-five thousand rands, Yudel was thinking.

"We have no doubt where you are going to find them. We have a comprehensive file that you can take with you if you decide to help us." He paused and gave Yudel his cunning look. "And to help yourself, of course."

Something about Stevens's sudden emphasis on the money drove Yudel's thoughts away from it and towards a more sober consideration of the task. "What happens if I discover that it's not the Special Branch who are behind it?"

Yudel could see by the look on Stevens's face that he had not even considered the possibility. "We're quite sure it's them."

"If I find proof that it is not the security police, do I still get the money?"

Stevens shrugged. "Well, I suppose you do. Of course." It was not said with a great deal of conviction. "But we are quite sure that it is them. The pattern is always the same. Someone of the Left is in trouble with the security police, then a few days later there is an attack. None of these crimes ever get solved. The whole thing is a conspiracy to stifle real opposition. They want to intimidate the people who want genuine radical change in this country. We know all about them." Stevens's voice had risen to a more normal pitch, some of the pretence had disappeared and he was getting into his stride. "One of our own staff members, Robin Du Plessis, has personal experience of the security police. Robin is right in your parish at this moment, Zonderwater prison, for refusing to give evidence in a trial involving one of our writers."

Yudel looked at Stevens. He was unsure about the man and afraid of the task, but the money . . . "You realize," he said, "that it is probably not just one person who is responsible."

Stevens nodded. He was looking closely at Yudel. "We are sure that it is a group," he said.

It was starting to get dark as Yudel left the publisher's office. The late afternoon traffic was flowing strongly, side streets and main arteries crowded with jostling manoeuvring cars, their headlights already switched on. He walked quickly along Jorrissen street, Blythe Stevens's file under his arm, up the steep slope of the hill to the place below the civic theatre where his car was parked.

Never before had he been paid for his work on a homicide. Where he had helped the CID, his bosses had seen it as nothing more than inter-departmental co-operation. Most often he had been led by his own interest. Twenty-five thousand rands. He allowed his mind to dwell on the money one last time, then he dismissed it from his thinking. If he was going to make any sort of decision on this, one that was not going to be completely foolish, he would have to leave the twenty-five thousand out of the reckoning.

Down the hill below and behind him was the Braamfontein business centre, a part of central Johannesburg. Many of its offices were occupied by businesses or organizations the function of which was communicating knowledge to other human beings. There were advertising houses, commercial artists, public relations companies, graphic designers, printers, typesetters, publishers of books and periodicals, film makers, little shops that made a business out of photo-copying, editing houses and a few small newspapers. Among these a surprising number were driven by political motives: liberal, socialist, trade union and religious; they ran small newspapers or information leaflets, published books and arranged seminars, all of which had the same purpose, to persuade the nation of Apartheid's evils.

Beyond the business centre, stretching right down the far side of the ridge to the edge of Parktown, was the largest liberal establishment of all, the University of the Witwatersrand – Wits to anyone who had anything to do with it. It was out of this section of South African Society, from among the people who worked in these organizations, that the victims would come. The editors, lecturers, writers, trade unionists who might one day go too far, upset some unspecified sensibility, cross an invisible threshold, cause an offence that could not be overlooked: they would come from places like this.

Yudel found his car, got into the driver's seat and sat quietly for a few minutes before he started for home.

Two

By the time Yudel reached home Rosa was in the kitchen, preparing to dish up the evening meal. As soon as she saw him she smiled. This was not altogether usual. It was a moment before he remembered the reason for her apparent goodwill. His meeting with Blythe Stevens had replaced the evening's gathering in his mind. "I was afraid you might be late," she said.

Yudel returned her smile. "I'll wash and change my shirt."

"Give me a kiss first." She pouted her lips and half-closed her eyes. It was an expression that was intended to be seductive.

Yudel looked interestedly at her before kissing her briefly on the lips. Down the years he had always refused invitations to address learned gatherings. That he had finally accepted such an invitation had been entirely at Rosa's insistence. She had felt that if he would not make the money of which he was capable, he could at least allow himself a modest degree of celebrity.

"Mother's here," Rosa said. "She's coming with us tonight." Yudel looked enquiringly at his wife. The occasion had not seemed to warrant a family outing. "Irena and Hymie will meet us there. Dad can't make it though. He's in Cape Town buying the site for a factory."

"Rosa, I don't know if this is necessary . . . " he started to say.

"Nonsense. You must have something to eat before going."

Rosa's mother was in the living room, drinking whiskey out of a short broad glass. Like her daughter, she smiled at him as he came into the room, but unlike the undiluted enthusiasm on Rosa's face there was a sardonic element here. "The man of the moment," she said. She was small, lean, close to seventy and she reminded Yudel of an angry farmyard hen.

He could not decide whether or not he was being goaded. "How are you, Mom?" he asked.

"I'm well." She rose to her feet and received his kiss on her cheek. She stepped back and looked carefully at him. "You aren't a bit overweight, are you, Yudel?"

"Not so far as I know."

"It's probably that liquorice you're always eating."

"I like liquorice, but I'm not always eating it."

"You can substitute anything oral for it." Her expression had become serious and she was imparting the information as if this was something Yudel needed badly to know.

For the first ten years of his marriage Rosa's mother had asked Yudel's advice continually for what she regarded as her friends' problems. Unthinkingly, he had given it. And in the course of those years, as her reputation among her friends had grown, she had forgotten the source of her knowledge. She began substituting her own suggestions for Yudel's and lately she had been giving Yudel advice on what she considered his problems to be. "Anything oral," she said. "You could take up smoking for instance."

"I'll bear it in mind," he told her. He was backing towards the door. "I'd better get ready."

Dinner consisted of a vegetarian pie. Rosa had been reading books about vegetarianism lately and slowly (unobtrusively, she would have said) meat had been disappearing from their dishes. This was not something that bothered Yudel. He knew that new fashions in Rosa's cooking seldom lasted for more than a few weeks. Apart from which she had the skills necessary to disguise the absence of meat. He also knew that to discuss these things with Rosa often served only to anger her. On a previous occasion she had decided to take all her recipes from a book recommended by a famous woman tennis player. When Yudel had remarked that the food did not taste bad, but it had done nothing for his backhand, Rosa had not spoken to him for two days.

She was eating quickly and looking happily at Yudel. "How many people do you think will be there?"

Yudel was thinking about making the sixty kilometre drive to Johannesburg a second time on the same day. He sighed. "Before midnight, I hope."

"How many people? I asked how many people?"

Yudel glanced at her. "Not many, I should think."

"I'm sure there will be many," Rosa said. She seemed a little offended.

"Definitely," her mother said, nodding determinedly at Yudel. "There'll definitely be a lot of people. Apart from those university people Rosa has seen to it that the whole family will be there."

Yudel looked from one of the women to the other, then gave the vegetarian pie his attention. If only they would not look at him, as if he was trying to sabotage their evening.

The meeting of the university Psychology Society was held in a lecture hall below ground level in a new concrete building. Rosa and her mother had been right. Close to three hundred people were crowded into a room intended for little more than half that number. Most of them were students, young people dressed in denim trousers, sweaters, unironed ankle-length dresses, sandals, boots, tennis shoes with or without socks, leather and canvas jackets, collarless shirts: arranged in every possible combination, often seeming to have been carefully selected to form a striking disunity with the other garments being worn. Scattered among the students were university faculty members, the men wearing shabby unkempt suits and the women dresses that might have been borrowed from the students. They were people who, like Yudel, gave little thought to appearance. All had found larger interests. Apart from the students and lecturers there were practising psychologists, journalists, lay men and women, and Rosa's relatives, seventeen of them.

Rosa was sitting in the front row and regretting the fact. She would have liked to be further back where she could see the faces of those in the audience. Occasionally she would glance down the row in which she was sitting, but that was less than satisfying. All she could see was her mother on one side and her sister, Irena, on the other and both were paying careful attention.

The chairman of the society, a fat fifty-year-old professor of

29

psychology in a rumpled suit and faded bow tie, had introduced Yudel as "the famous criminologist", a description that had caused Rosa to blush with pleasure, her mother to nudge her in the ribs with her elbow and Irena to nod solemnly. Yudel had begun hesitantly, his hands folded tightly in front of him, but as he became more deeply involved with his subject his awareness of the audience receded, his hands had unclasped and he gestured freely as he talked.

"The criminal world is a sub-culture," he had started, "and this has to be borne in mind when rehabilitation attempts are made. Most often if you teach a career criminal to be a bricklayer you have not turned him into one. What you now have is a criminal who is also a bricklayer.

"The true criminal is part of a separate group in rebellion against conventional society. Teaching him a skill in no way changes his essential view of life. It is this view that has to be challenged. Without that the most enlightened prisons stand to produce more sophisticated and better trained criminals . . . "

At one point a thin blond man had interrupted him to tell him that this was so much clap-trap, that he had no facts or figures to support it and that Yudel's ideas flew in the face of civilized liberal thinking. When the chairman had been unable to make the man sit down Rosa had joined battle and asked him how many criminals he knew. A male student had answered that he knew only the inmates of Italian One. The audience had laughed, the blond man had sat down and Yudel had heard Rosa's mother whisper hoarsely, "Well done. The cheeky little devil."

But the blond man had raised the point that Yudel felt lay at the centre of liberal society's failure to understand the criminal. He spoke directly to him. "The premise that if you treat people well they will respond favourably and if you treat them badly they will respond aggressively is an over-simplification. If aggression is only a response to frustration and injustice, I'd like to know what it was the Jewish people did to Nazi Germany. I'd also like to know what injustices civil rights activists murdered in our own society had inflicted on their killers to provoke such aggression." He paused for no more than a moment before returning to his subject. "What I am suggesting is not that criminals should not be

30

given study opportunities in prison or that they should not be taught skills, but that these alone have no rehabilitative effect . . ."

Yudel spoke for more than an hour. At the end of that time there were many questions, from students and lecturers alike. Some sacred prejudices had been affected and he had not expected to get away with that lightly. The blond man had tried to put another question, but more irreverent student applause had taken the edge off what he wanted to say.

When the meeting was over Yudel found himself surrounded by the society's chairman who kept saying that "it was so good of you to come" and Rosa's relatives, most of whom had just acquired the need to shake his hand. Irena took the opportunity to kiss him. She rarely missed such a chance.

"Who was that horrible man?" Rosa asked the chairman.

"I'm terribly sorry about that," the chairman told her. "He's a lecturer in the Italian department."

"Italian," she said. "The nerve."

By the time Yudel got outside the lecture hall most of the crowd had left. Rosa and her relatives were already climbing the broad wooden stairway to the front of the building, Rosa's mother giving her opinion on some aspect of the criminal mind and a few of the others nodding. "This is the first time in years that we've had anything on criminals," the chairman was saying.

Standing directly across the passage were a group of young men dressed in the same haphazard, apparently casual fashion of those who had attended the lecture. The one who spoke had a bush of crinkly brown hair, not too different from Yudel's own, but considerably greater in volume. His face was round and puffy, his eyes partially hidden by the swelling around them and revealing a suspicion of Yudel and what he stood for. He looked too old to be a student. "Mister Gordon, why are you taking the job?" he asked.

Yudel stopped to look at him, unsure as to the wisdom of answering, but knowing immediately which job he was talking about. The chairman looked from the group to Yudel and back again.

"Why did you take it? You're a government man, aren't you?"

Yudel knew what they wanted to hear, what they would believe regardless of what he told them. "The money," he said. "I'm doing it for the money."

He turned and started up the stairs, the chairman a few steps behind. Outside Rosa and the others were already moving in the direction of the car park. The money, he had said. Until that moment he had not realized that he was going to do it. The realization was disturbing, but not so disturbing as the knowledge that Blythe Stevens's secret was no secret at all.

Three

At the desk in his study Yudel started reading what Blythe Stevens had called a pretty comprehensive file. He found it to be little more than a collection of newspaper clippings and the names and addresses of some of the victims of attacks. A few typed pages, the work of different typewriters, were attached to some of the clippings.

For Rosa and her mother the excitement of the meeting had not yet dissipated. For a while he heard them, their voices still animated despite the lateness of the hour, fading only as his attention was absorbed by what he was reading. The early clippings began some twenty years before, dealing with attacks on members of the Liberal Party, a small idealistic group that had been led by a famous South African writer, but had not survived the middle Sixties. Yudel read about car windows being smashed, printing machinery damaged, offices burnt, shots fired into activists' homes, a prominent member questioned by the security police on one day and having a Molotov cocktail thrown through her bedroom window on the next.

The next batch was general, not relating to a specific case, and Yudel passed quickly over reports of iron filings and sand being poured into motor car engines, smoke bombs being thrown into meetings and petrol bombs against the walls of houses, anonymous threatening letters, shots fired at homes, family pets killed and left hanging on the front door, a fire being started in a church hall, more petrol bombs, telephone threats, smashed windscreens and slashed tyres, bricks hurled through windows, signs written on victims' homes with messages like "nigger lover", "Communist den" and "Jew" and more threats, more fire bombs, more wildly fired bullets.

Yudel took another wad of clippings from the file. Before he started reading he became suddenly and unexpectedly aware that there was someone in the room with him. "Ah . . . " The sound was involuntary.

It was only Rosa. She smiled. "Did I give you a fright?"

"Ah," Yudel said. This time it was a slower, long-drawn sound and he nodded in answer to her question.

"You were engrossed in your reading."

He nodded again and smiled at her. His impulse was to ask what it was she wanted, but he realized that would be unwise. Since he had announced his acceptance of the speaking engagement Rosa had been more favourably disposed towards him. It was not a situation that he wanted to put at risk.

"I was wondering," she said. She had not sat down and it was clear that she felt that she was intruding. "The meeting . . . what did they pay?"

"They don't pay for meetings of that sort."

"Oh . . . " Rosa was clearly disappointed. Being a celebrity was fine, but it was obviously not right that they did not pay.

"Societies of that sort are little more than informal groups, funded by contributions from their members, most of whom are students and academics. There isn't any money to speak of in their treasuries."

"It was a good speech," Rosa said determinedly, as if that settled something.

"Thank you," Yudel said modestly.

"You're making fun of me, Yudel." She spoke almost girlishly.

Yudel thought he saw the faintest trace of a blush cross her face. If addressing a learned society was going to have that sort of effect on her he should do it more often. He wondered vaguely who else there was who might invite him.

Rosa's eye caught the file of newspaper clippings, a file quite unlike those he normally brought home. "What's that?"

He considered for a moment. The thought of keeping Rosa in her present state of mind almost had him invent a story.

Reluctantly he acknowledged to himself that sooner or later she would have to know. "I've been offered an investigation," he told her.

Rosa did not look enthusiastic. "What does Freek want now?"

He shook his head and smiled slightly at the mention of his friend's name. "It's not Freek. It's a private group."

Rosa's eyes widened and she sat down. "A private group."

"They're offering twenty-five thousand rands."

Rosa leant against the desk. Her pupils had become rigid as if with shock. "What do you have to do?" she asked softly.

Yudel told her.

While he spoke the look on her face changed. "Don't do it," she said when he had finished.

"We could use the money."

Rosa's eyes rolled upwards in helpless supplication. They could certainly use the money. "The people . . . the ones who get attacked . . . "

"The victims."

"The victims. They have dealings with those other people . . . " Rosa's own brief experience with the security police had frightened her so much that she was barely able to talk about them.

"I'll be trying to help the police . . . "

"What if those people did it?"

Yudel looked at her. The twenty-five thousand was of no importance. Rosa's eyes were dark, the irises almost black, and set deep, adding a peculiar intensity to her expression. Yudel knew that he had often been unfair to her. When she nagged him about their shortage of money what she felt was anxiety, not greed. Now there was the possibility of a fairly large amount and she had immediately said that he should not do it. It was true that she was afraid for herself, but she also feared for him.

"You want to do it." It was not a question. In some respects she knew him well. After more than twenty years together she knew and understood some of Yudel's needs better than he did himself. At this moment she could see that he needed the stimulation that the investigation would afford. It was the facet of his personality that she found hardest to come to terms with. "If you must, then do it," she said. She left the room without looking back.

Yudel sat still with the file open in front of him, but not looking at it. After a few minutes he left the study to find that the bedroom door was closed, which probably meant that Rosa was inside and did not want his company. Giving up the idea of talking to her, which had not been a strong one in the first place, he went to the kitchen and made himself coffee. Coffee was the remedy Yudel sought in all crises, his source of relaxation in good times and a way to pass the time on unremarkable days. But today the coffee solved nothing. He had taken the job. And Rosa would have to find a way of dealing with it.

He went back to the clippings. The dates on the incidents were within the last ten years now. An anonymous letter writer had threatened a black trade unionist with death. An elderly woman who had spent twenty years living under a restriction order had been in her lounge when the windows had been blasted away by buckshot. In East London, a small coastal city, shotguns had been fired into the houses of a number of liberal and black political leaders. In Durban a time bomb had blown away the garage door of a politician's house. In Johannesburg the offices of the Institute of Race Relations had been set alight. Then across the border in Mozambique, six or seven hundred kilometres from Johannesburg, a prominent member of the Communist Party had been killed by a letter bomb. A single report told of a black activist being shot at in a city street, arrested by the security police two days later and found hanging in his cell shortly after that.

He picked a leaflet, compiled by a group that called themselves Delta Four, out of the file. Its purpose was to defame a liberal professor of law at Wits. He glanced through it quickly, then reread it carefully. According to its contents the professor was a Communist sympathiser. But it was the detail the leaflet contained that drew Yudel's attention keenly. For the first time he could see signs of what might be an organization. The information was too detailed to have come from a casual observer.

Another incident reinforced the impression. A gang of masked thugs had attacked a religious commune called the Attic. According to the report in the file there had been both blacks and whites among the attackers, a fact that suggested to Yudel that black mercenaries had been used. He would need to visit the Attic, if it still existed.

Two more sections dealt with the rare cases that had been brought to a successful conclusion by the police. In one, a small group whose members had obviously been influenced by some of Hollywood's worst products had been convicted of arson and firing at the home of the parliamentary leader of the opposition. In another a group of Italian immigrants, who had remained loyal to Benito Mussolini forty years after that protagonist of military glory had run out of luck, had been convicted of placing bombs in the offices of the country's only liberal political party.

A typed sheet listed two deaths and a few non-fatal motor car accidents where no second car had been involved. Cars had mysteriously left straight sections of road, refusing to respond to the controls. A black priest, who had resisted the removal of a clan to which he belonged to a barren rural area, and a white minister of the Dutch Reformed Church, who had preferred to serve a black congregation, had died in this way. The reports said nothing of what had been wrong with the cars, but Yudel could imagine steering linkages working themselves loose, the hydraulic fluid of the braking system leaking away: neither would be difficult to accomplish for an even moderately skilled mechanic. The hard part was getting them to break down at the right moment.

By the time Yudel stopped reading it was almost three o'clock. Perhaps a third of the file was still untouched. He flicked through the unread section. Most of it seemed to concern the killing of a trade unionist and that of an attorney who had appeared in political trials, both from Durban, as well as attempted assassinations of others in the same city. With its easy, winterless sub-tropical climate it was not a place where you would have expected to find extremism of any sort.

Two points had become clear to him. The police record of solving these cases was astonishingly poor and many of the attacks had been either immediately preceded or followed by a visit from the security police. Yudel accepted the knowledge reluctantly. He did not want to discover links to any branch of the police, but especially not that one.

He wondered what it was the assailants had in common, and could isolate only one point. They probably all felt threatened by the activities of the victims. But this knowledge was too wide and too vague to be of any use.

And the victims, what linked them? Of all the passionate civil rights workers breathing fire and indignation, the social scientists working out one fresh constitutional plan after the other, none of which would ever be employed, the black consciousness advocates who by a complex system of reasoning had decided that the hatred they felt for whites was not racialistic, the Marxist intellectuals who were going to save the country right after the revolution but seemed intent on destroying it in the meantime, the trade unionists who wanted to drive off overseas investors but did not want their members to lose jobs, the students who had redirected their resentment of their parents until it was now aimed at society, the religious objectors who had long since forgotten the religious roots of their rebellion: out of every kind of dissident, the thousands of active anti-government and anti-apartheid campaigners, what was special about those who had been attacked?

Perhaps it was they who had something in common, not their attackers. Perhaps Stevens had purposefully pointed him in the wrong direction. But why hire an investigator if you did not want him to succeed?

Rosa's mother, never a good sleeper, was sitting in front of the lifeless television set. She had her feet on a stool and was tilting back her head to blow a stream of cigarette smoke straight up at the ceiling. She raised her head as Yudel came in. "Oh," she said. "Rosa's gone to bed." Yudel nodded and turned to leave. "She's feeling very miserable," the cigarette-ravaged voice went on. He could hear the accusation in it. "You were secluded in there a long time." At the last remark her voice had adopted a jeering tone. It was not something that required answering, except perhaps in her eyes. He left without saying anything. Her inability to draw him into arguments was the cause of some strain between Yudel and his mother-in-law.

He found Rosa asleep in the centre of the bed. She was lying on her back and breathing through her mouth. In the half-light from the door, the dark-eyed belligerent front that Rosa adopted for the benefit of the world was gone. In sleep her face looked troubled and uncertain. As Yudel watched he saw the muscles on one side of her face twitch and her whole body jerk. He sat down on the edge of the bed, resting a hand on her shoulder, hoping that the contact would reassure her.

So often in the years of their marriage she had tried to persuade him to leave the department and go into private practice. She had never understood what kept him there. As she saw it Yudel had always chosen his convicts before her. Tonight she had surprised him. She had understood that he needed to take the job and had made no objection at all. This time it was he who was not understanding her.

He got into bed and closed his eyes to sleep, but before unconsciousness reached him, his mind had filled with the one previous occasion on which he had seen the worst side of the security police. He remembered the calm assurance that all power was theirs, the certainty that no one would be able to resist them. Yudel knew that in many ways they were typical white South African men. They shared the same fear of the great, voteless, barely literate, prolifically breeding black tide that seemed certain to engulf them all sooner or later, as other white men and women did. They shared the same hopes for their children and the same unspoken dread that these hopes could not be realized. But in them these feelings had become exaggerated. Fear had become obsession and hope had become tortured determination. He knew also that everywhere in the world the power that was given to such men attracted those most eager and least fit to use it.

He would have got up again, perhaps gone through to the kitchen to get another cup of coffee, but fear of disturbing Rosa kept him from moving. It was a long time before Yudel fell asleep.

Four

"Doctor Williamson?" Yudel said as he opened the door.

As soon as he could see into the office he knew that the time between knocking and entering had been too short. Doctor Williamson was coming away from a mirror that had been positioned so that the curtains normally hid it. He was still in the act of returning his comb to his jacket pocket. The thin layer of hair that was required to hide the large bald area on the top of his head had not yet been properly arranged, exposing patches of smooth gleaming scalp of uneven widths. "Oh, Yudel, come in."

Yudel detected a small flicker of annoyance in his eyes. The relationship between Doctor Williamson's dignity and the strands of hair in question was curiously close. "I'm going to take you to the brigadier," he said. He waited for the look of surprise to register on Yudel's face and Yudel obliged. "What have you been up to this time?" he asked, clicking his tongue reprovingly against the roof of his mouth.

"You tell me," Yudel said. He was thinking about Blythe Stevens and the twenty-five thousand rands. Technically it was against the rules for civil servants to add to their earnings privately. It was a regulation that was widely ignored and not likely to be enforced in Yudel's case either, but the manner in which he was to earn it was another matter entirely.

Doctor Williamson led Yudel down the passage to the lift they would take to the top floor where the brigadier had his office. The old psychologist's right hand made a quick pass over the top of his head in a vain attempt to correct the damage Yudel had caused. "Dear, dear, Yudel, you're always up to something, aren't you?" He was trying hard to look stern, but Yudel detected an element in his manner that was not altogether genuine. "I wish you'd learn to conform."

Brigadier De Beer's secretary ushered them straight into an office that by the size of the carpet on the floor, the glass top on the desk and the sculpted corners of the bookcase was designed to demonstrate clearly the difference in status between himself and the members of his staff. "Yudel," he said, "what have you been up to?" It was so like Doctor Williamson's reaction that they might have rehearsed it.

"Good morning, sir," Yudel said.

De Beer wore the uniform of the department. He was a little over sixty, just about twenty years Yudel's senior and still thought of him as a rather irresponsible junior. He was a genial man, his tanned face almost completely unlined, but his hair a deep steel-grey with almost no sign of its original black. He was a member of the influential secret organization, the Afrikaner Broederbond, a fact that had something to do with the regular promotions that had punctuated his career. He was also a leading figure in the reform programme that had done much to improve the country's prisons in the previous twenty years. In merit meetings he had always been Yudel's main defender. His remarks had come back to Yudel via fourth- and fifth-hand leaks. "I know he's a Jew," De Beer was alleged to have said on more than one occasion, "but when you get a good Jew, let me tell you, he's very good. And Yudel is a good Jew." He was approaching Yudel round the side of the desk and grinning at him. Suddenly he took Yudel's hand and shook it. "The very best of luck," he said. "From today you hold the rank of senior professional officer. Very well deserved, very well . . . shake this man's hand, Bill."

Then Yudel's hand was being shaken by Doctor Williamson who was telling him that it was "a good show, Yudel, a very good show."

Yudel looked from one to the other. Years before he had given up the idea of further promotions, reluctantly accepting the opinion of friends that he was far too unconventional to become a successful civil servant. Only the pleasure on the faces of the other

41

two men assured him now that this was real. "I'm surprised," he said. "I didn't think that I was in line for promotion."

"Sit down, Yudel. Take a seat. This doesn't happen every day. Have a cigarette."

Yudel accepted the cigarette and sat down. He was a social smoker in the same way that some people are social drinkers. On the rare occasions on which he could not avoid a social gathering he would buy a packet of cigarettes to have something to offer. In recent years though, as more South Africans had stopped smoking, the openings for social smokers had decreased considerably.

Brigadier De Beer even leant over the desk to light his cigarette for him. "You know, Yudel," he said, "this would have come a lot earlier if you hadn't come to the knowledge . . . er . . . attention of the minister a few times." In common with most senior civil servants he spoke English well, if a little hesitantly, sometimes searching for the right word.

Yudel looked helplessly at him, not knowing how to respond. He remembered occasions when his activities had come to the minister's attention, but on reflection his involvement had always seemed inevitable.

"Working for the government is like riding in a small boat," De Beer philosophized. "If anyone rocks it, we all get wet. People hate repercussions . . . "

"I'll remember that," Yudel said. He was thinking about Blythe Stevens's twenty-five thousand and the range of possible repercussions that could result from it. "I'll bear it in mind."

"I know you will, Yudel. You bear it in mind and you won't have to wait twenty years for the next promotion. I guarantee that."

In the lift on the way back to their offices Doctor Williamson smiled benevolently at Yudel. "Now that you are a senior professional officer I think you should call me Bill."

Yudel looked at the other man's face. They had been working together as Yudel and Doctor Williamson for almost seventeen years. The change would take a little getting used to. Along with a degree of condescension Yudel could see a lot of good will in the old psychologist's face. "Thank you," he said.

"It goes with the rank," Doctor Williamson said.

*

Yudel tracked Colonel Freek Jordaan of the Pretoria CID to a private hospital in one of the city's pleasant, tree-filled eastern suburbs. He had found the entrance to the parking area and had brought his car slowly through the entrance when a familiar sedan jerked suddenly in reverse out of one of the rows of parked cars, came to a momentary stop as the driver changed gears, then rushed forward, lunging awkwardly with a too-sudden release of the clutch. Its engine nearly stalled before the revolutions built up and it sped towards Yudel. The car was almost level with him when the driver braked to a dead halt, tyres sliding on the concrete surface. Freek, wearing a woollen dressing-gown over striped pyjamas, was at the wheel. "Yudel," he shouted out of the window, "what are you doing here?"

"I came to visit . . . "

"Park your car and get in here – quickly."

"But I . . . "

"Quickly, quickly . . . " Freek glanced over his shoulder in the direction of the archway that led into the hospital.

Yudel parked his car and came round to the passenger side of Freek's. As he was getting in a nurse appeared in the archway, waving both hands above her head. "There's someone . . . " Yudel began.

"Get in." Freek was employing the tone of voice he used on the least worthwhile of junior constables.

Before Yudel had the car door closed Freek was accelerating out into the street and away from the hospital. "Faster," Yudel said. "No telling what those nurses will do if they take us alive."

"This is no joke," Freek said. "The little bitches."

"Do you think you can explain this to me?" Yudel asked gently. "What were the little bitches doing to you?"

Freek's face adopted a hearty expression that was too complete to be natural. He leaned towards Yudel, took hold of his right hand and shook it as if trying to detach it from the shoulder. "So," he said, his voice booming in the confined space, "senior professional officer. I heard about it this afternoon. What would the equivalent rank in the police be? At least a general, I'm sure."

Yudel looked at him and raised his shoulders in the least perceptible of shrugs. If Freek thought such a feeble diversion would work on him he was going to be disillusioned. "The equivalent rank is probably a sergeant," he said.

"A sergeant? Come on, Yudel. Don't be ridiculous." Trying to shake hands while driving was causing the car to weave from side to side. An oncoming driver pulled off the road as a safety measure and waited until they had passed before resuming his journey.

Freek gave Yudel's arm a last jerk before releasing it. "And all that money? What are you going to do with all the money the department of prisons is going to pile on you now?"

Freek laughed at his own joke and even Yudel could not suppress a grin. The small rewards of civil service promotions were well known to both of them.

They were stopped by a traffic light and a young woman, waiting on the pavement outside a shop, put down a large framed print she was carrying to look curiously at Freek. With his right hand on the steering wheel, he used his left to draw closed the front of his dressing-gown. "Your style of dress fascinates her," Yudel explained.

Freek was Yudel's friend of many years, a relationship he had often found stimulating and occasionally regretted. He was a big man, both in body and spirit, and had been a CID colonel for longer than he should have. Recent chances for promotion had been impeded by his refusing transfers to the vice squad and the Special Branch. At this moment he was still trying to divert Yudel's attention from his reason for leaving the hospital. "Long overdue, that promotion – about fifteen years, I'd say."

"Let's talk about what the nurses were doing to you." It was rare that Yudel saw Freek discomfited and he was not going to yield such an opportunity.

"Nothing so far."

"What were they planning?" Yudel was remorseless. "Did you uncover a vicious plot on the part of the hospital staff? To have provoked your flight it must have been pretty bad."

"Look, I've got things to do and I was not going to trust my luck in that ward any longer."

"No telling what can happen to a man in a place like that," Yudel said.

44

Freek glared at him for a moment and saw that a confession was unavoidable. "There were four of us in the ward. I was the last to come in and one of the others asked me what I was in for. So I told him it was my tonsils. They all laughed and said, yes, they were in for their tonsils too. I didn't know why they were laughing. It was only a couple of hours later that I heard one of them talking to his wife. They were all talking about losing their tonsils, but tonsils was a sort of a code word for them." Freek stopped speaking and glanced angrily at Yudel as if he was in some way to blame for this.

"Yes?" Yudel said, nodding. It was a device he used on clients.

"The bastards were all going to have something quite different cut out. Every one of them was having a vasectomy."

Yudel looked at his friend's angry face and tried to suppress his own inner merriment. "So you got out before they confused you with the rest and operated on the wrong end of your body?"

"You can see the point?"

"Very wise." Yudel nodded. "Some things a man doesn't gamble with."

"I'm booking myself into a place that specializes in ears, nose and throat."

"After all what good is a policeman with a soprano voice?"

Freek chuckled uncertainly. "That was only part of it. There was also something I had to do." He was steering the car north on a minor main road that led towards a segment of the black homeland of Bophuthatswana. "And you? I suppose I shouldn't take you away from work."

"It's all right. I wanted to talk to you."

"About what?"

"Nothing to do with tonsils," Yudel said. He took a deep breath to arrange his thoughts, then told Freek as briefly as he could about Blythe Stevens and the job offer and the twenty-five thousand. His friend listened, nodding occasionally despite the sceptical look on his face. When Yudel was finished he shook his head slowly. "Twenty-five thousand is a lot of money."

"The truth of that hasn't escaped me."

"Don't do it, Yudel." His voice was calm, assured and not without determination. "They're all pinkoes."

"That's a very illuminating remark."

On Freek's face a small shade of amusement became apparent. "Don't sneer, Yudel. That remark's not so stupid. Did you ask him who's supplying the money?"

"Yes. He wouldn't say."

"Have you considered the sort of position you'd be in if the money was sent from East Germany and that became the subject of an investigation?"

"Maybe it's not coming from East Germany."

"Maybe not. But can you be sure that it's not coming from outside the country?"

"Would it be so bad, if it is?"

"You're an official of the state, Yudel."

There was no avoiding that argument and Yudel had no plans to change his status. "Anything else?" he asked.

"Isn't that enough? In any case, things have changed. The people who did these things ... they aren't operating in a favourable climate any more. These people that want to hire you, they want you to investigate old crimes. How many of these incidents took place in the last year?"

"Some did."

Ignoring his reply, Freek went on. "Old crimes, Yudel, I'm telling you. These things are drying up. We're a changing society. Don't rock the boat. It isn't going to do any good."

"That's what my boss said."

"What did he say?"

"Don't rock the boat."

"You discussed this with him." Freek looked almost as alarmed as he was surprised.

"No, of course not."

"I wanted to say ... " Freek began.

"There's nothing to say. I didn't discuss it with him."

Some thirty kilometres from the edge of town Freek turned on to a sand road. There were no fences along the road, no discernible boundaries between properties and no obvious attempts at farming. Scattered at intervals of fifty or a hundred metres in the light thorn scrub on either side of the road were dwellings that had been built of anything that had come to hand. Mud, brick, cement-block or wooden walls were topped with

46

roofs made from old packing cases, rusted corrugated iron, asbestos sheeting or even plastic water-proofing. A few had steel window frames with glass panes, in others holes with rough wooden shutters served as windows, but in many even this had been an impossible extravagance. Here and there in front of the houses old black women in clothing still darker than their skins watched the car go by. For every one of them there was perhaps a dozen children, from naked infants to ragged teenagers. Some of the smaller ones ran towards the road, open palms outstretched. "Cent, cent."

"Where are we going?" Yudel asked.

"To make a delivery. Not much further." But Freek's mind was with the other matter. "I know the sort of thing you're talking about, but times are changing. You're only going to open old wounds. Deaths of detained people are drying up . . . " Freek made the last statement without a great deal of conviction.

"I'm glad you said they are drying up, not have dried up." Yudel knew of one political detainee who had allegedly committed suicide in his cell during the past twelve months. Freek knew of two. Yudel was studying the expression on his friend's face, seeing the part of him that did not want to examine closely the crimes with which he was being confronted. Things were getting better. For a man like Freek, who loved his people as he did, they had to be getting better.

"You'd be scratching open cesspools that would be better to leave buried."

"I don't think you understand," Yudel said. There was not the smallest degree of irony in his voice, only the need to express himself clearly. "These are assassinations, not acts of petty hooliganism."

"I hear you, Yudel." Freek brought the car to a halt outside a hut with unpainted mud walls and just one small window at the side. There was a wooden frame in the doorway, but no door, a set of empty steel hinges recalling more prosperous days. A piece of sacking hung across the opening. By the time the car had stopped three small children, their slightly distended bellies and almost fleshless legs showing the early signs of malnutrition, and an angular woman who could have been any age between thirty

47

and sixty, had appeared in the doorway. "I hear you." Freek was looking at Yudel and ignoring the woman and children. "But, if you take this thing on, and it looks as if you're going to, I want to say just two things. Firstly, if there has been a campaign of violence against these lefties it has not been planned from the tenth floor of John Vorster Square."

Yudel was looking into Freek's serious face, his eyes flat with the screen he was unconsciously drawing over them. Yudel was not surprised by the reference to security police headquarters. He remembered the night six years before when the two of them had seen the very worst of security police vindictiveness. He knew that Freek remembered it too. "We know what they can do," Freek said, "but they don't plan assassinations." He got out of the car, his dressing-gown flapping in a warm afternoon breeze. "Mboya?" he asked the woman abruptly.

For a moment she did not respond, possibly afraid of admitting to her identity. "Yes, my boss," she said softly in Afrikaans.

He went to the back of the car and unlocked the luggage compartment. "Let the children come and carry," he said in the same language.

The woman looked uncertain and afraid, but she followed Freek's instructions. "Go and help the boss," she said.

Yudel had followed Freek to the back of the car. "Help me with this stuff," his friend said.

The luggage compartment of the car was filled with groceries, bags of sugar, mealie meal, jam, cheap soap, flour, a few vests and shorts for the children, some loaves of bread . . . "What is this?" Yudel asked.

"Now yes, don't just stand there." Freek was talking to the children. "Carry inside."

"My boss?" The tone of the woman's voice carried a question. She stood gauntly erect just outside the hut, her face suspicious, lean and empty, with the emptiness of much suffering.

Freek glanced at the woman, then turned away so that he would not have to face her. "Her husband was picked up for burglary last night," he explained to Yudel.

"And this?"

"This is what he stole."

Yudel looked at the children as they came cautiously forward and the woman's inscrutable face as she watched them. "Damn people are so slow to react, you'd think they didn't want the food," Freek said.

"The circumstances might have something to do with it," Yudel suggested.

"What circumstances?"

"How many times in her life do you suppose she has received a consignment of groceries from a strange police officer wearing pyjamas?"

Freek studied Yudel's face seriously for a moment, then chuckled from deep in his stomach. "Damn," he said, "Magda's never going to let me forget this."

"Nor am I," Yudel assured him. The children had started carrying the food into the hut, scurrying bare-foot over the dusty ground. "Do you always let burglars keep the spoils?"

"No. They don't usually steal food."

Children from the neighbouring shacks, sensing some especially joyous occasion and trotting closer to investigate, were driven off by the furious shouting of Mrs Mboya, suddenly drawn from her silence by the possibility of losing some of the spoils. Yudel and Freek carried the larger bags into a windowless dwelling so dark that they had to pause in the doorway for a few seconds before they could see the outlines of walls and floor, almost entirely devoid of furniture.

Yudel looked back as Freek drove away from the Mboya home. The woman was standing in front of the hut and had drawn her children close around her, all watching the car, perhaps doubting that the events of the last few minutes had been real. At a safe distance the children of the neighbours formed a wide circle, hyenas that had not been invited to the kill.

The people who had been the subjects of the attacks, the activists, civil rights campaigners, black consciousness leaders, trade unionists and rabble rousers, the whole strange amalgam of idealists, cynics and demagogues: whatever else was true of them, whatever Freek's opinion and his own reservations, at least they all had, as their stated aim, the elimination of scenes like the one he was leaving.

49

"Secondly?" Yudel asked. "Firstly, these crimes are not being planned from the top floor of John Vorster Square. What is secondly?"

"Secondly," Freek said, "you are certain to fail."

Yudel sat alone in his study. Rosa was already asleep. There was very little that he discussed with his wife. Early in his marriage he had tried to talk to her about matters that were important to him, but as the years had passed he had come to accept that both he and Rosa were alone in many ways. His problems and priorities had little in common with hers.

The decision had been made. Before he went with Freek on his friend's errand of mercy he had known. Even before the previous evening's meeting of the Psychology Society there had been no real doubt as to what he was going to do. He thought about his promotion and the trust Williamson and De Beer had shown in him. He thought about what Freek had said about there being a new climate in the country. He thought about the twenty-five thousand rands, and about the victims of the attacks. He thought about it all, but within himself he knew that none of these many factors had been the decisive one.

The final factor, the ultimate and over-riding consideration, did not have to do with the money he might receive or the good he might do. It had to do with a rising excitement within him, the growing joy of the hunt, the chance again to examine his species' immense propensity for violence from close by, his own irresist-ible curiosity. From the moment he had spoken to Stevens, refusal had never been a real possibility. He picked up the phone and dialled Blythe Stevens's number.

Five

Jackson had told him the whole story, but Yudel had heard no part of it. "He should be inside," the cleaner concluded. "What does the boss say?"

Yudel looked at the tea tray where Jackson had placed it on the same corner of his desk that it occupied at tea time every day. He glanced at Jackson's face and saw the righteous anger there. The indications were that he was expected to agree with something. "Quite right," he said. "Quite right."

Jackson stood where he was, nodding slowly. Every smallest gesture, from the annoyed blinking of his eyes to the rigid way he was holding his shoulders, indicated that there was something he expected Yudel to do. "Quite right," Yudel repeated, hoping that this would satisfy him and he would go.

"He should be inside," Jackson said again. "Locked up," he added in case further clarification was needed.

Yudel looked at Jackson's honest indignant face and decided reluctantly to expose himself to the cause of his wrath. "Who?" he asked.

"That man," Jackson said, his eyes growing larger with the determined emphasis he placed on the two words.

It was clear that there was no avoiding the matter. "I think you should tell me again," Yudel suggested.

Jackson told his story a second time. He came close to leaning on Yudel's desk to emphasize what he was saying, but the inhibitions of all his life prevented this degree of intimacy. He told Yudel that on Saturday night his son had been knifed while

51

drinking in a beer hall. He had caused no offence and been involved in no fight, but he had been knifed all the same. The boy was in hospital and in no danger, but his assailant was still walking the township streets, a free man.

"Do you know his name?" Yudel asked.

Jackson had the name and address written down. He handed the piece of paper to Yudel. Yudel sighed. It was looking more and more as if Jackson had decided his course of action for him. He lifted the handpiece of his telephone and asked the switchboard operator to get him the officer in charge of Mamelodi police station. Jackson took a step back and smiled. The forces of vengeance were gathering.

The policeman answered the phone with the words, "Captain Willemse." Yudel introduced himself as the assistant to General van Tonder, head of the Department of Prisons. "Yes, officer," Captain Willemse shouted into the phone. By the sound of his voice Yudel could imagine him coming to attention on the far side of the connection.

Yudel explained the problem, conceding that it was no more than an oversight on the part of Captain Willemse's staff and assuring him that all that was required was a rapid correcting of the situation. This man had committed a crime and he should be . . . arrested. Yudel avoided using Jackson's terminology.

By the time he hung up Jackson was smiling at him, large white teeth forming a striking contrast to his dark brown face. "Thank you. Thank you very much," he said. The old man normally avoided the more obvious obsequiousness of assuring Yudel with every sentence that he was the boss. He resolved the relationship between himself and all the white people, for whom he made tea three times a day and whose offices he cleaned each morning, by maintaining a rigid distance between himself and them. There was no familiarity and no servility either.

"It's a pleasure," Yudel said. "You'll know if they arrest him?"

"Me? I'll know. I'll tell the boss." Even Jackson could not avoid these things entirely.

After he had left, Yudel packed his briefcase slowly. He felt depressed and uneasy. He had come in that morning and gone straight to old man Williamson's office where he had asked if he

52

could take leave for the next week. He had lied to him, saying that he and Rosa wanted to spend a little time at the sea to celebrate his promotion.

Old man Williamson had gone off down the passage, leave form in hand, to clear it with Brigadier De Beer. Yudel knew that he would never do anything as important as granting leave without first consulting the brigadier. The old psychologist had barely had time to reach De Beer's office when the director was on the phone. "Of course, Yudel, of course, a very good idea. You and your wife go and have a good time. Don't think about prisons. Don't work the rest of the day. Go now."

A few minutes later Williamson had arrived back. His smile held the benevolence of one who spread largesse as a matter of course. "I've thought it over," he had said, "and you may have the leave. I suggest you don't bother about working the rest of the day . . ." Whatever his pretences it was clear that he was glad Yudel had what he wanted.

Despite the problems he had caused them down the years, despite the mildly anti-Jewish attitudes that had always existed in the department and despite the areas of his personality they saw as eccentric: despite all of this, these two old civil servants were happy because he had been promoted. Yudel had always felt that he was an outsider at work, but here in the pleasure they showed in his promotion and in their eagerness to grant him this sudden leave was proof of the extent to which they had accepted him. It had taken Yudel a long time, but now, beyond any doubt, they felt that he was one of them.

Not that any of this would make a difference to his course of action. He knew this too. It was just that it complicated everything more than he would have liked.

The professor of history was a tall thick-set man, heavy cheeks and brows giving him the misleading appearance of being perpetually angry. He was the only one known personally to Yudel to have suffered an attack that might be related to those in Blythe Stevens's file.

He gripped Yudel's hand firmly and invited him to sit down. "Yes, it was my book that started it all. I said everything in my book." His voice was deep and possessed a certain roughness in keeping with his appearance, but like most of his colleagues his Afrikaans was spoken with fastidious care, each word carefully formed and clearly enunciated. To a man like Professor van Deventer the language he spoke was more than just a vehicle for his thoughts. It was a gift from God, a bequest to his people.

The incident had been relatively minor, the professor having been tarred and feathered while in the middle of an address to an international history conference. The group responsible had been a fascist organization that called themselves the Afrikaner Revival Movement. Before that time the movement had not been heard of and the incident in question had given them the publicity they had been seeking. The thirty-six members who had been involved had all been convicted of assault and had paid fines of a few hundred rands each.

"They got it in my book . . ." van Deventer's voice was bitter with a subject he hated talking about, but was unable to avoid. Yudel suspected that it had come to dominate the professor's life. "My book's name is *The Development of Apartheid*. I explained in it that the day of the Covenant had never been intended as a holy day, never at all. I have the original documents . . . if you care to read them . . ."

Yudel did not care to read them. "And they attacked you because of this?"

"They wanted to make a name for themselves. They wanted to get into the newspapers. That's why they picked the conference. I was reading a paper on the same subject . . . I had it all written down and while I was reading I suddenly became aware that there were other people on the stage . . . I thought it was the press . . ." He shook his head in disgust. "We had guests from overseas countries, America, African countries . . ." And thirty-six young men had tarred and feathered one older man on the conference podium because he had suggested that the day of the Covenant, their national holy day, was not holy after all.

One hundred and fifty years before, a small group of Afrikaner pioneers had defeated the Zulu army at a place called Blood River by putting their faith in God and their gunpowder. The victory was one of a chain that had led eventually to Afrikaner dominance in South Africa. On the anniversary of the battle each year celebrations were held to thank the Almighty for his part in the victory. Their general behaviour since that day indicated that they had not forgotten the part played by the gunpowder either.

"How did they know about the subject of your paper?" Yudel asked.

"It was printed before the meeting and it was given to them by members of the staff of this university. Two other professors, both fanatics . . . they were the link. I saw it coming. They opposed me from the start. I'll give you their names." It was becoming clear to Yudel that van Deventer had been conducting a campaign. "We need to liberate the prisoners of the past. We have many."

"You would have the names of the men who took part."

He shrugged. "Of course. They're no secret. They are in court records. They were successful in getting into the newspapers." Suddenly the words came out with greater force, more intense bitterness, almost a desperation. "They are not ashamed. They want their names known. They are proud. They have made me ashamed."

"I don't understand," Yudel said.

"It is my shame, not theirs. People I thought were my friends tell me that I asked for it. It was my fault." He had been resting back in his chair, but now he was leaning towards Yudel, his expression almost accusing. You, he might have been saying, you are an outsider. People like you look for these attitudes in us, but you don't have to live with them. "I was continually invited to address meetings of cultural organizations, school camps, Christian associations . . . do you know how many invitations I've had since then?" The bitterness was welling over within him. He barely paused for an answer to his question. "Not one," he told Yudel. "Not one."

The discharge of bitterness left van Deventer tired. He rocked slowly back in his chair. The professor was not a man who wanted to be at war with his people. When he spoke again Yudel could still detect some of the bitterness, but the fury had been spent. "They phone my wife. They phone me. They call me thug. They say, be careful tonight, thug. They send anonymous letters. They say I am not a Nationalist." The anger flickered again briefly. "If I am not a Nationalist, what am I then? I am an Afrikaner. What else can I be? It is in any event no sin to be a Nationalist."

He got out of the chair, restless, as if by moving he could leave some part of it behind. "They are proud, Yudel, and I am ashamed. I sometimes think ninety per cent of all Afrikaners are against me." Standing at the window, he looked down unseeing at the pleasant gardens and scattered buildings of Pretoria University campus twenty storeys below. "A leper. They have made me a leper. But I am free. I have broken the chains that still bind them."

Yudel was preparing to excuse himself when the other man said something that cancelled the thought completely. "And there was the arrow."

"Arrow?"

"It didn't get into the newspapers. I reported it to the police. For the rest I kept it to myself."

The afternoon had passed and Yudel was back in his study. He had visited van Deventer's home and seen the place where the steel bolt, probably fired from a cross-bow had lodged in the study wall. The professor had been at home, but not in his study at the time. Judging by the point at which it had struck the wall, had he been at his desk, it might have ended its flight in the side of his head.

Yudel had also visited the two professors van Deventer suspected of complicity, but neither had been willing to see him. At the office of the first one he had been met by a broad woman with a round expressionless face who had relayed the reason for his visit to her boss. By the time he had reached the office of the other they had been expecting him. In this case he had been met by a small neat woman who seemed sure that she was a far superior person to Yudel or no doubt to any other person with his sort of interests. The professor would not be seeing him, not today and not in the future.

Van Deventer had leant Yudel a tape recording of a speech

made by the leader of the Afrikaner Revival Movement at one of their meetings. Yudel had also stopped at the libraries of two of the local newspapers to get clippings about the movement.

Now, with the tape recording starting its run on Rosa's portable recorder he paged through the photocopies from the newspaper libraries. There was a click from the recorder's loudspeaker and he could hear the mush from the machine itself and the sound of a hall waiting for the speaker to start, a chair moving, a cough, distant footsteps . . .

The first clipping had a photograph of Gys Muller, the movement's leader. He was standing in front of a microphone, one finger pointing heavenward as if suggesting the source of his inspiration. The face Yudel saw was broad, bearded and belonging to a man of about forty. The hands too were broad, the fingers short and thick, hands that you might expect to find on a farmer or manual worker, perhaps a carpenter. Another photograph showed Professor van Deventer, holding up a tar-impregnated jacket. A third showed the professor's smiling face. Yudel imagined that the last one must have been taken before the tarring and feathering.

Suddenly a rich confident voice was coming from the tape recorder. "Welcome to the Afrikaner Revival Movement meeting in Standerton tonight." Yudel had another photograph of the man at hand. The photocopies were distinct and he could see his features and expression clearly. He was shown in profile with his mouth wide open, in full flow. The brows were heavy, covered by a thick layer of flesh and the nose rounded. The expression was angry, confident and determined. "It is a special pleasure having you with us tonight," the full bass voice from the tape recorder was telling Yudel. "To have you here with us at this time of crisis, this time when Afrikanerdom, the Afrikanerdom of your father and my father, of your mother and mine, the Afrikanerdom we all love so deeply, is at the crossroads." The voice was restrained, almost muted, but even at this early stage Yudel, who was not an Afrikaner, could sense the drama that was being transmitted to the audience.

"This time of crisis when once again Afrikaner women and children are threatened, when once again the spectre of the

57

dying Afrikaner child, held by its mother, its mother who is powerless to help because those in power fail to use their power . . ." Yudel stopped listening to the voice from the recorder. It was not a conscious decision. In his paging he had reached a new press photograph that immediately monopolized his attention. It was larger than the others and showed a stage, heavily hung with flags, and in the centre Gys Muller stood at attention beneath a large Germanic eagle, probably made of fibre glass. It was the arrangement of flags that had drawn his attention away from the voice on the recorder. Some were the four colour flags of the old Boer republic. The others were also familiar. Their central adornment was a black swastika, differing only from the emblem of Hitler's Germany in that the foot of each leg joined the leg itself at an acute angle. Yudel had seen it all before in newspaper photographs, but talking to van Deventer had lent it far greater immediacy. On all the flags the swastikas were in the centre of a white circle which in turn was contrasted against some other colour. The originals had been in black and white, but Yudel could guess at the third colour. It was always a shock to see the black, white and red flag of Naziism in South Africa.

Yudel's Jewishness did not normally hold a conscious importance for him. He was not one to have nightmares dwelling on past horrors. He understood Zionism's motive force, but he understood it intellectually. For him it did not have the powerful emotional content it had for many Jews. Now he was faced with this, in the country in which he had been born, grown to maturity and reached middle age. Without any doubt it would be here in the city in which he lived.

The voice waas thundering from the recorder now, rolling in an even powerful cadence. "This man was allowed to call the day of the covenant a man-made Sunday . . ." The assault on Professor van Deventer had become an act of heroism. "This holy day when Sarel Celliers made a pact with God, when God himself gave us the victory, when he chose us as a people, and ten thousand heathen Zulus retreated before the wrath of the Almighty and the bullets of the small band of believers who had put their trust in him."

Gys Muller's voice was rising in intensity. The control and restraint had disappeared, the sentimentality becoming a gathering hysteria. "Not the Prime Minister, not one cabinet minister, not one of the leaders of Sarel Celliers's people spoke out to stop this man, this blasphemer of his people's most holy truth . . ." The voice dropped suddenly to a passionate whisper. "But he was not allowed to slander the Afrikaner and his God. Thirty-six men in front of his mulatto audience, in front of the Buthelezis, the descendants of those very Zulus, the overseas liberals . . ." Yudel found himself sliding slowly deeper into a world bordered by the limits of this man's mind, the images and the fantasies. "Found guilty by an Afrikaner judge . . . Outside the court the people are singing, Oh Lord, let your blessings on them fall." There it was. By tarring and feathering Professor van Deventer he had become a martyr, tried and found guilty of defending his people's most sacred beliefs.

"Children's corpses, mothers' tears . . . this land, this land of heart ache, this bitter chalice, death and struggle . . . blood . . ."

"Rise up, Afrikanerdom. Choose this struggle . . . the God of Blood River . . . the shed Afrikaner blood that enriches the soil of Africa . . ." Drawn by the magnetism of the voice, Yudel's eyes were still on the last of the photographs, held by the swastikas and the arrogant certainty in the speaker's face. "Kneel, kneel before your creator. The God of Blood River is your God."

It was over and the tape that had an hour's playing time shut itself off. Yudel looked at his watch. It really had been an hour since the speech had started. With an action that was almost involuntary he got quickly to his feet and opened the glass doors leading into the garden, letting the fresh evening air into the room. A light on the tape recorder was blinking, indicating that the end of the tape had been reached. On his desk the photographs of Muller, preaching his gospel, lay scattered, the swastikas proudly displayed. Proudly, Yudel thought . . . He was proud, sure of the rightness of his actions, sure of the approval of both God and his people. And the thoughtful, introverted man they had attacked: he was so ashamed that he had not even contacted the press about the bolt they had shot into his study. He was the man who had goaded these good Afrikaner boys, driven them too far.

On his desk Yudel found another picture of the professor, his clothing covered in tar, an outsider now, a leper.

Six

Sunday morning in Pretoria was not one of the busier times of the week. Young men and women, already wearing summer clothes, were out on the pavements, fingers entwined in innocent preliminary copulations. Mothers who seemed younger to Yudel every year were pushing their offspring in little carriages. Proud fathers, arms and legs bared to the sun, walked alongside. Here and there a black newspaper seller offered the Sunday papers to the drivers of passing cars and the people on the pavements.

The country's capital was a neat, almost antiseptic city. Outwardly it was a gentle and lovely place, softened by its thousands of jacarandas and the absence of either slums or heavy industry. Vice was buried deep, hidden beneath the bland outer respectability that visitors saw, as was the unease that pervaded Pretoria as it did all other South African cities and towns. It was still free of the wave of desperate black residents who in recent years had occupied empty buildings almost everywhere else.

It was a place of government department head offices, state-funded research centres and the army of civil servants who staffed them. It was also a city in which bribery, the rigging of tenders and the manipulation of the country's strict currency regulations were becoming major commercial factors. Many senior Afrikaners in key positions, sensing the coming end of white rule, were trying every device, legal or otherwise, to swell overseas bank accounts before the revolution ended the game.

But there were others in the same society whose members had no access to the levers of governmental manipulation. They felt the same threats and knew the same fears, but for them there could be no funds in safe places and no chance of flight. It was in their ranks, angry and increasingly helpless, that Gys Muller's followers would be found. They could see nothing beyond the clear fact that they were losing their country and, if blood had to flow to retrieve it, well, that was what it meant to be a man.

While Yudel waited at a traffic light, a large Mercedes Benz, its paintwork glowing with the pride of the aristocrat, drew up next to him. He glanced at the occupants, in front a middle-aged man in a grey suit and a woman of the same age group wearing a wide-brimmed hat and a lacy white dress that buttoned up to the neck and in the back three teenage children, dressed to be younger imitations of their parents. This was the traditional Afrikaner family outing to church. Together with nationalist politics, their language and rugby football, it had been part of the thread that kept a people intact. For a moment Yudel's eyes held those of the younger girl in the car, pretty, plump and not much more than thirteen years old. He grinned and winked at her. She blushed and turned away. The lights changed and the Mercedes pulled away quickly, as if to leave him behind.

Yudel parked outside the building where he had his office. The city street was almost deserted, a few cars nosing their way along as if afflicted by the same lethargy that gripped their owners. He pressed the bell and through the glass saw the old superintendent, who served as the security officer at weekends, blink open his eyes and glare angrily at the door. Seeing that it was Yudel, he took a bunch of keys from behind the counter and hobbled slowly across the lobby. "Gout, mister," he had often told Yudel. "Don't let anyone tell you that you only get it from boozing." He stopped on the other side of the glass door to inspect Yudel's identity card. That he had seen both Yudel and the card some hundreds of times in the past did not affect the performance of the ritual. Having satisfied himself that Yudel was still Yudel and still permitted to enter the building, he fingered his way through the keys until he reached the right one and unlocked the door. "Good morning, mister," he said. He was a broad, sloping-shouldered man and his face was an almost artificially pink colour. "Overtime on the dear Sunday?" he asked.

He had spoken Afrikaans and Yudel answered in the same language. "Just something I forgot in my office, Mister Volschenk."

Yudel started towards the lifts, but the old superintendent had little company at the weekends and did not intend letting him escape that easily. "What did mister think of the rugby?"

"Er . . . " Yudel stopped to give him a moment more of his attention.

"The Western Province game. Didn't mister watch?" Before Yudel could explain that he had not watched and would not have known what he was looking at, if he had, the old man continued. "My son-in-law brought in my television set for me. He brought it right up to the door, but I carried it in alone. Nobody comes in this door without a card." The last remark was added hastily in case Yudel thought that an irregularity had taken place. "I put it on the counter and I sat in my chair with my coffee . . . " A smile of satisfaction crept over his face as he recalled it. "That was now really nice," he said.

"Yes, well . . . " Yudel nodded, walking backwards towards the lift.

"But it was a scandal the way Western Province cheated us." The old man was not yet finished. "All that rough play . . . "

"Scandalous," Yudel agreed.

"That's what I say, mister, scandalous."

Yudel waved as he stepped into the lift.

In his office he filled out the authorization that would give him entry to Zonderwater prison. Zonderwater was not his territory. It fell under the control of Gert van Staden, his genial fellow departmental psychologist. Gert was one of the new breed of Afrikaner, sophisticated, educated and enjoying life in the city, but like many others a part of his personality longed back for the bushveld farming country that had been his forebears' home and that he had never known except as a visitor. Van Staden was currently on holiday on the Natal south coast. No one had told Yudel that he was to relieve Gert, but it was not an entirely unreasonable assumption.

Yudel affixed the office stamp to the form and signed it.

That was the only irregular part of the proceeding. The signature should have been Doctor Williamson's.

He leaned back in his chair and examined the sheet of paper. The thought came to him that there was a second irregularity. He was supposed to be on leave and did not have access to prisons at such times. They would not know about his leave at Zonderwater and they would probably not examine the permit that closely, he told himself. They might see the Sunday visit as unusual, but if they had the paperwork they would be satisfied.

Zonderwater prison, situated just outside the small and beautiful mining town of Cullinan, was something under an hour's drive from Pretoria.

In the town centre old stone mining houses were shaded by the thickening green of the jacarandas. Narrow roads, overhung by the trees that were already budding heavily as Yudel drove through the town, cut back and forth between the houses.

It always surprised Yudel that the streets of a town that had, as the reason for its existence, a diamond mine and a prison could leave such an impression of tranquility. The effect was the result of stone walls, old and narrow streets and mature spreading trees, rather than any real peace in the lives of the inhabitants.

The prison itself was a large orange and white building. Seemingly impregnable security walls were surrounded by fifty metres of open ground and a security fence almost as forbidding. Pretoria Central was more famous and, in the mythology of these things, a more feared prison, but of the many prisons he had known Zonderwater was the one Yudel would least have wanted to visit as a prisoner.

The form that he had completed in his office, together with his identification card, took him through the outer gate and past the door of the building where he was met by the lieutenant on duty. He was young, dark, wore a thin moustache, carried himself unfalteringly erect and had never questioned an order or any of the attitudes of his life. "On Sunday, Mister Gordon?"

Yudel nodded without answering. He looked boredly past the lieutenant.

"This is unusual." The lieutenant made a pretence of checking carefully through the authorization, but the fact that Yudel had not answered his remarks and that he now yawned slowly, barely concealing the gesture behind a lazily raised right hand, was putting him on the defensive. And to refuse something for which there was proper authorization was out of the question. "Carry on, Mister Gordon," he said, trying to make it sound like a command. "Viljoen."

A middle-aged warder who had heard himself summoned in the same military tone far too often came tiredly out of an adjoining office to receive the authorization from the lieutenant. Yudel smiled at him in sympathy.

While Yudel waited in the office reserved for such interviews he read Robin Du Plessis's file. He was thirty years old and had been sentenced to a month in jail for withholding information. The charge was the result of an article he had written for a student newspaper on the black underground resistance. The security police had wanted him to divulge one of his sources and he had refused. It was not in the file, but Yudel thought he remembered reading that Du Plessis had been detained by the security police before the trial.

The file photograph of Du Plessis showed his face as lean and angular, the skin around his eyes so dark that it appeared bruised. The eyes did not possess the acquired guardedness of criminals dealing with authority. Instead he stared angrily and defiantly back at the camera. To Yudel the arrogance in his face seemed to reflect the conviction of the rightness of his own actions and the evil and stupidity of his captors.

Robin Du Plessis was brought in by a warder and sat down in the seat Yudel offered him. What the photograph had not shown were the delicate features and limbs, the elfin, almost feminine qualities of face and body. His shoulders, wrists and hands were narrow, the limbs long. His skin, apart from the area around his eyes, was milk white and looked smooth and soft. It was an appearance that was not likely to make things easier for him in prison.

The warder left the room, leaving the door slightly ajar. Before

65

speaking Yudel got up to close it. Du Plessis was staring at him, much in the way of the photograph. "I'm Yudel Gordon." He reached out his hand and the other man took it briefly. The activist's hand was smooth, slightly damp and cold. Yudel felt no responding pressure.

"This means that they offered you the job, I suppose."

"I had hoped that it was not public knowledge."

"I'm not the public." He spoke coldly, with no apparent inclination to conduct the meeting on a friendly basis. "They've been talking about approaching you for some time."

"But you're against it?"

"Yes." The word was spoken with a finality and an emphasis that left Yudel in no doubt.

"Perhaps you could explain that to me."

Du Plessis directed his eyes ostentatiously around the room. "Look where we are. I've been locked up for something that isn't a crime in any civilized country and you sit there, an agent of the system, and you are going to help. They pay your salary, don't they?"

"You're suggesting that the government itself is involved in these crimes?"

Du Plessis got suddenly to his feet. "Don't try to question me. I don't need this."

Yudel looked down at the file. "You take part in running a student newspaper. Are you still a student?"

"I'm a former student."

"But you are not still a student?"

"I'm a former student. I told you." It was said angrily as if answering a challenge.

Yudel tried another angle. "According to Blythe Stevens you had a contact with the security police that might be helpful."

"Christ . . . " Du Plessis sat down again suddenly, the legs of the chair shuddering a few centimetres across the cement floor. "I don't need this. I don't know what these fools are thinking about. As far as I'm concerned you are system. It's that simple."

"But you have suffered some sort of harassment?" The activist stared at Yudel without answering, his arms folded across a chest that was heaving with indignation. "Haven't you?" Du Plessis

66

made no response. As far as he was concerned the interview was over. "Even if you don't have faith in me, what possible harm can it do for you to tell me?"

"Listen, Gordon. Everybody knows that the system is involved . . . " He stopped speaking, still staring at Yudel, his eyes revealing the resentment he felt.

"I must be the one who doesn't know."

He shook his head briefly, his disgust showing in his face, and when he spoke, registering in his voice. "I don't know what they are thinking about, hiring system people."

"Why not just tell me what you know?"

"You want to know what they do to people? You want to know?" He leapt to his feet and banged on the door with the flat of his hand. The warder came in and Du Plessis tried to push past him into the passage. "I'm finished here. I want to go back to my cell."

The warder looked at Yudel and Yudel nodded. After they had gone he closed the file and remained for a while, looking unseeing down at its cover. You want to know what they do to people? he had asked. It was an interesting question, especially as Yudel had not asked that. The last expression he had seen on the prisoner's face had seemed to him to be almost one of loathing.

The warder called Viljoen ushered Yudel through the series of doors that led to the courtyard where his car was parked. To reach it he had to pass the only other car in the parking area, a blue medium-sized continental sedan.

The lieutenant was standing near the open door on the driver's side, talking to a tall lean man who was resting against the car on one elbow. The lieutenant had to turn to nod a casual goodbye to Yudel.

It was the other man whom Yudel noticed. He was about sixty, his straight grey hair carefully combed, but long enough to touch the top of his ears. He pushed himself away from the car to stand upright, the movement surprisingly fluid for a man of his age, as if his body was that of a much younger man. He wore a dark three-piece suit and black leather shoes that someone had spent a long time shining. Yudel passed close by them and looked into his face.

It was only for a moment and Yudel had never seen the man before, but there was an element that he recognized immediately. He saw an embittered aspect to the mouth, a certain hardness, cynicism and suspicion in the eyes and an overriding contempt and confidence that he had seen in policemen before. It was the face of a man accustomed to the more brutal aspects of the exercise of power, the outer façade of a man deadened by experiences that he needed to hide deep behind the barriers of the mind.

The interest Yudel had provoked was not hidden by eyes that seemed more than half closed. Yudel had seen the slight cocking of his head, a gesture that suggested there was no doubting his own right to be there, but that the psychologist's presence might need explaining.

The car started at the first turn of the key and Yudel moved it slowly towards the motor gate. In his rear-view mirror he saw the two men at the other car. Both had turned to watch him drive away.

At the gate the guard came to the car window to inspect Yudel's identification. He had done it on the way in, but orders were orders and he would inspect it as many times as they told him to. He was a sturdily built young man with a puzzled look in his eyes that did not suggest unusual intelligence. "Who is the man with the lieutenant?" Yudel asked him.

"That's Colonel Wheelwright," the guard said.

"Of prisons?"

He shook his head. "Police."

"Do you know what branch?"

"Pretoria branch, I think."

It was not the answer Yudel wanted, but he thanked the man and drove through the gate as it was opened. In his last view of Wheelwright and the lieutenant, before the driveway turned and they disappeared from the mirror, they were still looking in his direction, watching him go.

Seven

Yudel had found a coffee shop in an arcade not far from the university. He had an hour left before his meeting with Blythe Stevens.

He had spent the last few hours talking first to a group of black trade unionists whose leader had died in a car crash some months before, then to the university professor who had been defamed in the anonymous pamphlet. He had asked the unionists if the crash had been an accident. "Some say so," had been the reply. The professor had told him that the information in the defamatory leaflet had been completely accurate, but selective. "There were no factual mistakes at all. I can think of only one organization that would have all that information. In fact only one that would be interested. But perhaps I don't need to tell you which one that is." He most clearly remembered the professor's parting remark, two wide-open innocent eyes sparkling with merriment. "It's an outrageous project you are tackling. You might come back if you find yourself in need of legal counsel."

With the floor carpeted and deep armchairs around the tables the coffee shop felt comfortable and looked expensive. Yudel ordered coffee. When it came he offered a twenty-five cent tip that the waiter, a dark brown man in a white jacket and trousers with a red stripe down the side, accepted with studied, condescending dignity. Never in all his life had Yudel felt confident about the amount to tip waiters. Ten per cent, Freek had told him. But the coffee had cost one rand and ten cents. He wondered what the waiter's reaction to an eleven cent tip would have been. Yudel knew that he would never have the courage to find out. Perhaps tipping worked on a sliding scale with more towards the bottom and less towards the top. He briefly considered having Freek explain it to him, but dismissed the idea. Freek would laugh.

The other customers in the shop were ordinary people, people whose primary motive force in life was to create lives for themselves that were well served by the trappings of suburban ease. They were much less complicated than the people of the other world that existed next to theirs: the world of Blythe Stevens, Professor van Deventer, even Gys Muller . . . Whatever the lust for power in any activist, the troubled childhood that might turn a Blythe Stevens or a van Deventer against the society of his parents, whatever insecurities drove a Gys Muller: all of them, radical and reactionary, had the same discovery in common. They had found something larger than themselves. It was this that the men and women in the coffee shop had probably never known.

Yudel could never wholly trust anyone for whom the pursuit of political goals formed the centre of life. In patients he had seen too much of the unconscious motives for apparently altruistic lives. Saintliness was an unreliable phenomenon. He was too aware of the twenty-five thousand to attribute any saintly motives to himself either.

He drank the coffee slowly and ordered a second cup. This time he left a tip of fifty cents. The waiter swept it smoothly off the tray, smiled and nodded. Yudel considered that he might just have been taught something.

Blythe Stevens's house was surrounded by a high hedge, interrupted only by the gate at the bottom of the footpath and a motor gate, both equally high. To gain entrance a push button with an engraved plate bearing the word 'bell' was mounted in an indentation in the cement gatepost.

Yudel rang the bell and through a thinner part of the hedge he watched Stevens come down the steps of an old well-kept house. The Venetian blinds in the front of the house were drawn and Stephens had closed the door behind him. Glancing down the street Yudel could see only one other car. It was parked a block away and there was no one in it.

The gate opened and Stevens smiled at him. "Yudel," he said, his voice low, but its tone seeming to indicate that this was a real pleasure. The hint of suspicion and slyness were there as they had been when Yudel first met him. "Come in, quick." He gestured towards the front door with a sharp jerk of his head. Before closing the gate he looked up and down the road. "Let's get into the house." It was said with a last glance in the direction of the parked car, before he hurried across the lawn and up the steps with Yudel following.

The front door opened into a thinly furnished hall through which Stevens led him into a large living room. In the dim light entering through the cracks in the blinds Yudel could see that there was another person present. He was sitting alone on a long settee. As his eyes became accustomed to the light he recognized the man with the unhealthy-looking, puffy face who had confronted him after his talk to the Psychology Society. "Mister Yudel Gordon." Blythe Stevens waved an arm in a grand gesture towards the other man. "Ralph Du Plessis."

The discovery of a second Du Plessis among Stevens's friends was a surprise. Yudel tried not to let it show. Du Plessis got to his feet as if to shake hands. Despite the brief nature of his association with them Yudel was growing weary of the radical Left. Their hostile attitudes, seemingly exaggerated fears, the closed blinds, earnest faces, lowered voices and meaningful looks all appeared theatrical to him.

He imagined the way they intended conducting the interview. Without shaking Du Plessis's hand he selected an armchair and sat down. The others followed, a little hesitantly. "Well, now we all know each other . . . " Blythe Stevens said, his voice hearty and again pitched too low. It was a device that Yudel was beginning to recognize.

"Have you got the money?" Yudel asked.

The question caused a certain discomfort among the other two. "At least you're true to type," Ralph Du Plessis said.

"Have you or haven't you?"

Blythe Stevens swayed forward in his chair. A brown envelope had appeared in one of his hands. "Let's keep the aggro to a minimum. We have the money. When do you intend going to

Durban?" He was making no effort to hand the envelope to Yudel, tapping it lightly against one knee.

Yudel held out a hand. "The day after tomorrow, Wednesday." The hand that held the envelope hesitated before moving in Yudel's direction. It was obviously no easy matter for him to hand it over, but Yudel's hand was outstretched and waiting. With an effort Stevens overcame his problem and parted with the money.

Tearing the end off the envelope, Yudel took out the twenty rand notes inside. He counted them one by one, placing them in a pile on the arm of the chair. There were forty, the amount he had asked for as expense money. He shuffled them into a neat pile and slipped them into the inside pocket of his jacket.

"You are not to bank that money or deposit it anywhere. You are to keep it in cash until you use it." Ralph Du Plessis's face was pale and waxen, even in the semi-darkness of the room.

"Where does it come from?"

"What . . . "

"The money? Where does the money come from?"

"I don't know that we . . . "

But Stevens interrupted him. "The West German churches." Yudel must have looked unconvinced because after a moment Stevens continued. "In Germany the state churches are financed from the taxes. As a result they are very wealthy, wealthier than religious organizations anywhere else. And they are very generous. The liberation movement inside the country is largely funded by the West German churches."

"Liberation of what?" Yudel asked.

"Of the country, of you and me, liberation from oppression . . . "

"I see," Yudel said untruthfully. He felt no need to be liberated from anything, excepting occasionally the members of Rosa's family, and he doubted that the German churches were going to be of much help in that area. "These criminals I'm looking for . . ." Yudel was speaking to Du Plessis. "What did you people do to them? How did you antagonize them?"

"We?" A small smile of disbelief appeared on his face. "How did we antagonize them?"

"At the meeting last week I kept being told that aggression is only caused by frustration. What did you do to these poor people? How did you drive them to their crimes?" Yudel knew that when he left them he would wonder about his own behaviour and probably find no answer. He always understood the motives of others better than he did his own. His puzzlement was not strong enough to stop him though. "What are the closed blinds and the locked gate for?"

The attention of the two men turned from the causes of aggression to their security arrangements. "The blinds are to shield us against listening devices outside. The closed gates are to prevent the wrong people knocking on the door unexpectedly."

"I wouldn't put much faith in either," Yudel said. "It would be more to the point if you" – he was looking at Du Plessis –"didn't question me about this project in public."

"All right. That was a mistake." Du Plessis looked resentful. "I admit it."

"Jesus, Yudel," Blythe Stevens interrupted. "Ralph and I have been through this . . . " Yudel looked at him in silence for a moment and Stevens used the opportunity to try to divert him. "Have you started your investigation?" The expansive rugged appearance that had suffered under Yudel's onslaught was struggling to reappear.

"I've seen a few people." He listed the names, ending with van Deventer.

"Van Deventer?" Du Plessis asked, looking at Stevens for confirmation.

"He's not one of us," Stevens explained. "He's a government man."

"Do you mean that it doesn't matter if he gets attacked?"

Ralph Du Plessis was no longer able to contain himself. "What we mean is that you are not being paid to investigate crimes against government supporters."

Stevens tried again to assume control of the meeting. "Look, Yudel, what's the point of that? The crime was committed in the public eye. Everyone knows who was guilty."

Yudel told them about the crossbow bolt that had been fired

into the professor's study. "You people think there is an organization behind all this . . . "

"We know it." Ralph Du Plessis spoke with the combined certainties of being young and politically convinced.

Yudel was not interested in his convictions. "I saw Robin Du Plessis. Are you related?"

"In Zonderwater?"

"Yes. He wouldn't say anything to me."

"You didn't tell me . . . " Ralph Du Plessis was speaking to Stevens. "I thought we agreed . . . I told you Robin doesn't want to be part of this."

Stevens raised both hands, a man appealing for peace. "Yes, I'm sorry. Yudel, I should have told you. He's Ralph's brother."

"So why doesn't he want to co-operate?"

"Just leave him alone. You don't know these people."

Yudel wondered uncertainly what it was they thought they knew that he did not and who "these people" were. "Do you also work on the student newspaper?" he asked Du Plessis.

"That's right."

"And are you also a former student?"

Du Plessis glanced at Stevens, as if to confirm that his ears were not deceiving him. "Yes. Is this important?"

"I'll tell you what is important," Yudel said. "What is it that the victims of these crimes had in common?"

"They are opposed to the government." Du Plessis's answer came quickly and emphatically, but not more so than any of his other answers.

"A lot of people are opposed to the government, but never suffer attacks of this sort. And you say that Professor van Deventer is not opposed to the government."

"What are you talking about, Yudel?" Blythe Stevens shrugged. "I don't follow."

"I want to know why these people were chosen and not either of you gentlemen for example." Neither responded. "Is there any chance that they all, or at least many of them, belonged to the same organization?"

"None at all," Stevens said.

"Could there be an underground movement of which many of

74

them were members?" Yudel looked for any sign that he was probing the right area. All he saw was puzzlement: a puzzlement that was coloured by exasperation in Du Plessis's case and weariness in Stevens's. Whether or not there was anything linking the victims, as he looked at the faces of the two men at least one point seemed certain, they knew nothing of it.

Yudel took the off-ramp that led down into the Fountains picnic area and on to an old main road that wound itself round a large traffic island and through the row of hills that formed Pretoria's southern boundary. It was early evening and a few cars from the outlying suburbs were coming down the hill into town for the evening's entertainment. On the left a thin screen of trees grew along the railway line and on the right the University of South Africa building, a kilometre long and seeming to overhang the road, looked to be an extension of the hill that supported it. He slowed the car where the road curved towards the station and turned right, up the steep incline towards his home in Muckleneuk.

As he made the turn his eyes picked out a sign on a light cardboard poster. He was past before he had been able to read it, but the small swastika in the lower right-hand corner had alerted him. Stopping the car on the dirt strip next to the road, he walked back the twenty or thirty paces to where the poster was hanging.

Against the background of a South African flag, waving in the wind, bold black lettering exhorted the nation to "Let the land of the fathers for their children remain". In small lettering next to the swastika the Afrikaner Revival Movement took credit for its existence.

Nothing could be more natural than that the fathers of any tribe would want to see their piece of earth pass into the hands of their children. It was hard to reconcile these entirely normal sentiments with Gys Muller's hysterical oratory.

The message on the poster was a warning to all Gys Muller's people. It was also a warning to the many who had been dispossessed, who because of the military defeats suffered by their forefathers were no longer masters of the earth on which they had been born and where they would die. There was to be no part of this earth for their children.

*

75

"Mother has gone home," Rosa said. "She said she felt in the way." All the lights in the house were on and Rosa was sitting in the lounge smoking.

Yudel had seen fear in Rosa before. He saw it in her now and he knew what was causing it. "They aren't going to come here," he said. "Please don't worry about it." She looked at him without speaking, the only response coming from her eyes "They have no reason to come." The ash-tray on the floor next to her contained more than its usual quota of cigarette ends. She must have been sitting there for some time.

"I'm sorry, Yudel," she said at last. "I hate myself now." He had not seen the guilt as being hers and he could find no way to frame an answer. She shook her head and when she spoke again her voice had an uneven, almost breaking quality. "I'm such a coward."

Yudel drew a chair up next to hers and took her hand. He wanted to suggest that he drop the investigation and they go away for the rest of his week of leave. But before he could start she spoke. "I know you have to do it. I've been sitting here thinking about it all day." She waved a hand towards the ash-tray. "I suppose you can see that." Yudel was strangely troubled by Rosa's new humility. It was altogether unlike her usual lack of consideration and insufferable self-assurance. "I know you have to do these things. At least it's better than having other women. You don't have other women, do you, Yudel?"

"No," Yudel said, "I don't have other women." As a general rule this was true and as a matter of absolute truth it was not far off.

"I know you don't," she said, "and I appreciate it. It's terrible for women whose husbands have other women."

Yudel patted her hand softly. "Did you want to talk about unfaithfulness in marriage?" he asked.

"No, not really. I didn't want to talk about that at all."

"Oh, I thought you did."

But Rosa was too involved with what she was trying to say to acknowledge his pointless attempt at teasing her. "No. No." Suddenly the hand that was holding the cigarette shook violently. She had to steady it with her free hand while inhaling. "That other time I was so frightened. You remember, when those people came."

Rosa never gave them their name, but Yudel knew who she was talking about and he remembered the incident well. It had been the briefest of contacts and there had never been any real threat to her, but the barely conscious fear she shared with all South Africans and the gentlest hint of security police power and ruthlessness had been more than she had been able to bear. "You don't have to be afraid," he said. "They know that we are not political people."

"But this case . . . the ones that were attacked . . . most of them . . ." Rosa was having difficulty putting her fears into words.

Yudel tried to help. "Many of the victims have been security police clients and you are worried about who might be responsible. Is that right?"

"Do you think they might be?"

"These things are not being planned by the special branch or any other branch of the police. I assure you of that."

"Are you absolutely sure, Yudel?"

"Absolutely. Freek says so."

"I'm glad. He should know. Freek knows all those things." She blinked slowly and the tight band around her brain seemed to loosen a little.

"All the same, why don't you go to Irena for a few days?"

"I did last time, didn't I?"

"That doesn't matter. Do it again. I think you should."

"Perhaps I'll go on the weekend."

"Or sooner, you could go sooner." He got to his feet, still holding her hand. "Why not come to bed now? I have a few things to do. I'll be along in a moment."

"You won't be long?"

"Not long at all."

He led her down the passage to the bedroom, then went around the house, putting out the unnecessary lights. Finally he made his way to the study and, with the glass doors and curtains open wide to let in the gentle warmth of a premature spring, he took out the clippings he had not yet studied. They concerned attacks that had taken place in the pleasant sub-tropical city of Durban. It was a lazy holiday place where the climate itself seemed to militate against anything as vigorous as violence. For half an hour he read with the complete concentration that shut him off from all but the most intrusive sounds and that allowed him to absorb almost all the information in what he was reading.

By the time he had finished he knew the superficial outline of the killing of Ray Baker. He had seen photographs of his beautiful Indian widow and his suffering, tormented eighty-year-old mother who, according to one of the reports, had spent the years since her son's death searching for the killer. He had learnt about the attempts to kill Lionel Bensch, an artist who had once been a restricted person. He had read about Fellows Ngcube, the attorney who had been shot through the front door of his home. He had also read about Morris Subramoney, a man who had the audacity to organize a swimming league that had no racial restrictions and how the screams of a neighbour had saved his life.

Durban, Yudel thought, I'll go the day after tomorrow and stay till the weekend. I'll see Baker's widow, Bensch and the others. He was still telling himself what he was going to do in Durban, his mind no longer completely alert, his thoughts drifting, when a sound from the air and the wall above him drove all else away. The brief quivering in the air, followed by the crack of steel against brick, superimposed over the duller blow of force meeting force, threw him from his chair to the floor.

Yudel rolled on to his back as a piece of plaster cracked away from the wall and fell to the carpet. In the far corner, just below the ceiling, dully reflecting the half-light from his desk lamp, he could see the steel shaft of the crossbow bolt.

He started to his feet in a movement that would have taken him into the open doorway, but resisted the impulse and turned instead in a crouching run towards the door leading into the hall. He found Rosa standing next to her chair in the lounge, her eyes rigid and the crumpled remains of a cigarette between her fingers. "Sit down," Yudel heard himself say, his voice higher in pitch and hoarser than usual. "Sit down on the chair." He reached her before she had moved and dragged her down. "Stay there. Don't

78

move." He could hear the panic in his voice, but he had no way of controlling it.

He was at the front door before the intention had formed properly in his mind. He ran across the lawn and stopped in the deep shadow at the side of the house. From the road beyond the hedge he heard the sound of a car accelerating. For a moment he could see it in outline against a street light, largely obscured by the hedge, a dark shape moving quickly away from him without lights.

He passed carefully among his wife's rose bushes. Even under these conditions a part of his mind warned him about Rosa's probable displeasure if he flattened some of the bushes. He went through the small side gate in the hedge and stopped on the pavement. Now the street was quiet. The car was gone and nothing moved on the street or under the jacarandas down either side. Looking back in the direction of his study, he saw the open doors, his chair lying on its side and Blythe Stevens's file open on the desk.

Rosa, Yudel thought, remembering her shocked immobility where he had come upon her in the lounge. He hurried back, again picking his way among the roses with care, then trotting across the lawn. The sight of her at the hall telephone stopped him in the open door. She had her back towards him and was holding the handset in one hand and trying to dial with the other. Her hands were shaking so badly that, while Yudel watched, she had to stop twice and begin again. Eventually she dialled the number successfully and waited for the reply, holding the handset with both hands to steady it. "Irena," Yudel heard her say, "please come. Come and get me. There's been a terrible thing . . . "

Eight

After breakfast Yudel made a call to confirm the booking of his flight. Then he sat down to wait for Freek. He had given the servant leave for the time that he would be away and the house was altogether quiet.

The last thing Rosa had said before leaving with Irena on the night before was, "I'm not good at this sort of thing, Yudel. You married the wrong kind of woman." She had been careful not to look at him while speaking. Then she had fled down the drive to Irena's waiting car without looking back.

Irena seemed to have enjoyed the drama. Before going she had come close to Yudel and murmured, "I'll look after this end. You go and do what you have to do."

Yudel wondered idly if he might ever have to live without Rosa. She had been a part of his life for so long that suddenly being in his home without her left him with the feeling that all was not as it should be.

The feeling ended with Freek's knock on the door. Yudel let him in and took him through to the study, watching him get up on the chair to get a good look at the bolt. "It hit very high," Freek said. "Let's go outside."

Yudel followed him into the garden and pointed to the corner where the road frontage met his neighbour's fence, near the small side gate in the hedge. "It must have been fired from the pavement over there."

Freek looked doubtful. "It may have come from a lot closer than that." Together they walked to the corner Yudel had indicated, turned and looked back at the study. "You can't see it from here." Halfway back to the window Freek squatted down on his haunches. "I can just see it," he said, "but this is a hell of an uncomfortable position." He took another five paces forward and crouched again. "This is about it, Yudel." Freek was no more than fifteen steps from the glass doors of the study.

"Here?" Somehow it was worse that they had come so close to the house.

"It looks like it."

"Politically they're ignorant," Yudel said.

Freek looked curiously at him.

"You said they aren't operating in a favourable climate. They haven't realized that."

Freek had come to expect remarks of that sort from Yudel. He ignored it. "Where were you?"

"Sitting at the desk with the doors open."

Freek went back inside, with Yudel following, and looked at the bolt again. His usual exuberance was gone. "This is a warning. From that range they could have bisected the space between your ears beautifully if they had chosen to. This was just a demonstration of what they could have done." Freek looked straight at Yudel. "You don't want to make a statement to the local boys?"

"No."

"I can't do much if it's unofficial."

"I don't want to attract attention."

Freek looked at him from beneath raised eyebrows. "I would say you already have."

They looked thoughtfully at each other for a moment. There was no denying Freek's logic. "I don't want my career affected. If it's reported it will become public knowledge and there are plenty of people who will wonder why I am becoming a target."

"And you're still going on with this?" Yudel was looking for the words in which to frame his reply when Freek continued, "Of course you are. And it's not for the money. And it's not for justice. It's a compulsion." Yudel shrugged. "All right. I just want to tell you for the last time that these crimes are not now and never have been planned from the top floor of John Vorster Square."

81

"Okay," Yudel said, "but there are problems." He told Freek about the pamphlet defaming the law professor and the amount of detail it contained. He also told him about the assailants at the Attic, how there were both black and white men and how so many of these incidents followed trouble with the security police.

"This only means that one or two, perhaps a few more are involved. It might not even mean that."

"Okay," Yudel said.

"Another thing: obviously the word is out by now. They might come looking for you seriously next time."

"I can't see it."

"You can't see what?"

"Me, with a bullet in me. I can't see it."

"Boetie." Freek shook his head. The word meant 'little brother' and the tone was exasperated. "What about a crossbow bolt? Can you see that?" When Yudel did not answer, he changed the direction of his attack. "So where's Rosa?"

"I sent her to Irena for a few days." Freek was observing him sceptically and Yudel looked out of the window to avoid his friend's eyes. "Actually she left after it happened." He turned his head to study Freek's earnest face. "Why don't they ever find the people responsible?"

Freek was not enjoying the conversation. His face was set hard, but controlled, and his eyes were without their usual warmth. "It's not because they're involved. It's because they lack enthusiasm. If a part of you secretly agrees with the crime it becomes a little hard to get enthusiastic about finding the criminal." It was said almost with irritation, as if it was self-evident and Yudel should not have needed to ask the question. "You don't want a file opened. So be it. I'll get prints taken. We can compare them to those of the crowd that shot at Eglin's place and that mob that blew up the PFP offices. I'll have them checked unofficially." The cases to which Freek had referred were minor ones and neither he nor Yudel expected to find a connection. "Don't hope for anything," Freek added.

"I won't."

"In the mean time, see that you keep your windows closed at night. Keep your curtains drawn so that no one can see in. Make sure you know who's outside before opening the door and don't let anyone sleep in direct line of fire from a window."

"Is all this necessary?"

"I don't know, Yudel. Do you?" The policeman was not joking, nor was he trying to frighten him. He was suggesting what he saw to be a simple necessity.

Yudel remembered the other matter he wanted to clear up. "What happened with the tonsils?"

"They're coming out this afternoon."

"Ear, nose and throat specialist?"

Freek nodded, but there was no longer anything amusing in the matter. He tilted his head in the direction of the crossbow bolt. "I'm surprised by how fast they reacted."

The building where the Reverend Markus Mbelo had his office was just a few years old and provided premises for black organizations only. No law or town ordinance prevented white businesses from occupying offices in the building, but no businessman would ruin his business for the sake of his address. The lobby was littered with used cigarette packets, transparent containers that had once been filled with potato crisps, plastic cold drink bottles that had been emptied of their colourful and artificial contents and grease-proof sorghum beer cartons that gave the ground floor a heavy sour smell.

Mbelo's office was on the fifth floor and Yudel went up in a crowded lift that stopped at each landing. The building made an impression of crowded corridors, people standing in groups talking or just waiting with endless African patience, leaning against a wall or squatting on their haunches.

The fifth floor was even more crowded than the others, dozens of women thronging the open doorway of a family planning clinic. A sign on a wall near the door extolled the virtues of the loop in ten languages, English and Afrikaans among them. The office next to the clinic had an engraved sign announcing that it belonged to the Black Christian Fellowship. Yudel knocked and entered a small office where a fat woman was seated at a cheap pine desk and typing a letter on an electric typewriter. She kept him waiting while she finished the paragraph on which she was

83

working, then looked up without smiling. "Yes?" The face was expressionless, the eyes studiously bored.

"I would like to see Reverend Mbelo," he told her.

"Have you got an appointment?" It was said with the same deliberate boredom that held within it revenge for hundreds of small humiliations suffered at white hands.

"No, I haven't got an appointment."

"The reverend won't see you unless you have got an appointment."

"Please tell him I'm here and let him decide."

"Name?" She pushed a sheet of paper across the desk towards him. Yudel took it and wrote, Yudel Gordon, the Attic.

The woman took the paper, read what he had written and looked quizzically at him, clearly not understanding what the last two words were about. Leaning heavily on the desk, she pushed herself to her feet and went into the adjacent office. In less than a minute she was back. "You can go in," she said resentfully.

Markus Mbelo remained seated at his desk when Yudel entered. He pointed Yudel to a chair and attempted a smile that was not entirely successful. He was broad in both shoulders and head and his face was heavily pockmarked. "Mister Yudel Gordon of the Attic?" His voice and face both reflected his puzzlement. "The Attic has been gone for a long time." Mbelo addressed Yudel in Afrikaans. It was a rare ability among black political activists. According to the common perception of that group Afrikaans was the language of the oppressor and English, because there were so many competing African languages, was the medium of the revolution. The exceptions were those, scattered widely throughout the black resistance, who had been educated within the Dutch Reformed Church. "The Attic has been gone for a very long time. I haven't heard it mentioned in years."

"Reverend Mbelo," Yudel said, reaching out and shaking his hand. "I don't come from the Attic. I'm writing an article on its history." Yudel lied easily when he felt the lie had a valid purpose.

"It was a short history."

"I know, but I have heard that you were a member of the fellowship and that you might be able to help."

The smile had not left Mbelo's face, but it was not a convincing expression. He looked less than enthusiastic at the idea of helping Yudel in any way. "What do you want to know?" he asked.

Yudel felt sure that if he wanted to spend any time in this man's company he would have to interest him quickly. "I believe the people of the Attic suffered some harassment."

The false smile was still in position and the man's expression had not changed in any obvious way, but in his eyes Yudel could see the beginnings of interest. To people like Mbelo the suffering of the oppressed and the persecution of their champions were subjects that could not be exhausted. "Harassment? Oh yes, there was harassment."

"I'd like very much to know about that," Yudel said. "I wonder if you can spare five minutes."

The intentness in Yudel's manner and the urgency in his voice when talking about something important to him had often persuaded people who had been reluctant to be questioned. And now, despite the smile, it was clear that he was at least a source of interest to Mbelo. "You want to know about harassment? The security police were the main culprits. Once they came and took away all the typewriters. I don't remember if they ever brought them back . . ."

"Why did they take the typewriters?"

"Probably to compare the letters to those used on some document. I don't really know that much about it. If Bernie Miller was still here . . ."

"He's the man who ran the Attic?"

"He ran the Attic and he ran all the way to Canada." Mbelo pressed a button on his intercom system. "Bring us two cups of coffee," he said into the device. "There is a man who knows more about the Attic than I do. He was more deeply involved, Reverend Dladla of the Presbyterian church. I don't know where he is now, but he was a regular at the Attic. The Presbyterians will know."

"And the Attic's aims?" Yudel was disappointed by what the preacher was telling him, but years of experience had taught him that sometimes all you needed to do was keep the other person talking. If the information you needed was in his memory it was going to come out in his conversation sooner or later.

"The Attic's aims?" The preacher's habit of repeating a question as if it surprised him seemed designed to put the questioner on the defensive. "The aims were . . . " He paused to allow a measure of contempt to show itself. ". . . to employ the Reformed tradition to bring all South Africa's people together." The smile had never left his face but now it had a sneering quality. "Some of us thought it was just another trap to keep the black man down. I think I have some of the literature." He pulled open a drawer of his desk and began searching through it. "A piece of paper called the RACC declaration."

"Rack?"

"R.A.C.C. Reformed Action Christian Conference." He pulled a thin black and white booklet from the drawer and waved it at Yudel. "The RACC declaration," he said. "Take it away if you want to."

The fat sullen receptionist came in carrying a tray with two cups of coffee as Mbelo had ordered. Yudel got to his feet as she crossed the room and put the tray down on the desk. Mbelo glanced at her, then at Yudel, watching him wait for her to leave before he sat down again.

"I'll read this," Yudel said, slipping the booklet into an inside pocket. "The Attic was on an old mine property, I believe."

"There's a map on the back cover of the booklet. It was a big old house. Bernie lived there. He had a study in a little basement at the back of the house. He called it the Hole. I don't know who else lived there. They had a library and a room for meetings." He had indicated the coffee to Yudel with a wave of his hand and had taken a cup himself. "I went a few times. I was not closely involved. I only heard the stories about the security police . . . "

"And Miller fled to Canada?"

"When it gets too hot the white activist finds a cooler place."

A fair number of black ones too, Yudel thought. He had almost said it out loud, but his internal censor suppressed the remark. "Miller was one of those?"

"He used to wear pretty clothes. He liked boots. One night he was attacked there. They tried to stab him. He pushed the knife hand away and got a deep gash across one of his beautiful leather boots. I recall that it was a most upsetting injury." Mbelo seemed to enjoy recounting the incident.

Yudel recognized it as one in the file. "Three of them and they were wearing masks?"

"You know about it?"

"Just the broad outline."

"I think they knew he was alone that night. On many nights there were a lot of people, but on this night there was just him. They were wearing black masks and gloves. They hit him and tried to stab him."

"Do you remember anything else about it?"

Mbelo thought for a moment, still favouring Yudel with his smile. "I remember one other thing. Bernie said he could hear by their voices that one of them was black and two were white." This was not what Yudel wanted to hear. He knew that he needed to hear it, but he would rather that Mbelo had something else to tell him.

Memory was awakening in Mbelo. "I remember that as they were leaving one of the Attic people who was just arriving and did not know about the attack saw them without their masks. There was a lot of excitement, Bernie telling everyone what he was going to do and so on, because this man said he recognized one of them." He recounted the incident as if it was of little consequence and nothing could be done about it. "I soon stopped attending the meetings. There was no point in trying to liberate the country by means of the Reformed tradition."

"The man who saw them, what was his name?"

"A character called Fred One-night Tuwani, a trade unionist. He was coming to the Attic on foot and he saw them get into a car and take off the masks. I think the car's inside light came on by accident." His smile's vindictive aspect had returned. "See Dladla. He's a bit sensitive, not an easy man to talk to, but he knows all about the Attic. And he knows Fred One-night very well. If you can find Dladla I don't think Fred will be far away." An insinuation was present in what Mbelo was saying, but Yudel had no way of deciphering it.

The bar at the Hotel Veld Kornet was a pleasant place to have dinner. It overlooked an illuminated pool area that had palms and ferns planted densely along the far side. The menu offered a mushroom steak for twelve rands and a kiddie's portion for seven. Yudel never managed to get a hotel or restaurant steak into his one hundred and thirty-five pound body. He considered for a moment the waiter's possible reaction to his ordering a kiddie's portion.

The waiter wore a gleaming white jacket, shining black trousers and a black bow tie. On his head a red fez was mounted at an angle that suggested confidence and the possibility that he might not suffer nonsense from patrons. "One mushroom steak," Yudel said.

"Yes, sir." The waiter made notes on his pad. "To drink, sir?"

"Coffee," Yudel said. "And could you bring it now . . . if it isn't too much trouble."

"No trouble at all, sir." The waiter clicked his heels and hurried in the direction of the kitchen as if Yudel was the only customer he had served all day.

Yudel took one last look at the kiddie's steak on the menu before closing it and pushing it away from him. What the hell, he thought. Feeling in his inside pocket, he brought out the RACC declaration, a document potent enough to bring down violent assaults on the heads of its authors.

"Anything from the bar, sir?" This was a second waiter. He wore a red jacket and silver bow tie.

Yudel had a table in the corner. At the bar a number of well-dressed young people were talking with alcoholic exuberance. "Nothing," he told the wine steward.

"Nothing, sir?" This was clearly a response that was not altogether acceptable.

Yudel yielded the point. "A glass of sherry."

"Thank you, sir."

The waiter went away and Yudel went back to the RACC declaration. He read fast, consuming both the information and the tone in which it was written. The language was ecclesiastical and the approach was cautious, slow getting to the point, but purposeful. It started by professing love for those in authority, thanking God for them and suggesting that Christians pray continually for them to be granted wisdom.

By the next paragraph it was exhorting those same people in

88

authority, who apparently had not yet received the wisdom, to submit themselves to the word of God. By the third it was quoting scriptural grounds for propositions that all people should have equal rights before the law, that relatives should be allowed to visit political detainees, that detention without trial obstructs the proper exercise of justice . . .

Yudel's sherry came and he emptied the glass with a single swallow. It surprised him that such humble material, so full of religious language and so littered with biblical quotations could be the cause of such fury. Then his eyes fell on a list of signatories that did not include either Dladla or Tuwani. An understanding started to form itself in his mind. Apart from Miller himself all of them were university faculty members. In brackets after each of the approximately twenty names was the university and the department each represented. A few came from departments of philosophy, but overwhelmingly they were theologians and, surprisingly to Yudel, from Afrikaans universities, soul mates of Professor van Deventer. Perhaps it was this that could not be forgiven. The English or black rebel revolted against a system in which he had no real power anyway. If the Afrikaner once started to yield, no resistance would remain.

This Fred One-night Tuwani actually claimed to have seen Miller's assailants without their masks and to have recognized one of them. And Reverend Dladla would know where Tuwani was. But who knew where Dladla could be found? Yudel had phoned the offices of the Presbyterian church that afternoon, but Dladla had resigned from their ministry three years before and they did not know his whereabouts. He had tried Blythe Stevens, but Stevens had never heard of him.

The fact that one of Miller's assailants had been a black man was troubling to Yudel in the same way that the detailed information in the pamphlet about the professor of law had been troubling to him. Where, he asked himself, would a black mercenary find employment of this sort? The options were not wide.

The waiter brought the steak. It was very good and so was the mushroom gravy. He ate it with great enthusiasm, leaving nothing. Now the only problem was what to tip the waiter.

*

Yudel took off his watch and placed it on the surface of the desk next to Blythe Stevens's file. The digits on its face told him that it was eleven o'clock. From outside he heard a few distant cars and the bored and mournful barking of a dog. Otherwise the night was silent, a silence somehow brought into sharper relief by those far-away sounds.

The place in the wall where the bolt had lodged looked innocent now. The steel shaft had been removed and the hole patched. Freek would have arranged that, probably to make sure that Rosa did not see it.

The events of the last few days were so strongly in Yudel's mind that thinking about anything else was difficult. Even Rosa's unhappiness slipped quickly away to leave space for the job in hand. Aspects of the entire thing had become distasteful to him. That the money came from outside the country was a problem. That the Du Plessis brothers were not students, but involved in the running of a student newspaper was also troubling.

Yudel tried with little success to turn his thoughts away from it all. He had heard too many stories, examined too many coincidences and studied too many crimes in the past few days. They were beginning to merge in his mind, a poorly defined blur of violence, anger and fear. He was being asked to find some unity in it all, a strand of culpability that would draw them all together.

His flight would leave at seven. That would mean boarding the airways bus at five-thirty. He set his desk alarm for ten to five. He was glad of the few days in Durban. Perhaps his mind would clear. Perhaps new sights would make the old ones more understandable. Perhaps newer questions would answer older ones.

He slept in his chair until the alarm woke him.

Nine

Yudel had parked the hire car on the grass verge of the road and followed the curving lane through the cluster of dense tropical trees. Now he stood at the open gate of the property, looking at the house where Doctor Raymond Baker had spent the last years of his life.

Like the other houses in the neighbourhood it was old and large, but had been kept in good condition. It had a broad untidy lawn in front with patches where the brown Natal soil showed through. There were broad windows down the front and a glass panelled door with stairs leading up to a wide veranda.

The part of the file devoted to Baker had been filled with notes in Blythe Stevens's handwriting. Stevens had been a close friend and the contents of the notes would probably have come from personal knowledge. One of them had said that the widow did not want to talk about Baker's death. Another had said that she was now living in the house with a director of radio programmes.

He had seen photographs of Dahlia Baker. In one she had been laughing, her mouth wide open, an exuberant uninhibited expression. In another she had been smiling with the slow slyness, the soft knowing eyes of the sexually promiscuous. Yudel realised that he might be wrong in an assessment based on two photographs. He told himself that he was always willing to revise a first impression. Then he told himself that this was not always true.

He crossed the lawn slowly. It was a suburban property like any other. The comfortable looking house, the stand almost an acre in size, the broad lawn and the trees along the drive: all combined to make it look like a good place for kids to grow up. No sign remained of the events of six years before.

Yudel stopped in the centre of the lawn. He wanted to see all that could be seen, hear every possible sound, even smell whatever was being carried on the air. The years had taught him that the most significant pieces of information often came at moments when they were least expected.

He crossed to the foot of the short flight of steps that led up to the front door. He would have started up, but the door had opened and he recognized the woman in the doorway from the photographs. "Good afternoon, Mrs Baker," he said. "My name is Yudel Gordon."

Her skin was fairer than he had expected and her hair was waved and full around her head, looking more European than Asian, but it was the eyes that held his attention. They were deep brown and friendly, but with a shade of panic in them. It was the face he had seen in the photographs, but some of the excitement seemed to have left it and been replaced by the anxiety he saw now. "Hello, Mister Gordon," she said. "I've heard about what you're doing."

Yudel thought briefly about Stevens's closed Venetian blinds and locked garden gate. "Why not?" he asked. "Everyone else has."

"I hoped you wouldn't come here."

"But you thought I might?"

Neither of them had moved, Yudel at the foot of the stairs and Dahlia in the doorway. "Yes, I thought you might."

"It must be done, you know that." It was not a question.

"I suppose it must." Her face was troubled and for a moment she seemed to be thinking about something else and to have forgotten Yudel. Then she looked at him and stepped aside. "Do you want to come in?"

Yudel mounted the stairs and went past her into the hallway. The floor was uncarpeted and the only furniture was a cane table and chairs against one wall. A few mediocre water-colour paintings hung at irregular intervals on either side.

"They took him outside his office, not here," Dahlia told him.

"Someone saw it, I believe?"

"A shopkeeper across the road from the building where the union had its offices heard the hooter of Ray's car and went outside. While he was watching the hazard lights came on and the car pulled away suddenly, jerking like mad." Her expression was neutral and her voice quiet and unemotional. She had told the story often before and she would tell it again if it was unavoidable.

"You weren't here that night?"

"No." There was a finality about the way she said the word, that interested Yudel, a flatness that precluded the possibility of an explanation.

"So when did you hear about it?"

"Early that morning."

"Someone phoned you?" Yudel was trying without success to make his interest sound casual. He did not want to appear to be cross-examining her.

She shook her head briefly. "I arrived home." Yudel was sure that she would prefer not to talk or even think about that night. "Will you sit down?" She waved a hand towards the open door of the living room.

He went through the doorway, chose a seat and sat down. Dahlia remained standing. "A cup of tea?" she asked.

"Thanks," he said. She left the room and he looked around it. The furniture was old and the lounge suite had needed upholstering long before. A number of simple wooden bookshelves along one of the walls were filled with books that had probably belonged to Baker. Their titles indicated that the subject matter of most was probably classified under headings like Sociology and Politics.

But Baker was dead and Dahlia was alive and sharing her house and bed with another white man. Yudel wondered about it. For years she had been contravening the racial provisions of the Immorality Act by having intercourse with a white man and for as long she had been ignoring the Group Areas Act by living in a white area. Yet neither she nor Baker had ever been prosecuted.

A magazine stand next to the chair in which Yudel was sitting was filled with very recent and very cheap fiction. He wondered if this was the reading matter of her new man. Among them in a plain blue jacket was a book with the title *The Kingdom is Within You*.

The name of the author was Raymond Baker. The back cover bore a quotation from the book. Yudel read, "To achieve the ideal of a perfect society we must consider first every human being and his need for personal liberty."

Dahlia came back into the room. She stopped before him, holding a small steel tea tray on which the paint was wearing away. Yudel got to his feet and accepted a cup. He sat down again and she sat opposite him. He held up the book. "Do you think I could borrow it?"

"Do," she said. She sat with her hands on her thighs and her knees touching. Something in her posture seemed intent on convincing Yudel. He read in her face a weakness and vulnerability, a possible inability to be alone for long.

"I'll return it in a few days." She shrugged as if it was not a matter of importance. "It won't take me long to read."

"It's not a very long book."

"No," Yudel said. It was clear that Dahlia was going to tell him little that was not in answer to a question. "Your husband was a noted opponent of the government." She nodded in slow, thoughtful agreement. "Overseas visitors with political interests often visited him?"

"He was part of the tour."

"The tour?"

"Since he became banned. They didn't feel that they'd found out about South Africa unless they'd been to Ray. Overseas liberals just have to visit certain people while they're in South Africa. They can't go home without seeing Winnie Mandela, Bishop Tutu and so on. It doesn't matter who they are, film makers, journalists, politicians, they just have to meet the real opponents of apartheid." There was a degree of cynicism in Dahlia's voice. "In Ray's case there were sometimes three or four a week."

It was interesting to Yudel, but not what he had come to discuss. "The night he died . . ."

"As I told you, I wasn't here." She looked straight at him and her expression was somewhere between annoyance and pleading. "Look, Mister Gordon . . ."

"Yudel."

"Yudel." Her expression weakened a little. "I've talked about Ray a lot, to all sorts of people. None of it has done any good. I don't want to talk about him any more. Why don't you talk to his mother? She loves talking about him."

"I'd like to but she lives a long way from here . . ."

"She's living with Lionel Bensch and his family."

Bensch was next on Yudel's list. "With Bensch . . . ?"

"She's here to harass the police. She spends her life trying to force them to find Ray's killer. She just can't leave it alone."

"And you?"

"He's dead. Nothing can change that. I have a new relationship. I want to make it work this time."

This time? Yudel thought. He wondered if the last time had not been a success. "Will you tell me about yourself, if you won't tell me about Ray?"

For a moment she looked really surprised. "Me? Why would you want to know about me? I'm not very interesting."

"I'm sure I'll find you interesting." Yudel was the least flirtatious of men. Little that was temporary appealed to him. He admired high and lonely hilltops, the churning waters of a mountain cataract, the long curve of a sea shore, the inexorable passage of the seasons: all that was unchanging in human terms. They were not the tastes of a man who drew much from the transient or superficial. For all this he realized that his voice had adopted a flirtatious tone. He also realized that it was Dahlia who was the cause of it.

"Interesting?" She tried to suppress a smile. "What do you want to know?"

"I'd like to know why you've never been prosecuted under the Group Areas Act." He was trying to sound businesslike. "Not to mention the Immorality Act." His determination did not help. His voice was thinking for itself.

At the mention of the Immorality Act Dahlia had to work at looking serious. "I suppose they felt sorry for me."

"I'd be surprised."

"You'd be astonished," she said, "to know what our life was like. The security police once came here while Ray was banned. They said that the CID had wanted to prosecute us, but they had stopped them. They were so busy watching Ray that they didn't want little things like us sleeping together or me living here to disturb them. They said they get first option."

"They spent a lot of time watching you?"

This time she did not bother to suppress the smile. "Actually Ray," she said.

"How did they watch?"

"They tapped the phone, of course. Sometimes they questioned us about things we had only said over the phone. They often came here, just walking in. You know Ray was allowed to be in the company of just one person at a time. They would come round to check up. They also got some of our neighbours to spy on us. Old Mister Maartens at the back even cut his hedge low so that they would have a clear view of the house."

"And your immunity has lasted?"

She sucked her cheeks in slightly, trying not to smile. "It looks like it."

"There are children?"

He was again touching on something she did not want to discuss. She answered quickly. "A son by his first wife. They've left the country. His mother took him to England."

"And the woman, Beryl, who was staying here?"

"She's left the country." She looked resignedly at Yudel. "I really know little about that night."

"Perhaps you could tell me something else. I read somewhere in a newspaper that you were a trade union worker at one time . . ."

"I was a branch secretary for the Garment Workers' Federation." She raised her eyebrows in surprise that this should interest him.

"Did you ever know a man called Fred One-night Tuwani?"

This time Dahlia laughed loud, the pain of other memories forgotten. "I haven't seen him for years, but I knew him well. He was always trying to organize unregistered unions. In those days blacks were not allowed to register trade unions."

Yudel could not resist the question. "Where did his nickname come from?"

Dahlia's eyes were alive with merriment. "Oh, I can laugh at that. No woman ever kept Fred for more than one night. And plenty tried."

Yudel tried to break through her amusement. "He saw something that is very important to me. Where can I find him?"

"I haven't seen him in years. He was picked up in '77 with hundreds of other people. That was the last time I heard of him." She grinned. "He was a real rubbish."

"He had a friend, a Reverend Dladla . . ."

The memory of Fred One-night's friend amused Dahlia even more than Fred had. She rocked forward on her chair, her hands clasping her knees, and laughed. "His wife . . . " she said. "His wife was always with Fred. And he was a Presbyterian minister . . ." In Dahlia's mind that was the funniest part.

"And Dladla? Where's he?"

She shrugged. "Somewhere in the Transvaal, I think. If I know Fred you only have to find Dladla to find him. Better still, find Dladla's wife . . ."

It was clear to Yudel that he was not easily going to learn much from Dahlia. Either the memory was too painful or some area of guilt was getting in the way. Perhaps there had been too many wanting to know: whatever the truth of it was, it seemed that what she did know was buried deep beneath other, brighter, less painful recollections. "May I use your phone?" he asked. "I'd like to phone Lionel Bensch's house. Perhaps Mrs Baker is there now."

After he had phoned and found that Mrs Baker was there and that she would be pleased to talk to him or anyone else who would help her find her son's killer he allowed Dahlia to walk him to the door. "If you think of anything that might help me . . . "

"Yes?" She was sucking slightly at her cheeks again, holding back her laughter, a new amusement this time that seemed to have something to do with Yudel.

"I'm at the Rajah for the next few days." He held up the book. "I'll return this."

"All right."

"Try to think about it. I know it's not easy." But Yudel's attempt at ending the conversation with a serious request was lost. Something he had said or the way he had said it had amused Dahlia greatly. "I . . . " But he left it there, not knowing what he had wanted to say.

"Yes?" She was looking into his eyes, her head cocked slightly to one side.

Yudel could find nothing to say in the face of her amusement. "The Rajah hotel," he said finally.

This was even funnier. She laughed again as he retreated down the stairs. He crossed the grass, glancing back twice. On both occasions she was still in the doorway, grinning after him.

"I saw him die. I saw blood pumping into his dirty great beard." Mister Maartens was a man of about sixty. His face was unhappy, deeply lined and belligerent. His eyes were damp and fearful behind glasses that were lightly tinted. "I used to keep an eye on him. I was watching that night. They put the knife into him up to the hilt." The old man seemed to enjoy the memory. "The blood was pumping out like a water pump."

"And into his dirty great beard," Yudel asked.

"Right into his dirty great beard, like it was coming out of a pump."

"Could you show me the place from which you watched?"

"Come on." He turned and went down the passage, rocking from side to side with the rolling gait of the bandy-legged. He glanced back more than once to see that Yudel was following. It was not often these days that anyone was interested in what he had to say.

The floors were covered by cheap linoleum. There were vases holding plastic flowers and Yudel noticed two prints of little girls with disproportionately large tear drops running down their cheeks. He stopped next to the old man on the back stoep. "You see I let the boy cut my hedge short," Maartens said, "so I could keep a good eye on him."

From where they were standing Yudel could see the back and one side of the house as well as the tiny cottage where the woman, Beryl must have stayed. "You were standing here?"

"Right here."

"On this spot?"

"This very spot?"

"And you saw the blood pumping into his beard?"

"Like it was coming out of a water pump."

"He had no beard," Yudel said. The old man's face was startled as he turned to Yudel. "When he died he had no beard. And he was not killed here."

"I saw it." His face was indignant. "I was working with the police. I was the first . . . "

But Yudel was already on his way down the passage to the front of the house. He heard Maartens shouting behind him. "I saw it. It was my job . . . " He went down the path to the place where he had left the car. As he drove away he saw the old man's angry face framed by the front doorway.

He drove slowly through the quiet suburban streets, past the homes of white working-class people, their gardens filled with Durban's bright, large-leaved, sub-tropical plants. A few yellow and brown leaves still clung to trees that were bright green with the freshness of the false spring that had settled over the country. The warm weather had come too soon and brought out the new leaves before time.

Yudel reached the main artery that wound down the long hill towards the city centre and let the car run. For a moment he had felt stimulated by his visit to Dahlia. But whatever she had done for his state of mind Maartens had undone. What was it, he wondered, that would make a man boast that he had seen another die when there was no truth in it? What was it within him that made him play the part of a security police spy when it had never been anything more than a pretence?

Ten

Yudel rang a bell that was mounted in a wall almost a metre taller than he was. When Maureen Baker opened the door to him he saw an old house, smaller and narrower than Baker's. What had originally been a low brick rail along the edge of the stoep had been extended until it touched the roof. Along the front wall of the house to the right of the door he could see a row of small cement patches which had not yet been painted over. "You heard about the machine-gun attack on Lionel's house?" she asked.

"Yes, I've heard about it."

"Those are the holes the bullets made."

"One went through the front door, I think."

"Yes, but Lionel has fixed the door. I'll show you where it entered the floor." She led him into a dim windowless passage with the doors of bedrooms leading off to either side and stopped, bending over, six or seven paces from the door. "Here you are." Yudel examined the place. The bullet had entered obliquely, tearing a long deepening furrow in the surface of the wood. "The children took it very badly. Especially the little boy, Willie. He often sits in a sheltered corner, doing nothing. He seems to choose places from which they can't shoot at him."

According to Blythe Stevens's clippings she was over eighty years old. She wore a shawl around her shoulders and she stooped slightly, but her movements were decisive and vigorous, and her eyes and, Yudel was sure, her mind were clear. Her hair was completely grey and drawn tightly around her head to a bun at the back. A network of very fine wrinkles followed the natural lines of her face around features that, even now, were a source of admiration to Yudel. At the corners of her eyes deep lines of anguish had become a permanent part of her face. It was the face of one who had loved to the exclusion of everything else. "Shall we sit in the dining room? The Bensches don't really have a parlour."

The passage opened into a large room that was dominated by a long wooden table surrounded by straight-back chairs. Maureen Baker sat down on one side of the table and Yudel on the other. Through the windows at the far end of the room he could see a fruit orchard that was just starting to bloom. "Is the back as well fortified as the front?" he asked.

"Almost. Lionel did his best to close it off from the road. He has dogs there, a Doberman and an Alsatian."

"Mrs Baker," Yudel asked, "how do you come to be staying with the Bensches?"

"I thought that the same people who are responsible for my son's death might have attacked Lionel."

"Do you think they are the same people?"

"I think they might be." She considered for a moment. Her eyes were faded, soft and blue and what she felt was reflected clearly in them. "I'm sure they are," she said.

Yudel did not pursue that line. He had been exposed to the same sort of certainties among Blythe Stevens and his friends. He intended drawing his own conclusions. "You spend a lot of time looking for your son's killers?"

"He was all my life. When they killed him they killed me." It was said simply, not as if it was intended to impress him. He could see that something of warmth and love in her may well have perished with her son's death. He could also see that it was not just the dying, but rather the manner of the dying. "My blood turned to ice water when they killed him."

"Will it help if they are found?"

She looked at Yudel as if she was not sure that she understood him. "I don't know." But the resolve he could see in her was strongly reflected in her voice when she spoke again. "I must do it. There's nothing else for me." When Yudel did not reply she said, "I've made a lot of notes. I've got a copy for you. Shall I get them?"

"I'd like to read them later. I'd also like to see a photograph of your son."

"Of course you wouldn't have seen one in Dahlia's house." It was said with a strong resentment that Yudel suspected was never far from her. "I'll give you a picture of him."

"And I want you to tell me about him. His widow lent me a copy of one of his books . . . "

"There is only one, *The Kingdom is Within You*. Dahlia always says that she'll talk to no one about Ray, but if the someone who wants to talk is a man . . . " She left completion of the sentence to Yudel's imagination.

"I'd like to know about him, the sort of man he was."

"He was a very good man. Some people thought he was a saint. If he had chosen he could have been a great scientist." She nodded to emphasize the point, her serious pain-racked face suddenly drawn with the force of her concentration.

"They started to hate him while he was still at university. He was an executive of the National Union of South African Students. Even then other students used to bring their problems to him. Anyone could talk to Ray. Later, when he got married, students and workers would come to discuss something with him and stay a month. His first wife, Rhonda, never came to terms with that sort of thing. He married her while he was still at university. I was against it, but he wanted to get married and he wanted Rhonda.

"She went with him to Paris. He learnt French specially to study under Sartre. He felt Sartre's philosophy was just what he'd been looking for. Sartre didn't want to teach him at first and he only agreed when he saw that Ray was not going to go away. Eventually he admitted that Ray was the best student he'd ever had. He wanted him to stay in France, but Ray felt that he had to come back. He had work to do in South Africa.

"When he came home everyone expected him to take a university posting, but he surprised them all by doing a very humble job in a union office. That lasted for a few years, but he wanted to try out his own ideas so he and Rhonda came to the farm. I have a fruit farm near Paarl and I agreed to let him run it his way.

"The labourers loved him. He was everybody's big brother. They brought him their problems and he lent them money that never came back. He organized Saturday evening bioscope shows. They had the best year of their lives. Of course we made a huge loss that year. If I'd let Ray go on there would have been nothing left of the farm. No one wanted to work. They worked about two or three hours a day and Ray would spend his time looking for reasons why they were so lazy. The next year I had to get a really hard foreman to straighten things out.

"After the farm he got an important union posting. By this time he and Rhonda weren't even living together. She was in Cape Town with my grandson and leading her own life. She had become quite a different person from the shy dependent girl he had married. I don't think Ray wanted an independent wife.

"Those people who killed my son hated him because he influenced so many others. He ran an industrial research programme that big industry hated. He held evening classes to teach black workers from every industry how to run a trade union. They saw what effect he was having and in 1974 they banned him. It was about the same time that he married Dahlia according to Muslim rites. Of course it could never be legal. She calls herself Mrs Baker, but she isn't really. I was no more sure about that marriage than the one to Rhonda. I knew she would hurt him terribly and she did. The way she used to carry on with other men, even in his company. You can't imagine it. I used to tell him to do something about it, but he would just say, Oh Mom, it means nothing. He was like that. He saw no harm in anyone.

"From the time he was banned Ray's life changed completely. His phone was tapped. They often came round to make sure that he was not breaking the provisions of his banning order. They would phone and say that they knew about his braaivleis or his dinner party and that he had better be careful. He also started receiving threatening calls.

"The telephone, Yudel. It was the telephone that played a major part in my son's death. They were listening in and they acted accordingly. He phoned Dahlia to say that he would be leaving the office late that night and they intercepted him. Of course she was too busy with her own plans to care.

"That same week a man with a very cultured English-sounding voice had phoned all five R. Bakers in the book, each time asking if he could speak to Doctor Ray Baker. Eventually he spoke to Ray and when Ray said, yes, the man just hung up. About a month before one of the other R. Bakers had received two threatening calls.

"It has all been so ugly. When the police arrived after Ray went missing they unplugged the phone and would not let anyone use it. The lieutenant pulled it right out of Beryl's hands. He said he was in charge there and he did not want any trouble from her. They seemed to want to keep my son's death a secret. Afterwards the CID would not let me discuss the case over the phone with them. They said I could phone them, but I should say nothing until they came to see me.

"While he was alive they made life difficult for him in every way they could. More than once his car was stopped on the freeway and searched. They always said that they were acting on information received, but they never once found anything incriminating. His passport applications were refused without any reason being given. They never bothered to look for his killer. They never even questioned the neighbours.

"Strangest of all, his banning order was due to expire two months after he was killed. And his son's passport had just been renewed. I'm sure they were expecting him to leave the country, but they wanted to kill him first.

"It's no wonder Rhonda took their son and left. I would leave too, except that if I go I'll never find my son's killer. And I have to, Yudel. If you do it for me you'll be restoring a small measure of life to an old lady."

Yudel smiled at her. "When will the Bensch family be home? I'd like to talk to them too."

"Not till tomorrow. They have a place they visit in the mountains, near Underberg."

"Oh? Nice if you can afford that."

"No, no. They inherited a little house up there." She said it as if the Bensches being able to afford much was unthinkable. "They only have what Daisy earns as a teacher. Lionel is very talented but he rarely finishes a painting. He does a bit of restoration from time to time. Living with them is very difficult. They're so Bohemian I'm always hungry. There are no meal times. When you want to eat you just cook for yourself. It takes a little getting used to."

"I'll come back to see them," Yudel said.

"You must. You'll be very interested in Lionel's story."

"You can depend on it."

"There are connections, Yudel. If you speak to them, Lionel and Daisy, you'll see the connections." Her gentle, pain-ravaged eyes were on his, pleading with him to see the connections that would reveal the identity of her son's killers.

"The policeman who told you not to talk on the telephone, what was his name?"

"Sergeant Visser of the CID."

"And the security police officer your son had most dealings with?"

"Major Heunis."

"You're sure of their names?"

She was sure. Her eyes were sure. "Their names are carved in my memory. I'll never forget any of them."

Yudel was aware that he was in the process of destroying whatever chance he had of keeping his activities away from Doctor Williamson and Brigadier De Beer. "What do you mean?" Lieutenant Visser was saying. He had moved up a rank since his last dealings with Maureen Baker. He was a man of a little over thirty. His straight brown hair was cut short like that of a schoolboy complying with regulations. His open, boyish face had become troubled in the few minutes Yudel had been in his office. "What do you mean, investigating the Baker murder?"

"I've been hired by friends of his."

The policeman sat stiffly upright behind his desk, his elbows pressing hard on the armrests of his chair. "We've been investigating the Baker case for six years. It's not closed. If we can't find the guilty party, how are you going to?"

"I might as well have a go." Yudel was being overly casual. "You don't seem to have got very far."

"How would you know? How would you know how far we've got?" The lieutenant's indignation was that of someone on whose territory an outsider was trespassing.

"I was going by the number of arrests you've made."

"And what are you going to do?"

Yudel could see nothing sinister in the policeman's face. He decided to meet the charge head on. "I'm going to ask you why you told old Mrs Baker not to use the telephone when discussing the case with you."

Indignation and exasperation seemed for a moment to become alarm.

"Agh, the old lady's mad," he said. "Why would I have said something so stupid?"

"Was it so stupid?" Yudel was watching his face with the complete fascination the mongoose has for the cobra. "Who was tapping their phone?"

"Please, man. What are you talking about?" Visser was shaking his head and rising from his seat. Yudel had the definite feeling that, brief though it had been, the interview was ending.

"If the security police were tapping Baker's phone, why didn't you want them to overhear what the old lady had to say?"

Visser was on his feet. He had been pushed beyond reasonable limits. "You just stop right there. You better give me your name and address."

"Why didn't you want them listening to the old lady's complaints?"

"That old lady, let me tell you . . . " He was shaking his head and sliding a sheet of paper towards Yudel. "You know how old she is? She's completely unreasonable. Write your name."

Any interrogation that Yudel had been attempting was clearly over. He wrote his name on the paper.

"Now your address, occupation and employer."

Yudel wrote it down.

"Department of Prisons? You work for the Department of Prisons?"

"Yes . . . "

"You're not supposed to be doing this. You stationed in Pretoria? What rank are you?"

Yudel told him.

"Yissis, Mister Gordon. I'm sorry about this, but I'll have to report this to my Captain. You're not allowed to do this. Didn't you know? If you interview potential witnesses you might even be prosecuted for defeating the ends of justice. I don't say it will happen, but it might. You aren't allowed to interfere in a police investigation. Didn't you know that?"

Locating Major Heunis of the security police proved to be more difficult. After leaving Lieutenant Visser's office he had spoken to the policeman on duty in the charge office on the ground floor of the building. The policeman had looked worried and called his sergeant. He had wanted to know why Yudel was looking for the security policeman. When Yudel told him that the matter concerned the death of a restricted person he had raised both eyebrows and passed him on to an office further along the corridor. Here a new officer had asked the same question and received the same answer. He had then asked Yudel his name. Yudel had told him and he had asked how to spell it. Yudel had spelled it slowly so that the officer could keep pace, had offered his address, occupation, identification number, place where he was staying in Durban and, reluctantly, his employer. "You work for the Department of Prisons?" the officer had asked, unbelieving. Then he had made a telephone call and directed Yudel to a building three blocks away. Yudel had followed his directions and given his story to a man in civilian clothing who had introduced himself as warrant officer Rossouw. He too had written down Yudel's name and particulars and had made a telephone call. After that Yudel had been directed to a warrant officer Holtzhausen who had his office in a building near the harbour.

"You say friends of the family hired you?" warrant officer Holtzhausen asked.

"That's right," Yudel said. "I came to see Major Heunis."

"Major Heunis asked me to handle this for him."

The hell he did, Yudel thought. "I didn't come here to talk to you. If he's not available I'll be going." Yudel got to his feet.

Holtzhausen remained seated. "Sit down, Mister Gordon. You are being questioned by a police officer. You can't just go."

"Questioned about what? I came to see Major Heunis. You didn't ask me to come in."

The policeman's face was lean and suntanned, his straight black hair cut as short as Visser's and neatly parted along the side of his head. His eyes had opened a little wider in mock curiosity. His voice was altogether calm when he spoke. "That doesn't matter," he said. "You are still being questioned by a police officr and you may not leave."

Yudel sat down. "And Major Heunis won't see me?"

"It's not that he won't see you. It's simply that he is very busy at the moment." The warrant officer lied without skill. "He asked me to deal with this for him."

"Perhaps I can see him tomorrow when he isn't so busy."

"He won't be available for the next few weeks. He's in the middle of a very important investigation."

"I see."

The policeman nodded, apparently glad of Yudel's new clarity. "And you are investigating the death of Doctor Baker?"

"That's what I said."

"You are aware that civil servants are not allowed to augment their salaries in any way whatsoever?"

He had not told Holtzhausen that he was a civil servant, but the news was bound to have travelled ahead of him. "I've heard it said."

"Something to think about?" The question was again accompanied by a raising of his eyebrows. In Yudel's experience members of the security police were more than usually adept at making ordinary citizens feel that they were in the presence of a superior breed, but Yudel had devices of his own. One of them was not to answer hostile questions. The warrant officer waited until it became clear that Yudel was not going to reply. "Don't you think this matter is the CID's job?"

"Either theirs or yours."

"Ours?"

"He was one of your special babies, wasn't he?" This time the policeman chose not to reply. "So aren't you interested in who killed him?"

He waited long enough so that when he did speak it was not in answer to Yudel's question. "You are trying to interrogate me, Mister Gordon."

"No, I'm not. But I would like to question Major Heunis."

He smiled slightly and briefly, an amused but not a friendly expression. "Nobody questions Major Heunis." He held up a hand to check Yudel's reply. "You haven't told me why the police can't handle this murder."

"You tell me. You people have had six years to work on it. You tell me why you can't handle it. I wouldn't be here if you had been successful."

Holtzhausen nodded again. He was not yielding the point, merely conceding that Yudel had made a mildly interesting observation. "You know we were good to him. We were recommending that they lift his ban. Another few months and he would have been able to come and go as he liked."

Yudel found it a strange statement. The policeman might almost have been looking for approval. "We protected him from the CID. Do you realize that? They could have had him under the Immorality Act any time they chose. They only had to walk in there and pull him out of bed. He contravened the Act every night of his life." It was said with the leering expectancy of a peep-show patron. "We could have picked up his coolie woman under the Group Areas Act. But we aren't interested in that sort of thing. We are interested in the safety of our people." He frowned and pursed his lips. It was an expression that indicated the superior knowledge and wisdom of the one wearing it. "You know of course that there is a theory the African National Congress terrorists killed Baker."

Yudel had heard the rumour that the national resistance itself was responsible for Baker's death. "Yes," he said.

"There's quite a lot to be said for it," Holtzhausen said.

Except all the evidence, Yudel thought.

"You know that the night he died an ex-ANC terrorist was murdered in Kwa Mashu. It makes you think. Do you also know that he once gave evidence in a treason trial. The ANC didn't like what he said, I can tell you." It was all said with the air of a man sharing a secret. "What do you think about that?" Before Yudel could answer, the door of the office directly behind him opened and someone came in. There was quiet as the newcomer stopped just inside the door. The warrant officer repeated his question. "What do you say about that?"

Yudel was strongly aware of the man behind him. He spoke without carefully considering the words. "I say that if he was such a great friend of yours and an enemy of the ANC it seems strange that he was living under a restriction order at all."

This was a conclusion the security policeman had not expected. For a moment his eyes flicked towards the man behind Yudel. Then the self-assurance that was not really self-assurance, but an attitude that came with the job, reasserted itself and he shook his head as if to rid it of erroneous thinking such as Yudel's. "These things are very complicated and the information is top secret. I'm afraid I can't explain it to you."

"I suppose not," Yudel said. The new man was standing altogether still, not betraying his presence in any way. "But there are a few things I'm sure you can explain to me."

Holtzhausen brightened. "Try me," he said. He had learnt the expression from a girl he had once known. He had tried her without success, but the words had remained in his memory.

"I'll do that," Yudel said. He was not allowing himself to be deceived into thinking that this was an invitation to interrogate. "Firstly, during the last years of Baker's life, while he was restricted and you people were tapping his telephone . . . " Yudel paused. He wanted to be sure that he had the complete attention of the man behind him. Then he moved, spinning round suddenly and rising to his feet, his right hand outstretched. "Yudel Gordon," he said.

The man was lean, blond and balding, perhaps forty years of age, and he answered on reflex. "Varrevich," he said. His face was lined and tanned, his eyes barely visible behind heavily tinted glasses, and he knew that he had been tricked into revealing his identity. "Milan Varrevich," he finished, the sound of his voice resentful now.

"Pleased to meet you," Yudel said. He studied the other man's face for a moment longer before turning back to Holtzhausen. "While you were tapping his telephone, could anyone else have been tapping it at the same time?"

"Who says we were tapping it?"

"I say so. But let's not waste time debating it. Could anyone else have been tapping his phone without your department knowing it."

"Th . . . this is not something I can discuss with you." He stumbled over the words. "This is not for public . . . "

Yudel saw the poorly disguised confusion on his face. He was sure that if Holtzhausen had known the answer to his question he would not have told him. He was equally sure that the warrant officer did not know.

"There's only one other thing," Yudel said. This time the policeman looked less enthusiastic. He said nothing. Yudel could see a certain humiliation in his expression. He seemed to be feeling that this little Jew had outmanoeuvred him somehow. "The only other thing is this: I would like a list of the names and ranks of every security policeman stationed in Durban between December 1977 and December 1981. That shouldn't be too much of a problem."

Yudel turned to look at Varrevich. He had been in this line of work far longer than the warrant officer. His face was altogether impassive. Yudel could not see his eyes.

Eleven

The rain fell softly over the city in the late afternoon, the clouds moving off the surface of the sea to settle in a low bank along the shore line. From the window of Yudel's hotel room he could see a smooth heavy swell, grey with cloud and rain, running in to break against the concrete blocks of a pier and down the long flat approach to the beaches. With the clouds twilight had come early and was already deepening towards night.

He was beginning to doubt the wisdom of having approached Visser and Holtzhausen. He had known from the start that contact with the police was going to be unavoidable at some point, but the sooner it was made the sooner he was going to have problems at work. And there was the matter of his recent promotion and the goodwill of Brigadier De Beer and old man Williamson. Damn, he thought. Couldn't they have waited a few months?

The sea slowly disappeared into the growing darkness until only the bright crests of waves gave away its uneasy presence. Down on the street the rain was heavier now, gleaming curtains of water swirling downwards in the light from cars and street lamps. He would take the evening off. On nights like this street crime dropped to almost nothing, violently inclined citizens having the good sense to exercise their unlawful skills in better weather. If it was all right for the bad guys, Yudel wondered why he should endure the discomfort of going out on such a night. Besides that he was tired.

He thought briefly about Maureen Baker and the way she used

the word 'they' when talking about the police. She said that when her son had been alive they had harassed him in every possible way. And she had said that they had never really looked for the killer. It was clear that she suspected the police of not trying, but she suspected them of a great deal more than that. Yudel found her confusion understandable, but he had no doubt that it was confusion. Someone had phoned a number of R. Bakers a few days before the killing, looking for the unionist. If this had been the killer or a member of the organization that was responsible, he could not have had police connections. It was true that the matter of when Baker was to leave his office could have been learned from a phone tap; but by itself that was hardly evidence at all.

Yudel turned away from the window. He felt he should phone Rosa. Every day without effort he remembered the essential details of the hundreds of prisoners whom he dealt with regularly in his work. He even remembered a great many irrelevant details of the lives of thousands of prisoners who had passed through his hands over the last twenty years. Almost every small incident of all the murder cases that had involved him were fixed in his mind as if they could never be erased. For matters that interested him his memory was almost flawless, but at this moment it was proving to be of no use. He was trying without success to remember the telephone number of Rosa's sister, Irena. After some intense and fruitless concentration he recalled that Rosa had written it down on a sheet of paper and placed the paper in the bottom of his suitcase. He took the case from the top of the cupboard, found the paper with the number in Rosa's careful handwriting and asked the switchboard operator to dial it for him.

Irena's voice whined plaintively across the trunk connection, repeating the number that the operator had dialled.

"Hullo, Irena . . . " Yudel started.

"Oh, Yudel . . . " Irena was Yudel's most constant admirer. "Are you safe?"

For a moment Yudel was startled by the thought that something might have happened to prompt such a question, but his knowledge of Irena dispelled the alarm almost before it arose. "I'm well, Irena. Are you safe?"

"Me?" Her voice sounded surprised and a little enthusiastic. "Why? Is there any danger?"

"Not that I know of," he told her.

"Oh. You're making fun of me." Her disappointment was complete. "I suppose you want to talk to Rosa."

"If it's possible."

"Yudel." Rosa's voice came on to the connection almost immediately. He could hear the fear in her voice. No one else had the ability to make him feel guilty the way Rosa could. He had enjoyed his first day in Durban, but the soft, querulous sound of her voice made him wonder if he should be there at all.

"Everything's all right, Rosa."

"Are you sure?"

"Yes. Everything's fine."

"Come back, Yudel." It was a plea. Leave this thing alone, she was saying to him. Come back and let's be as we were before.

"I'll be back on the weekend." His own voice was uncertain, not sure that he could ask this of her.

"Must you stay on?"

"Rosa . . ." He needed to know if there was any new reason for her fear. "Has anything happened since I left?"

"No, Yudel. I'm just such a damned coward." He could hear her tiredness now, a deep exasperation with herself.

"There's no reason to be afraid," he said. His memory, acting independent of his will, resurrected the image of the crossbow bolt in his study wall. "You just stay with Irena and Hymie."

"It's not me . . . It's not me I'm thinking about. Good Lord . . ."

Yudel's natural reflex was to tell Rosa that the Lord was not involved but he managed to inhibit the impulse and said, "There's really no reason to be afraid for me."

Someone knocked on the door of the room, a soft sound, the knock of a person unsure of his welcome. "Just a moment, Rosa," Yudel said into the telephone.

"Was there a knock? I'm sure I heard a knock."

"Yes, there was. I'll be back in a moment."

Yudel went quickly to the door. In the back of his mind was the barely conscious idea that it might be warrant officer Holtzhausen or one of his colleagues. But the knock had been too gentle.

Dahlia Baker was waiting just outside the door. She was wearing a soft pink dress that contrasted subtly with the colour of her skin and holding a rain-wet yellow mackintosh at arm's length. Her teeth shone white in the sallow tones of her face. She was smiling with the same uncertainty he had heard in her knock. It was an expression that said, here I am, please don't send me away.

"Hullo?" Yudel said, not moving from his position in the doorway. His greeting was also a question.

"Hullo." She grinned at him, the expression almost fearful.

Yudel was looking at her face, wondering at the apprehension he saw, unconsciously waiting for her to explain what she was doing there. "Hullo," he said again, awkwardly aware of the lack of variety in his conversation.

She glanced down the passage and back at his face, immediately averting her eyes. "May I come in?"

Yudel leapt back from the door as if he had been pushed. "Of course, of course. Come in." She still seemed to hesitate. "Come in," he repeated. She came in, eyes cast down as if in extreme modesty. "Can I get you something?" he asked, wondering at the same time what he would possibly be able to get her and hoping that any request would be reasonable.

"What would you like to get me?" The question was accompanied by a little teasing smile and a quick sidelong glance.

"Well, I . . . "

"You're on the phone."

"The phone?" Yudel was looking at her face, admiring the smooth almost glowing skin.

"The telephone," she explained. "You're busy on the telephone."

Yudel turned to the telephone, the handpiece lying on the table. It seemed to be staring back at him with Rosa's face, Rosa's accusing face. He picked it up thoughtfully, watching Dahlia all the time and spoke. "Rosa?" Dahlia was hanging up her mackintosh behind the door.

"Where were you, Yudel? I heard a woman's voice." The uncertainty in her tone had made way for intense interest.

"It's just a person from the hotel," Yudel said. Dahlia was looking down at her feet and making no effort to hide her smile.

"What does she want?" Rosa asked.

"To make the bed," Yudel lied again, but with no easier facility. "She came to make the bed."

"To make the bed? At this time of night? Wasn't the bed made yet?"

"Not yet. I suppose they thought they wouldn't use the room tonight."

"That's terrible." For a moment, her anger having found a target, Rosa had forgotten her fears. "To come along making beds at this time of night, it's unheard of."

"Yes," Yudel said.

"You should complain to the manager."

"I will," he told her.

"Don't forget now. Go there and complain."

"I will."

"You're not just saying that, are you, Yudel?"

Yudel was looking at Dahlia and she was looking at him. Her eyes were deep brown and the pupils were large, seeming to merge into the irises. "No, I'm not just saying that," he told Rosa.

"Oh Yudel." She had dismissed the incompetence of the hotel management. He could hear in her voice that earlier preoccupations had returned. "Come back, please."

"On the weekend," he said. "I'll be back on the weekend." The neckline of Dahlia's dress formed a sharp vee that ended just above her breasts. It was edged by little vertical frills of the same material.

"Can't you come before?"

"There's no need to be afraid." Around her waist and hips the material fitted tightly, fanning into a broad skirt.

"Are you sure?" Rosa's voice pleaded across the six hundred kilometres.

"Quite sure. Rosa, I have to go." Dahlia's shoes had very high heels, little openings through which the toes protruded and thin straps that encircled each ankle.

"Why? Why must you go?"

"I'm running up a terrific telephone bill." The ankles were narrow and the toes were small and neatly rounded.

"Are they still making the bed?"

"Bed?"

"The bed, are the people from the hotel still making it?"

"No. They've gone."

"Don't forget to go to the management and complain." Dahlia took a deep breath and her breasts moved with the movement of her lungs.

"I will complain. I must go. I'll phone again tomorrow."

"Be careful, Yudel."

"I will. Goodbye."

"Goodbye. I'll wait for your call tomorrow."

"Goodbye, Rosa."

"Goodbye . . ." Yudel hung up.

"Would you like summer or winter sheets?" Dahlia asked. Yudel's face must have reflected his confusion. "Since I have to make the bed . . ."

"It's just . . ." Yudel thought about it, but he was not sure just how it was.

"I know. She wouldn't understand."

"She certainly wouldn't." He looked at Dahlia, at the sharp vee point of her neckline and the smoothness of her neck, the way she stood with her ankles close together, one foot rocking back on its heel and her hands, the only part of her that betrayed nervousness as they tightened and loosened their grip on her purse.

"May I sit down?"

"Of course." He had to look round the room before discovering the table at the window and the two chairs on either side of it. He gestured with both hands. "Would you . . ."

She smiled again, this time without looking at him. "I don't mind if I do," she said.

Seated at the table, Yudel looked at her. The question, Well? came to his mind, but he was glad that he edited it away before it reached his lips. He was looking into her eyes again and his mind was not especially clear. He was also not sure that his voice would follow the instructions of his brain well. In every way it was best for him to wait for her to speak. He waited.

"I forgot something this afternoon," she said. "I didn't give you the name of the shopkeeper who saw them take Ray."

"No, you didn't."

117

"After you left I realized that I should have given you his name."
She was grinning at him, the expression of her face seeming to bear little relation to what she was saying. The panic that he had seen in her eyes earlier in the day was there again.

"You should certainly have done that," he said.

"His name is Luis Rodrigues."

"I'll speak to him."

"He calls his shop Greyville Greengrocer." He was looking at her face, trying to read the smallest emotion or slightest pretence. He looked at her hands where they were spread, palms-downward on the table. The fingers were long and narrow and would have been beautiful if it had not been for an ugly thickening of the joints. Suddenly she drew them away and hid them below the surface of the table. "You're looking at my hands."

"Shouldn't I?"

"No. They're ugly."

Her face had his attention again. "And you came to give me this information?"

She looked at her hands that were now folded in her lap. "It's important, isn't it?"

There was a new knock on the door. Yudel got quickly to his feet, looking first at the door, then at Dahlia. "I think you should open it," she said, as if this was an idea that might not have come to Yudel without her.

He opened the door. A young African, even smaller than himself and dressed in the uniform of the hotel, peered at him out of the relative gloom of the passage. "Excuse me, sir. Mister Gordon?"

"That's right," Yudel told him.

"Excuse me, sir. I'm very sorry, sir." He paused, possibly unsure about the reason for his sorrow.

"Yes."

"I'm sorry, sir . . . a lady came to the room . . . "

"Which room? Which lady?"

"Sir's room. A lady came up . . . "

Yudel realized which lady was being referred to. He was suddenly aware of Dahlia seated behind him and of the fact that she was not white. What did the law say about Dahlia being in a hotel room with him? Would she be allowed there at all? And would there being alone together be seen as conspiring to contravene the Immorality Act? Yudel had heard that such a charge existed. "I think he's talking about me, Yudel," Dahlia said.

Yudel turned to her. She looked at ease and a little amused. The hotel employee was not amused though. "Sorry, sir . . . " he stuttered.

"Yes," Yudel said. "What about the lady?"

"Sir, sorry, sir. The manager says if the lady is going to stay for the night . . . sir must pay for the extra person . . . "

"Ah . . . " Yudel felt Dahlia's presence behind him more acutely than before. The man from the hotel looked down the passage to his left, then to his right, up at the ceiling and down at his shoes. The only direction he was avoiding was the one filled by Yudel.

"Tell the manager . . . " Dahlia was speaking. " . . . that Mister Gordon has not yet made up his mind. He'll let you know."

"Thank you, ma'am, thank you." He executed a few quick bows and backed away down the passage, only turning after he had put six or seven paces between himself and Yudel.

Yudel watched him go, closed the door and turned round with difficulty. Dahlia was again studying her hands. He sat down opposite her. When she did look up it was with a brief sidelong glance, the same pleading smile and fearful eyes. The apprehension and amusement in her face were all part of the same expression. "Do you want me to go?"

"No. I don't want you to go." He answered without thinking, but no amount of thinking could have added anything to it. He wanted her to stay.

She opened her bag and took out a packet of cigarettes. "Smoke?" she asked. He accepted the cigarette and took the lighter from her hand to light both cigarettes. She inhaled the smoke deeply and leant back in her chair, seeming to relax for the first time. "Well," she said.

"Well, indeed," Yudel said.

The appearance of relaxing was superficial. Dahlia moved in her chair, rocking her knees from side to side, ankles and knees held elegantly together. "I didn't know you smoked," she said.

Their eyes met, then moved off in different directions. "I didn't know you did. Did you know about my athlete's foot?"

"Do you have athlete's foot?" The idea seemed to distress Dahlia.

"No. Do you?"

She smiled again. There was embarassment in her smile, but also something of a shared secret. "You're teasing me."

She smoked in silence and Yudel could find nothing further to say. There are men who talk easily to women, finding no difficulty in making them smile and respond. There are others who find it less easy, but not a great problem. Yudel belonged to a third group who found it all but impossible to make conversation with a woman unless he had something important to say. Now, failing in his effort to find something to say, he did nothing but look at Dahlia. "Perhaps I shouldn't have come," she said. Yudel looked at her. Her hair was thick, strong and black with dusty brown highlights along the edges. "I think I shouldn't have come. Would you like me to go?"

"No," Yudel said. Her neck was long and smooth, disappearing into the frills of her collar.

"Are you sure? I'll go if you want me to."

The dress had no sleeves and her arms were lean like her neck and a yellow brown colour that seemed to hold an inner radiance. It was a while before he answered her question. "I'm sure," he said.

Dahlia had her purse in front of her on the table and was kneading it with both of her rather ugly hands. His silence and apparent lack of response was something she had rarely dealt with before. The third knock on his door that evening relieved her of trying to manage his silence. "Busy night," she said.

The knock had been brief, sharp and businesslike, not the hotel porter this time. Yudel opened the door to Lieutenant Visser of the Durban CID. The lieutenant's face was set and serious. He was still wearing his raincoat and causing a darkening circle of moisture on the hotel carpet. "May I come in?" It was not a demand.

Yudel stepped aside for him to enter and he came in slowly, frowning slightly. He started taking off his raincoat. Underneath he was wearing a grey sports coat and slacks. He saw Dahlia and his eyes widened with surprise. Then he looked quickly at Yudel as if expecting an explanation. "Good evening, Mrs Baker," he said.

"Hullo, lieutenant." Dahlia was leaning back in her chair, neither alarmed nor surprised.

"I didn't expect to see you here," he told her.

"I could say the same." She looked vaguely amused.

"I wonder . . . " Visser looked round the room. "Mister Gordon . . . "

Yudel was watching his face. Visser seemed to have a problem composing what he wanted to say. "I think the lieutenant wants to speak to you alone, Yudel," Dahlia suggested.

"I'd be glad."

Dahlia stretched her legs in front of her, pointing her toes. After they had the attention of both men she allowed them to sink slowly to the floor, then got to her feet. "Is that the bathroom, in there," she asked Yudel.

"Yes."

"All right if I wait in there, lieutenant, or are you going to be a long time?"

"I'll just be a few minutes. I'll be glad if you wait in there." His face was troubled and he did not look at Dahlia as he spoke.

"You know where to find me, Yudel," she said. She walked smoothly into the bathroom and closed the door, happily conscious of the male admiration she was leaving behind.

"Won't you sit down?" Yudel asked.

Visser sat down in the place Dahlia had vacated. "This afternoon . . ." he began, speaking English for Yudel's benefit. "This afternoon I'm afraid I was very unfriendly to you." His eyes examined Yudel's face for the effect his admission was having. "It was unnecessary."

"That's okay, lieutenant." There has to be more than this, Yudel was thinking.

"Yes, I shouldn't have acted that way."

"Think nothing of it."

"I don't think any laws were being broken. I'm sure you would be careful."

"Well, good."

The policeman was having trouble getting to the next step. "I hope you don't hold it against me," he said.

"Not at all." Yudel was giving him no assistance.

"This investigation of yours . . . " They were moving into more significant waters. "I got the impression . . . " His face was set and troubled. What he was doing was not easy for him. "You seemed to think that the CID and the special branch were not working together." He paused for Yudel to respond. When he did not, the policeman continued uncertainly. "I got the impression you thought that."

"Did I say that?" Yudel asked innocently. "I don't remember saying that."

"I think you said something like that." It was clear that he was struggling. "I think you got the idea that we didn't want them to know everything about the murder."

"Oh yes," Yudel said, his face brightening. "I gathered that you told old Mrs Baker never to contact you on the phone, or at least only to contact you, but never to tell you what she wanted."

Visser shook his head slowly. "That old lady, she never gets anything right."

"You mean you didn't tell her that."

Visser smiled with friendly exasperation, still shaking his head. "Of course not," he said. The policeman was an honest man to the extent that it is possible for policemen and other human beings to be honest and he lied badly.

"She seems a bit confused," Yudel agreed.

"Not just a bit. She gives us a hard time. She's always starting some new rumour about what happened to her son and she expects us to take them seriously."

"None of her ideas have been helpful?"

"Her ideas?" The thought was ridiculous. "She's not looking for her son's killer. She's just trying to incriminate the police."

"I'm glad you came to clear this up," Yudel told him.

"I thought I should." The policeman seemed to relax a little. The discussion was going better for him now.

"So," Yudel said, looking utterly guileless, "you don't mind that I continue with my investigation."

"What's the point?" Visser was on Yudel's side, the friend who did not want him to waste his time.

"The point is that I might come up with something."

"How? Do you know how many men we put on this case? Do you know how many man-hours? Do you really think you can compete?"

"I can question the people whose properties border the cycle track."

The lieutenant looked surprised, not understanding the point Yudel was making. "The cycle track?"

"I believe all the men you've got on the case never got so far as to talk to the people who live around the cycle track."

"Who says so?"

"I've heard it said."

"Old Mrs Baker, I suppose." It was beyond his understanding that Yudel could take the old lady seriously.

"Have you questioned them?"

"Well . . . " His hesitation was momentary. "I'm not sure of the complete details . . . "

"Aren't you the officer in charge of the case?"

"Not really. I've worked on it." If Lieutenant Visser had ever been enjoying the conversation, that time was past. "It's really Major Nortjé . . . What could they have seen anyway?"

"Perhaps I should speak to Major Nortjé."

"What for? You've spoken to me. He's very busy."

"I see." The flow of Yudel's questions stopped as suddenly as they had started. He leant back in his chair and looked at Visser.

It was a few seconds before the policeman regained his balance enough to continue. "I assure you we've done everything. I promise you . . . " He went on assuring and promising. Yudel listened to the meaning of the words with diminishing attention. He was interested in the face of the other man, the troubled frown around the eyes and the determined mouth, the face of a man telling lies that he would rather have avoided.

When eventually he stopped talking Yudel nodded as if in agreement. "I see your point," he said.

"Will you drop it then?"

"I might as well."

"You'll go back to Johannesburg?"

"Pretoria," Yudel said. "I'll go back to Pretoria." He was a far better liar than the policeman.

"There's really no point in going on."

"I can see that now."

"Another thing . . . " His eyes flickered towards the closed bathroom door. "That woman . . . "

"Yes?"

"It doesn't look too good."

He stood at the window of the darkened room, watching Visser run along the pavement in the rain to a small blue sedan on the other side of the road. Yudel was wearing Dahlia's yellow raincoat. It was a little tight in the shoulders, but otherwise it fitted him well. "You look fetching," she said.

"You don't mind?"

"Not at all."

"I might have to be in the rain for some time."

"It's all right." She looked amused. "Yellow suits you."

"Thank you. I'll drop it off at your house tomorrow. Why don't you stay until the rain subsides."

"Thanks."

Visser was opening the door of the blue sedan. "I've got to go," Yudel said. "Thanks again." He ran for the lift.

By the time he passed through the front doors of the hotel the car was pulling away from its parking place. Yudel stepped out of the direct light from the hotel door and drew the hood of the raincoat over his head. The car passed slowly on the far side of the road. By the light of a street lamp he saw Visser's worried face in the moment the car was opposite him.

Yudel's car was a block away in the direction Visser was travelling. As he reached it Visser turned to the right, across the oncoming traffic to take one of the roads that led in the direction of the harbour. Yudel started the engine and moved the car into the light flow of traffic, the wipers working at keeping the windscreen free of water. A traffic light stopped him at the intersection where Visser had turned.

The lights changed, but he had to wait for the traffic from the front to pass before making the turn. He was now driving directly into the rain and the wipers' best efforts could not keep the windscreen clear. Four blocks ahead a car that might have been blue and about the same size as Visser's turned right, moving towards the city centre. Through the flowing water on the windscreen Yudel searched the road ahead for any other sign of the policeman's car. He found none.

This time the lights were in his favour. He covered the four blocks to the corner at which the car had turned and found himself on a quiet side street. Two cars were approaching from the front, both moving slowly because of the rain. Apart from them the street was empty. He turned right again at the next corner, stopping immediately to look back in the other direction. There was no sign of the car. The street was only a few blocks long, ending against the closed motor gates of a service station. He eased his foot off the accelerator, slowing to little more than walking pace. If it had been Visser's car that made the turn it was gone now. Yudel took a deep breath and sighed. The idea of following Visser had been based on nothing more than intuition, but he had learnt not to disregard his hunches. He had no way of understanding their origin, but the results had often been satisfactory.

Yudel parked the hire car and slipped out of the raincoat. Reluctantly he acknowledged that the colour was too bright. He walked back along the pavement to the intersection. Immediately the rain started soaking through his trousers, finding the seams in his shoes and creating a minor torrent down his neck. He noticed none of it.

The buildings on either side of the street were old and small, no more than two or three storeys. They seemed to house stores, secondary industries and car repairers, with here and there a dry cleaner, fast food outlet or shipping agent. The cross street at the intersection was almost as quiet. In the distance a car's tail lights wavered uncertainly through the rain.

He paused for a moment, then turned in the direction of the harbour. After only a few steps he almost collided with a man coming out of the building that occupied the corner of the block. The man had been moving slowly, seemingly without purpose and wearing regulation police oilskins. His sudden movement as he drew away from Yudel was no more than a reflex.

Yudel was careful to continue walking at an even pace. At the first corner he looked back. The man was watching him with what appeared to be great interest.

Turning at the corner, Yudel walked two blocks and turned again, making a wide arc around the building. By the time he was again facing it almost fifteen minutes had passed and there was no part of his body that was dry. He had to wait a few more minutes before he saw the man again, coming slowly down the pavement through the rain. Security guard, Yudel thought. Then he recognized the building. He had approached it from the opposite direction to the one he had taken this afternoon and the rain and bad light had added to his confusion. But now he knew where he was. During the afternoon he had visited warrant officer Holtzhausen of the special branch there. Yudel returned to the car, careful not to be seen by the guard.

Twelve

Dahlia had not left. She had drawn the curtains and was asleep in the armchair near the window.

He closed the door carefully, but the small sound of door against door frame woke her. She sat up quickly, a low grunt of alarm reaching Yudel's ears. He had never heard a sound quite like it, but some part of it defined its nature in his mind. It was a sound of fear, a desperate animal sound, one that might come from the prey in the moment when avoiding the predator becomes impossible.

"I'm sorry," Yudel said. "It's just me."

She took more than a moment to look round the room and remember where she was, then at Yudel to piece him into the picture. When she had it all in place she closed her eyes and breathed deeply as if to chase away the evil spirits. "I got a fright," she said.

"I saw that." Six years, he was thinking, and you're still like this.

She rubbed her forehead with the fingers of both hands, massaging away all that was bad, ridding herself of the dreams. "When you followed that man . . . " She paused to consider. "I was afraid. I thought they might see you." For the first time she saw how wet his clothing was. "You're wet. Why are you wet? You didn't use the raincoat."

"It was too bright . . . the yellow was too bright . . . "

"So you got wet?" She was on her feet and pulling loose his tie before he could protest. "Did you find what you wanted to know?"

Yudel lost both his tie and jacket while thinking about how he should best answer her. He decided that nothing would be gained by telling her what he suspected. "He went back to his office."

"So you learnt nothing?"

Dahlia was busy with his shirt. "Nothing at all."

She had his shirt off and hung it over the chair on which she had been sleeping. With a hand on his chest she backed him towards the bed until he sat down on it. "If you'll lift your feet I'll take your shoes and socks off."

She was already lifting one of them and Yudel did no more than passively assist her. "I didn't think you'd still be here," he said.

Dahlia paused, holding his cold, lean and naked foot in her hands. "Would you rather I had left?"

Yudel thought about her question. He thought briefly about her arriving while he was on the phone to Rosa and about his lying to Rosa. He thought about whether it was a good idea for her to be there and decided that it was not. But no one had taken wet clothing off his body for a long time, perhaps not since he was a child, and she was kneeling in front of him and her eyes were so dark that pupils and irises ran into each other and became one. "I'm glad you stayed," he told her.

She knelt motionless in front of him, still holding his foot in both hands and looking into his eyes. The anxiety, almost panic, that he had seen in her face earlier was present again. It was a fear of rejection, of being turned away once more. He suspected that Dahlia knew only one way of dealing with any man, one primary level of communication, and she was afraid that she might fail in this one sphere.

She released his foot and moved quickly to sit down on the bed next to him. Then she was looking down at her hands, her change of position an embarrassment. Yudel had turned his face towards hers and their heads almost touched. She lifted her face and he kissed her.

Yudel and Rosa had travelled through a long sexual desert together. The dreary mechanical ritual of their intercourse had probably been more Yudel's fault than hers. Other interests had intruded and quickly dominated his life. A sexual relationship that had not been exceptionally passionate at the start had withered until making love had become a social duty, fulfilled occasionally, without enthusiasm, unplanned and uncelebrated.

Making love to Dahlia was something altogether different. It was not accomplished quickly and put behind him so that he could go on to more important matters. It started slowly. Haste would have been almost blasphemous. They kissed without holding each other and Yudel was surprised by the coolness of the inside of her mouth. He felt her move closer to him, her shoulder against his chest so that he could enclose her in his arms. Apart from his trousers he was still wearing one wet shoe and sock. He wondered if there would be a suitable point to rid himself of them without interrupting the flow of events.

Dahlia solved the problem by slipping away and removing them for him. Her eyes had become calmer, the earlier uncertainty gone. She was next to him again, the warmth of his mouth again finding the coolness of hers. His hands ran the length of her back, cupped the smoothness of a shoulder, touched the softness of her breasts. Hers were flat against his chest, then on either side of his neck, around his waist and on his thighs, touching lightly, stroking, knowing, assuring herself that he was there, with her, that she was acceptable.

Dahlia's naked body was long, her legs smooth and lean, her hips a little narrow and her buttocks round and small so that his hands almost covered them completely as he drew her towards him. The softness of her body as she received him was probably no different to that of any other woman, but Yudel was being reawakened to something he had left far behind, unaware of the extent of his loss.

He joined her in an exultant celebration of their bodies, an unexpected crescendo of passion such as he had not experienced for twenty years. When it was over he looked at her face anxiously, suddenly and belatedly hoping that it had been as satisfying for her as it had been for himself. He found the answer in the softness and surprise on her features. She smiled at him, her hair spread fan-like over the pillow.

When he saw her again she was still looking at him, but now he was seeing her by the city lights coming into the room through the partly drawn curtains. The light in the room had been switched off and the sheets had been pulled up to cover them. He realized that he had been asleep. She was smiling at him. "I must have worn you out."

"Was I sleeping long?"

"I don't know. Half an hour."

"Did you sleep?"

"Somebody had to keep guard."

"Against what?" Yudel's senses were not yet functioning properly and he glanced toward the door as if there might be a threat from that direction.

Dahlia chuckled. "The hotel management."

"Have they been back?" He pushed himself up on one elbow and looked down at her.

"Relax, Yudel. Lie down again." No one could have looked more relaxed than Dahlia did. "I'm joking."

He slid back on to the pillow. "I thought I was going to have a quiet evening."

She grinned at him. "We weren't very noisy."

"I was thinking about the whole evening: you, the hotel management, the police . . . "

"I'm glad I got first mention." Her voice was teasing, but sleepy, almost tranquillized. "You're a surprise to me."

"Then we're both surprised," Yudel said.

"I didn't know what to expect with you."

"I didn't know that there was anything to expect."

"That's what I mean. You're so innocent."

Yudel was up on his elbow again, faster this time. "Innocent? I am not innocent. This evening proves I'm not innocent."

"You're a man of the world, in fact." Dahlia sounded as if she was trying not to breathe. Yudel looked stonily at her without answering and her breath exploded in a rush of small giggles. "Oh, lie down, Yudel. In that sense you're no more a man of the world than I am." He sank slowly back on the pillow. "How many times have you been unfaithful to your wife?"

"Why?" It was clear that this knowledge was going to be linked to whether or not he was a man of the world. He considered lying to her. He remembered an occasion on which Freek had wrung the same confession out of him, and he remembered Freek's laughter at the time. "Twice." He told Dahlia the truth. "Actually three times."

"I'm the third?" She was not laughing.

"Yes."

"In how many years?"

"Twenty-two . . . twenty-one . . . "

"Ah." She nodded. "That's why I didn't know what to expect. Also there are holes in your underpants. Men who have affairs don't have holes in their underpants." Yudel wondered if he needed to respond to this unusual piece of information. Dahlia was smiling at him, a slow accepting expression. "I suppose everyone has a perfect sexual partner. You're mine."

Yudel was not sure that he wanted the honour. "What about your husband?" he asked.

"That's another reason I didn't know what to expect. Who else would have asked that question? Which husband do you mean, the man I'm living with now or Ray?"

"I meant Ray."

"Of course you meant Ray." Her voice sounded suddenly resigned. "Who else would you have meant? Everyone only wants to talk about Ray." She was silent for a while, looking up at the ceiling, until Yudel thought she was not going to answer. "Our marriage was a grand demonstration, a political gesture. I've thought about it a lot since he died. When he was alive we often talked about our love that society's strictures would never inhibit. I think the whole thing had more to do with defying society than it had to do with love."

So Dahlia told him about Baker. It was a different story to the one his mother had told. She told Yudel about her first meeting with Baker at a gathering at which he had been teaching black labourers how to start their own trade union. She told him about her own desperation to break away from the life she had known as a child in Sparks Estate, one of Durban's Indian suburbs. She had heard of Baker many times from friends. Even then his reputation had begun to reach proportions that would become almost legendary with his death. She told Yudel how Baker had been different from all the other radical whites. During times

131

when the heat was on and police patrols were roaming township streets; the lists of detained activists growing and newspapers starting to count the death toll: at such times the most dedicated white was always able to disappear back into his whiteness, to flee to his own suburb where the streets were still peaceful, where the police were a reassuring rather than an intimidating presence, where he could suffer the agonies of his conscience in safety and survive. Baker was different. He would share the supper of a poor black squatter family and spend the night on the floor of their hut to be ready to continue with his work among them on the next day. And his message was always essentially the same. "You are human beings too," he would say. "God has given you full right to the earth. Hold up your heads. Demand what is yours." And when they did make their first tentative demands he was among them, accepting the same hazards and risking the same penalties.

Dahlia told Yudel how they continually discussed their love, how they would defy the law to be together, how nothing would ever be able to keep them apart, how no political system would be able to regulate their lives and how eventually it was only the political system that kept them together. She also told Yudel how she deceived Baker with his friends and colleagues, while all the time the public image of the white crusader and the brown trade unionist who would not allow apartheid to destroy their love had to be kept in place.

She spoke at length, lying next to him in the semi-darkness and staring up at the ceiling. When she stopped it was thoughtfully, remembering all that had passed between them, remembering things that perhaps she was never going to tell Yudel. The silence in the room, interrupted only by the sound of their breathing and the now gentle falling of the rain against the windows, was filled with Baker's image, his life and his work. Only his death was absent. Dahlia had said nothing about his death.

"You never took the final step in your defiance of society," Yudel suggested.

"The final step?" Dahlia could not believe that there was anything they could have done, but had not. "What final step?"

"You never had a child."

"My God, Yudel, a child? Do you think I want to bring another human being into this world? And this country?" She was lying on her side, facing him. The faint light coming in at the window was falling on her face. The darkness of her eyes was darker still, only the occasional reflected gleam indicating their presence in the hollows below her brows. Yudel knew that people who did not want to produce children for reasons of that sort always had other less conscious reasons as well. The subject was not an easy one for him either. "And you? I'm sure you are a family man."

"No," he told her. "I don't have children either."

"Out of choice or because you can't?"

"We can't."

"Your fault or hers?"

"Good Christ, Dahlia, does it matter?"

"It would to me, very much."

It mattered very much to Yudel too, but he had no intention of discussing Rosa's barrenness with Dahlia. "Was he ever unfaithful to you?"

"In a small amateurish sort of way." In the poor light he thought he saw the sly knowing smile that was often Dahlia's expression when sex was the subject. She looked away from Yudel, seeming to take in the room afresh. "Oh, God, Yudel. This place has seen me before." It was said wearily, by one who had travelled a long road to reach his bed on that night, but also with a hint of satisfaction. Perhaps, at least partly, the journey had been worth while. The chain of thought revived another memory. "Why did you ask me about old Fred One-night this morning?"

"He may be a useful witness. And you said I should find Reverend Dladla if I wanted him. You are the second person to give me that piece of advice."

Dahlia chuckled. "Old Fred was a rubbish of the worst kind. He was supposed to be a trade unionist. Ray trained him. But the union was his hobby. Women were his life. He had plenty, all ages and all colours, but he had a special liking for poor old Dladla's wife. If the reverend has any influence in heaven, they're both finished, Fred and Flora. The Almighty will send the pair of them one way."

"And you?" Yudel asked. He had not meant to ask it, but the question had come out, unbidden.

Dahlia understood immediately. "Me? Me and Fred?" She reached out and rested her hand on Yudel's arm, as he lay on his side, facing her. "Let's forget it. I don't want to shock you more than I have already."

There was something more important than her relationship with Fred One-night. "The night that Ray died, you are sure that you can tell me nothing else about it?"

Her hand slipped away from Yudel as if repelled. "How could I? I wasn't there."

He lay still, watching her fall asleep and wondering what it was about that night that could not be told.

With Dahlia asleep on the bed Yudel switched on the table lamp and settled in one of the chairs to read Baker's book. He turned to the first page to sample for himself the work of this dangerous man who needed such intensive police surveillance.

It was a slim volume, some hundred and twenty pages. Yudel read fast, trying to understand not just the book, but the man who had written it. He felt that he needed to know Baker and these were the very outpourings of his soul.

The hours passed and he read without any lapse of concentration and without moving his position. When he had finished he turned back to some of the passages that had most clearly illuminated Baker's thinking. "For us to construct an ideal society, our only consideration should be for the individual and his deep need for freedom and love, according to the gospel of Christ.

"How is it possible that a Christian businessman can avoid offering his assets to the workers, freeing himself to labour as an equal with them in love and deep fulfilment? Without question the lesser matter of financial sacrifice will be far outweighed by the spiritual and emotional benefits such a man will enjoy.

"Absolute control of the means of production by the workers must take place before a truly Christian society can be achieved." He went on to offer as examples of Christian societies a number of East European states, all of which to Yudel's knowledge had been less than enthusiastic about Christianity and none of which were well-known for their concern for the individual and his need for freedom and love.

"The phenomenon called human nature does not exist," Baker had written. "Every person is simply the product of the conditions under which he has lived all his life. In the ideal society the human beings that are produced will unquestionably be ideal. To reach this level the greed and avarice that are found everywhere must first be eliminated. Only then will we achieve the spiritual heights revealed to us in Christ."

Yudel lay the book down on the table, allowing the pages to fall closed. Maureen Baker may have been right about her son being a saint, but she was wrong about him being a scientist. All of genetics, the very process by which humankind had evolved, had been ignored. Aggression, invention, art, thought, genius, even motherhood and the sex drive, every human state, good and evil: all had been reduced to nothing more than the result of conditioning. In his life and work Baker had not been seeking the facts. He had been seeking Utopia. And the world had seen too many seekers after Utopia who had eventually come to believe that any means justified so noble an end. He looked at the photograph of her son that Maureen Baker had given him. It was a younger version of the old woman's face, lean and refined. The expression he had adopted for the picture was one of thoughtfulness, the philosopher, the aesthete.

Yudel rose and stood at the window. The darkness was no longer complete. The night was ending and he could see the long rising and falling of the breakers, grey against the softness of a lightening sky. Yudel loved the waves. He loved the movement of the tides, the rising and setting of the sun. He loved the permanence and stability of things natural. They seemed to him a bulwark, a buttress against the transience of matters human and a respite against the immanence of man-made insanity.

Someone or some group had found Baker sufficiently dangerous or at least hated him enough to kill him. Of all the government's many political opponents, why had the choice fallen on him?

Yudel wondered if Baker had been aware of the extent of his

wife's promiscuity. Probably not, he thought. It was the sort of thing people often hid from themselves if there was nothing they could do about it.

He sat down on the edge of the bed, bent over the woman's sleeping form and kissed her. Her sleep-hooded eyes flickered open and she smiled, a slow vague expression. He kissed her again and her mouth opened to renew the intimacy of their contact.

In the early Durban morning with the beginnings of dawn filtering through the lace curtains and the sound of the traffic limited to only the occasional passing car, Yudel made love to Dahlia again. When it was over she smiled up at him, the expression, made indistinct by sleep and softened by the twilight in the room, was warm and at peace. "You're a horny little devil," she said.

Thirteen

For the second time in two days Yudel was seated at the dining room table in Lionel Bensch's home. "I am the last remaining free member of Umkhonto we Sizwe," Bensch was saying, "at least the last one the police know about. All the others are still on the island. I was the first to be arrested and I spent three years in Pretoria Central for making a bomb. At that stage I don't think they realized how big the movement was. A year later they were picking up our members by the score and practically everybody got life. Mandela was one of the last to be caught."

The events that he was recalling had taken place more than twenty years before and Bensch was no longer a young man, but there was a leanness about his figure, a lightness of movement and a keenness in his conversation that would have been more at home on a thirty-year-old. Superficially his appearance was one of wildness and an inability to compromise. Most of his face was covered by a spreading poorly-trimmed beard, a large hooked nose that had been broken many years before dominating the narrow space between beard and long brown hair that hung in a sweep across his forehead. It was the eyes that revealed what the rest of the face seemed to be trying to hide. In them Yudel saw an inner gentleness and concern for other human beings that should not have been present on the face of a convicted member of the military wing of the national resistance.

"But I'm a political dinosaur, Yudel. I haven't been involved in anything for a long, long time. These people that came looking for me are either operating from an old list or they are from the old days themselves."

The table was large and square. Yudel sat directly opposite Bensch. Next to the artist was his twelve-year-old son, a pale blond child whose face bore signs of tension out of place on one so young. To one side Dahlia sat next to Daisy, Bensch's wife, a pretty woman in whom Yudel believed he could see an unusual capacity for patience. She said little, watching her husband while he talked. From time to time he looked directly into her eyes. In such moments the exchange between them, brief as it was, seemed to speak of great pain they had caused each other and a determination never to hurt each other again.

Dahlia, for her part, was sitting primly upright on the edge of her chair, her hands neatly folded in her lap. The effect was only spoiled by a certain ostentation in her primness. She looked so respectable that Yudel hardly recognized her.

"Fucking arseholes, Yudel," Bensch went on, "it smelt like Guy Fawkes. And the sound of it. In the dead quiet of night you can't imagine the noise. I think that was the worst part. But I'm ready for them, if they try again." He patted the canvas cover of a shotgun that leant against the wall behind his chair.

"That was the second time?" Yudel asked. "The first time he knocked on the back door, I think."

"That door there." Bensch pointed and Yudel could see into the kitchen and the back door where it led into the yard. "Daisy opened the door and he was standing there, stripped to the waist, his body covered in oil and holding the gun in both hands. I think he'd seen too many movies. I was sitting behind Daisy and I just got a glimpse of him. He fired immediately. Then he ran like hell. We thought it had been a blank, but the next day we found a hole in a picture that was hanging above my head. The bullet was lodged in the wooden panel behind it."

"The police didn't find it?"

"No, but on the other hand I told them it had been a blank and they didn't search for a bullet."

"But the man who was charged was found not guilty. In fact, Mrs Bensch, I believe that you did not pick him out at the identification parade." Yudel had turned his attention to Daisy

138

Bensch where she sat modestly upright, for her an altogether more natural posture than Dahlia's overblown propriety.

She answered softly, but not so softly that she might be retreating from what Yudel wanted to know. Yudel saw in her a strong personality, a woman who, like women in every age and all societies, absorbed whatever life had in store for them and somehow bore and cared for their young, kept their husbands away from some of their most foolish excesses and held the species together. "I think he got off," she said, "because of me. I said he was the man in court, but at the identification parade I didn't. His lawyer made a lot of that. I had to put my hand on his shoulder and I just could not do it. It seemed so damning. I told the officer as we left the room that he was the man, but I could not do what they wanted."

"And was he the man?"

"On my oath, I swear it." It was said simply and without emphasis. Whether it was true or not Yudel could not say, but that Daisy Bensch believed it, he had no doubt.

"Here comes Maureen. Here we are, Maureen. Join us," Bensch called, disregarding the fact that she was coming straight down the passage with the clear intention of joining them. "Yudel," he continued, his attention again diverted, "what about some wine. Would you like a glass of wine." Yudel glanced at his watch. It was a quarter past eleven in the morning. "Don't look at your watch," Bensch berated him. "It's all right to drink wine in the morning. What do you say, Maureen?"

Daisy was looking at her husband with an amusement and affection that she had not quite succeeded in suppressing. Maureen Baker did not answer Bensch. Yudel turned to greet her but the look of disapproval on her face aborted his words. She was looking at Dahlia, who in turn was looking at the ugly hands that caused her such embarrassment. Bensch had gone into the kitchen in search of the wine. "Are you here with Yudel?" the old lady asked Dahlia.

Dahlia's eyes were directed at her for only an instant. "You're not the only one who's interested in finding Ray's killer."

The old lady sat down at the table, withdrawing into a cold dignity that would not admit to such heresy. "I expected better of you than this," she said to Yudel.

Bensch came back with a five-litre vacuum pack of wine. "Here we are," he said. "This is quite nice."

Yudel nodded in agreement that it was bound to be nice while Dahlia looked down at her hands again and Maureen Baker looked from Dahlia to Yudel as if she could see their writhing bodies copulating on her son's grave. Yudel tried not to look at her. Bensch poured the wine into tumblers and handed them round the table. "Hair of the dog," he said.

For Maureen Baker that Dahlia lived in her son's house with another man was sacrilegious and the idea that she was going around with Yudel who said he was looking for her son's killer was unthinkable, but despite the degree to which Dahlia and Yudel offended her, there was a matter of greater importance. She spoke to Yudel. "Do you think that the people who killed my son might have been responsible for the attacks on Lionel?"

"I don't know," Yudel said.

"It is an organization though, isn't it?" the old lady persisted.

"I don't know that either."

"One thing you must have realized by this time is that the authorities cooperate with the killers." Both Lionel and Daisy Bensch looked at the old lady with calm impassive faces. They had been over all of this many times before.

"I'm not convinced of that."

"What about Lionel's fire-arm licence? Why did they refuse him one after all this?" Maureen Baker would not be diverted.

Yudel's eyes focused unconsciously on the shotgun behind Bensch. "Daisy has the licence for this," Bensch said. "Even after the second incident they won't let me have a hand gun." With a quick gesture he seemed to brush away the thought. "But I think it's just the bureaucracy. I was a banned person and if you were once banned you may not have a gun licence. It's that simple. I don't think there's anything sinister in it."

There was both distress and anger in Maureen Baker's voice as she turned on Bensch. "They just wanted you unarmed, that's all. They wanted you to be an easy target the way Ray was."

This was also territory that they had covered many times before. Lionel Bensch looked at his guest without replying. His long hair had fallen away to either side, exposing a high pale forehead. It had the effect of completely removing the original impression Bensch made. There was an innocence about the man that belied his past. At length he said, "Oh, I don't know if it's the Afrikaner at all. Mark my words, Yudel. If you find them, they won't be among the government boys. They'll be among the English-speaking he-man types, the gun club boys who spend their spare time watching videos about vigilantes popping off everyone they don't like. That's where you'll find them."

Yudel did not want any preconceptions as to where he might find them. What he wanted to know was the question that had troubled him throughout his investigation. "Why you, Lionel? Of all the activists, why did they pick on you?"

The other man shrugged. He looked at his wife. Her eyes had never left his face. "I'm not an activist, Yudel. I was one a long, long time ago, so long ago that you wouldn't think anyone would remember. When I came out of jail I wrote a series of newspaper articles about conditions in prison. In court it was my word against theirs and I went back to jail for another three years under the Prisons Act. Since then there's been nothing. Take my word for it, whoever is running this is either pretty old himself or he's working from a very old list."

Yudel was ready to go. He got to his feet and thanked Lionel and Daisy Bensch. Dahlia rose too, smoothing out her skirt with modest, downcast eyes. Maureen Baker looked sharply from one to the other. "Are you two leaving together?" she asked.

"I don't even like Morris," the woman said, "but I saved his life." She was a simple person who had survived in South African society by observing the most obvious ground rules. One of them was that Indian women did not consort with white men. She looked from Dahlia to Yudel and back to Dahlia. Dahlia yawned, the back of her hand, with fingers elegantly spread, shielding her mouth. Yudel was aware that a minor matter of status was being established. "It was two or three o'clock in the morning. I couldn't sleep it was so hot. These Durban summer nights are terrible."

The little houses, part of a municipal scheme, were spread along the steeply sloping hillside that rose from the flats through which the Umgeni river flowed. From a distance they were barely visible, the dense overhanging branches of the avocado pear and mango trees that grew in every garden shading and softening the entire scene. No place was good to be poor in, but this one was better than most.

"I stood on the stoep for a while and I heard their combi coming up the hill. It came very slowly. I think they were looking for the place, watching the street numbers, you know. I still thought, what would people be doing out so late? By the time they stopped I could see the headlights, over there, just by that big tree. I heard the doors open and close and I saw them coming on foot. I couldn't see them properly, but there's a street light and I could see their outline. I only saw them properly when they came into the light from that lamp there." She pointed to the street lamp just outside her garden wall. "I dunno why, but as soon as they stopped the combi and got out I stepped back into the shadow. It must have been woman's intuition.

"But when they came into the light outside my gate I said to myself, here is trouble. They were wearing these balaclavas the natives wear on cold days so you can't see their faces. And they had guns. I dunno what kind. I dunno what kind you get.

"They first looked up at my house, then I think they saw the number and one of them pointed to Morris's house. I saw him pick up a stone and throw it against the front door. He didn't come out straight away, but they threw another one and I saw Morris's light go on. Then Morris's front door opened and then . . . " She paused for effect. ". . . I did a very brave thing. I screamed. I screamed to Morris, get off the stoep. They going to shoot you. Morris heard me and he fell on the floor and the next moment they were shooting everywhere, his house, my house . . . I don't think it lasted very long. Then they ran down the road. I heard the combi start and drive away."

"How do you know it was a combi?" Yudel asked.

"Mrs Naidoo down the road saw it."

"I agree," Yudel said.

"What with?"

"You were very brave."

"I know," she said happily. "Even Morris said so. And we hate each other."

Yudel allowed the car to free down the hill, slowed only by the engine compression. He turned into Quarry Road where it ran alongside the river and drove in the direction away from the coast. Dahlia was sitting neatly upright, her stockinged knees touching and her hands folded, still playing her newly adopted role. "She's a cow," she confided in Yudel.

He glanced curiously at her without answering.

"Did you see the way she looked at us? Some people always think the worst."

Yudel wondered what the woman might have thought that had not in fact taken place. "She has a suspicious nature," he said solemnly. "Anybody can see that we aren't like that."

Dahlia considered this for a moment. She glanced sidelong at Yudel in time to meet his eyes in the briefest of contacts. Suddenly she threw back her head and released a short loud squawk of laughter. "I know why I like you, Yudel. You can see through me."

"This is attractive?"

"Not really. But it gives me confidence in you. It's not easy to find a man who inspires confidence these days."

"Thank you," Yudel said.

"Who is this Morris Subramoney anyway? I thought I knew everyone in the struggle and I've never heard of him."

"He ran a swimming league."

"And they tried to kill him for that?"

"It was non-racial."

"Jesus," she said, "Rhonda was right. She was right to go. Why should we all stay here to be killed? Ray had only been dead for a month when she took her son and left. She was right."

Yudel thought about it. He wondered about whether Rhonda had been right to go, or should she have stayed and, if so, to what purpose? He did not know the answer, but he did know with a fair degree of certainty that he would never find himself before such a choice. Yudel was as South African as the river that flowed, brown and slow, down the flats to the sea. He could no more live anywhere else than he could, at this point, close the book on these cases and forget them. For him, there were no alternatives.

"When did it happen?" Dahlia asked.

"This thing of . . . " He searched for the man's name.

"This thing of Morris Subramoney, yes."

"Five years ago. Twenty minutes after the second attack on Lionel Bensch, when they fired through his front door with the repeating rifle."

"It was the same people?" The hands that had been sedately clasped in her lap were now clutched together more tightly. They released each other as she lit a cigarette for herself. Yudel saw her hands shaking as she brought it to her lips. "Do you want one?"

His mind was absorbed by the first question and he did not hear the second one. "Yes, the same people were responsible in both cases. There was the same combi and the same military issue automatic rifle. And the twenty minutes that separates the two incidents is very close to the time it takes to travel from one to the other. There were two men and, at least in those cases, they were the same two."

Dahlia was inhaling from the cigarette again, her hand shaking as much as before. Even the smoke seemed to emerge from her mouth in staccato fashion. "Jesus, Yudel," she said, "isn't it too bloody awful, just thinking that they can come in the night to kill like that and nobody stops them." She shifted in her seat to look more closely at him. "Except you. You have actually come here to stop them." From the corner of his eye Yudel thought he saw her shudder. "God, Yudel, they're going to eat you alive."

Elizabeth Ngcube let them in the front door herself. "Why, Dahlia my dear, I didn't expect you to come. Are you looking after Mister Gordon? It is Mister Gordon, isn't it?" It was said in gently mocking amusement, without bitterness.

Yudel shook her hand. She was a small, mild-looking middle-aged woman. Soft and gentle colours were dominant in her dress and turban of West African design. The dress hung almost to the

144

floor and to Yudel it completed a sense of worth and dignity that was a part of the woman. "I'm afraid that I don't understand what this is all about, Mister Gordon."

He told her what it was about. What the hell, he thought. Is there anyone who doesn't know?

"That's very interesting," she said. "It's also quite ambitious. There are those who might not approve of what you are doing."

Yudel had always admired understatement and Elizabeth Ngcube's was a well-rounded example of the art. "This has been brought to my attention," he said. He was trying to match her.

She seated them in the lounge of her home. It was a pleasant room in a pleasant house and looked down on green Natal hills that folded gently into each other on the far side of a narrow valley. On the closer slope the township's tiny brick houses peeped out here and there among the dense greenery in many gardens and in the empty patches between the houses.

Elizabeth Ngcube was one of the small group of black business and professional people. She was also one of the strange sub-culture of restricted persons to which Baker and Bensch had belonged, the pariahs who, although they had never been convicted of any crime, had their every move monitored, were not permitted to leave the city in which they lived even for a few hours, were not allowed to spend a night under any roof but their own, had without fail to report to their local police station daily, had to live with the knowledge of the tape recorder waiting patiently and always on their telephone lines, were not permitted to prepare material for publication or attend public meetings, even if such a meeting was the baptism of a long-awaited child: she was part of this informal association, the members of which were presumed so dangerous that they were compelled to live under a set of regulations completely different to those which applied to other citizens. "May I offer you some tea?" she asked gently.

She went to the door of the room to give instructions to a servant. As she came back she spoke to Dahlia. "Of course I knew your late husband very well, my dear." She smiled. "Intellectually, I mean." Yudel could see Dahlia bridle at the other woman's words, but she said nothing. "He was a remarkable man."

"You shared his views?" Yudel asked.

145

"Certainly."

He sighed inwardly. He wondered if, after all her years as an attorney she could really see intra-specific love as a solution to humankind's problems. "I've read about the murder of your husband of course.

"Of course. That's why you're here." Her voice was still soft and friendly. She could have been talking about a subject far more pleasant than the one Yudel had come to discuss. "I'll tell you a few things you did not read. I'm sure you didn't read that our dogs were poisoned on the night before. They prepared the way before they came.

"I'm sure you did also not read about my daughter's experience on the way to Lesotho that night. My younger daughter was with her father and I was in Johannesburg for the week. She was going to spend a few days with a friend in Maseru. She reached the border post exactly three hours before they shot Fellows. They were expecting her. They took her to an office, the police not the passport control people.

"Mister Gordon, they kept her in that office for the entire three hours, while outside the passport control officers almost took the car apart. Again and again they asked her what she was going to do in Lesotho and they repeated the same questions about her father. They said they knew she had contacts with the African National Congress and if she never arrived in Lesotho no one would know what had happened to her.

"There were two of them and they were the worst sort of scum. They were dressed in jeans and lumber jackets, not suits and ties as you would have expected. After a couple of hours of interrogation they got up and left her in the room, telling her to wait till they came for her. They said there would be a guard outside the door.

"Well, after a while a different one came in. He pretended to be friendly. He was older and he wore a suit, the typical father figure. She had been crying and he asked her what was wrong. So she complained about the other two. He said that their behaviour was shocking and he would have them reported. He was the worst scum of all. He had his arm around her, pretending to be concerned, trying to get her off guard. But he never got anything out of her. The Lord knows, Mister Gordon, the child had nothing to give them.

"When he was finished he said that he was going to fix everything up and she should just wait a few minutes for him. But he wasn't the one who came back. It was his two friends. They told her that they were going to make sure that she took nothing across the border into Lesotho. So they stripped her naked, then searched her. They looked everywhere. There was no place on her or inside her where she could have carried anything over that border.

"While they were busy the phone rang. One of them spoke for a few seconds, then they lost interest in her. They threw her clothes on the floor and went out, leaving the office door open. People were moving around, walking past the door. They had even taken off her watch and she had to pick it up to put it on. It said ten minutes past nine. Fellows was shot just before nine.

"They knew, Mister Gordon. They knew all along that my husband was going to die that night."

"I don't suppose your daughter heard the names of any of them?" Yudel asked.

"I'm afraid not."

"Did she describe them to you?"

"She only said that two were young and the other was old." She stopped to think about it. "What she did say was that the older one had something wrong with one of his eyes."

The road climbed steadily away from the coastal lowlands into the green hills beyond. The previous night's rain had stopped, but the clouds still hung low, resting lightly on the higher hills. They passed among beautiful sub-tropical gardens, their colourful large-leaved plants adding an element to the scenery that would always be absent on the dry brown undulations of the highveld where Yudel spent most of his life.

The last thing Elizabeth Ngcube had said to him was that Baker had been a visionary, a man centuries ahead of his time. She had smiled at Dahlia and added, "But I'm sure you know that better than anyone else, my dear."

"The old cow," Dahlia said to Yudel. "She's jealous of me. She

147

used to have long discussions with Ray. For hours they would talk as if only they knew anything. But I slept with him. On the other hand she's probably past it." She finished with a certain amount of both satisfaction and finality. This was an aspect of life that was so important to her that if Elizabeth Ngcube was past it she could safely be ignored in future.

Yudel was tiring of Dahlia's company. She interrupted his thinking and so much of what she said was trivial. He found it strange that a woman like her should be attracted to men whose interests were not trivial. She was looking gloomy and morose, like a little girl who has been made to stand in the corner. "Well, she is an old cow. You heard how she spoke to me. Why don't you say something?" Yudel still did not reply. He was surprised at the degree of insult Dahlia seemed to feel at the other woman's very mild jibes. "Say something," Dahlia said. "You sit there with an expression on your face like you don't even know that I'm here. What are you thinking?"

"I'm thinking that there may be danger and allowing you to accompany me is irresponsible." Also, if you stay at home I won't have to listen to this, he thought.

Dahlia said nothing for a while. When he looked at her he saw that she was grinning at him. "Is something funny?"

"No." She reached out and squeezed his arm briefly. "You're concerned for me. I like it."

Yudel sighed. She was full of surprises, this Dahlia. But then, no doubt there had been men who had made use of her and had not been concerned for her.

"But you don't have to worry. I read my horoscope this morning and I'll be all right today."

"That's very comforting," Yudel said.

"Don't sneer at me, Yudel. Isaac Newton believed in astrology and so do I. I'm a Gemini and anyone who knows me well knows that I have two personalities. Astrology is perfectly logical."

There was a martial tone entering Dahlia's voice. Yudel feared that she was just getting into her stride. "I'm sure it is," he said.

"You're still sneering. One day last year my horoscope said that I should be especially careful around machinery. And I was involved in a six-car pile-up on the freeway."

"There you go," Yudel said in his most conciliatory manner.

"That's not all," Dahlia said.

She said nothing more, looking straight ahead and waiting. This was his cue. He knew that he now had to say, so what else is there? He breathed deeply once. "So what else is there?" he asked.

"All the other drivers were Geminis too."

His head spun towards her, as if on ball-bearings. "You're joking."

Dahlia retained her composure for only a moment. She laughed loud, a brief explosion arising from the tension within her. For Dahlia joy was always brief. Yudel reached across and rested his hand on hers. The gesture said that it was all right. She could relax with him.

William van Ryneveld was the grand old man of South African sculpting. He received Yudel in his study. "Thank you for seeing me, Mister van Ryneveld," Yudel said.

"Doctor van Ryneveld," the great man said. It was an honorary doctorate, but he did not want it forgotten.

"Doctor van Ryneveld," Yudel said respectfully. "I explained why I wanted to see you."

"Yes, you did." The sculptor was at an age when he would have described himself as being in the latter part of middle age while others would have said he was elderly. Forty years earlier his work had been of a standard and originality that had gained him international recognition. With the passing of the years he had lost the originality, but outlived his contemporaries and now occupied a position of such eminence in South African art that his pronouncements, which were many, were treated as being beyond debate. "It is some years since I was involved in politics. In those days there were a number of such incidents." He nodded to himself while he seemed to contemplate what he had been saying. "Of course they are very efficient."

"They?" Yudel asked.

"The security police. They are very efficient. We are talking about them, are we not?" He glared angrily at Yudel, his round balding head and the long folds of wrinkled and leathery skin around his neck making him look like a belligerent old tortoise.

"I didn't know that we were," Yudel said.

"Certainly we are. Who else would we be talking about? They broke the windscreen of my car once. Very efficient."

Yudel wondered how their efficiency was related to the damage inflicted on the old sculptor's car. He did not share van Ryneveld's view. If you were empowered to tap all telephones, pay thousands of informers, lock away your adversaries for indefinite periods without having to prove a case against them, place restrictions on the activities of any that you mistrusted: if all this was possible, efficiency did not come into the question. "There have been many small incidents. A load of concrete was dumped in my front garden once. By the time I came home it had set, incidents of that sort. I am really the wrong person for you to speak to though. I had young colleagues at the time who were subjected to far more serious harassment, even assault."

Through the study's large bay windows Yudel could see Dahlia and van Ryneveld's wife, moving among the roses in the garden. Dahlia was wearing her modest, eyes-cast-down, hands-primly-folded demeanour. The other woman's mouth was moving, but the sound of her voice was cut off by the closed windows. "You were saying that we are talking about the security police. Do you have any reason for believing this?"

The question seemed to annoy van Ryneveld. The old tortoise head performed a quick sideways twitch as if ridding itself of an irritation. "There were many small things. I don't remember them precisely. It was a long time ago. Many things pointed in that direction." He blinked angrily at Yudel. "Once one of them threatened to put two bullets through one of my knees." He looked away with another quick twitch of his head, dismissing Yudel's doubts with the movement. The new direction he was facing caused his eyes to settle on the women in the garden. "Is this woman your wife?"

"No . . . " Yudel started to explain.

"Do you have a wife?" The angry blinking took on a more intense aspect.

"Yes." Yudel was feeling uncomfortable and wanting to say more, but the old man's disapproval was strangely intimidating.

"Where is she?" van Ryneveld demanded.

Yudel took a deep breath and steadied himself. "My wife is at home. The lady is the widow of Raymond Baker, the trade unionist. She's an interested party."

He glared out of the window, inspecting Dahlia across the distance that separated them. "Shocking business," he said. Yudel pondered uncertainly whether the shocking business was Dahlia accompanying him or Baker being assassinated. Van Ryneveld cleared up the point. "We had nothing as bad as that." Yudel reasoned that if he had been talking about Dahlia's presence there was a fair chance that they would have had incidents that bad.

"The man who threatened to put the bullets into your kneecap, you wouldn't know his name?"

"Certainly, I do." He glared at Yudel in silence for so long that it became doubtful that he intended providing the name without being asked directly. Yudel had started to frame the request when the effort became unnecessary. "Varrevich. Lieutenant Varrevich, he was at the time. Imagine an East European name on a South African security policeman."

Yudel did not need to try hard in order to imagine it.

Fourteen

"Size thirty-four," Yudel told the sales lady. He was buying new underpants. Dahlia had made him aware of the cluster of little holes in the seat of some of his present pairs. Men who have affairs don't have holes in their underpants, she had said.

"For yourself, sir?" the saleswoman asked. She was vulgar-looking, about Yudel's age and at that moment casting an appraising eye over the pelvic section of his body. "Could be thirty-six," she decided. "Would you like to try a pair on?"

"No, thank you," he said coldly. "Thirty-four will be fine."

"Can't be too careful," she said archly. "You wouldn't want to get a pain in the middle of your forehead."

On three or four occasions Freek had told Yudel the joke about a man whose underpants were too tight and how he developed a pain in the centre of his forehead as a result. Telling jokes more than once was a failing of Freek's. "Four pairs," Yudel said.

She rang up the amount. "Don't hesitate to come and change them if they're too small."

Yudel paid, took his change and walked back to the hotel along a busy, late afternoon pavement. He had phoned Rosa, listened to her pleading for him to come home and told her that he was nearly finished and would be back on the next day, or maybe Saturday, and definitely not later than Sunday.

Going up in the hotel lift, he was accompanied by a middle-aged man wearing a polished leather jacket and trying to arrange depleted reserves of hair in order to hide a broad pink area of scalp. He saw Yudel watching him and his eyes took in Yudel's own crinkled bush. "You're lucky," he said. "You've still got plenty."

"You don't have to comb mine. It has a mind of its own."

"At least it's there. You could try hair straightener. You know, like the coons use."

"Thanks," Yudel said.

"That's okay." His fellow traveller was a well-meaning soul. "Even Brylcreem might help. A coon once told me they rinse their hair in olive oil and that makes it softer."

The lift stopped on Yudel's floor. "Thanks again," he said.

"Any time," his new friend said. "A cup of olive oil in a basin of water."

The lift doors opened and Yudel went down the passage to the room where Dahlia was standing at the window, watching the surf running up on to the beaches and the kids on the surfboards riding the swell. "You bought something."

"It's nothing," Yudel said. His nonchalance was total.

Dahlia came closer. "Let me see."

He transferred the parcel to the hand furthest from her. "It's really nothing . . . " then with a smile, "How are you?"

"Perfect. Let me see, Yudel."

With Dahlia swarming round him to get hold of the packet, Yudel finally surrendered it. "It's really nothing," he said. "I needed them."

She inspected the contents briefly, then grinned at him, the expression spread across her face as if held there by some happy inner pressure. "Part of your campaign towards becoming a man of the world, I presume." She sounded as if she was choking.

"I needed them," Yudel said weakly.

"Of course you did." She put her arms around his neck. "God, I can see how a woman can love you. Do you know what sort of sacrifices I'm making to be with you?" she whispered. "I promised to sleep with one of the people at work tonight, but instead I'm here. What do you think of that?" Dahlia's face was so close that he could not focus on it. He tried to think about the sacrifices she was making, but the feel of her body against his and the smell of her interfered with his thought processes. She drew her head away and looked at his face. "It's okay," she said. "You don't need to answer." Then she kissed him and it was all as it had been the evening before and as it had been that morning.

Yudel's first sexual experience had been on his wedding night twenty-one years before. It had satisfied an urgent and long-neglected need, but a measure of inhibition had always remained. Rosa might close her eyes, writhe appropriately and gasp at the required moment, Yudel might do his best to make proceedings pleasant for her and feel this particular thirst quenched, but there was a part of each of them that stayed remote, spectators at the feast, rather than revellers.

Most men enjoy the sort of experience that honeymoons are supposed to produce just once in a lifetime. There is a meeting, because of some psychological or physiological compatibility or perhaps only because of a certain happy timing, a meeting at the right moment in two lives, which assumes an importance and a glowing perfection that neither had ever reached before and that neither ever experiences again.

Dahlia's only way of dealing with the other sex was to make love with them. She possessed no other skills for handling the men in her life. She loved them warmly, physically and without reserve, or else there was nothing. And she drew Yudel with her into this unfettered physical nihilism. All thought, all memory, all earthly contact except that one, all conscience, all pain: every possible element of awareness was suspended while the meeting of their bodies lasted. It had never before been that way for Yudel and it would never be that way again.

They made love for the third time in his hotel room, her face soft with the discharge of emotion, lit gently by the failing afternoon light from the window. The sound of the traffic, the rolling of the breakers, the room itself: all of it was gone, absorbed into the moment, dissolved by a superior force, until there was nothing that existed anywhere for Yudel, but Dahlia and his need for her.

They slept for an hour, then dressed and walked down the length of the promenade that passes between the holiday hotels and the sea, the stretch described by the Durban Tourist Association as the Golden Mile. Along the way they found a small Italian restaurant, deep in an arcade, where the manager and the head waiter conversed anxiously for a few minutes before deciding if it was possible to serve them. Yudel thought that he heard the words "a white man and a sammy woman" whispered at a table nearby. Eventually veal piccata became possible, if only to prevent a scene that might have been even more repulsive to customers than the sight of Yudel and Dahlia dining together.

Afterwards they went down to the beach and walked still further away from the hotel. The tide was out and they took off their shoes and walked barefoot on the damp hard sand just above the water. On one side the sea, insistently moving as always, was dark to the point of being invisible, except for the foam close to shore. On the other, the long row of hotels, windows alight, signs flashing, determinedly worked at banishing the night.

They walked slowly, close together and talked. They talked about the lives each lived, about spring in this warm, gentle, lazy and sometimes terrible city, about the sea and about the people they had spoken to during the day. They did not talk about the weekend when Yudel would be returning to Pretoria. And eventually, perhaps inevitably, they talked about the man who had been Dahlia's husband.

"Tonight," she told him, "in the restaurant you experienced a tiny bit of what my life with Ray was like. There was no end to such incidents. Eventually we hardly noticed them.

"They would force his car off the road and search it before allowing him to continue. Once they did it three times in the same month. We used to have parties that Ray was not allowed to attend because his banning order said that he could only be in the company of one person at a time and that included me. So he would sit in another room and the guests would come in and visit with him separately, one by one.

"At one of these parties they came swarming up the drive and over the garden walls, five or six of them in plain clothes. We were all outside in the garden, except Ray, and they shouted to us all to stand still. They took photographs from every possible angle and actually measured the distances from the closer guests to the room where Ray was sitting while we stood rooted to the spot.

Finally they took the names and addresses of everyone. The American envoy in Durban was there that night with his wife, but it was the last time we ever saw them. Oh God, Yudel, we were so self-righteous. Even now I can't believe it. Only our happiness was perfect in an imperfect world. Our love transcended the state's efforts to destroy it. My God, what a load of shit."

Eventually the hotels fell away and were replaced by the dark uneven presence of the hedge bordering a golf course, separated from them by the broad expanse of the beach and the bright humming presence of the main road running northwards up the coast. In quiet moments on the road the sounds of loud talking and laughter reached them across the beach from the club house. Out to sea, near the horizon, a few freighters, given away only by their lights, lay at outer anchorage.

They reached the point where the Umgeni river spills round the sand wall of its lagoon into the sea. The hotels were far behind and the broad dark belt of beach sand reached back towards the brightness and exuberance of the Golden Mile. They stood together at the edge of the water, Yudel's left arm resting lightly aound her waist, and looked back the way they had come. For the moment, despite the strange nature of the project with which he was involved, despite the knowledge that his relationship with Dahlia could never be more than brief, he was at peace. "He really was wonderful, you know," she told him. "He was always so gentle with others, even when they were angry with him. He was so lovely to me, no matter what I did. He didn't even mind other people in my life."

"Other people?" Yudel asked.

"Yes. He didn't mind if I had other people in my life."

"You mean, other men," Yudel suggested.

Dahlia giggled, a brief nervous sound. "Don't put it that way, Yudel. At any rate he didn't mind. If I spent a night away from home he never said anything. God, there were times when I only came home to take my pill."

The headlights of a car swept along the edge of the golf course, leaving it again briefly in darkness. Yudel's eyes were on the hedge when the flash of light momentarily pierced the even shadow of its outline. It had been no more than a brief punctuation of the dark mass along the roadside, a single flash and then darkness. He had heard no accompanying sound, except perhaps a splash in the water behind him. But the moving sea was full of sounds and it may have been nothing at all, the jumping of a fish or a wave slapping against one of the concrete blocks of the nearby fisherman's wharf.

Yudel drew Dahlia down, till they were crouching low on the sand. His eyes were fixed unblinkingly on the section of the hedge from which he had seen the flash. "Yudel." She spoke his name fearfully, her voice soft and its sound uneven.

"I think it's nothing." He glanced back at the sea. Except for the crests of the waves its darkness was complete. It was a good background. Crouched on the sand they would not be easy targets. They might possibly not be targets at all.

"What was it?" Dahlia asked, her voice so soft and the tightness of her throat so constricting that the words barely reached Yudel's ears.

"Probably nothing," he said again. He was accustomed to dealing with Rosa and a more truthful response would have been out of the question with her.

"For Christ's sake, I'm not a child." She was getting her breath back. "What was it?"

The section of the hedge from which the flash had come was still in complete darkness. A car came past, the sweep of its lights picking out branches and leaves, but nothing that should not have been there. "There was a flash from across the road. It may have come from a gun."

"I heard nothing."

"Nor did I."

In the little light that reached them from the street lamps along the road Dahlia's eyes were wide and darker than ever. "There's a path," she said, "along the lagoon. I'll show you." She took his hand and they ran the last few yards until the fisherman's wharf, across the car park at its base and on to the path that followed the sandy edge of the lagoon into the light tropical scrub that fringed the river. Yudel cursed intermittently as they ran. They stopped out of breath beneath the road bridge where it crossed the river. "What's wrong?" Dahlia asked.

"My feet. Let's put our shoes back on."

Her face was incredulous. "What's more important, your feet or our lives?"

Yudel sat down on a concrete slab at the base of the bridge to dust the sand off his feet. "If someone did shoot at us, they will not follow us now."

Dahlia was looking back down the path, its sandy surface showing light against the darker vegetation. "In the cinema the killers always follow the victims. Especially into places like this."

Yudel had one shoe on and was shaking the sand out of the second sock. "We aren't victims yet and fortunately this is not the cinema. If there was someone, they want to live to shoot again. They won't come after us."

"Are you armed?"

"No."

"I don't know how you intend to manage, Yudel. On television all the detectives are armed. Even the previous detective who looked for Ray's killer was armed wherever he went. He had a shoulder holster. I saw it."

Yudel had his second shoe on. He got slowly to his feet, took Dahlia by the arm and drew her close to him. "There was another investigator?"

"Didn't you know? Blythe Stevens and that lot hired him as well."

Yudel was trying to see her face, but the light was poor. "Dahlia, what are you telling me?"

"Well, I thought you knew. Six months after Ray's death they hired this man, a Mister Du Toit from Johannesburg. They chose him because he had been a security policeman in Durban at the time Ray was killed but I thought you must know this."

"How do we get out of here?" Yudel asked. She led him through the fringe of light tropical vegetation into a small amusement park where a few young adults were playing miniature golf. "So tell me, what did Mister Du Toit find out?"

"I don't really know. He gave a report to Blythe Stevens, but I never saw it. All I ever heard was the name of the man that he thought killed Ray."

"Would you like to share this information with me?" Yudel asked gently.

"But I thought you knew. It was a funny sort of name, Polish or Russian or something."

"Varrevich," Yudel suggested. "Milan Varrevich."

"That's it. How did you know?"

"I'm the investigator, remember. I'm supposed to know these things."

The light in the hotel room was on and Yudel sat facing Dahlia across the table. She had talked for much of the evening, trying to rid herself of the lingering images, the still living, still scarring memories of times that would have been better forgotten. But she had not rid herself of it all. Yudel could see the signs, the unease and the lack of fulfilment that came with a partial confession. There was still something that lay unrevealed, something of which Dahlia needed to free herself. She looked back at him from the other side of the table, the blackness of her eyes an unfathomable view into her soul that told Yudel nothing at all. For a moment the strange intensity of her expression and the deep colour of her eyes reminded him of Rosa. They were different in almost every way excepting the strange fragility they held in common.

Dahlia was speaking and Yudel knew that at last he was going to hear the part of the story she had been avoiding. "There were plenty of nights when they could have done it. I don't know why they had to kill him on that one. I don't know why they had to choose a night when I wasn't there. The man I was with was nothing. I think he was a friend of my sister. If he came into this room now I wouldn't recognize him.

"You can't imagine what it was like coming home and the police were there and right away I knew what it was all about. That damned Beryl was standing there, looking at me as if I killed him. She had always been in love with Ray, but she'd never had the guts to do anything about it."

Dahlia was leaning towards him, her eyes holding his and her face tense with the pressure of the memory welling up within her. This was why she had come on the previous evening. It had not been to make yet another conquest, to test her unquestionable attractiveness one more time. Although she had seemed to be trying to avoid it, Dahlia had come to tell him about the night that her husband had died.

"His mother blames me too. While he was alive she often told him that I was bad for him. She complained because I saw other people from time to time. What difference would it have made if I had been there? They abducted him on the pavement outside his office. How could it make a difference that I was screwing somebody else at that moment? It's not my fault her precious boy is dead."

Dahlia's pupils were dilating until the irises, themselves almost completely black, were just thin rings around the edge of the strange ballooning pupils. She was seeing it all again and her capacity for vision was increasing so that she should miss nothing, that everything should be revealed and no part of it left unrecorded.

"I don't care what they think. That isn't the worst part. The worst part was looking at his body. He had been stabbed fourteen times, but there was not a drop of blood anywhere. His clothes were perfect, completely undamaged. His hair was combed, carefully combed, not a strand out of place. His feet were together and his arms at his sides. It was almost a loving presentation, everything perfect, his body washed clean.

"He was naked when they killed him, Yudel. Then they washed him and put him back into his clothes and combed his hair and laid him out neatly on the cycle track, waiting for an old vagrant to find him there. What kind of people would do such a thing?"

She stopped speaking. The story had been told. Now, for the first time, she was free of it. All the tension, the pressure within her had leaked away. The rigid posture had softened and she leant heavily against the table. "I never told his mother or the rest of them. What for? They can go to hell."

Fifteen

It was late Sunday morning by the time Yudel got home. The airways bus had broken down and as a result had been an hour behind schedule. After that the driver had seemed to be in no hurry to get to the city, guiding the bus with elaborate care through traffic that was never heavy enough to be even a modest hindrance.

He had spent much of Friday and Saturday searching Durban for Duncan Jones, the man who had been tried for attempting to murder Lionel Bensch, but Jones had resigned his job, changed accommodation a number of times and seemed to have left the city. He had also questioned Morris Subramoney, Elizabeth Ngcube's daughter and Luis Rodrigues, the shopkeeper who had seen the struggle in Ray Baker's car and none of it had illuminated anything.

Dahlia had taken him to the airport. On the tarmac before boarding he had turned to see her at the observation area on the upper floor of the building. She had been wearing a light blue sleeveless dress that contrasted sharply with the yellow-brown of her skin. He had waved and she had returned it, a quick almost abrupt gesture. The brief movement told much about her, a sudden flash of warmth, immediately inhibited, replaced by the barrier to keep out the pain that always followed.

At the top of the stairs to the aircraft he had looked back, but the place where she had been standing had been empty. Yudel had found his seat between a young woman with a tight sweater, dyed blonde hair and a jaw that was grinding determinedly at a gob of chewing gum, and a lean man with a bobbing Adam's apple who was reading a magazine called *Soldier of Fortune*. His eyes had fallen on the article the man had been reading. The headline had exhorted readers to *Fire your repeating rifle with one hand*. The journey had seemed unusually long.

Rosa was still away with Irena and Yudel moved quietly through the house as if afraid of advertising his presence. In their bedroom he sat down on the edge of the bed. He could see his reflection in a standing mirror against the wall and he looked at himself with surprise and curiosity. He was forty-four years old, but his image in the mirror looked older. A small, rather frail-looking middle-aged man, obviously Jewish, his skin sallow and his eyes tired, looked back at him. The wild unkempt tangle of his hair was laced with grey to an extent that surprised him and the lines on his forehead and around his mouth were deeper than he remembered.

He lay back on the bed and closed his eyes. The few days he had been with Dahlia rested heavily on him, part of the weight of the many things he had wanted to do in his life, but left undone, and the many things he would rather have turned away from, but had done anyway. What the hell, he thought. Nobody's life is perfect.

The weariness of losing Dahlia so soon and the hopelessness of the task he had set himself swept irresistibly over him. He slept until late afternoon.

Yudel woke with the telephone ringing. Rosa was on the other end of the connection. "How long have you been home?" she demanded. "You said you'd phone when you got in."

"I've just got in. Last night's flight was full."

"Are you coming to fetch me? Should I come back?" Her voice was uncertain, seeming to ask if it was safe now.

"Why not leave it till tomorrow?" Yudel suggested. "I'll make an excuse to come over and pick you up."

"Okay, Yudel. Are you all right? Did everything go well?" The questions came out quickly, partly from a desire to know the answers and partly as a reflex. "Is everything all right at home? The hotel you were in was terrible, making up the beds in the middle of the night."

"Everything's fine, Rosa. I'll fetch you tomorrow."

"I'll be ready," she said, then stopped as her thoughts changed direction. "The things you found out in Durban . . . You did find things out, didn't you?"

"What is it, Rosa?" he asked gently. "Do you want to know if I am going to continue with this?"

"Yes." The single word was said softly, almost experimentally, hung out to test the wind.

Yudel's usual response to such a question would have been to answer, almost without thinking, yes of course he would be going on. It was a surprise to him that his answer did not come readily. There were too many victims, too many stories, the endless contradictions . . . "I don't know," he answered.

"Are you saying you might stop?"

"I don't know, Rosa. I'll tell you about it when I see you."

"Yes, you must. You must tell me all about it."

After he hung up Yudel consulted his notebook, then dialled Dahlia's number. A male voice answered and he hung up without saying anything. Christ, he thought.

He dialled Freek's number and one of the children answered. She recited the number, then said in Afrikaans, "Jordaan residence, Bapsie Jordaan speaking."

"Good evening, Bapsie," Yudel said. "May I speak to your father?"

"Hullo, Uncle Yudel. My father says Uncle Yudel's busy on a big adventure and if Uncle Yudel is not careful Uncle Yudel will lose his tail feathers."

Yudel thought briefly about Freek's colourful symbolism before answering. "I'll be very careful," he told the child.

"It's very exciting, Uncle Yudel. When I'm big I'm going to come and work with Uncle Yudel."

"You'd better discuss that with your father first. Is he at home?"

"Yes, he's here, Uncle Yudel. Uncle Yudel, I just want to say to Uncle Yudel that I won't tell anyone. I'll die before I say."

"That's all right, Bapsie. I don't think you need to go that far. Most of the country seems to know anyway."

"Oh." The child sounded disappointed. Dying before saying

163

seemed to have held a special appeal for her. "Shall I call my father, Uncle Yudel?"

"I'll be glad."

Freek came on the line. "Yudel." He spoke his name almost as an exclamation. "I'm glad you're back. Are you going to be at work tomorrow."

"Sure. What's happened?"

"Word of what you are doing seems to be out. You may have a difficult month or two."

"Or longer."

"These things subside in time," Freek said. "You'd better keep your nose clean for a while . . . if you can."

Yudel thought about the losing of his tail feathers and the keeping clean of his nose and about what it was exactly that had gotten out. "Anything specific?" he asked.

"There've been a couple of security meetings, that sort of thing."

Yudel thanked . Freek and hung up again. The worst part, maybe not the altogether worst part, was the way Williamson and De Beer had entrusted him with their precious promotion. The party to celebrate it was scheduled for the Tuesday.

He went through to the kitchen to switch on the coffee percolator. He had little decent coffee in Durban and his body was reminding him of his addiction. Before he could pour it the phone was ringing again. He answered it in the lounge and the voice of a young man asked to speak to Mrs Gordon. "She's not in," Yudel told him.

"When will she be back?" the voice asked.

"Tomorrow. Phone tomorrow afternoon and you can speak to her."

"Don't you want to know who this is?" The voice was that of a white English-speaking South African. By his way of speaking he was little educated or possibly had started life in a household where there was little education. "Don't you want to know who this is?" he asked again.

Until that moment Yudel had not been in any way interested in his identity, but that had changed with the question being put to him. "No, I'm not interested," he said.

164

"Don't you think you should be interested? Rosa's often alone, you know. I wonder if you should leave her alone so often. Strange things happen to women who are left alone. You might not want her afterwards."

The hell with you, Yudel thought. "That's you, isn't it, Willie?" he asked.

"No, Yudel. This isn't Willie."

"Come on, Willie, I know your voice. You can't fool me."

"You're making a mistake, Yudel, a very big mistake."

"You can come clean, Willie."

"You don't know me, Yudel. I've seen you, but you've never seen me. Even if I kill you, you won't see me." For all its pretensions the voice was showing signs of irritation. The only thing that would satisfy him would be for Yudel to take him seriously. "When your wife meets me she will be sorry she did."

"A joke's a joke, Willie, but . . . " Yudel knocked softly on the telephone stand.

"What was that?" Something of the easy confidence had left the voice.

"Pack it in, Willie," Yudel said.

"You're a sneaky little bugger, Yudel. You're trying to keep me on the line while you have the call traced. I can see I'll have to talk to Rosa." Yudel heard the sound of his hanging up. The experience Elizabeth Ngcube's daughter had at the Lesotho border post returned to his mind. He knew that they were trying to frighten him, but he also knew of what they were capable.

He went into the study and paged disconsolately through Blythe Stevens's file. None of it made any sense. It was no more than an untidy catalogue of fairly random crimes. Only the common interests of the victims gave it any coherence at all.

The phone rang again. Yudel spoke his name into the mouthpiece, but there was no answering voice on the other side. He replaced the handpiece and went back to the file. Fifteen minutes later the phone rang again, and again after another fifteen minutes. Yudel unplugged the instrument and rocked slowly back in his chair, his hands behind his head. The game was on. There was no doubt about that now.

Sixteen

In the passage outside his office Yudel passed the head clerk from the stores section. A garrulous man of about Yudel's age, he was rarely one to pass up the opportunity for a bit of friendly conversation. This time he hurried past Yudel with only the briefest glance in his direction. The mumbled greeting, "Morning", was no more than a reluctant afterthought.

"Good morning," Yudel said. It could just be something personal, he thought. He did not believe it, but he did not want to be seeing things that did not exist. Perhaps it was just your average Monday morning depression.

He gave his attention to an in-basket that was showing the signs of the previous week's neglect. Two requisitions for fuel needed signing, a leave roster for the next six months had to be made out, five reports on new prisoners needed completing, three submissions to the parole board were awaiting attention, requisitions for a new mop and a replacement for the element in the coffee urn also had to get his signature, while the graphs showing the fuel consumed by the section's vehicles had to be made out in three colours, one for each vehicle. Before he could start on any of it the phone rang. The hand holding his pen shook with the suddenness of the sound. Since the night before the telephone had become an almost hostile presence. "It was the telephone . . . " he remembered Maureen Baker saying. Old man Williamson was on the other end of the line. "Yudel, I want to see you immediately." His voice was cold and pompous to a degree unusual even for him.

"I'm coming," Yudel said.

Williamson was at his desk when Yudel entered the office, his shoulders drawn tensely together. "Good morning," Yudel said.

The section's senior functionary was in no mood for greetings or other pleasantries. "I would have thought that I might have been taken into your confidence. You said you wanted a few days in Durban with your wife." Yudel sat down tentatively, without being invited. He was looking for the words with which to answer, but Williamson was only getting into his stride. "I take the strongest exception to this. This sort of thing often has very wide repercussions."

"Sort of thing?"

"This jaunt of yours . . . " The older man's indignation held an element of injured dignity. "I take the strongest exception . . . I thought our relationship was good enough."

"I shouldn't have . . . " Yudel tried to frame an apology. Deceiving Williamson was something he did not feel good about. But he did not believe that being deceived was Williamson's main objection.

"There is a clear departmental ruling, embodied in our administrative instructions that employees may not augment their incomes outside. It's a specific rule." Nor did Yudel believe that this was the cause of his boss's outrage. "There is a right way and a wrong way to do things, Yudel. I am the head of the section. I should have known . . . " Williamson was angry, even humiliated, but he was avoiding the real problem. "I have been in the department longer than you . . . " It was true. He had been employed by the Department of Prisons for thirty-five years while Yudel was a relative newcomer with a little over twenty years of service. " . . . and I have seen the repercussions this sort of thing can cause".

Yudel doubted that any departmental employee had ever been involved in anything of the sort before. He decided to get to the heart of the matter. "I believe that I've been the subject of security meetings."

"I don't know anything about that," Williamson said quickly. He lied badly, turning his head away and shaking it too vigorously in denial. "I don't believe there has been any such thing."

"Oh, there has," Yudel said.

"Obviously you know more about it than I do." Williamson shuffled a sheaf of papers on the desk in front of him. "In any case, if there are no grounds for that sort of investigation, my experience shows that it goes away on its own. If it does not go away, then there are obviously reasons for it."

"You are saying that if suspicions survive long enough they become facts."

"What I am saying is that, if there are no grounds for something like this, it goes away." Williamson's irritation was increasing. Yudel was in the wrong. He had no business confusing the matter in this way.

"Who reported me?" Yudel asked.

"A fact is a fact and who reported you is of no consequence."

"I apologize for lying to you," Yudel said. "It was inexcusable."

Williamson stared across the desk at Yudel, for a moment unable to find a direction from which to renew his attack. "The whole thing has become public knowledge in other sections . . . they get an unfair advantage . . . they try to take the credit . . . " Then he remembered that he still had an angle. "You saw a prisoner in Gert van Staden's section for private reasons."

"I counselled him against the foolishness of withholding evidence." The old psychologist thought about this. It had a certain usefulness, if he needed to defend his section against attacks from outside. "Van Staden was on leave. I thought I'd help out."

His visit to Robin Du Plessis had been on a weekend and at this point Williamson should have been able to see the fabrication in Yudel's story, but in any government department it was bad to have something wrong in your section and good to have a cover for it. "I must say that I'm disappointed in you, Yudel," he ended lamely. "Have you filled in your fuel consumption graphs yet?"

"I'm working on them at the moment."

"I want them on my desk before lunch." He had found a safe area in which to assert himself.

Yudel went directly to Gert van Staden's office. His colleague was in the process of drawing a staff attendance graph. He grinned as Yudel came in. "Ja, Yudeltjie," he said, the diminutive indicating a vague endearment. "What have you been up to now?" Van Staden spoke Afrikaans to Yudel. He was ten years younger, prematurely balding and the possessor of an astonishingly calm and even temperament.

"You tell me," Yudel suggested.

"I don't know." The grin was still on his face. "I hear the holy ones, Poena van der Merwe and them, are upset with you for something." Van der Merwe was the senior administrative officer in the transport section, an elder in the Dutch Reformed Church, a card-carrying member of the National Party which had run the country for thirty-six uninterrupted years and a patriot. A few months before he had tried to persuade the regional director that each day should commence with a prayer meeting, involving all staff members. When Brigadier De Beer had remained unconvinced he had drawn up a petition to present to him. He had given up the idea when only five signatures were realized. The five were all people who fell directly under his control and had thought it wise to comply with his wishes. "Also," Gert van Staden went on, "I hear you've been scratching in my salad."

"I just wanted to talk to Du Plessis and you were away splashing in the Indian Ocean, remember?"

"Clearly." He leant across the desk and spoke softly. "Agh, Yudeltjie. If you want something in my section, you can have it. But the way you've been acting lately is making some people uneasy."

"Listen, Gertjie," Yudel said, returning the endearment. "I don't think you reported my visit to Du Plessis to the old man."

Van Staden shook his head slowly and now he was not smiling. "A policeman by the name of Sydney Wheelwright, a colonel."

"I saw him. What is he, CID?"

"Special branch, little brother, special branch."

Yudel returned to his office to scribble aimlessly at the fuel consumption graphs while at the same time making telephone calls that had nothing to do with his activities in the department. First he tried Dahlia's number and listened for a while to the sound that meant the telephone on the other end was ringing. There was no point to the call. Yudel knew it, but for all that he dialled again when it was not answered and listened to the sound a second time.

He phoned Rosa and apologized that he would not be able to fetch her and could she stay one more night? She sounded relieved at the question and yes she was able to stay another night. Irena would not mind.

He turned again to the graph. He had bought a set of coloured pencils especially for the purpose and the effect was not displeasing. Gert van Staden came in while he was busy. "You're an artist," he said admiringly. "May I borrow them for my graph when you're finished?"

"See you bring them back," Yudel said.

"Old Williamson is going to like yours." Van Staden sounded a little envious.

He had just left with the coloured pencils when the phone rang again. "Hullo, Yudel." It was the voice of Brigadier De Beer.

"Yes, sir," Yudel said guardedly. He wondered just how far the whole thing had gone. There was also the promotion. By all accounts De Beer had supported him throughout.

"I've got a bit of a problem with the leave allocations." His voice sounded unusually hoarse and he had to interrupt himself once to cough. "I'd like you to come over and help me sort it out. I'm at home. I've got a bit of bronchitis. Come at lunch time. Tell Doctor Williamson you'll be late."

After he had hung up Yudel stood for a while at the window, looking down into the car park. Not only was there nothing wrong with the leave allocations, but the brigadier had never showed the slightest interest in them. In the car park a black attendant was waving a car into an empty bay. A member of the uniformed staff came out of the building, jangling the keys of a vehicle in one hand. It was an entirely normal scene, one that he saw almost every day of his life, but now he no longer felt part of it. The events of the last week had contrived to alienate him from everything that was usual and trivial. In his own mind he had lost normality somewhere during the last seven days.

As he watched, Poena van der Merwe and his entourage of junior clerks came out of the building. They were carrying briefcases and were without doubt on their way to one of the prisons where they would conduct one of the mysterious exercises on which civil service administrative clerks spend their lives. They reached the car and van der Merwe opened the door on the driver's side. At that moment he turned and his eyes made contact with Yudel's. He said something and the others in the group followed the direction in which he was looking.

Yudel was careful to stand completely still. He made no attempt either to acknowledge or avoid them in any way. The group at the car stared passively back at him for a few seconds, then van der Merwe broke the spell by getting into the driver's seat. The others followed immediately. As the car drove away Yudel could see the two in the back seat, their faces still turned towards him. The fascination of the free for the condemned, he thought, the living for the dying. The car turned into the street in front of the building and they were gone. And fuck you too, he thought, bringing his thinking to a more prosaic level.

Brigadier De Beer was sitting down to lunch on the glass-enclosed stoep at the back of his home. His wife of many years, a lean fussy woman, led Yudel through the house, asked if he would like lunch, accepted his refusal with a polite smile and disappeared into the kitchen to make coffee. The regional head of the department was wearing flannel pyjamas and a woollen dressing-gown. "Sit down," he croaked, looking at Yudel inquisitively, even sympathetically and altogether without hostility.

Yudel sat down across the small table from him. "I agree that we need to clear up this leave business immediately," he said.

De Beer smiled weakly. He was an Afrikaner, a senior member of the country's dominant group and he possessed the confidence that went with his position. Most English-speaking civil servants were of a far more timid variety, never sure just how far they were entitled to question orders, never quite understanding the ground rules and always careful not to give offence. De Beer was also not a man to waste words when something important was being discussed. "Yudel," he said, "I don't know what you were doing in Durban last week and I don't want to know. I just want to say that I don't believe you have terrorist connections."

"I didn't know anyone believed that," Yudel said innocently.

"I don't know what they believe, but two security meetings were held last week and you were the subject under discussion." He was speaking slowly, stopping to breathe between sentences. "The first was just the building security meeting, Poena van der Merwe and that bunch. The other, on Friday afternoon, was more serious. I had to attend and they had two security police officers present. The issues raised were your visit on a Sunday to a political prisoner who falls under Gert van Staden's jurisdiction and what you were doing in Durban and the kind of people you were meeting there. As far as the first is concerned I told them you were van Staden's senior and you went to see this Du Plessis with my blessing. As far as the second is concerned . . . "

Yudel interrupted him. "Thank you," he said, "for coming up for me that way. As far as the second . . . "

De Beer held up a hand. He turned his head to direct a cough away from the table. "As far as the second is concerned, I don't want to know about it." The brigadier's face was calm, but a little tired and he was looking straight into Yudel's eyes. "This regulation about civil servants not being allowed to add to their incomes, I know we all ignore it, but there are people who will not hesitate to use it against you, if they need to, and if they can't find any other stick to hit you with."

"Thanks again," Yudel said.

"We've known each other for what, five or six years . . . " Mrs De Beer arrived with the coffee and her husband stopped speaking. Politics was a man's business. She poured two cups, asked Yudel if his wife was well and if they had enjoyed the few days in Durban and, oh, congratulations on your promotion. Yudel made all the required responses and Mrs De Beer returned to her kitchen. "We've known each other for some time," De Beer went on, "and I don't believe that you are a danger to anyone. Nobody has told me this, but your telephone is probably tapped at the moment. Your mail might be opened. I think you should be careful."

"I don't suppose I can ask who the security policemen at the meeting were."

"You can ask. I can't answer."

"I don't know what to say . . . "

"Say nothing. How's Rosa?"

"She's all right."

"Give her my regards."

It seemed to be a signal that the interview was at an end. Yudel got to his feet. "The only thing I'm sorry about is causing you embarrassment."

De Beer waved a hand in a way that suggested that the only thing that caused him embarrassment was this kind of talk. "I told them at the security meeting that I felt I had been correct in promoting you. I still feel that way." Yudel edged towards the door. "One more thing, according to the grapevine you are going to be raided."

Yudel stopped. "You didn't hear when?"

"Tonight," De Beer said. "I can't guarantee it, but that is the story."

Yudel stayed late at his office, ostentatiously, flamboyantly late. At five o'clock, a bunch of papers in one hand, he fought his way down the corridor through the evening stampede as his colleagues threw down their daily chains to take themselves home to chains of a different variety. At the corridor's end he went up the stairs to the floor above where he coasted with the stream of liberated humanity, leafing vigorously through his documents as he was swept along. He went down a different flight of stairs and back to his office. On the way he elbowed past Poena van der Merwe, gruffly instructing him to "Excuse me". The purpose of his performance had been to display to all that, no matter what the rumours, he was still very much part of the department.

After five o'clock the building quickly subsided into the silence that pervades all government buildings the world over after hours. It only remained for Yudel to go home to await the raid. He put the incomplete leave roster into his briefcase, straightened his tie and ran an aimless set of fingers through his hair. It was going to be a long night.

He took the road that skirted the fountains area, noticing that the Afrikaner Revival Movement's signs had not been taken down. He parked his car in the garage and, once in the house, closed all the windows, made sure that the doors were locked and drew the curtains. At least Rosa was away. She would be expecting him to fetch her on the next day, or would she? Yudel wondered if she intended coming back at all. She was not a brave woman and she hated the thought of becoming a pariah in the community. It was fortunate that she had been born into a time and place in which discrimination against the Jews was of an innocuous nature.

He tried Dahlia's number, but there was no reply. Christ, he thought, she knew about this sort of thing. She'd been through it. But tomorrow Rosa would probably be back and they would be sharing a bed. And Dahlia? Dahlia was a brief and meaningless incident in the past. He told himself that in his life she had no more substance than a shadow. He dialled her number again. Still there was no reply.

Yudel inspected the window latches a second time. If they were going to come in, he wanted them to do it through the front door. Outside, beyond the curtains, the city was sinking into deep twilight. Stopping at his study window, he could see the Union Buildings across the valley, the executive office of the government dark grey against a still bright northern sky. Down below in the Sunnyside shopping area, a few neon lights had come on as businesses peddled the wares of the evening. He could see part of an intersection and a short queue of cars, stopped by a traffic light.

I'll try her again, he thought. Don't be a fool, he told himself. Other men have one or two night stands. By all accounts it is a not uncommon phenomenon. But I'll try her just once more.

Yudel left the window, but before he could reach the phone it rang. Perhaps it's her. In his anxiety to reach it he knocked the handpiece from its cradle, sending it crashing to the ground. He picked it up in both hands, trying to steady them that way, and pressed the instrument to his ear. "Gordon," he said. But the line was already dead. He thought about dialling Dahlia again, but if she was at home the man she was living with would probably be there too. He thought about unplugging the phone, but Rosa might call.

The phone rang again, the two bursts of ringing following each other in monotonous succession. On the twentieth ring he answered. "Gordon here." He heard the click as the caller hung up. They wanted to soften him up before the time came.

Jesus, Yudel thought, getting quickly to his feet. The purpose of such raids was to find things. He did not want to lose Blythe Stevens's file or his own erratic note-taking. The file was lying innocently in the centre of his desk for all the world to see. As Yudel picked it up there was a knock on the front door. It was a strong confident sound, the knock of someone who expected to have the door opened to him.

Yudel ran into the kitchen, found the plastic bags Rosa used for cakes, dropped the file into one, sealed it with the wire binder intended for the purpose and slipped that into a second bag to make doubly sure. The visitor knocked again, as forcefully as before, and Yudel started for the bathroom. He threw his parcel into the automatic washing-machine, stuffed a handful of clothing from the washing-basket in after it and turned open the tap to flood it. A moment later he was standing just inside the front door, trying to compose within himself the illusion of the suburban male at peace with the world and those in authority. He reached for the door handle as the person on the other side knocked again. Yudel waited for him to stop, then he turned the key and opened the door.

The boy who delivered the newspaper every evening had already started down the steps towards the gate. He turned an innocent thirteen-year-old face, uncluttered with resentments or premature notions of independence, to Yudel. "Hullo, Uncle," he said. "I didn't know if Uncle was away or what. Uncle did not take Friday or Saturday's newspapers inside." He held all three out to Yudel.

"I was away," Yudel said, "thank you."

"That's all right, Uncle." The boy trotted down the path, leapt on to his bicycle that had been leaning against the gate and pedalled away.

Yudel locked the door again, took his three newspapers into the lounge and switched on the television set. The programme was an American situation comedy in which three young adults share an apartment. It was not one of that country's better exports. Yudel stared at the flickering tube while the mundane dialogue and the pre-recorded laughter droned meaninglessly on, far in the back of his consciousness.

The telephone rang again and one of his hands lifted convulsively as if to ward off a blow. He lowered it slowly, surprised by the degree of tension within himself. His arms pressed against the armrests of his chair and the muscles across his chest and shoulders had become taut. The sound of the telephone formed a nagging intrusive presence behind the jocular inanities of the television script. Each twin burst of ringing followed the other at precisely structured intervals. He waited for it to stop. In the left side of his chest a glowing blunt-edged pain had appeared.

The programme came to an end and an advertisement for the local front company of a mighty international motor conglomerate appeared on the tube. The company had, amidst a prolonged public relations fanfare, announced that it was divesting itself of all South African interests. The manoeuvre had served the combined purposes of calming the souls of anti-apartheid activists everywhere, easing the consciences of the corporation's shareholders and allowing them to pursue their usual goals unhindered.

The telephone stopped ringing. A new programme started, filling the room with the raucous sound of its electronic theme music. He got up to switch off the set. His hand had barely left the button when the phone started again. It might be Rosa, he told himself. If it is, I must put her mind at rest.

He answered it in the study. By the time the handpiece had reached his ear the call had been disconnected. He took hold of the cord that connected the instrument to the wall and jerked the plug out of its socket. Then he went back to the lounge and sat down in one of the easy chairs to await their coming.

He was still in the chair when morning's first light woke him from a restless and dream-filled sleep. The night had passed and they had not come.

Seventeen

The job they had done on his office had been carefully executed, carefully enough that he had been at his desk for some fifteen minutes before he realized what had happened. De Beer had been right about the time of the raid, but wrong about the location. The surface of the desk was free of all dust and the disorderly pile of paper that normally occupied its right-hand side had been neatened, not completely, but enough to make a discernible difference. It had also been moved until it was touching the government issue blotter in the centre of the desk. The blotter was an ancient innovation that had somehow outlived the fountain-pen in the South African civil service.

Yudel inspected the filing cabinets that housed his case studies. All the drawers had been closed and, inside, the files were neatly positioned on the runners. He went down the passage in search of Jackson.

The cleaner was in the small kitchen at the top of the stairs, pouring the early morning tea. He looked up curiously. "Jackson," Yudel started, "how many times have I told you not to touch my desk or my filing cabinet?"

"Hou!" Jackson's exclamation carried all the injured dignity of a good man wronged. He drew himself upright, squaring his shoulders and pulling in his chin. "And I never touch it."

"And no one else has been in my office to clean?"

"Who's touch it? Nobody's touch it." The idea of someone else dusting and sweeping on his territory was appalling.

"And you touched nothing?"

"Not once. Never, never."

"Thanks," Yudel said. He glanced back once as he went down the stairs. Jackson's outraged face, appearing round the door frame, watched him go.

The security guard on the ground floor was letting in a visitor through the two-stage armoured glass door that provided the only entrance to the building. "Take the lift to the fifth floor," he was telling the visitor. He was nearing retirement age and possessed a face that suggested both suspicion and discontent. He looked uncomfortable at Yudel's approach. "Yes, Mister Gordon." He spoke more loudly than necessary, working at sounding confident and in control.

"Who was on duty here last night?" Yudel wanted to know.

"Nobody." The man's answer was so absurd that Yudel made no response to it. "I don't know," he amplified it.

"Was Volschenk?"

"Perhaps. I'm not sure."

Yudel's manner and tone of voice indicated no attempt to make things easier for him. "Who was here when you came on duty?"

"Volschenk."

"I see." Yudel's voice was cold and ungracious. If there was a need to restore the pecking order he was ready to start.

He took the lift to the top floor and the stairs to the roof. Mister Volschenk, the building's elderly superintendent, had not yet gone to bed. He was limping slowly, watering-can in hand, on gout-affected feet among the pot plants that surrounded his roof-top apartment.

Like the security guard he did not appear pleased to see Yudel. "Who was in my office last night?"

The old man had averted his eyes, not even looking at Yudel when he stopped directly in front of him. "I don't know." His voice was resentful and the area around his eyes had acquired a deeper shade of pink than the rest of his face.

"You were on duty. Who did you let into my office?" The old man had his back towards Yudel now, still weaving his way amongst the pots. Yudel manoeuvred to face him. "You have responsibilities in this building. Are you going to answer me?"

"Nobody. I let nobody into your office. The whole thing has got nothing to do with me."

"Must I take this matter further?" Yudel demanded. "You can answer me or you can answer Brigadier De Beer."

"It's not right." The old man's anger held a degree of desperation. "It's not right that you should question me like this. It's not my fault that you're in trouble."

"What were their names?"

Volschenk looked straight into Yudel's eyes for a moment before averting his own. "It's not right. They say I may not say anything. You say you'll drag me in front of the brigadier. It's not fair. I'm sorry, Mister. I know nothing."

Yudel looked at the flushed and agitated face of the old man. He was right. It was not fair.

On his way back to his office he passed Doctor Williamson in the passage. His senior nodded grimly in his direction without allowing his eyes to focus fully on Yudel and slipped into his office. Yudel followed close behind. "Someone's been searching my office. I take the strongest exception to this . . . " It was a favourite expression of Williamson. "I trust that as my senior you had nothing to do with it."

Williamson's eyes found something on the desk top that demanded his close attention. His fingers fiddled with a loose sheet of paper. "I can't imagine what you're talking about."

"I'll take the matter up with the brigadier." Yudel started towards the door.

"You can't go over my head. It'll cause repercussions . . . "

It was this very civil service fear of repercussions that Yudel was seeking to exploit. "Who was in my office?"

"So far as I know, there was no one." That he had to qualify the statement was typical of Williamson. There had always to be an escape hatch. "In any event I feel that you're in no position . . . "

Yudel interrupted him. "I expect action on this or there will be repercussions such as this department has never seen." He was careful not to bang the door as he left.

In his office Yudel went through the contents of his desk and files, but so far as he could see, nothing was missing. But nothing connected to the Blythe Stevens matter had been in the office. They had searched and found nothing at all.

Jackson brought in the morning tea. The old Sotho's look of disapproval was a lesson in self-expression. "Me, I never once touch the desk. I never once touch the cabinet."

"All right, Jackson. I accept what you say and I apologize."

"How many years I work here?" Jackson's indignation was by no means spent.

"Many years, Jackson. I said I'm sorry and . . . "

"Me, I do how the boss say." Jackson backed through the door with his tea tray, looking marginally less wounded than before. The brigadier and the cleaner were honest men. At least he had shown the rest of them that he would not be going down without a fight.

Yudel weighed up the matter and came to the conclusion that his working late on the previous evening was good for half an hour now. He had to fetch Rosa from her sister's home before the promotions party and, if he was early enough, he would be able to attend to another matter that was growing in importance in his mind.

Late afternoon on the Transvaal highveld is beautiful. The soft shades of dusk are especially lovely because they replace the bleached landscapes of the high altitude midday. The beiges and whites of frost-burnt grass become rich reds and browns. Even the tired grey bluegums grow rich in colour. The mud wall of an old farm building, a washed out pink at noon, becomes a lustrous red. The dusty opaque African streams assume a wonderful subtlety of shade and depth.

Yudel drove quickly, not insensible to the beauties of the closing day. He had never been indifferent to Durban's rich subtropical green, but the highveld reflected both Africa's harshness and its gentleness. The extremes of heat and cold, the blinding white sunlight and the scorching night-time frost: he loved it all.

In the half-hour that it took him to travel between the two cities the pressures of the past week fell away just a little. Fingers that gripped the steering wheel too tightly started to loosen, the iron band that had begun almost unnoticed to constrict his breathing, the blunt-edged pain in the area of his heart: all yielded slightly to the soothing sound of the car's engine and the calmness of the late afternoon.

He parked the car outside a new and expensive office building in Sandton, a wealthy dormitory suburb to the north of Johannesburg. The building was only three or four storeys high and surrounded by a broad strip of carefully landscaped garden. Its outside was tiled and the cars in the parking bay probably cost three or four times the price of Yudel's. If you had premises in such a building, you had either arrived in business or so over-extended yourself that you were sinking fast.

He took his briefcase with him and told an attractive confident-looking teenage girl at the reception desk of Sandown Private Investigations that his name was Milan Varrevich and he would like to speak to Mister Du Toit. The girl's skin glowed a rich cream-brown, the colour of a synthetic creation that was advertized to give your skin a lustre no man will be able to ignore. It was not unsuccessful. Her hair too was carefully cut, styled and positioned. Just as her skin had no wart, pimple or other blemish to disfigure it, so the hair had no misplaced strand to disturb its structured equilibrium. It was a wondrous thing to Yudel. The number of daily woman-hours that went into such a production was a matter of awesome proportions.

In brief and businesslike fashion she completed an unfinished telephone call, then called her employer on the intercom system to tell him that Mister Milan Varrevich was in reception to see him. Du Toit showed considerably greater interest in the news than his receptionist had. In the few seconds that it must have taken him to come from his office he appeared next to the reception desk.

The private investigator had hair that was greying, the red cheeks that go with high blood pressure and a waist line that was showing the effects of too many business lunches. "Where's Varrevich?" he asked the girl.

Before the girl could reply Yudel extended a hand. "Attorney Gordon for Mister Varrevich," he said.

Du Toit's eyes searched Yudel's face for a moment, then he looked enquiringly at the girl. "He said he was Varrevich," she explained.

Du Toit gestured to Yudel to follow him, then led the way down a tiled passage, into a large office, the floor covered by a dense deep-pile carpet, the walls wood-panelled and the desk of genuine walnut. Du Toit had done well out of the sexual and industrial misdemeanours of the city's wealthier inhabitants. He sat down behind the desk and pointed to a chair. His face bore an expression of carefully imposed inscrutability. He left Yudel to start speaking.

"My client would like to arrange a meeting to discuss damages. We are willing to settle out of court for a reasonable figure. I am sure that, in view of the nature of your business, you would prefer us to do this discreetly."

"Your client, Mister Varrevich?"

"Major Varrevich," Yudel corrected him.

"Of course. And you said you are . . .?"

"Attorney Gordon."

Du Toit looked thoughtfully at the wall behind Yudel. "And why does Major Varrevich feel that I owe him damages?"

Yudel opened his briefcase, took out a sheaf of papers, appeared to glance at them, and said, "Major Varrevich feels that your assertion that he murdered Doctor Raymond Baker in 1978 is a severe blow . . . "

Yudel did not finish speaking. Du Toit's structured pretence had fallen away. His mouth hung open in astonishment. His voice was no more than a hoarse croak. "I deny it."

Yudel waved the papers at him. "According to information passed on to me by Mister Blythe Stevens, who is willing to testify on our behalf . . . "

Du Toit was sliding back into his chair, seeming to shrink with the weight of his problems. "God Almighty," he said. "What does that mad bliksem think he's doing?" He pressed the fingers of both hands against his temples. "God, I can't believe it. Little Lord Jesus, doesn't he know who these people are?" He was talking to himself. Yudel's presence in the room made no difference.

"We are looking for damages of fifty thousand rands, if you want this done discreetly."

Du Toit had covered his face with his hands. For a while he

said nothing. When he did speak it was to vilify Blythe Stevens further. "That fucking mad bliksem . . . " His voice faded as his thoughts branched away in a new direction. "You ask Varrevich from me if he will be satisfied with damages." He sounded tired. The last few minutes had taken much enthusiasm out of the life of the proprietor of Sandown Private Investigations. "You don't know that mob, my friend. You tell him from me, I want to know if damages will satisfy him."

"This is not a criminal matter," Yudel said. "My client's only recourse is via civil action."

Du Toit's laugh was short and without humour. "You think I'm worried about court action? You think I care about that fifty thousand?"

"If you are willing to meet my client's demand, there is no further problem."

"Is that so?" It was said heavily and with sarcasm. In Du Toit's mind Yudel might have been a child to be humoured. "I'm worried about staying alive, my friend."

Yudel slid the papers back into his briefcase, placed it flat across his knees and folded his hands on its closed lid in what he imagined to be a businesslike, legalistic sort of way. "I don't think this presents a problem. I'll have Mister Varrevich place in writing that he will not interfere with or assault you in any way. You give the paper to your attorney to keep. Varrevich will, of course, know of the document's existence. If anything happens to you, suspicion will immediately fall on him." He looked smugly at the private detective, wondering irrelevantly if he might not have made a fairly good lawyer.

Du Toit was less impressed. "That mad, fucking bastard," he said, thinking again of Blythe Stevens whom Yudel had so viciously defamed.

It was time to start pulling in the line. "There is another way out for you," Yudel told him. He was being generous and it was reasonable to expect Du Toit to show a suitable degree of appreciation. The private investigator looked impassively at him. He did not seem to have much faith in ways out of his problem. "My client is not particularly interested in enriching himself at your expense. What interests him . . . "

"I know what interests him." Du Toit came briefly alive. "Having my gut for his necktie, this is what interests him. I know about Milan Varrevich's interests."

Yudel would have liked to know about Varrevich's interests too, but pressing the matter would have its own problems. "My client's main interest is to clear his good name." Du Toit snorted derisively. This, clearly, was a good one. "I might be able to persuade him to drop the matter completely if you are willing to hand him the evidence on which you based your findings."

The way out that he was being offered did not please Du Toit in even the smallest degree. "Bliksem," he said. The word was an adulteration of the Afrikaans for lightning and was widely used to provide relief for a range of emotions beginning at anger and journeying through disgust and exasperation to amazement and wonder. Du Toit's use of it was somewhere towards the centre of the range.

"I think it's a very generous offer." Yudel was the kind officer of the law, giving the undeserving offender a chance. "I think it's something you should grasp before he changes his mind."

"Bliksem," he repeated sadly. "Little Lord Jesus. That mad bastard. How the hell could he hand that stuff over to Varrevich?"

"But I don't see the problem. Just give Mister Varrevich the information that he wants and he'll leave you alone. I guarantee it."

"You guarantee it." The tone of his voice was both miserable and mocking. Du Toit leaned across the desk towards Yudel. "I can't give him what he wants because I don't have anything to give. I had just left the police when that bunch of commies approached me to find Baker's killer. I needed the money so I took the job. They believed it was done by the Durban special branch and I had worked in that very office for three years. All I did was pick the man I thought most likely to have done it. They wanted a security cop and I gave them one. I supported it with some fictitious evidence that I said came from my own phone taps. I didn't think they'd have the nerve to try to lay a charge and I was right. All they did was smuggle it out of the country. After the revolution they'll have Varrevich shot. Oh, bliksem."

184

"That's it?" Yudel asked.

"I swear to God."

Yudel got up and made his way through reception and down the stairs. In the parking area Du Toit caught up to him. "We've got to talk about this a bit more. I don't really think they'll shoot Varrevich after the revolution."

Yudel laid a hand on the other man's shoulder. "Never mind. I'll put in a good word for you. My client is a gentle and forgiving man."

"Varrevich?"

As Yudel drove away Du Toit was still standing among the parked cars, a man in the hands of fate.

She was standing at the corner of the children's park near her sister's home. As he approached Yudel could see by the rigid way she held herself and the stiffness of her smile that Rosa was having difficulty dealing with the events of the past week. "Hello, Yudel." Her smile was the result of so much effort and the attempt to keep her voice light and cheerful was so obvious that the effect was the opposite of what it should have been.

"How are you, Rosa?" It was the question of a man, estranged from his wife, formal, not expecting an answer that would be more than polite.

"I'm well. How was the trip to Durban? Did you find what you wanted?"

Yudel shrugged. "I'm not sure."

The sun was gone behind trees and houses and the day had unexpectedly turned cold, winter making itself felt one last time against uncovered skin, up nostrils and on the damp surfaces of the eyes. Rosa was wearing a woollen coat, buttoned up to the neck and Yudel had his hands deep in his pockets, his shoulders hunched up as if to shield his head. They stood stiffly upright, facing each other, she not knowing how to proceed, and he fairly sure of what she wanted to say, but finding himself unable to help her.

"It's cold," she said.

"Yes, after such a nice day."

"Since you've been back, has everything been fine at home?"

He shrugged again. "Of course." It was not true and he guessed that his manner probably gave that away.

"I tried to phone last night, but there was no answer. Perhaps you were out."

"No. I . . . " No explanation was going to be useful to Rosa.

"Perhaps you had an appointment somewhere and had to go out." Rosa needed a reason for the telephone not being answered.

"It was disconnected accidentally. I noticed it in the morning."

"I tried on Sunday night as well, about nine. Were you out then?" She was not asking Yudel where he had been, what he had been doing or with whom. What she wanted to know had to do with the telephone and why it had gone unanswered. Yudel was trying to structure the explanation that would satisfy her when she spoke again. "You unplugged it on Sunday night as well, didn't you?"

The dark shadow around her eyes was more than usually deep in the fading light. He would rather have provided an answer that would have put her at ease, but he feared that the time for such answers was past. Whatever he said Rosa already knew the answer. "Yes," Yudel said.

"You were getting calls?"

He knew what sort of calls she was talking about, how she feared them and how she hated herself for her fear. "Yes."

"Oh God." It was said with much control and a curious lack of passion. "I had a call too. I think it was those people."

"You were here, with Irena?"

"Yes. They asked to speak to me. They said that you were not doing what I thought you were doing in Durban. They said you were going around with an Indian woman. This afternoon there was an envelope in Hymie's letter box for me. It just had a photograph of you and this woman. You seemed to be in a shopping arcade. She's holding on to your arm and laughing." Rosa breathed deeply, seeming to try to draw strength for what she still had to say. Her voice had remained soft and restrained and her face expressionless, except for the small lines between her eyes that gave away the tautness and pain within her. "I want you to know, Yudel, that I don't believe you were going with another woman. I know what they can do with photographs. I'm not a

186

child. I know what those people are capable of. And if the picture is real, I'm sure it was just part of your investigation."

Yudel resisted the impulse towards self-congratulation. The look on Rosa's face and the quiet desperation in her voice were sobering enough. He could find no way to answer her fears or to respond to her misplaced faith in him.

"I don't care about what they said. But they phoned me here. They know I'm here. They know everything, Yudel."

He stood with her for a while longer as the day gave way to night. It seemed to him that lately his whole life centred around the twilight part of the day and his activities with the twilight parts of society. The uncertainties of fading light merged in his mind with the new insecurity that had become part of his life, the deepening dark with the gathering fear that was coming to dominate every moment.

He walked back with Rosa to the gate of Hymie and Irena's home. She did not believe about the other woman, but she knew about the telephone. She would be coming back, but it was not possible for her to do it yet.

Eighteen

The hotel was on Pretoria's more prosperous east side. On this end of town hotels looked better, smelled better and charged more for drinks. The promotion parties of lower ranks in the departments of police or prisons were normally held in hotels on the west or north of the city where the hotels were older, the waiters shabbier, the price of brandy more affordable and it was less unthinkable to puke on the floor. Wives, girlfriends, sisters, even female staff members were not invited. This was an all-male affair. Six promotions were being celebrated, the advancement of three new majors and one colonel in the police, and in prisons one new colonel and a senior professional officer in the person of Yudel.

The party was going well by the time he arrived. It flowed out of one of the conference rooms, spilling into the garden. Officers in uniform and out of it, with ranks anywhere between lieutenant and general, clustered in large and small groups, glasses in hand, talking loudly and laughing even louder. Laughter was a prerequisite for such parties. As you came in the door you started grinning and from that moment on you were ready to burst into unrestrained laughter at the smallest hint of amusement.

Beer was the lubricant that oiled the wheels of conviviality during the early stages. It was expected that each man would drink a considerable volume of the country's most popular beverage, would strain to capacity the hotel's refrigeration system, and excessive visits to the urinal would not be necessary. A man stayed at the party, only deserting it every sixth or seventh beer to pee like a horse. You had to be able to hold your liquor both in the head and in the bowels. The rules were tacit and informal, but everyone acted in accordance with the norms that provided the qualifications for manliness in this most interesting social sub-group, the departments of police and prisons.

Later in the evening the beer would give way to brandy. It was true that the occasional aberrant soul might order gin, vodka or cane, but with few exceptions and much conviction, a real man drank brandy when the time for beer was past. And he mixed it only with coke.

This party had a problem. It had been going well enough, the beer flowing in its usual excessive quantities, the laughter loud and prolonged, the jokes crude and undemanding, but Yudel's presence, as much as his promotion was a damper on the merriment. Many of the three or four hundred men were aware that there was something happening with the little Jew in prisons. Very few had been told in clear language that Yudel was now a security risk, but oblique hints, looks, small gestures, unfinished sentences, snubs, shrugs suggesting that I know nothing about it and don't want to know anything, all had the effect of directing him towards the outer fringes of the group. He was not yet cast out. That time might come and most were getting themselves ready for the possibility that it was not far off. No one wanted to be too close when the time came.

Brigadier De Beer, a scarf wrapped around his neck as defence against the evening air, was in conversation with Brigadier Visagie of the CID as Yudel came in. He nodded and smiled briefly, not pausing in what he was saying. On the far side of the room Gert van Staden, Yudel's genial fellow psychologist, was part of a large group in civilian clothes. He waved, but made no effort to join Yudel. Poena van der Merwe, of the intense patriotism, stared in Yudel's direction, apparently surprised that he had dared to attend the party under such circumstances. Others either shook Yudel's hand briefly and slipped back into the crowd or pretended not to notice his presence.

He went over to the bar that formed one end of the room, sat down on a high stool and ordered a beer. The hell with them all, he thought, looking among the many figures in a room that was already hazy with cigarette smoke to see if Freek had arrived. He could not see Freek, but old Williamson was not far from him. He had sidled up to a group of uniformed officers and was trying in his own suppressed way to be genial. It was clearly not proving easy. Two black barmen, over-awed at being in the presence of that many senior white police officers, scurried back and forth along the end of the bar, trying to meet the needs of their customers. One of them brought Yudel his beer. It was cold and bubbled on his tongue in a way that might have been refreshing if the circumstances had been different.

One of a cluster of officers near him, a large, heavy man with coarse features, was spoiling the mood by raising the sort of matters that were normally forgotten on such occasions. Yudel recognized him as Brigadier Momberg, head of the special branch in Pretoria. He was waving the index finger of his right hand back and forth as if it was a sword he was using to defend a righteous cause. "One thousand cheap watches," he was saying. "In 1976 the Anti-Apartheid Movement in London advertised for one thousand cheap watches. If they were not intended to set off bombs right here . . . And they tell us that these people are not in Moscow's pocket." Momberg was jabbing the same finger at the air in front of him with a fury that boded ill for any member of the accused organization who might wander far enough from his safe London accommodation to gatecrash this gathering. "They mustn't tell me," he continued, "that liberalism is . . . "

Yudel's attention was drawn by the only man apart from Momberg in civilian clothes in the group, the more sharply so because the man was looking directly at him. Yudel had seen the face once before and then only briefly, but he recognized it immediately. Despite the nature of the occasion, the loudness of the voices and the general lowering of inhibitions, Colonel Wheelwright's guard was still carefully in place. The brittleness, scepticism and suspicion that Yudel had detected in him on that one previous occasion were unaffected by the beer or the lightness of the mood.

The look that met Yudel's eyes was too restrained to be one of complete hostility, too calm to hold at this moment the threat of physical violence and too measured to be the forerunner of rash or unplanned action. For all that, Yudel knew that he was looking into the eyes of an enemy. It was not the look of one who might arrange for Yudel to meet with a few bruises, a broken rib or a ruptured spleen in a dark place some night. Wheelwright was one who would not move until he was sure that he would be able to neutralize his adversary utterly.

Someone was clapping his hands and calling for attention. "Gentlemen. Gentlemen." The language he was using was Afrikaans, the medium of most of the men. With an effort Yudel turned away from Wheelwright. "Gentlemen, we are not going to make speeches tonight." A loud cheer from a group of young officers greeted this announcement. The man speaking was Brigadier Visagie who had been in conversation with De Beer earlier. "I mean it. We don't want speeches tonight. Tonight we are going to enjoy ourselves. I just want to say two words of congratulation and then have each of our men who have been promoted say a word." He held up a finger. "One word."

Yudel looked at Wheelwright again, but the colonel was paying attention to the speaker. "First of all I want to say that each of these men deserves . . . " Freek had come in at the door and was pressing carefully through the knots of revellers. " . . . maintaining high standards . . . " The brigadier's voice was firm and emphatic. He had forgotten his pledge about speech-making. " . . . loyalty and discipline are the qualities . . . "

Freek had reached Yudel. "Sorry I'm late," he murmured. "Bapsie was sick."

Yudel looked curiously at his friend. Dealing with sick children had never been a part of his life. "Why are you here? You don't have to be here."

"Take it easy. The child's mother is there."

"I'm finishing, gentlemen, if you can just give me another moment." The brigadier was looking at Freek and Yudel. "It just remains for me to offer my congratulations and for each of these men to come forward and say a word."

"It must be a short word and he must say it fast." It was one of the group of young officers.

"We've still got a lot of drinking to do," a colleague added.

"Now yes," the brigadier said, "promoted from major to colonel in the murder and robbery squad, Charles van der Spuy."

Newly promoted Colonel van der Spuy had been drinking single-mindedly since half past four. He made his way unsteadily to the brigadier, shook his hand enthusiastically, made a short speech that was almost completely incoherent and drank a toast to himself. The brigadier called up the others, one at a time, and each made a speech of no more than a few words to loud alcoholic cheering by the entire gathering. Yudel was last.

He had consumed only half a bottle of beer and Yudel's liver, an organ in fine condition, was capable of processing a great deal more than that before its owner's reflexes and judgment were impaired. Since the speeches had commenced he had been preparing himself for his turn. He squared very modest shoulders, held his head erect and marched to the brigadier, seized his hand and shook it with a vigour that surprised even himself. "Thank you, gentlemen." He had pitched his voice a shade lower, something he had learnt from Blythe Stevens. "Thank you, each and every one, for the loyal support that you have always given me in my work in the department. I especially thank my senior officers, Brigadier De Beer and Doctor Williamson, for the faith they have placed in me. Also the senior officers of the South African Police, especially the CID and the drug squad, sections with which I have worked closely in the past. I thank them for the great trust they have placed in me. Indeed trust has been the very basis of our relationship." Yudel was getting into his stride. He found addressing a gathering wonderfully impersonal, far easier than meeting the problems and objections of an individual. In making a speech he felt he was dealing with a certain lowest common denominator of the gathered intelligence. He always did it with confidence and usually he did it well.

This particular crowd had lapsed from drunken good humour to a sort of puzzled solemnity at what he was saying. Yudel saw a wry and sardonic amusement on Freek's face as he looked around him to gauge the effect of the speech. "It is because of this trust that I have been able to do my work to the best of my ability and to earn this promotion. And, I would like to say, that it has been a singular honour for me to have been associated with so many brilliant officers in the CID and outstanding colleagues in my own department."

Doctor Williamson was studying his feet as if there was something strange about them that he had not noticed until this moment. De Beer was looking straight in front of him with unfocused eyes, a dreamlike expression on his face. Poena van der Merwe was shifting uncomfortably from one foot to the other. One man in Yudel's audience was neither surprised, amused nor disconcerted by the small psychologist's discourse. Wheelwright looked at him through steady unblinking eyes. Yudel could play whatever game he liked. The time would come when he would realize that all games would be at an end.

"I look forward . . . " Yudel was closing. " . . . to many more fruitful years in the department. It is the place where I have worked all my adult life and the place from which I intend to retire. I am sure that the atmosphere of trust that I have always known, will continue in the years ahead. I feel that I am only beginning. Thank you, one and all."

There was a moment of silence. Some of the officers in the room were looking in puzzlement at each other, some at Yudel. He was making his way back to the bar by the time Freek started to app-laud. De Beer joined Freek almost immediately. Some others start-ed clapping uncertainly and there were a few drunken shouts of "Good old Yudel" and "There he is, Yudel." It took a few minutes for the party to get back to its former level of enforced pleasure.

"That was a very interesting speech," Freek said. "Whether or not that kaffir psychology of yours is going to have the desired effect we shall have to see."

The group of young officers who had wanted the speeches to go faster because of all the drinking they still had to do had moved close to Freek and Yudel, their glasses clutched tightly and their free arms around each other's shoulders for a measure of doubtful support. One of them peeled himself away from his friends and leant heavily on Yudel. "Sir," he addressed Freek, "may I ask what you are doing in the company of this man?" Behind him Yudel saw Wheelwright shaking hands with a few of the men around him. With each handshake he made a little bow. A poor imitation of an old-world gentleman, Yudel thought.

"This man is a Communist," the young officer, who was leaning on Yudel, said. "I have that on the highest authority."

"Whose authority?" Freek's voice was flat and utterly without humour.

The young man was far too drunk to take note of his senior officer's disapproval. "I have it on the authority of Mister Poena van der Merwe, a transport clerk in the Department of Prisons. And I would say to you that if we do not trust the clerks in our sister department, who can we trust?" He raised his glass, possibly thinking that a toast to transport clerks was in order.

Wheelwright had completed his round of handshaking and was moving towards the door. To reach it he had to pass close by the knot of young officers. He nodded towards them as he shouldered his way past, the quick irritated gesture of the sober for the inebriated. "Evening, evening," Yudel heard him say.

A few of them turned to watch him leave. As he went through the door the one who had his arm round Yudel's shoulders shook his head sadly and said, "These old men with the scorpions in their pockets." At this the rest erupted into unrestrained laughter that had the effect of making them cling more tightly to each other.

The young officer turned his attention back to Freek. "May I have your explanation, colonel, for why you are drinking with a known Communist?"

Freek's change of manner was too sudden to be natural. Yudel knew that it was a deliberately calculated device. "I am staying close to him to keep an eye on him, lieutenant. If I see that he is in possession of anything dangerous, such as a bottle of brandy, it is my intention to dispossess him and drink it myself."

The lieutenant released Yudel, made a determined attempt to stand upright on his own, almost overbalancing, and saluted Freek. "Thank you for that explanation, colonel. If you need any help with confiscated brandy, the men of Sandfontein are ready to come to your assistance." He executed an insecure right turn and overbalanced, falling against his friends and pushing the entire group a few paces across the floor.

"So," Freek said, studying Yudel's face. "You look like hell. What happened to you in Natal?"

*

One of his junior officers had given Freek a lift to the hotel. Yudel drove him home and on the way he told him about Durban, about Ray Baker, Fellows Ngcube and Lionel Bensch, about the name Milan Varrevich coming up in a few different places, about the Durban CID apparently not wanting the Baker case discussed on the telephone and about the suspicion, no more than that, that the police at the Maseru border post knew that Ngcube was going to die the night his daughter passed through.

Freek listened to it all in silence. "Very interesting," he said. "But there is an aspect you are glossing over. This woman, Mrs Baker, it sounds as if you spent a fair amount of time in her company."

Yudel shrugged. He was being unbelievably nonchalant. "A bit."

"A bit? From what you've been saying it sounds like you were with her all the time."

Yudel could see all of Freek's teeth as his friend was unable to suppress his grin. "Not all the time. I did spend some . . . " Yudel was explaining the matter very seriously.

"Good-looking, isn't she? I've seen pictures of her."

"Yes, I suppose . . . "

"Now, Mister Gordon, I'm only going to ask this question once . . . "

Yudel again took his eyes off the road to look angrily at Freek. There were supercilious features of his friend's personality that were unbearable.

"Did you make love to this woman?"

"Jesus Christ, Freek . . . "

"Hah, you did. That makes three, I believe."

Yudel looked straight ahead and concentrated on driving the car. Some conversations were best left to themselves.

"You also broke away from your habit of only cheating with Afrikanertjies, which seems to disprove your theory that your previous affairs were a form of rebellion against Afrikaner domination . . . " Freek's grin was now so wide that it seemed to be in danger of permanently disfiguring his face. " . . . a theory, I might add, to which I imputed a fair degree of credibility." He was very proud of his English.

"Do you suppose we might change the subject?" He was doggedly going to bring Freek back to more important matters. "I was hoping for a little help . . . "

"With Mrs Baker?"

"No. I was hoping you might be able to get your hands on a list of the membership of the Afrikaner Revival Movement and also of the archery clubs in the Transvaal."

"Nothing else?" Freek's voice was heavy with sarcasm.

"Well, yes. What about the names of all the security policemen stationed in Durban between January '78 when Baker died and November '81 with Ngcube got his. That might also prove useful. There may be a name that appears on all the lists." He was speaking quickly, to draw Freek as far as possible from the discussion on Dahlia.

"Nothing else you want? I hate to feel that I'm not needed. Please don't be shy."

"No. That's about it." He was being careful not to look at Freek.

"I'm sorry to hear that. After all, what are friends for?"

"I do appreciate the things you do for me and I understand that it is not always easy to do this sort of thing . . . "

"Yudel, for God's sake. I am not one of the stupider members of that crowd you sold all that horse shit to tonight. If you want something from me, at least pay me the compliment of trying a more subtle brand of psychology."

"Is it all right if I say thank you?" Yudel asked. At least they weren't discussing Dahlia any more.

Freek chuckled humourlessly. "It's all right if you piss off," he said.

Nineteen

It took Yudel three telephone calls to get the office address he wanted. It was time to flush out the other side and meet them in the open. He wanted them to feel that he was watching them too. He did not want an adversary lying in the undergrowth, waiting for him to slip.

First though he had business in Pretoria Central, the old prison overlooking the city from the ridge of hills that form its southern limit. It took Yudel only a few minutes to get there. The man being questioned was a former railways employee who was accused of stealing mail bags from trains. According to the charge sheet he had enriched himself by the amount of seventy-eight thousand rands in defence bonus bonds. It was past noon when Yudel took the officer in charge of the CID team out of the interrogation room. "You'll have to give him a breather," he said.

"He's ready to break."

"I know, but you've got him so confused he doesn't know what he's saying. If you want his confession to tally with what he says in court, you'll have to give him time."

"God, you okes." The officer disgustedly called off the interrogation, rescheduling it for later in the afternoon. "I'd like to know whose side you okes are on," he told Yudel.

It was almost lunch time when Yudel reached the office in the police building in Pretorius street. A harassed looking guard on the far side of a double perspex screen asked through a loudspeaker to see his identification. Yudel showed him his departmental card and told him that he wanted to see Captain van der Vyfer. The guard checked with van der Vyfer's office and a puzzled captain said, "Yes, if someone from prisons wants to see me, let him come up."

Yudel knew that once past the checkpoint it would be assumed that he had the right to be inside. He asked a female clerk, sitting at a computer in the first office he passed, where he would find Wheelwright. "At the end of the passage, last office on the left," she said.

Yudel opened the door without knocking and stepped inside. Wheelwright was at his desk, reading a departmental circular. By the time he looked up Yudel was already sitting down in the chair opposite him. The security policeman's head came up with a jerk and his eyes widened involuntarily. It was only a momentary reaction, but it was enough for both to know that Yudel had won the first point. Wheelwright recovered immediately. The twin shields of superiority and deceit settled over the policeman's eyes and he looked at Yudel without saying anything. Yudel had never before seen him in good light from close by and now he saw that the lid of Wheelwright's left eye hung permanently almost halfway down the eyeball. The policeman turned his head slightly to favour the good eye.

"You laid a complaint against me," Yudel told him. He was surprised at the anger he heard in his voice. "Perhaps you'd like to do your complaining to my face." Wheelwright raised his eyebrows in feigned surprise, the gesture exaggerating the effect of his drooping eyelid. For a moment Yudel thought that he might deny the charge. "That is the way a man should do things, I think."

Wheelwright turned his head away from Yudel before speaking. "Complaint?" he asked. It was also the first time that Yudel had heard his voice clearly. It had a dry and brittle sound, the voice of someone who had been a heavy smoker for many years. Yudel heard in it the reflection of a harsh and ravaged personality. "My departmental reports are confidential. If someone from another department has access to them, then something is wrong."

You bastard, Yudel thought, it's nice to see you on the run.

"Perhaps you had better examine your section for security leaks."

"Not this section," Wheelwright told him. He was still not looking at Yudel. "There are no security leaks here."

"Why should there not be security leaks in a department as inefficient as this one?"

Wheelwright was looking straight at him now. He had recovered from the surprise of seeing Yudel in his office without invitation or arrest, but there was still an element of chagrin and resentment, almost humiliation, in his face. "Inefficient?" The word was a question, the response to the almost unbelievable suggestion that this one of all government departments was not competent. It was the branch of the police that monitored thousands of telephone taps, kept a close watch on the reports of its hundreds of informers, administered bannings and house arrests, held thousands of unconvicted prisoners, conducted interrogations that ran into tens of thousands each year, that kept in check the restless tide of Communists, rabble rousers, black nationalists, university Marxists and other malcontents and allowed little blond children to grow up in safety and security. Only a madman could call them inefficient.

"I think that's the correct word," Yudel said. "A few years ago one of your special babies, a Doctor Raymond Baker, was assassinated, yet to this day your department does not know who did the killing. I would not call that efficiency."

"Murders are investigated by the CID."

"He was a client of yours. Don't you wonder who killed him? Don't you want to know who else is part of the game?"

"He's dead." Wheelwright's voice scratched like a nail across a steel plate. The eyelid too was bothering Yudel. "Why should I care?"

"If you were doing your job properly you would know. You would know who is involved and why. You would know about both friends and enemies. You would know who was playing in your backyard."

The insult implicit in all that Yudel was saying was starting to crack the policeman's carefully imposed control. "We know all that we need to know." He was trying to shield behind the illusion of total control, the ragged pretence that was always employed by his section of the police. "The question is not what we know. The question is why are you so interested in it? That is the question." He waited for an answer. Here he was at an advantage. If he insisted, Yudel would have to answer his questions, while he would never need to answer Yudel's.

"I could see that you needed help. I could imagine how you must feel with such a poor record. I thought that a little assistance for a weaker brother would be in order."

Wheelwright smiled, but it was a forced and unhappy expression. Without warning he changed the direction of his attack. "But why are we arguing? After all we are on the same side. We are friends after all."

It was not a statement with which Yudel agreed, but he knew that neither did Wheelwright. "Of course," Yudel said. "We should not be arguing."

Now that they were on the same side Wheelwright tried another smile. "This man who died was after all an enemy of the State." The smile had not extended to his eyes and he watched Yudel carefully while he spoke.

"He was definitely guilty then?"

"Without question. He was the enemy of all of us. Perhaps whoever killed him was nothing more than the hand of God, bringing punishment to the evildoer."

Yudel was looking to understand every smallest expression of Wheelwright's face, the meaning of even the slightest vocal intonation.

"I never thought of it that way."

"Perhaps that is what it was, the sword of righteousness, cutting down the ungodly." Yudel wondered whether he believed what he was saying, or if this was just another device to achieve some goal that would only be of importance to those like him. "For many, many years I've been involved with these people and I know them. It might be that it is not important to know who did the killing. Perhaps the only important thing is that it took place." He was completely confident now, safe on his own territory, knowing that Yudel could never repeat any part of the conversation. Both men knew that Yudel would never be believed by any court, that his career would be over and that there were laws governing what could be printed about the police. "Perhaps it is simply the will of God."

Yudel had enough of Wheelwright's tortuous entertainments. He decided to reach to the heart of the matter. "Perhaps your section was the instrument of God's will."

"We are here to serve the national interest. If it had been our work, we would in any event have been serving the nation."

"That's an interesting admission."

Wheelwright too had tired of subtlety. He leaned across the desk towards Yudel and now there was no attempt to hide his animosity. The hatred that he felt was evident in every word. "I did not ask you to come here today. You walked into my office as if you have every right here. Now let me tell you that I have made no admission to you and, if you take what I said as being an admission, you will be making a very big mistake. If you try to use it against this section you will learn how big the mistake was.

"Let me tell you something else. If murder is in the national interest there are plenty of men here who have the balls to do it. We know what we have to do to defend our people, and if murder is needed we will commit murder. Let me also tell you that working for a government department does not make you safe. If we need to take you in, we'll take you in. If we need to interrogate you, we'll do it."

"If you need to kill me?" Yudel suggested.

"We'll do whatever we need to protect our people. You liberals would let us be overrun. We'll level you all with the ground before we allow it." The words had been waiting inside Wheelwright for a long time, the pressure building mercilessly. Too much restraint made the release all the more violent. Now it was coming out as if there could be no stopping it, no end to the flow. "This Baker friend of yours and his coolie whore that you've been enjoying . . . " Yudel bit down hard on his teeth. If he lost control he would learn nothing. "Those people want a revolution. They want Nuremberg trials with me and everyone like me in the dock. They want to see us at the end of a rope. Do you think I'm going to allow that? Do you think I'm going to hand over the Afrikaner people to genocide?"

He leaned back in his chair. The rush was over, the storm's anger spent. "I want to tell you something, my clever little Jewish friend, that you don't seem to understand. Afrikanerdom is not a loose group of people like the Americans with their Poles, their Puerto Ricans, their Irish . . . Afrikanerdom is not a recipe for chaos like Canada with its English and French. We are altogether different. Afrikanerdom is a closed circle, complete and perfect. There is no way in except by birth and no way out except by death. It is a perfection that is of God. And if anyone tries to interfere with it, a Ray Baker or a Yudel Gordon, let him watch out. I can't be responsible for what happens to him."

Yudel phoned the CID officer whose interrogation he had spoiled an hour earlier. He was out, but expected back at half past four and would want to continue then. That gave him three hours, too little to get out to Leeukop prison where most of his duties lay, do something sensible there and get back in time for the interrogation. There was always the leave roster. It was not yet complete and Williamson was asking for it.

Yudel took it out of a desk drawer and placed it on the blotter in front of him. The whole thing was beginning to take on the dimensions of a major diplomatic exercise. The men who had children of school-going age had leave allocated to them during the school holidays, Williamson insisted on his in little bits adjacent to public holidays to give him the illusion of having more than the regulation number of days and Brigadier De Beer wanted the week that coincided with his club's annual bowls tournament. There were loose ends that needed attention. A clerk from the stores section wanted to go to the Drakensberg mountains after the worst of the winter cold had let up and there would be little chance of snow, one of the new boys wanted three weeks late in the year to complete his masters and somehow all of it had to be combined to have them all present in January when a visit from the minister was expected.

There was an alternative. It had been waiting in the back of Yudel's mind since before he had gone to Durban. The image that he had invented appeared continually in moments of idleness. It was the only place where one of these assailants had been recognized, where Fred One-night Tuwani, himself unseen, had watched one of them remove his mask. And what sort of man could he have been to be recognized by an activist like Tuwani? Yudel wanted to see the place they had called the Attic.

It did not take him long to win his argument with the leave roster. It was very complicated and he would bring a fresh mind to it later. Three hours were not enough. For continuity's sake it would be better to tackle it when he had more time. He could have thought of other arguments, but already he had persuaded himself.

Yudel wanted to do just one thing before going. He dialled the Durban number that he now knew by heart. Dahlia answered. "Yudel here," he said.

"Yudel, my God." Her voice sounded breathless, as if she was struggling for oxygen.

To Yudel she sounded alarmed. "Dahlia? Is something wrong?"

"No, there's nothing, nothing at all." She was still struggling for breath.

"You sound like something is wrong."

"I'm fine. I'm fine." He could hear her breathing. "It's you, my God."

She was not making sense and to Yudel almost anything was a source of anxiety now. "What do you mean? What are you talking about?"

"It's you. My God, Yudel." There were brief pauses between each sentence. He thought he heard her swallowing. "I didn't think you'd phone. I didn't think I'd hear from you again."

Her reaction was in the nature of her relationships with men. Hearing her voice, he could see her again at the parapet of the air terminal, walking on the beach or lying next to him in the uneven light coming in at the hotel windows. He could see in his mind her way of walking, her head hanging forward as if in thought. "You're sure nothing is wrong?" His nervous system was alive, racked by the calls he had been receiving, the security meetings of which he had been the subject, Wheelwright's tirade: it was barely possible that she could be all right.

"There's nothing wrong, Yudel. I just can't believe I'm speaking to you. I thought that when you left that would be the end of it. I've been good since you left. I haven't been naughty once, not even with my fiancé."

Yudel was not sure how he should react to this. Clearly Dahlia was proud that she had been faithful to him for the entire three-day period. It was a considerable achievement and he was not one to sneer at other people's moral accomplishments. "That's very nice," he said.

"Are you teasing me?" She was recovering from the shock of speaking to him and her voice was starting to regain its flirtatious note. "When are you coming to Durban again?"

"I don't know if I will be coming again."

"You have to come." The statement was short and emphatic. "You haven't found out everything here yet. There's still a lot to do."

"I know there is. I'm not sure that I'll be able to do it though." Yudel was confessing to her what he had been hiding to himself until that moment.

"You have to. There's no one else who will do it. Please." He was not sure if he was being asked to go on with the investigation or if she was asking, please come back to me. "Please come again."

"I tried to phone before, but there was no reply. Once I got your fiancé."

"He didn't say anything about it."

"I didn't speak to him. I hung up."

"That's what I like about you. You're so innocent. You could have spoken to him. It wouldn't have mattered."

"I don't want to speak to him."

"Can't you come back, Yudel?" It was a plea and now there was no doubt about what she was asking. To hell with the investigation, to hell with the killings, to hell with the country and its troubles, just come back to me. "For a weekend, anything."

Rosa was not a wife to be pleased about having her husband away from home without a reason. But Rosa was not at home herself. "I'll try," he said. "I'll arrange something." Nothing else was important. He would go back to see her again.

"When? When will you come?"

"I'll phone you."

"Soon, come soon."

"All right," Yudel said. "I'll come soon."

Twenty

The sign, clumsy and hand-painted by an amateur sign writer, cracked and weathered by the years between, still hung on the rusted steel gatepost. The large ungainly lettering announced 'the Attic' to anyone who might be interested. Yudel turned the car into a gravel drive. It curved slowly to the left, losing itself in a cluster of willows, bluegums and peppercorn trees. Under the trees kikuyu grass that had not been tended for many years grew in straggling, waist-deep disorder.

The track ended some distance from the house at a place where it had been widened to allow a car to turn. The house was made of wooden planks and corrugated iron sheeting. It stood high off the ground, rough wooden stairs leading to a stoep that ran the length of the two sides of the house Yudel could see. At the back it seemed to merge with a second building that might have been a store in earlier days. The house itself had probably once been the mine manager's office.

Behind it the mine dump, yellow clay deeply corrugated by rain, rose to the height of a five- or six-storey building and extended for some hundreds of metres, until it disappeared from sight behind another grove of trees and a disused and rusting headgear.

Yudel approached the house via a well-worn footpath that passed through the peppercorns and ended on the fringe of bare ground in front of the building. From a distance it had still possessed some of its former dignity, but from close by Yudel could see that the lower end of a number of planks had rotted badly and the corrugated iron was rusted through in places. It was clear that the mine had not been in use for many years, but the property was probably still owned by the mining house. They would hold on to it until its value was almost as great as the gold they had dug there.

Yudel went up wooden steps that were still firm underfoot, his feet crunching the peppercorn seeds that were spread in a light carpet over them and along the edge of the stoep. He tried the front door. It was locked but through its glass panels and in the windows on either side he could see that frayed and ancient lace curtains had been tied back to let in the light. Pressing his face against one of the windows, he found himself looking into a large room. A number of rough wooden benches without backrests were arranged in neat rows and at one end a small table stood before a blackboard that had been fixed to the wall. He followed the stoep to the side of the house, then down the side to a narrow opening between an old corrugated iron coalshed and the building's back wall.

He tried the back door, but it seemed to be latched on the inside. Yudel turned to look in the direction of the mine dump. A few steps away, across a dusty courtyard, stood the large shed that from the front had seemed to be joined to the house. The courtyard was in shadow, the scattered remnants of a cold afternoon sun having barely the strength to penetrate the leaves of another row of ragged bluegums.

A stout black man appeared in the doorway of the shed. He was wearing denim overalls and sandals. He came straight to Yudel. "You?" he said. It was clearly a question and as clearly without hostility. "You East Rand Mines?" The man had a broad innocent face and he was extending his knowledge of English to its limits.

"No," Yudel said, "I'm not from East Rand Mines. I'm looking for a man who lived here long ago." He waved an arm towards the house.

"No." The man smiled. He had a few discoloured teeth, scattered at irregular intervals along his gums. "No. Nobody. Empty. You police?"

"No," Yudel said. "I'm not police."

"Not police?"

"No." Yudel pointed a finger at him. "You? You here long? Five year? Six year?" His use of language was being affected by the company he was keeping.

"Me . . . " The man patted his broad chest. "Ten year, East Rand Mines." He thought for a moment. "Caretaker," he concluded.

"Here, in house," Yudel said. "Bernie Miller? You know him. Bernie Miller?"

The caretaker thought about it. "Bennie Meeler," he said.

"Bernie Miller," Yudel said.

He nodded thoughtfully. "Bennie Meeler." The smile returned to his face. He bent over and made extravagant passes with his hands over the area of his calves. "Boots," he said. "Bennie Meeler, boots." His hands flickered quickly back and forth, apparently indicating that the boots had been especially shiny.

It sounded like the man. "That's right," Yudel said, "Bennie Meeler."

The caretaker looked disappointed. "Gone. Bennie Meeler gone." He would have liked to help.

"Do you know what happened to him? Cape Town? Durban?"

"Kep Town? Debun?" He looked as puzzled as Yudel was trying to sound. "Bennie Meeler. Boots."

Yudel gestured in the direction of the house and twisted his right hand from side to side, imitating the action of turning a key. "Key?"

"You police?"

"No. Key?"

"No key."

The communication problem was beyond Yudel's ability to penetrate. The man had complicated matters. Yudel could not imagine that he would be happy about breaking and entering on his domain. He thanked the caretaker, said goodbye and told him that he was going to look for Bennie Meeler among the mine dumps. A footpath, much like the one from the car track, led through the bluegums in the direction of the dumps. Behind him the caretaker watched him go in apparent puzzlement.

Among the trees vagrants had been making rough shelters from cardboard and plastic refuse-bin liners, temporary refuges against the harshness of Transvaal winter nights. The path crossed an old walled canal by means of a discoloured concrete slab, only a small trickle of water finding its way along the canal bottom. Yudel came out of the trees. The dump was some fifty metres away, the ground between covered by a fine white dust, part of the gold-carrying sub-soil that had been brought from deep beneath the earth's surface. At intervals clusters of hardy reeds somehow survived in the lifeless ground.

Everywhere there was evidence of past industry. In the way of gold mines it had flourished briefly and died. In the space of a few decades the gold had been taken from the earth. Some had been enriched. Some had died. Now they were all gone. Only the caretaker who remembered Bernie Miller but spoke little English, and the few passing vagrants seeking a night's shelter among the trees remained.

Yudel climbed the side of the dump slowly, stopping to catch his breath every fifty or sixty paces. It was steep, but not so steep that he needed to use his hands. The vertical ruts down its sides were deeper than they had seemed from a distance, deep enough to hide a man. It took him a few minutes to reach the top, the surface of which provided openings for dozens of pale caves that had formed as the soft clay-like material had collapsed during wet weather and the water drained through the openings.

Looking back the way he had come, Yudel could see the corrugated iron roofs of the house and shed, both red-brown with rust, protruding amongst the trees. To his right the old mine headgear looked like the soot-blackened fossil of a long-dead giant insect. He thought about the names Sydney Wheelwright and Milan Varrevich. Neither were Afrikaans, yet their owners saw themselves as Afrikaners. He wondered if it was uncertainty about their status that had driven them to actions that were the most grotesque caricature of their people. It was an irony, if in their determination to be part of Afrikanerdom, they succeeded only in giving strength to the lie that all Afrikaners were violent and racist.

The cold September wind, not truly a wind, little more than a movement of the air, had dispelled the false spring of the week before and he shivered. Suddenly Yudel was afraid. Standing out on the edge of the mine dump he felt vulnerable and exposed. It was not the mine dump he reasoned, nor the position in which he was standing. The reason for his fear was all that had happened in the past two weeks. The telephone calls, Rosa's inability to come home, the security meetings, even Poena van der Merwe's hostile face had something to do with it. But most of all his fear had to do with the nature of the crimes he had confronted and the conviction growing inside him that they were a phenomenon that his society could not afford to face. His fellows, friends and relations, men and woman, would rather turn away from them, hide from themselves that such things had ever taken place. For a moment he struggled with the urge to run down the steep slope of the dump, get to his car and flee, hide somewhere far from this place among ordinary people, retreat into the safety of blessed obscurity.

For Yudel there had been too much in too short a space of time. Too many facts competed with each other in his mind. The crimes seemed to merge with each other, suffering that had been inflicted on one victim seeming to be the suffering of them all.

They all wanted him to find that it was the work of an organization. But why these particular victims? What provided the link between Fellows Ngcube, the attorney, and Ray Baker, the seemingly saintly trade unionist?

Yudel's thoughts moved from one victim to another, pondering each for a moment, then passing to the next, wondering . . . Then, suddenly, without warning and without a concise pattern of thought, he knew. Beyond any doubt, he knew. And it was no use to him at all.

Fellows Ngcube was a black man, low on the ethnic status ladder, who had stood up in court to cross-examine and humiliate policemen and government witnesses. Ray Baker had contravened society's most sacred commandment by sleeping with an Indian woman. He had not done it surreptitiously, hiding his sin from the world, but openly living with her in a white area, ignoring his neighbour's sensibilities. Lionel Bensch was the only person who had ever been a member of the military wing of the national resistance and was living free, coming and going as he chose, within the country's borders. Professor van Deventer had spoken blasphemy against Afrikanerdom's holiest day. The signatories to the RACC declaration had employed the reformed tradition by which the country's authorities lived as a weapon with which to challenge them.

Yudel knew what linked them all. It was not membership of the same organization or even political aims held in common. What linked them was audacity. They were the people who had not only resisted the workings of the system, but had resisted them in the most audacious possible ways. Society's most hallowed decrees, scriptures that were especially sacred because we all doubted that they were valid, codes of behaviour that were accepted without question because we had persuaded ourselves that our lives depended on them: the victims of these crimes had ignored them all. And it was the fury that their audacity had generated that had been unleashed upon them. It was not a common organization that had been to blame, only a common anger.

He looked down, over the trees, to the place where the old building that had once housed the Attic slowly deteriorated under the combined influence of neglect and the elements. It was time for him to go if he was to be back for the interrogation.

He paused on the edge of the dump a moment longer. He saw the trees, bluegums, willows and peppercorns, leaves shining silver in the white highveld sun. He saw the gaunt framework of the headgear. One last time he saw the rusted roof of the house. He did not see the flash of steel on the edge of the clearing. Nor did he see the glint of sun on gleaming projectile. He felt it, a quick sharp spasm in the bottom of his chest.

The trees and sky disappeared and he saw the yellow dirt of the mine dump's surface. There was no pain, only warmth, the gentle warmth of warm liquid flowing over the lower part of his abdomen. Yudel knew that he was falling. He saw the bolt where it had entered his body just below the rib cage. He tried to turn as he fell, knowing that he must not drive the shaft in deeper.

Part 2: THE CIRCLE, CLOSED
Pretoria, November 1984

Twenty-One

Yudel rose slowly through a drug-induced nightmare to the surface of complete consciousness. His mind had reached out to the pain as something on which to anchor his senses, but they had buried it deep beneath the layers of drugs and again and again it slipped away from him, swimming ahead beyond his reach into the glowing mist of his distorted perception. At last, after a long time, a time that he had no way of measuring, he overtook it, held it fast, felt its hot knife-sharp presence right through his abdomen and met clearly and lucidly the dark anxious eyes of his wife.

The hospital was on the cool southern side of one of the parallel chains of hills that runs through Pretoria. Yudel spent more than a month in a bright ward with high windows that reached from the ceiling to the floor, filling one wall of the room. The view from his bed was of one of Pretoria's endless avenues of jacarandas. While he was there summer's first buds appeared on the trees and they burst into the dense extravagant purple canopy that had been responsible for many ill-considered proposals of marriage.

The point of the bolt had sliced obliquely across his heart without puncturing it, but tearing a hole in the liver. His life had been saved by the old caretaker who had watched him walk out towards the mine dump and, not having seen him return, had gone to look for him. He had carried Yudel down to his room, run to a nearby filling station and with a combination of gestures, Zulu and his few English words persuaded the manager to call a doctor.

Rosa had come on each of the five days before he recognized

her and she came on every day afterwards. She had returned home and there had been no further telephone calls. She never asked if the attempt on his life meant that the investigation was over and neither did Yudel raise the matter again. Even before his thoughts had cleared completely he knew that his state of mind had changed. It was partly the result of a fear that, until then, had been alien to him, the sudden unbidden realization that something as mundane as a shaft of steel was capable of ending his life. Yudel had been threatened on other occasions, but he had never before been able to imagine meeting death except on his own terms. Rosa had always called it arrogance. Freek had explained it by proposing that even clever people are all stupid in some way. As for Yudel, he had never given the matter more than five seconds of continuous thought.

Since the age of four he had been fascinated by violent death. Lying in the hospital bed, he remembered how at that age he had been standing on a railway station, holding his mother's hand. It had been just before the end of the Second World War and a young sailor had come sprinting across the station to leap for a moving train. He had missed his foothold and slipped between train and station. For a few seconds his body was wedged in that narrow space, only his head, arms and shoulders above the level of the platform. The train had spun him round and round and Yudel had ever after been able to hear the tattoo made by his arms drumming against the wooden panelling of the coach. Then he had been drawn beneath the wheels and was gone, as if nothing had happened. Yudel had tried to run to the edge of the platform to see what had become of the sailor, but had taken only a few steps when his mother's hand on his collar had brought him to a sudden and unplanned halt. No amount of pleading had been able to persuade her that he needed a closer look.

Now he had visited death more closely and personally and he was afraid. It was not only his closeness to death that ended the investigation though. It was also everything he had learnt and his belief that it was the national state of mind that made such crimes possible. To Yudel it was not so much a wave of crime as a condition of the nation and he knew there was nothing he could do about it. This too, the acknowledgement of his own ineffectiveness, was an area of introspection that was new to him.

There was still a third aspect to his withdrawal. To his great surprise he had been visited one evening by Blythe Stevens and Ralph Du Plessis. The conversation had followed lines that had not been intended to encourage Yudel's continued involvement. Perhaps the whole thing was unwise, they had said. We wouldn't want to be responsible for anything happening to you. Frankly, your investigation has blurred some of the issues. And twenty-five thousand is a lot of money. Do you know how many people can be fed on that? In any event you've been getting your salary all the time. And this is covered by a medical aid, isn't it? Do you know how much my wife and I live on?

Freek spent a few mornings with Yudel. He told him that the official CID position was that the bolt had probably been a stray from an archery range that adjoined the mine property. He had spoken to the secretary of the archery club that used the range and discovered that none of their members used crossbows and that the bolt was definitely from a crossbow. Also, if it had been a stray from the range it would have had to travel some three hundred metres and climb twenty-five to have struck him. But the area did not fall within Freek's jurisdiction and there was nothing he could do officially. The local CID were questioning club members and getting nowhere. Freek had obtained membership lists of all the local archery clubs as well as an incomplete register of Afrikaner Revival Movement members, but neither had revealed anything.

They had talked about Lieutenant Visser of the Durban CID and on one astonishing morning Freek had been accompanied by the lieutenant, on holiday and wearing short trousers and a bright check sports shirt. Visser had seemed truly disturbed by what had happened to Yudel, but he had directed most of his comments at Freek. "Yisis, colonel, you know how it goes with this sort of thing. No one ever knows where such a thing might lead and none of us wants to take the chance of finding out. What if you find out that security want to take over and you are in their way? You know what I mean? You know, there's a point, if the investigation starts going in a certain direction, everybody stops asking questions. Hell, Mister Gordon, I'm glad you're getting better."

"Tell Mister Gordon what you did after you visited him in the hotel," Freek had suggested.

"It was Varrevich sent me. I went to report back to him. He wanted to get rid of you without a fuss. I'm sure he would never be involved in something like this though. He's a friendly oke. He's often bought me a beer."

"Who is this Varrevich?" Freek had asked.

"Major Milan Varrevich. He escaped from Hungary as a youngster in the early sixties and came here. It just shows that there are worse placs in the world than South Africa. Those overseas people who are always complaining about us can just shut up."

Dahlia had phoned the hospital daily until he regained consciousness. The next week she saw him between official visiting hours. She had been attending a seminar on the "Role of Muslim women in the liberation struggle."

"I've found Dladla," she told him. He was glad to see her, but not interested in Dladla's whereabouts.

The next morning he woke from a deep, leaden sleep to find Dahlia seated on one side, Rosa on the other and Freek hovering uncertainly round the foot of the bed. Involuntarily he tried to rise, but the tensing of his stomach muscles was accompanied by a sudden and deeply penetrating pain that cause him to fall back on the pillows. "May I introduce you?" he groaned.

"That's all right," Freek said. "I've already . . . "

"Hello, Mister Gordon," Dahlia said. "I've been telling Mrs Gordon how grateful we all are for your willingness to take up this matter and for your courage. I was saying how proud she must be of you."

Rosa was looking at Dahlia out of her dark, unfathomable and almost unblinking eyes and saying little. She had recognized Dahlia as the woman in the photograph. On her next visit she told Yudel that she had read a magazine article on the dreaded disease, AIDS, and how it was not just homosexuals that got it now. It was cutting down loose-living heterosexuals in large numbers. It served them right and it just showed how careful you had to be and only unswerving, single-minded monogamism could ensure one's survival.

On Dahlia's last day in Johannesburg Freek was there too and he left with her. When he came again a few days later he looked to Yudel's eyes more than usually satisfied with himself. "What the hell did you slip away to on Thursday?" Yudel snarled at him. "I know you, Jordaan. You're a real bastard with women."

Freek sat thoughtfully down next to the bed and looked impassively at him. "Perhaps you need to bring this thing into some kind of clearer perspective," he said.

"You take advantage of women, Freek. Don't deny it. She's not . . . " He looked for a word that would describe Dahlia, but did not find one that suited him. " . . . strong."

Freek allowed himself the smallest smile. "There are other ways you could describe her. For the record, I walked her to her car and said goodbye there. I apologize for my many failings." He was grinning broadly by this time. "But they were not exercised on Dahlia."

Yudel turned to the window to avoid looking at Freek. "I'm being a damn fool, right?"

"Right," Freek agreed. "Listen, Yudel, I know what sort of effect she's had on you. It's happened to me from time to time, but believe me it passes. Girls like Dahlia are fine for an interlude, but more than that is impossible . . . even without the race thing."

"Do you think you could find it in your heart to spare me the fatherly advice?"

"We all have our areas of expertise." Freek ignored his request. "This is mine . . . "

"One of yours," Yudel suggested.

"All right, one of mine." Freek was being very modest. "You aren't married to her and you'll find that once the initial itching of your balls has been satisfied it's Rosa you really want."

"I'm sorry for my outburst," Yudel said carefully. "Please may we discuss something else."

It was not only Yudel's state of mind that changed while he was in hospital. The country changed too. In a black township an hour's drive from Yudel's home the population protested about the way they were being treated by the local authority by refusing to pay rent and overnight law and order disappeared from township streets throughout the country.

Police vehicles were stoned, barricades thrown across

thoroughfares, government buildings burned, cars hijacked and their owners assaulted. The number of burglaries in white suburbs increased by the day and were conducted with growing audacity, burglars sometimes returning with reinforcements to a house from which they had been driven a few hours earlier. A generation of black children were seized with a frenzy that made it impossible to continue schooling until they had been released from their position of subservience, proclaiming to the world, or at least the milling township streets that there could be no education before liberation.

For an instant, a bright flickering moment of history, the revolution was upon us and it was met first with rubber bullets and teargas, then with live rounds. There were massacres in Winterveld, Langa and Mamelodi and individual killings over the length and breadth of the country. For those who saw the way ahead as leading through revolution's fire it was necessary to keep the anger alive. Even death was nothing more than a necessary offering on the altar of a glowing egalitarian future. The funeral of every victim of police bullets was turned into a political jamboree and the police obliged by creating new victims. So the chain that led from automatic rifle to cemetery led back to the automatic rifle again.

Eventually the fury, bottled up in the townships by the police, turned inwards. Collaborators were found everywhere and the word, necklace, took on a new meaning as victims had motor car tyres forced over their shoulders to pinion their arms before the mob poured petrol over them and set them alight. Africa purged itself, removing the weak, the suspected collaborator, the overly introspective, the forgiving, ridding herself of all who were not possessed by the single-minded obsession to destroy everything that seemed to hinder the revolution. Three and four-year-olds learned to make and throw petrol bombs. On farms along the borders land mines dismembered white farmer and black labourer alike, while in the towns explosions in fast food outlets, parked cars, rubbish bins and supermarkets punctuated the life of the nation, bringing brief diversion and casual death.

In the white suburbs fire-arm dealers ran out of stock, as did the manufacturers of security gates, mercury arc lamps and closed circuit television systems. Burglar alarm companies worked sixteen hours a day to stay ahead of the demand. Gun clubs could not cope with the number of applications for membership, an industry for the training of guard dogs came into being and private security companies were registered daily.

White society as a whole, and Afrikanerdom in particular, took on a schizophrenic aspect as it sought both to reform the nation and to defend itself. The cabinet ministers who ardently promoted reformist measures to their constituencies were the same ones who made speeches excusing the massacres.

In the townships no one was unaffected. Old Daisy Matshogo, the charwoman who came in twice a week to help Rosa, for the first time in fifteen years asked Rosa for an advance on her pay. Her week's groceries had been torn from her hands, the containers broken open and the food scattered over the pavement. The youths who were responsible had screamed at her that there was a consumer boycott taking place and if they found her supporting white shops again she would get the necklace.

Daisy's son, Jonathan, who had just finished law school, came one day to fetch his mother from work and fell into conversation with Yudel. He was one of the new and growing tide of black graduates. Just as it was impossible for his mother to address Yudel as anything but Mister Gordon, so he only felt comfortable calling him Yudel.

"Where are you doing your articles?" Yudel asked him.

"No articles, man," Jonathan said. Then in explanation: "I'm a barman now. My brothers will kill me if I become part of the legal system."

"And your studies?"

"Times will change," Jonathan said. "I'll still have my degree when they do."

A few months later a three-year-old grand-daughter of one of Daisy's sisters was killed by a police rubber bullet, the heavy, unyielding projectile having struck her over the heart with such force that it had broken a rib. Yudel and Rosa, lone white faces in a sorrowing and embittered gathering, found themselves standing next to the grave of a child they had never known. They listened to speeches that first denounced racism, then all government supporters and finally all that was white. "We have to do it," Rosa had said after Daisy told them. "They must see all of them, that some of us care about what happens."

The violence swept through 1985 like a bush fire, the flame of each day igniting the one that followed until it seemed to be running of its own inner volition, without purpose and serving no aim. And among the general and random deaths there were other, more specific assassinations. The bodies of four activists who had been travelling by car from Port Elizabeth on the coast to a town a few hundred kilometres inland, were found stabbed and burnt in scrub along the roadside. Three others from the same town had gone missing a few months before and were never again seen by their friends or families. Chief Ampie Mayisa was hunted for weeks and hacked to death by vigilantes when he was found. A youth leader was shot from the distance of a few feet, his lifeless body left in the dust of the township street. Another was beaten to death.

Yudel's list that had from the beginning been too long and included too many cases would have grown into something beyond the most sordid imaginings, except that now no one was counting. Yudel himself turned away from the newspaper reports on these incidents. He saw no point in knowing the details.

After two months in hospital and another at home he had returned to work. For a long time he only felt comfortable lying down. He walked slowly, resting often, and found himself perspiring heavily after only minor exertion. At work he paid little attention to the averted eyes of Poena van der Merwe and his friends or the determined friendliness of some of the other staff members. And the tension was gone. Perhaps he had paid his dues for the aberrant behaviour of the past or perhaps guilt saw itself reflected too clearly in his obvious physical weakness. Whatever the reason, the awkwardness that had surrounded him for the few days before the attempt on his life no longer existed. He spent his working hours either in his office with the door closed or at the prisons doing the work for which the department paid him.

On one occasion he saw Wheelwright in Brigadier De Beer's office. The door had been standing open and the security policeman was leaning back in one of the chairs intended for visitors, trying, without conviction as far as Yudel was concerned, to look jovial and relaxed. He saw Yudel, but turned back to De Beer immediately, the smile never leaving his lips. It was a practised deception and, like the joviality, it lacked conviction. De Beer did not mention the visit and Yudel never discovered whether he had been the subject under discussion.

The family of the boy who had delivered the newspapers in his street had moved to another town and, as part of his convalescence, he walked to the Sunnyside shopping centre on most afternoons after work to buy the newspaper. The walk back up the hill was slower and he often stopped to rest three or four times, leaning against a jacaranda, before he got home.

In his study or sitting up in bed, while Rosa busied herself with her perpetual and as far as he could see pointless activities, he would glance through the newspaper, taking in only the broadest outline of the day's events. The sounds of her doing things with crockery in the kitchen or the intermittent buzzing of her sewing-machine reached him as from a great distance. Occasionally she might say something to which he would have to respond, first pausing to pick up the traces of what she had said where they were still floating along the outer edges of his attention.

It was on a Friday evening six months after he had been discharged and had undertaken his evening walk, for the first time without stopping to rest at all, that Yudel sat in his study, the unread newspaper folded on the desk before him, and thought about the events of the past ten months. He remembered the exhilaration of his trip to Durban. He thought briefly about Dahlia. Since he had left the hospital he had spoken to her three times on the telephone, but the conversations had become laboured, with neither having much to say to the other and it is impossible to make love over a telephone connection. There had been nothing to mark the last call, no acknowledgement from either that this was the end of it, only a growing restlessness in Dahlia and a lack of attention on Yudel's part.

Arrogance, he thought. Rosa had always said that he was arrogant. But it had been a long time since she had last used that word to describe him. He was aware that he had skirted the nearer fringes of a deep and destructive depression, but he had recognized it and employed the only cure which for him was certain. He had immersed himself so deeply in his work that there was room for little else.

Even Yudel's relationship with Rosa's endless relatives had changed. Since he had been wounded they had treated him with a degree of consideration he would not have thought possible. To Irena, Rosa's sister, he had always been a hero. Now he was a martyred hero, a role from which he derived no pleasure.

The thoughts of the immediate past rolled away, leaving him with only the present, the empty, despairing present. His eyes travelled idly over the unusually tidy surface of his desk, seeking something with which to occupy his mind and finding it in the folded newspaper. He made to take it, but before his hand had reached it his eyes picked out a single line of text at the bottom of a column, the rest of which was hidden. The line read, "Mrs Ngcube was a senior executive member of . . . " Yudel's hand stopped just short of the newspaper. It was the tense in which the report had been written as well as the subject's name that held his attention. "Mrs Ngcube was . . . " With an effort of will he unfolded the newspaper and spread it on the desk in front of him. The headline stretched two thirds of the way across the front page. "Ngcube's widow slain." Yudel's eyes fled over the words as if pursued. "Well known civil rights attorney, Mrs Elizabeth Ngcube (43), was gunned down and bludgeoned to death in front of her children in the driveway of her Umlazi home last night. Four years ago, in November 1981, her husband Mr Fellows Ngcube was assassinated . . . "

In the kitchen Rosa was trying to sing a popular song. She had probably been singing it for some time, but now her rather plaintive, off-key rendering had become irritating to Yudel. Then everything was absorbed, Rosa's song, his recollections, even the strange apathy that had become part of him, in the indescribable pathos of it all. Where will it end? he asked himself. Where in God's name will it end?

He started to his feet to go to Rosa, but stopped abruptly. It won't do for her to see me this way, he thought, suddenly realizing that for the first time in all of his adult life he was crying.

Part 3: THE CIRCLE, BROKEN
Pretoria and Johannesburg, April 1986

Twenty-Two

The door to Yudel's office opened quietly without knocking and he heard a brief whispered consultation in Tswana. He looked up from the report he was completing to see the cleaner from the floor above being pushed inside and the door closed behind him. "Yes?" His voice sounded more abrupt than his state of mind warranted and he immediately tried to soften the effect. "Yes, what can I do for you?"

The man looked down at his feet, then in Yudel's direction but not directly at him. He was small, not much over thirty and although he was sober now his face showed the signs of excessive drinking.

"Yes?" Yudel tried again in Afrikaans. Few of the lower ranks of black staff members could speak English. "Phineas is it? What can I do for you, Phineas?"

"My boss . . . " He was trying to frame the words in terms both clear and inoffensive. "My boss, Jackson he say . . . "

"Yes? What does Jackson say?"

"Jackson he say the boss can get me the house."

It took Yudel a moment to digest the meaning of Phineas's statement. When he did understand he leapt to his feet, sending Phineas backing towards the door in alarm. "No, it's all right. You've done nothing wrong." He held up a hand, gesturing to the cleaner to stay where he was. "Wait here. Just wait here."

Yudel threw open the door to go looking for Jackson and found him pretending to sweep the passage just outside. "Come in here, Jackson." The old man came in, walking proudly erect, his broom tucked under his right arm. When he was inside and the door closed, Yudel spoke to him. "So explain this to me. I smell your work here."

"For the boss is easy," Jackson explained.

"What is easy?"

"Get a house for Phineas. For the boss is no problem." Phineas looked from the assurance on Jackson's face to the puzzlement on Yudel's and nodded. "The boss can just phone."

"And say must give the house."

Yudel looked at Jackson's confident face and tried not to look at Phineas's anguished one. "What are you talking about, Jackson? The waiting list for houses is more than ten years long."

"The waiting list is nothing." Jackson sounded indignant. "The boss can phone."

"What difference will it make if I phone? It won't make any difference if Brigadier De Beer phones."

"He's bigger than you?" Jackson sounded unbelieving.

"Brigadier De Beer . . . " Generally Yudel followed Jackson's use of Afrikaans. For the moment though, he had lost him.

"He's not bigger than you."

"Who's not bigger than me?" Yudel suspected that there might be unforeseen ramifications to almost any admission now. "What are you talking about Jackson?"

"Boss De Beer, he's not bigger than you." With a vigorous nodding of his head he gave Phineas his attention, speaking animatedly to him in Tswana. Yudel understood no word of it, but he could see how Phineas was being impressed. "The boss can phone," Jackson said with a finality that seemed to sort out everything.

Whatever Jackson had told Phineas the result had clearly been to cause Yudel's prestige to grow in his eyes. Yudel did not want to think about the home circumstances that were at least partly responsible for Phineas's drinking. He hardly dared ask the next question. "What have you just told Phineas?"

"I tell him the boss can phone. That man stab my son. The boss put him inside – one time."

It was a moment before Yudel understood what Jackson was referring to, then he remembered the incident in which the old man's son had been stabbed. It had been ascribed to the power of Yudel's position. "A house is different," Yudel said. He turned his attention to Phineas's unhappy face. "I will phone, but I don't think I will be successful."

"Boss?" The word held both a question and a plea.

"I don't think I can get you a house. I'll try. Where are you living now?"

"Single quarters," Phineas said.

"Wife in Mafikeng," Jackson added.

Christ, Yudel thought. How do I get involved in these things? "Have you been to see the social worker?"

"He's bigger than you?" Jackson looked scornful.

"It's not a question of who's bigger." Yudel was aware that his voice had acquired a thin edge. "I'll try, Phineas." The two cleaners made no move to leave and Yudel repeated himself. "I'll try to get you a house. You can go now."

"The boss can just . . . "

"You also, Jackson. You can go now. I'll do what I can." Yudel held up a hand to stop Jackson expanding on the subject. "Go on now. I'll see what I can do."

After they had left Yudel dialled the number of the social worker and explained the problem to him. "You can forget it, Mister Gordon," he said. "I know the man. He's got TB and we've tried to get him to the front of the queue with doctor's certificates and everything. There's a ten-year waiting list for the hard-luck cases. The rest can forget it. How come you're involved?"

Yudel started telling him, but decided that the truth did not make a lost of sense. "His wife works for my sister," he said.

"I didn't know you had a sister," the social worker said.

Yudel hung up and looked at his watch. It was after four and Freek was going to give him a lift home. Phineas's problem was just another part of the country's endless inter-linking chain of more or less insoluble difficulties. In the black areas, except for the few who were relatively wealthy, everyone got their houses from the authority, and houses that the authority did not supply simply did not exist. Yudel's position in the matter was not something that Phineas and Jackson were going to understand though. A man who could pick up the phone and issue an order to have someone thrown into jail should not have a problem getting one of his subjects a house. Yudel sighed. The hell with it, he thought. Although there were still ten minutes of his working day left he packed a few prisoners' files into his briefcase and was about to clip it shut when the door opened and Gert van Staden looked in. "Ja, Yudeltjie," he said, "slipping away early?"

"If it hadn't been for you," Yudel said.

"I brought back your pencils." He handed over the box of coloured pencils he had borrowed from Yudel two years before.

"Not mine," Yudel said.

"I borrowed them for my staff attendance graph," van Staden said, smiling benignly.

Yudel reached into the box and took out a pencil that was now about a quarter of its original length. "They've seen better days. How long have you had them?"

"Some time. I don't know."

Yudel dropped the pencils into one of his desk drawers and snapped closed his briefcase. "Thank you," he said. "Anything else I can do for you?"

"Agh, don't be like that, Yudeltjie." He sat down on the edge of the desk. "I hear your friend Robin Du Plessis is in trouble again." Yudel looked at van Staden's friendly guileless face. Despite himself he was interested in what his colleague had to say. The part that chose rather not to hear about Du Plessis's trouble was dominant though and he said nothing. "My sources tell me that they want to detain him, but he got to hear about it and he's on the run."

"We all have problems," Yudel said. "Do your sources also tell you that you are stopping me from going home?"

Van Staden looked at his watch. "Still five minutes, but I see I've come at a bad time. Thanks again for the pencils."

"Any time," Yudel said, scooping up his jacket from the back of his chair and his briefcase in almost the same movement.

He accompanied van Staden into the passage. "They say Du Plessis has gone underground. They're talking about limpet mines and AK47 rifles and things like that. They say he's a soft Jo'burg socialist who's gone hard. They say your other old friend,

Colonel Wheelwright, is not amused. He detained your lefty friend the first time." The nature of the information he was transmitting conflicted with his friendly smiling face and the gossiping eyebrow-raising way in which he told it.

Yudel took him by the arm and brought his mouth close to van Staden's ear. "This information," he whispered, "is all governed by the official secrets act. You tell your sources that I will report them to Mister Poena van der Merwe, senior transport clerk in our department." He nodded gravely at van Staden, releasing his arm as they passed the door of his office. He looked back as he reached the lift. Van Staden was still where he had left him, grinning and waggling an admonishing finger at Yudel.

Freek was waiting in the parking area when Yudel got downstairs. He was seated at the wheel of his thirty-year-old immaculately maintained Jaguar coupé, a car he rarely used and of which he was immoderately proud. Yudel got in on the passenger side. "You trying to impress me?" he asked.

He acknowledged Yudel's presence by a preoccupied nod and moved the car into the city's late afternoon traffic, a weary gaggle of economy cars bearing homeward the capital's army of civil servants on their nightly migration. "My car's having a new diff put in," he said. "Do you mind if we take a detour?"

"To get the car?"

"No, no. We've got an interesting necklace murder up near Monument Park."

"Funny place for a necklacing."

"You're telling me," Freek said. "A damn long way from the nearest township."

The three bodies were in a thin screen of eucalyptus trees that ran along the edge of open grassland. Freek parked the Jaguar next to the row of police vehicles that had formed at a barbed wire fence a hundred metres from where officers on his staff and others from the city's forensic laboratories were already at work. As they approached, one of the forensic men, who had been crouching over the bodies, straightened up to speak to Freek. Under the spindly, anaemic-looking trees two CID men in plain clothes were searching the ground while others in uniform walked back and forth through the long dry grass. At a distance a man wearing khaki trousers and a discoloured white shirt with sleeves rolled up above the elbows, probably the owner of the land, looked on with an expression of distaste on his face.

It was only when they reached the end of the grass that for the first time they could see the ground underneath the trees and the three bodies in a neat row, close enough to be touching. Their clothing was charred and the skin of all three blackened, twisted and pitted by the heat of the flames. There was no sign that tyres had been used. The ground around the bodies was also black as the petrol had run and burnt where it soaked into the sand. "Well, they were burnt here," Yudel heard Freek say.

"But they didn't die by burning," the forensic man said.

All three had been lean long-legged youngsters, probably between fourteen and eighteen. The way they had been laid on the ground indicated special care, a sense of neatness and correctness. They were wearing open-neck shirts, only one of the three with long trousers and shoes. The other two had short pants and their feet were bare. The faces were particularly disfigured as if the killers had given them more than one treatment in order to obliterate the features. The rest of the burning had not been as thorough. Here or there a leg or an arm had not been touched by the flames at all. Sections of the clothing too had remained unburnt. But it was the care with which the bodies had been arranged that held Yudel's interest, the way the shirts were buttoned, right to the throat, the feet together, heels touching, and the arms, elbows tucked in at the waist in parade ground fashion. Someone had paid an almost loving attention to their appearance. "They had not been dead long when they were brought here," he found himself saying.

"That's right," the forensic expert said, immediately following his agreement with "Who is this man?"

"It's all right," Freek said. "He's a friend of mine from the Department of Prisons."

The man accepted the explanation without comment. "This is the interesting part," he said. He looked harassed and had his laboratory dustcoat over his uniform. "Look at this." He had cut away the burnt shirt to reveal the torso of one of the bodies. Yudel moved closer to see what he had found. Despite the burning, the stab wounds that covered his stomach were clear. " . . . nine, ten, eleven, twelve, thirteen," the forensic man counted. "Unlucky thirteen for him." The flesh had erupted in little raised portions through the wounds, looking like thirteen sets of fried pouting lips. It was not just the wounds that interested Yudel though. It was the piece of scorched and blackened shirt that had been cut free and folded away from the body. The material was altogether intact. Whatever the instrument was that had been used to kill the boy, it had not passed through his shirt first.

Yudel and Freek watched in silence as the shirts of the other two were cut away to reveal that they had been killed in the same way. "Very interesting," Freek said at length. "Very interesting. What do you think, Yudel?"

But Yudel was not thinking about the three boys and the manner of their dying. He was remembering a conversation with Dahlia and the condition of her husband's body when it had been found. "Yes, very interesting," he said.

Yudel sat in the lounge of his home, watching the news service on television. He recognized the eucalyptus trees he had seen a few hours before. The cameras showed only the burnt ground under the trees after the bodies had been removed, while the commentary told viewers that the boys were victims of black-on-black violence that was sweeping the country. The disembodied voice went on to say that the necklace method of killing was often used to eliminate enemies by the so-called comrades, gangs of youth who opposed the government.

The newsreader moved on to deal with a report about the war between Iran and Iraq and Yudel found that Rosa had come out of the kitchen and was standing next to his chair. "I don't understand it," she said. "Why do they do it? Why do they kill each other? I understand why they're cross with us, but why do they kill each other?"

Yudel got up from his chair and put an arm around her shoulders. "What's for supper?" he asked.

Rosa pulled away. "Don't do that. Don't treat me like an

ignorant female. At least allow me the dignity of a serious answer. Why do they kill each other?"

He looked at her face, tilted belligerently towards his, the dark eyes demanding. No, he thought, you don't really want to know. "I don't know," he told her.

Rosa did not look satisfied, but the ringing of the telephone gave him the chance to escape her. He went into the study to answer it and she returned to the kitchen. Dahlia was on the line. "Yudel, I'm glad you answered. I was afraid it might be your wife, and I don't think she likes me. She always gives me those looks."

"Hello, Dahlia," he said. It was more than eighteen months since they had last had contact. "I'm surprised to hear from you."

"I'm coming up tomorrow. I thought we might get together."

"Er..." The thought of seeing Dahlia again, perhaps making love to her, was beguiling. The range of convolutions that it might add to the currently uncluttered path of his life was not.

"Don't sound so enthusiastic. A lady could get a complex."

"I'd love to see you," he said. What the hell, he thought.

"We can be legal now."

"Legal?"

"Sure. They've taken away the Act. We can be friendly without the danger of being thrown into jail. We're legitimate."

"That's nice," Yudel said.

"I'm only going to be up your side for the weekend. What about tomorrow afternoon?"

Yudel's eyes took in the calendar on his desk. The next day was Friday, a notoriously easy day for slipping away during the afternoon. Almost the entire upper level of the department's hierarchy had disappeared by three on Fridays. "Okay. Tomorrow afternoon."

"Bring your toothbrush."

"Dahlia." An unformed thought skittered along the edges of his thinking. It came out in words before the more circumspect side of his personality could stop it. "You told me once that you know where to find Reverend Dladla."

236

Dahlia was slow to answer. "You want him?"

"Yes."

After he had hung up he went slowly through to the kitchen where Rosa would be finishing the preparations for dinner. She had to repeat herself twice before he heard the question. "Well, who was it? Who was on the phone?"

He watched her moving purposefully around her domain and told himself that she did not want the answer to that question either. "Freek," he said. "It was Freek." He sat down at the table. Bring your toothbrush, Dahlia had said. Yudel wondered idly why he would need his toothbrush.

Twenty-Three

Friday afternoon had not worked out the way Yudel had planned it. Dahlia had phoned to say that the afternoon had become impossible, but what about the evening? He told her that he doubted that he could manage the evening, but he would try. Otherwise the next day. "Phone me," she had said.

He left the building at three without his briefcase. If you did not have your briefcase with you it looked as if you intended coming back. Friday afternoons saw many briefcases left in offices throughout the civil service. Most were employed only to bring sandwiches to work and to provide a cover on Friday afternoons, but not to have one made it look as if you never took work home.

He walked down the long arcade in the adjacent building. Where it emptied into Pretorius Street, he struggled against the throng on the pavement until he reached the building where Freek had his office. The security man at the entrance let him in without enquiry. He was supposed to check with the person being visited, but Yudel was a regular caller and there is nothing like owning a familiar face to get you past security checkpoints.

Freek was at his desk, his elbows on the armrests, his hands folded in his lap and his head bowed in thought. It was a typical pose. Yudel paused in the doorway out of respect for the process and waited until he looked up. "Yudel," he said, the frown lifting enough to allow a smile. "I'm glad to see you."

"What about a beer?" Yudel asked.

Freek picked up the phone to tell the operator that he would be in Mamelodi for the rest of the afternoon, that it would be impossible to reach him and please to take messages. "Who's paying?"

"You are," Yudel said. "Why do you think I came to get you?"

At Freek's insistence they stopped at a hotel to the west of the railway station. It was old and beyond repairing successfully, the rooms now rented only by Pretoria's small and intimidated band of prostitutes, themselves no fresher or brighter than the building. The only part of the hotel that was still a commercial success, and it had increased in profitability while the rest of the establishment had declined, was the bar. The hard-drinking manual workers from the railway yards whose wives complained that they spent too large a part of their salaries on beer had not yet arrived. The men along the bar and at the tables were the early drinkers, salesmen who had been avoiding the afternoon's rounds, others who had fled work, but did not have the courage to face their wives, no-hopers who had begged money for a drink God-only-knew-where, men who were desperate to blur the sharper, more painful edges of consciousness.

The barman was a man of about sixty with a mass of crinkly grey hair and a face that looked like mud flats during a drought, lines and cracks interlacing from every possible angle. The emotion in his eyes, the vestiges of past pain, were plain to see. He was standing at the far end of the counter when they sat down. Yudel saw his hesitation before he came towards them. He had tried to catch the man's eyes, but the barman was looking at Freek, his face wearing an expression that was not easy to read. Yudel saw a keenly held interest, but also reluctance, perhaps an element of the unhappiness that seemed to be reflected in his face. He came slowly down the counter, his eyes never leaving Freek. Without looking up Freek ordered two beers. When the man brought them he paid, left a one-rand tip and asked, "Doesn't Johnny Sinclair work here any more?"

"He works here. He's gone out."

"You expect him back soon?" The question was asked casually. Freek had hardly looked at the man.

The barman's eyes examined the coin, then Freek's face. "Five minutes. He'll be back in five minutes."

"Good." Freek lifted his drink.

But as far as the barman was concerned the exchange was not over. He was holding up the coin that Freek had left. "What's this?" he asked. The man was offended, but Yudel saw more than just offence in his face. Freek started to answer, but instead left his mouth hanging open in surprise. "You gave me money." The barman was recreating the incident to make sure that he remembered it correctly. "I gave you change and you gave me this."

"That's right," Freek said.

Yudel looked from Freek's embarrassed face to the barman's humiliated one. It interested him that someone who normally had things so well under control should have the sort of problem Freek was experiencing now. It gave Yudel encouragement for future dealings with waiters. There is no sweeter ointment to soothe the pain of adversity than a fellow sufferer.

"Why did you give it to me? Because I'm so pretty?"

"It must be," Freek said.

The barman had adopted a chagrined smile to hide what he was feeling. He pushed the coin back at Freek. "You give it to me because I'm so pretty?"

Freek picked up the coin and pocketed it. "Okay."

"I don't need it," the barman explained.

"That's okay."

He took a few steps away from Freek, still looking at him with an expression of puzzled hurt. Yudel leant towards Freek and spoke very softly. "I find this very interesting," he said.

"Shut up," Freek said.

"I really do."

The barman was looking at Yudel. "You want to give me a rand too?"

"Not at all," Yudel said innocently. "I wouldn't dream of it."

A new customer came into the bar, drawing his attention away from Freek and his tip. "I don't think he wants to be tipped," Yudel explained.

"What an amazing observation. Have you any other thoughts you'd like to share with me?"

"No."

"Drink your beer."

"I do find it interesting though. This is the sort of thing that happens to me. You are usually so well in control on all public occasions. You have this air of confidence . . . "

Freek brought his face to within a centimetre of Yudel's. "I don't believe in hitting old friends, but I can be pushed too far. So just shut up and drink your beer."

"Okay," Yudel said. As an afterthought and a little maliciously he added, "You're paying."

A man of about the same age as the first barman came in from behind the counter to take over from him. The one who did not need the tip gave Freek a last hurt look before he went through an inside door into the main part of the hotel. The new man's nose was bent and flattened from the bridge down and he had old scar tissue along his brow ridges. He glanced round the room and noticed Freek, looking a little startled in the moment of recognition. He came over slowly, his eyes wary. "Hullo, colonel."

"Hullo, Johnny, who's your friend?"

"You mean the oke who stood in for me?"

"That's right."

He told Freek the man's name. "He's not really a barman. He works in the hotel."

"I thought he was going to throw me out because I tried to tip him."

"This is not the tipping side of town, colonel. Nobody tips around here." He was watching Freek's face, offering nothing and asking no questions.

"I want to ask your advice."

"Any time, colonel." The tone of voice was guarded and it was clear that the advice was going to be carefully weighed and edited before being dispensed.

"Somebody is burning bodies to make it look like township business. You saw that thing on the news last night."

"You know about Meiring," Sinclair said. He was referring to the murder of a jewel thief that the perpetrators had tried to disguise as a township killing. "It can happen."

"I was thinking about the dagga boys, that sort of thing."

"The coons?" Sinclair asked.

"Yes."

"I dunno nothing about that, colonel. True's God, I never had nothing to do with them."

Freek pushed himself away from the bar to go to one of the tables. "All right if I leave a tip?"

"Why not, colonel?"

Yudel followed Freek to a table and sat down opposite him. "On the news they said that the comrades were responsible."

Freek shrugged. "The PR would have given them that. We've identified the three. Nobody's saying it, but talking to their families it looks like they were comrades. If they were killed by other blacks it would have happened in or near a township and they would have left the bodies there. Multiple stab wounds might sometimes turn up in a mob killing, but mobs don't undress their victims before killing them, put them back into their clothes, drive them to a quiet place, arrange their bodies neatly on the ground, then set them alight. Whoever did it, it isn't the comrades."

Yudel saw that the stand-in barman who had been offended by Freek had rejoined Johnny Sinclair at the bar. He was still looking at Freek, his eyes and the down-turned corners of his mouth reflecting the depth of his humiliation. Freek, seeing that something had drawn Yudel's attention, glanced towards the bar, but immediately looked down at his beer. "Some mothers' fucking children," he muttered. "I can't believe this."

There was something beyond indignation and humiliation on the barman's face. Yudel detected a strange sort of disappointment. For a moment he thought the barman might come over to them, but the man turned suddenly and went out through the connecting door. Then suddenly Yudel understood. He understood the barman and with the understanding came memories, a sudden flood of images and words, imperfectly heard, superficially bearing no relation to each other, but clearly remembered. He reached out and took Freek by the sleeve and found that he was shaking his friend's arm. "What the fuck is going on with you, Yudel?" he heard Freek say.

"That man finds you sexually attractive," he told Freek.

"Let go of me." Freek tried to disengage himself without upsetting the table and with it the two beers. "Have you gone out of your fucking mind?"

Yudel had hold of his sleeve and was clinging determinedly to it. His throat was so tightly constricted that speech was almost impossible. "I'm telling you . . . "

"Don't tell me anything." Freek was trying to keep his voice down. "Have you gone mad? What is it with you?"

"Don't you understand . . . he resents it." The intensity of Yudel's expression was a growing problem to Freek. If Johnny Sinclair's stand-in did find him sexually attractive, he did not see it as a matter of urgency.

Freek pulled his arm free and rose so violently that he threw over the chair on which he had been sitting. "I'm getting out of here."

Yudel ran after his friend's angry, long-striding figure and caught up to him on the pavement. "Listen, you don't understand . . . "

Freek swung round and took Yudel by the shirt front. With one broad powerful hand he lifted him to the tips of his toes. "So help me, Yudel, this has gone far enough."

His big angry face was a few centimetres from Yudel's and his great fist was pressed against the underside of Yudel's chin. "They're homosexual killings," Yudel mumbled, Freek's fist impeding the movement of his jaw.

Freek let him down slowly. "What?"

"We've been staring at the political thing and missing everything else. They're homosexual killings, so was Ray Baker's."

The anger on Freek's face had been replaced by an interest that was equally intense. "What are you telling me, Yudel?"

"We must have the pathologist check their arses for traces of sperm."

"For Christ's sake, the bodies were burnt."

"On the outside. They're not cooked right through."

The pavement, thronged with hurrying commuters, trying to get to the station before their fellows, was a bad place for a discussion. Yudel was elbowed aside by a buxom young woman with parcels under both arms. "I hope you don't want the official list of queer security policemen now," Freek said.

"That won't be necessary," Yudel shouted above the traffic noise. "You remember the promotions party . . . my promotion . . . "

"Get in the car."

Inside, sheltered from the jostling mass on the pavement, speaking was easier. "Some young officers came over to us. A lieutenant hung on me. I could barely keep the two of us upright. He asked you if you knew you were consorting with a known Communist."

"Uys," Freek said. "Neels Uys."

"Where can we find him?"

"At Sunnyside, I think."

Lieutenant Cerneels Uys of the Sunnyside police was twenty-six years of age and lived with his nineteen-year-old girlfriend in a tenth-floor bed-sitter in a building containing some two hundred similar apartments. She was fair-skinned, had dark brown eyes and hair of almost the same colour that curled luxuriantly down to her shoulders. When she opened the door to Yudel and Freek her eyes looked bewildered and her hair freshly disarranged. She wore a dressing-gown that did not quite reach to her knees.

"Daughter, where's Neels?" Freek asked. His voice was friendly, but there was no doubting that whatever had been interrupted could only be continued after he had spoken to Neels.

She started to reply, "Just a second, Uncle. I'll . . . " but Freek was already lumbering forward and the girl retreating before him into the apartment's only room. Neels Uys was in bed, his naked head and shoulders protruding above a single blanket.

Freek sat down next to him on the bed and placed a large hand on his chest to stop him from rising. "Evening, Neelsie," he said. "What's going on here?"

"I . . . " He tried to cover his confusion. "We're both consenting adults."

"Uncle can't just come in like this." The girl tried to defend him. "Neels is a police officer."

"Is that what he tells you?" Freek grinned at her.

"It's true. His uniform's in the cupboard." She reached towards the cupboard door as if to provide the evidence.

"It's all right, Skattie," Neels said, still pinioned by the considerable weight behind Freek's right hand. "This is Colonel Jordaan of the CID and his friend, Mister Gordon, of the Department of Prisons. They cause trouble wherever they go."

"Child, you wait in the bathroom," Freek told her. "If he co-operates, I won't throw him out the window."

The girl looked doubtfully at her now alarmingly helpless lover and fleetingly towards the window. "It's all right, Skattie. Do what the colonel says."

After she had gone Freek released Neels and went to sit in a chair in front of the window that filled one end of the room. "Now, Neelsie, you answer Mister Gordon's questions clearly and honestly."

Yudel drew up a chair to the side of the bed and seated himself in it. He leaned towards the lieutenant. "I want you to think back to my promotion party." Yudel's way of speaking was calming and friendly, the therapist rather than the interrogator.

"That was a long time ago."

"About two years. Think back. You'll be able to remember it."

"Vaguely," Neels Uys said. "It was at the Union Hotel. To tell the truth, Mister Gordon, I drank rather a lot and I remember it through an alcoholic mist." He looked puzzled at the need to remember it at all. "Why?"

"Now do you remember coming over with some of your friends to speak to Colonel Jordaan and me. You held on to me for support."

"Ye-es." The way he said the word was slow and guarded, but amused.

"Good," Yudel said. "Don't ever let a potential witness tell you that alcohol clouds the memory. Now you think back carefully and tell us what you said."

Uys looked away from Yudel towards Freek and shrugged apologetically. "Look, Mister Gordon, if you're worried about that nonsense that I said, that about you being a Communist . . . I apologise. It meant nothing. I'll put it in writing . . . "

"You remember saying that?"

"Yes, but . . . "

"It's all right. That's very good. Immediately after that, something else took place. Try to remember what happened after that."

"You and the colonel went home, I think."

"We went home shortly after that. Quite right. But before we left another senior police officer went home and you made a remark that caused your friends to laugh." Yudel was speaking smoothly and gently, trying to ease the young policeman back through the passages of his memory to the moment that was important. "He was leaving and you made a remark about him. Your friends laughed."

"A senior officer . . . " He was genuinely puzzled, searching his recollection of the party for the incident that interested Yudel. "Don't you wa it to tell me who the officer is. That will help me . . . "

"It occurred immediately after your discourse on my being a Communist, immediately after. Think back. Give yourself time. We're in no hurry."

Uys's mind fastened on to it. Yudel was watching his eyes and he saw them draw tight with recognition. "Colonel Wheelwright."

"What did you say when you saw him leave?"

He shook his head briefly. "I can't think." But now the directness and openness of a few moments before were gone and Yudel knew that he was lying.

"Yes, you can." The gentleness in Yudel's voice had disappeared. "It made your friends laugh. Repeat it now."

"No. It was a long time . . . "

"Don't try to sell us that shit." Freek's voice came from above Yudel's head. He was on his feet and leaning over Uys. "What did you say?"

"No. I . . . " Both hands were raised in a gesture of helpless puzzlement that was clearly false.

"What did you say about Colonel Wheelwright?" Freek had not raised his voice, but a new harshness in his tone carried a demand that for the young policeman was reinforced by the authority of his rank.

"Yisis, colonel. I only hear what everyone else hears. He never tried anything with me. It's just stories. I can't testify to anything."

"Repeat the words you used that night," Yudel said.

"I don't remember the exact words. I said something about Colonel Wheelwright having a scorpion in his pocket."

Yudel leant back in his chair and Freek sat down. "And what does that mean?" The tone of Yudel's voice was gentle and coaxing again.

Uys's cheeks puffed up as he released air from his lungs, a blowing off of undesirable inner pressure. "Meaning that . . . " He considered for a moment. "Meaning that, according to rumour, he has made homosexual advances to some younger members of the force."

Freek steered the Jaguar from the side street above the narrow stream that borders Sunnyside on the north, over Esselen street where the cafés and fast-food establishments were attracting their usual early evening trade and up the hill towards Yudel's home on Muckleneuk ridge. He said nothing. They did not need to discuss the uncontrollable fury with which some men lived all their lives, the continually simmering desperation that Yudel believed had cost the three young comrades their lives. Both Yudel and Freek had experience of men who had destroyed themselves and their victims because of a sexual need for other men that they had found impossible to acknowledge. Such men spent their lives in a continual struggle with this part of their being. They got drunk to forget it or to submerge the pain of exercising it. They spent much of their lives in a desperate pursuit of women to pursuade themselves that there was nothing wrong and made love roughly to demonstrate their manliness.

If approached by another man the reaction was sometimes so violent that the man died for it. If advances to another man were refused the anger roused could be as vicious and unforgiving. And, having used another man or boy, the self-disgust and the agony of possible discovery were so intense that often only the complete destruction of the victim would satisfy the aggressor. Yudel recalled a case in which the victim's skull had been shattered into more than thirty pieces after intercourse. Often such a man would choose an occupation like the police in order to convince himself of his wholeness.

Yudel knew too that these crimes were more than a matter of sexual desire. The rape itself was an exercise in power that went beyond sexuality. In each case the victim's degradation was an integral part of the aggressor's triumph. The only more complete form of dominance was that of killer over victim.

Yudel was convinced that the killing of the three boys and that of Baker were not simply executions. He believed they were crimes of passion. A single bullet was enough to end the life of a troublesome activist. Thirteen stab wounds to kill a man who had already been undressed was a different matter entirely.

Freek stopped the car in Yudel's driveway. "I'll phone tomorrow after I've gotten hold of the pathologist."

Yudel barely heard him. His mind was busy with memories that were now two years old. He was thinking about Robin Du Plessis's almost feminine beauty and the loathing in his face when he had asked, "You want to know what they do to people?" He was remembering Lionel Bensch, his angry face and innocent eyes. "I'm not an activist, Yudel. I was one a long, long time ago . . . whoever is doing this is either pretty old himself or he's working from a very old list." He was wondering about the man who had humiliated and degraded Elizabeth Ngcube's daughter at the Lesotho border post eight years before. She had told her mother that he had something wrong with one of his eyes. But, more than anything else he had learnt, his thoughts were held by the way the bodies of first Baker, then the three township kids had been laid out, the care, the loving attention to detail. And the boys' youthfulness and Baker's refined elegant features.

In his mind there was an interlocking of events, an entwining of strands to form a pattern that up to now had been absent. He had only to take hold of it. For the first time in more than two years his thoughts were again seized by it all, and for the first time it was within reach.

Twenty-Four

Rosa was out when Yudel got home. It took him a few minutes to recall that she had said she was going to a sewing-machine demonstration at five and would be home late. He sat down at his desk and wrote her a note, explaining how there had been a crisis surrounding the prisoners' food at Leeukop and she should not wait up for him.

He felt weary at the thought of again deceiving Rosa. He told himself that it could not be otherwise though. The truth would start her worrying and probably inspire another flight to Irena and it seemed possible that Hymie might be tiring of that sort of thing.

Of course there was Dahlia. The thought slipped in, unbidden, through the back door of his mind. It would be a lot easier explaining things to Rosa, if Dahlia was not in Johannesburg, awaiting his call. Contacting her is unavoidable, he told himself. She knows how to find Dladla.

There were other things about Dahlia though. There were those dark eyes and the way she looked at him, that little sly, amused expression that suggested every sort of possibility. There was also that strange, in Yudel's experience, complete surrender to the stimulation of the senses, and that long, cool, lean body, the colour of coffee to which you've added little too much milk.

He dialled the Johannesburg number that she had given him.

She was waiting on the pavement opposite Joubert Park in front of one of the area's many old grey characterless buildings. From four blocks away he recognized her. She had her hands folded in front of her and was looking down at the pavement, a despondent posture that he knew would change as soon as she saw him. A light wind that gusted intermittently down the city's concrete corridors was ruffling her hair, sending it swirling and swooping around her shoulders.

She flew in through the car door with something of the wind's freshness and exhilaration. Despite the position of the steering wheel she fell straight into his arms. In a moment all that Yudel had felt about her, the way in which she had briefly brightened and rejuvenated his life, was back with him. "I can't believe it," he heard her say. "I never thought we'd be together again." The embrace was brief and she slipped back into the passenger seat, her face alive with pleasure and expectation. "This is wonderful. Tell me I look good."

It was true. To Yudel she looked more than good. "You look terrific," he said.

"I know. It's because I'm in love."

The idea troubled Yudel. "With whom?"

She laughed and reached out to touch him. "You're hopeless," she said.

Alexandra was only five minutes away on the highway and as they drove Dahlia talked in the same exuberant, bird-like way he remembered. Every word, exclamation, every quick gesture: all contrived to charm him again as completely as she had the first time.

Just outside the township he stopped the car and walked round to the passenger side while she wriggled past the gear lever and into the driver's seat. "You pretend to be asleep if anyone comes to the window," she said. "Bend forward and make sure your face and both hands are hidden. The way things have been going in Alex we don't want to advertise you." She examined the position he had adopted before engaging the gears. "Turn up your lapels," she added.

"I thought it was an advantage to be white in this country."

"Not in all situations, not any more." She reflected for a moment, then added absently, under her breath, "Power to the people."

Alexandra was one of the smallest black townships and also one of the oldest. It was different from most others in almost every way. Most townships had been built outside the cities with broad expanses of open veld providing a buffer between their people and the inhabitants of white suburbia. Alexandra was a black island in Johannesburg's wealthy northern suburbs as the city had grown and stretched and eventually surrounded it. It was not made up of the seemingly endless rows of tiny identical houses, but had developed naturally, most of its houses large, rambling and privately owned. They were old now, the roof sheeting rusted and the mud-coloured plaster crumbling away to uncover sections of naked brick. And they were crowded, families sharing houses to ease the burden of rent, sometimes a group of five or six occupying a single room. In many backyards, roughly erected shacks housed still more families.

The streets were almost completely empty, those who were not at home hurrying to get inside and close out the dangers of the night. Everywhere a heavy curtain of smoke from the thousands of cooking fires hung grey and evil-smelling in the air. There were no street lamps and the faintest lights, the unsteady flame of a candle or the smoky yellow glow of an oil lamp, gleamed uncertainly from the windows. Only the car's headlights lit the dusty, rutted streets.

As they turned at an intersection the furthest reach of the lights, reflected and attenuated by the smoke, picked out the shapes, quick in the wavering beams of light, of a number of young boys. Their long spindly legs moved lightly like antelopes as they bounded out of sight down a side road. Dahlia stopped at the corner where the boys had disappeared. With the headlights aimed in the wrong direction the darkness in the side street was complete. They could see no light or movement of any sort. A pair of headlights, far down the long road that ran the length of the township almost to the muddy stream that was called the Jukskei river, came into view and ground slowly up the slope towards them. The lights were mounted close together and set high off the ground.

"Hippo," Dahlia said. "Police hippo." She let the clutch in and allowed the car to move forward. "No point in waiting for them. Maybe they've seen us."

They passed two more intersections before she turned the car on to a street running parallel to the one where they had seen the armoured car. She allowed it to freewheel to the next corner and stopped next to an ancient corrugated iron fence that had lost many of its sections and even some of its supporting poles. From their position they would be able to see the hippo two blocks away when it passed opposite them. "There's something happening, Yudel. The cops and the kids are both on the streets tonight."

"Can't we just find Dladla and go?"

"Where's your spirit of adventure, Mister Gordon?" It was an interesting question, but before he could answer she did. "Shame, Yudel. That's not fair. Forget I asked that." She scratched in one of her coat pockets and brought out a crumpled cigarette packet. "Want one?" Yudel accepted the cigarette and allowed her to light it. By the brief glow of the match he saw the eagerness in her face just the way he had remembered it. "I'm waiting for them to come past. I just want to be sure we avoid them."

She had turned down her window and Yudel could hear the deep rumble of the armoured car's engine as it came slowly up the long gradient, hidden from them by the houses in between. The night air also came in at the window, heavy, tepid with the last vestiges of summer's heat and fouled by the smell from the latrine buckets and the coal smoke of the cooking fires.

Yudel was suddenly aware that he could see shadows, projected by a dim and moving light at the corner where the armoured car would have to pass. The light was gradually growing in strength, moving with the quick vertical bumping and slow lateral swaying of the vehicle. It was throwing elongated shadows, sharply delineated breaches of the light, that were themselves moving, a group of people being herded along in the headlights.

From out of the darkness of the road behind them an old woman, carrying a bundle of washing, little more than a deeper shade of the surrounding gloom, walked heavily past. Yudel saw her head turn quickly as she passed the corner, her attention drawn by the strange interplay of light and shadow and the sound of the armoured car's diesel engine. He thought that she increased her stride before disappearing completely into the enveloping depths of smog and darkness.

Now he could see the figures as they emerged from the shelter of the corner house and stopped in the intersection. There seemed to be some thirty or forty of them and they were not being herded as he had supposed. The engine revolutions of the hippo fell until they droned away to a steady idling and the headlights steadied. The men who now filled the intersection seemed to be armed, some with rifles and others with long-bladed pangas or knives. They had reached the corner in almost complete silence and still only the occasional spoken word, too far away for Yudel to distinguish it, reached them across the intervening space. "Vigilantes," Dahlia said. "They're vigilantes."

One of the men, broad and sturdily built, his white shirt unbuttoned and hanging loose outside his pants, his brown face gleaming with sweat in the headlights, was holding up a sheet of paper to read from it. Suddenly he folded it and set off in silence, directly away from Yudel and Dahlia. They watched as the group moved out of the headlights into darkness. A few seconds later the engine revolutions of the armoured car rose in pitch as the driver pulled away. It appeared, a great top-heavy beetle silhouetted against the grey curtain its own lights made in the smoke, and turned to follow the vigilantes.

Dahlia let the car roll forward without using the engine and suddenly the grotesque procession was gone. She waited until they were out of the intersection before switching on the lights and restarting the engine. "What was the paper they were looking at?" Yudel asked.

"Probably an address list. They've got business around Alex tonight."

"Supported by the police? Maybe they aren't vigilantes."

"Maybe not. Maybe there'll be no sunrise tomorrow." She was sounding like Freek in the way that she made his suggestion seem naïve.

Dahlia brought them to the house they were looking for by a slow tortuous route that led from one narrow dirt road to the next, between rows of old and crumbling houses, along the edge of a precipitous ditch, dug by the comrades as a trap for police armoured cars, to stop in front of a low prefabricated building that looked more like a storage shed than a dwelling. Walking in front and gesturing for him to follow, she led Yudel down a narrow lane between a roofless fire-blackened ruin of a house and the shed and knocked on a side door. The glass of the windows on their side were both papered over with newspaper. Through the paper Yudel saw the movement of a light, first at one window then at the other. Dahlia knocked again, still softly. It was not a place nor a night on which to draw attention to yourself. A man's voice, muffled by the closed door, answered in an African language.

"Reverend Dladla, it's me, Dahlia Baker." Her voice was low, hoarse with urgency. "I sent a message."

Yudel heard him unlock the door and it opened to reveal the shape of a fat man, lit faintly by a candle on the far side of the room. "Yes, yes. I know you. We met in Durban. Come in."

He backed into the room, retreating to its far side and waving a hand towards the plain wooden table that stood in its centre. "Please sit down. Please. Oh, you didn't tell me you were bringing a white friend. A bit dangerous, you know. Tempers are running high. No one can control the kids at the present time." He reached out a limp and excessively well-padded hand. "Dladla," he said.

"Yudel Gordon," Yudel said.

"Yudel Gordon," Dladla repeated. "Jewish. Very liberal people, the Jews." Yudel's eyes had become accustomed to the light and he could see Dladla clearly now. He had very thick lips and a wide mouth that hung open slightly when he smiled. Apart from the table and chairs Yudel could see a double bed, a few cupboards and a pile of sealed and bulging cardboard boxes in a corner. There was also a washstand with a jug and basin, of a sort Yudel remembered using on visits to the country as a child, and a small paraffin stove on an upturned wooden crate. "Please sit down," the reverend was saying, indicating again the table and chairs. "These are temporary quarters. We haven't been here long. There's very little accommodation in Alex. What about some tea? Can I make you some tea?"

Yudel and Dahlia sat down at the table while Dladla lit and pumped the stove, his large body hovering over the flame and casting a broad shadow across the room, as it sputtered, hissed and flared before bursting into life. He joined them at the table,

254

his hands folded over his broad stomach. It was a pose that was intended to look relaxed, but in Dladla's case it succeeded only in reflecting his unease. "I've known quite a number of Jewish people and I've always found them very liberal."

"Thank you for seeing us," Yudel said.

"And you, Dahlia?" The reverend grinned at her with his open-mouthed, thick-lipped smile, a large fleshy tongue seeming to block the space between the lips. "I was sorry to hear about your husband."

Dahlia looked down at her hands in what she imagined to be the prescribed way for grieving widows. "I'm well, Reverend," she said. "Do you have a congregation here?"

The grin seemed to grow wider, the eyes merrier. "I had a fall out with the church a few years ago. I'm the librarian here, but the people still call me Rev. Wherever I go in the township they all know me. You can hear them calling me Rev, kids, adults, everybody."

"How's Flora?" Dahlia's voice and manner were too casual not to be concealing something.

At the mention of his wife's name Dladla got quickly to his feet and started doing things with cups and saucers on the edge of the box, next to the buzzing stove. "Very well, thank you. She's out at the moment. She has a lot of community work." Dahlia's eyes widened meaningfully as she glanced at Yudel. "Did you have a problem finding the place?" Dladla's back was turned to them. "There's never been street lighting in Alex. We call it Dark City. Did you know that, Mister Gordon?"

"No, I didn't know that."

Dladla turned off the flame and came back to the table with cups of tea for Yudel and Dahlia, his eyes crinkling into a smile and his broad lips quivering. "Yes, we call it Dark City. Without electricity and with the smoke from the coal stoves every night, you can understand why."

The cups were cheap, fragile and decorated with pink roses. Yudel tried the tea. It was weak and tasted of dust. "Yes, I can understand that." He was finding it difficult talking to Dladla. Something about the man's eagerness to be acceptable inhibited him.

"Mister Gordon is an investigator, reverend," Dahlia said. "He is trying to help us uncover the truth about some of these attacks on the people."

"Oh, an investigator." But Dladla's expression had clouded. Some inner defence, sensing that this could be trouble, had descended to cut him off from his visitors. "I thought that in real life investigators only deal with divorce cases."

"Normally," Yudel said, "but at the moment, with winter coming on, there are fewer cases of infidelity."

"Truly? I had no idea that sin was . . . " He seemed to search for the word, " . . . seasonal".

There was a strange tension about Dahlia's face and the sound of her voice when she spoke. "Mister Gordon is very knowledgeable. He does a lot of fieldwork."

"That's very interesting, but I don't know how I can help."

Yudel told him, but while he spoke Dladla was shaking his large fleshy head slowly back and forth. "I'm sure you must remember the Attic," Yudel finished.

"Vaguely. Vaguely. It was a long time ago, even before I met Dahlia."

"A group of masked men broke into the premises and assaulted Miller. You must remember that happening."

"I heard about it, but I wasn't there when these incidents took place. I'd like to help, but what can I say?" The great mouth hung open, the tongue like a piece of liver suspended from a hook in a butcher shop, and he nodded slightly. "What can I say? I'd like to help you. This is a very valuable project, but I only heard about these things."

"We need to find someone who actually saw the assailants. We believe a man by the name of Fred Tuwani . . . " Yudel felt that it was prudent to avoid Tuwani's nickname. " . . . saw them without their masks and recognized one of them. You knew Tuwani, I believe."

But the inner defences, more determined now, like the shutting of a gate, had closed to remove even the possibility of acknowledgement. "I may have met him," he said. The grin had not left his face, but he was looking past Yudel, not at the wall behind him or the papered-over windows or any other tangible object, but at a past that he was never going to confide.

"He was also a member of the group . . . " Yudel started, but he was interrupted by Dahlia.

"We saw vigilantes in the street tonight," she said. "Would you mind if I peep outside? I won't be a moment."

"Vigilantes?" Dladla's smile was an unchanging mask, a cover for every occasion. "We've had vigilantes from time to time. I don't know what they hope to achieve."

Dahlia had reached the door. "Don't be seen," Yudel said. Then she was gone and the door closed behind her. He turned his attention back to Dladla and the minister smiled, the same unfailing reflex that masked every hatred and hid every fear.

With the stove dead the only light came from the clean, wavering flame of the candle. "Have some more tea," Dladla suggested.

It was half an hour later that Yudel left Dladla. Dahlia had not returned and all that he had been able to get from the reverend was that yes, perhaps, Tuwani had been a member of their prayer and study group, but where he was now was anybody's guess. As he opened the shed door and stepped into a night that had lost what remained of its warmth he immediately heard the flat sound of distant voices, shouted exclamations, and a banging, as of a heavy hammer being used in a demolition. There was another sound too, less obtrusive, but more consistent than the others. It took a few moments for Yudel to realize that he was listening to the sound of flames.

Dahlia was at the entrance to the lane, pressed against the wall of the shed. Behind him he heard Dladla close the door, shutting out Yudel, Dahlia, the vigilantes and every other unwelcome part of the night. "They're burning the people's houses." Dahlia's voice sounded thick, the words blurred. "They're punishing the leaders."

The fire was a street or two away. He saw the occasional uncoiling of flame above the roof of a closer house and a dense cloud of smoke, made orange by the reflected flames. "I got nothing out of Dladla," he said, surprised for a moment by an element in his own voice that sounded like fear.

"It's nothing." Again her voice had the strange blurred quality. She had seemed to want to say more, but stopped abruptly.

"Come on," Yudel said. He had taken her arm to lead her to the car, but she did not respond, still pressing herself against the shed wall. "Come on. We've got to get out of here." This time she came, allowing him to guide her to the passenger side of the car and getting in without objection when he opened the door.

He brought the car round and drove back in the direction from which they had come. At the second intersection he turned to get above the fire, stopping just before the street corner and walking the last few paces. The vigilantes were gathered outside a blazing shack in an otherwise deserted street. On the side of the street away from the fire two of them were standing watch over a few five-litre petrol cans.

A barefoot woman ran into the road from the direction of the shack. Yudel saw a thin line of flame, seeming to spring into existence from nowhere, appear along the hem at the back of her skirt. She spun over on to her back on the dirt surface of the road, her hands beating furiously at the flames. From the shack a man followed, limping slightly as he ran. He was also without shoes, wearing only a vest and trousers. Yudel saw him fall to his knees next to the woman and scoop dust over her burning dress with both hands.

A wave of dirt fell against the dress, extinguishing the flame. The woman rose slowly, her eyes held by the much larger fire that enveloped what remained of their dwelling. The man too was facing the shack, not looking at those around him. He took a step forward, an involuntary move towards saving something, but stopped. One of the vigilantes moved up close behind him. Yudel saw the knife a moment before the blow was struck. It was held low, a little under waist level, the blade horizontal to find the openings between the ribs more easily. The vigilante's arm thrust forward in a move so quick that Yudel thought the knife might have missed its target except that the man who had fled the house was now writhing on the dust of the road. Then he heard the woman's cry, a keening, an animal sound, unmistakable in its agony.

Yudel wanted to leave, but he hesitated a moment longer. In

some way the scene was incomplete. It was not so much something he knew, as it was an unframed question, hovering somewhere in the back of his mind.

He did not have to wait for the question to be answered. On a change of the wind, or perhaps through an opening in the buildings, the sound of the armoured car's engine reached him. By its loudness and high pitch it was moving quickly and was not far away. Yudel ran for the car. He had the engine started as the pair of high, close-set headlights swung heavily into the street behind him. The wheels spun for a moment on the loose dirt of the road before they found traction and drove the car foward. For a few seconds the sharp yellow-white of the hippo's headlights seemed to fill the rear-view mirror, then he turned hard into the street where the vigilantes were burning the shack, but in the direction away from them. The sound of the fire had retreated behind the car's insulation. Now the rear-view mirror showed the dark figures of the mob, each trimmed down one side by the light of the flames. Then the armoured car's headlights again burst into view, extinguishing all else. The driver flicked them on and off, a signal for Yudel to stop. The scene he had just witnessed persuaded him against it.

He turned hard at the next intersection and again at the next. The armoured car was following, but falling behind as the driver struggled to bring its cumbersome body through the corners. Yudel lost it altogether when he reached the tarred road of the adjoining industrial area.

But they'll have the number of the car, he told himself. At least three or four times we must have been close enough for them to see the number.

The knowledge brought Rosa to his mind and thinking of her made him glance towards Dahlia. She was bent over, her head resting on her knees and her face covered by her hands. He laid a hand on her shoulders. "Dahlia?" he asked. The only answer was a quick shake of her head.

Twenty-Five

The flat where Dahlia was staying was situated in a relatively well-kept building in an area that looked more decayed every time Yudel visited it. Joubert Park was one of the city centre suburbs where the buildings had emptied of whites in the Seventies and were now filled by black South Africans in defiance of the Group Areas Act that prohibited their presence, except in the servants' rooms on the rooftops.

On the way back from Alexandra Dahlia had said nothing, remaining in the same, almost crouching position for most of the journey. When she did sit back in the seat, she looked away from him, out of the window on her side. Only once while waiting at a traffic light did he get a clear view of her face and he saw that she was crying.

A young Indian woman, wearing a T-shirt with the lettering "Free Mandela now" across the front, denim trousers and tennis shoes, opened the door after inspecting them through the plastic lens mounted in the wood panelling. "Dahlia, what happened?" She bent forward to get a better view of Dahlia's face, then glared accusingly at Yudel. Dahlia shrugged past her and, taking Yudel by the arm, led him to a bedroom and closed the door.

He did not truly understand what had happened to have this effect on her. "It was awful," he suggested.

"Sit down." Her eyes were swollen, but she had stopped crying and her voice was steady. The room contained only a single bed, a built-in cupboard and a steel kitchen chair. Yudel sat down on the chair. Dahlia unwrapped her scarf slowly without looking at him, then started unbuttoning her jacket. "What did the old monster tell you?"

"He pretended not to remember Tuwani."

"Jesus, Yudel."

"What is it? I don't understand."

Dahlia slipped out of her coat and dropped it on the bed with her scarf. She was standing a few paces from him, her hands hanging helplessly at her sides. He was surprised, looking at her wearing only a light cotton dress, at how lean and narrow she was. Her face reflected complete emptiness, the sort of devastation that Yudel realized he had perhaps never experienced himself. "Fred is dead. He was necklaced by the comrades." The restraint that her pain had imposed on her was released and she rushed to Yudel, seeming to collapse at his feet, her head coming to rest on his lap and her hands in his. "The people's court sentenced him to death as a spy." Dahlia's back heaved as she spoke. She seemed to be struggling for breath as if the universe would never again have enough oxygen for her needs. "Dladla pointed him out. Flora left the same day. She's not busy with community work. She's gone. It happened during the height of the unrest, two weeks ago. When I went out it wasn't to look at the vigilantes. I went to talk to the neighbours. They told me this and they all believe it. The Rev would never lie, they say." She looked up at Yudel, her eyes fastening on to his with a strange rigidity. "These things are not supposed to happen, Yudel. The system acts like that, not the people. How could they listen to him? He got his revenge at last. After all those years he finally got his revenge. He's a monster."

"But surely they knew Tuwani."

"He's been living in Thembisa and only occasionally coming to see Dladla, or rather Flora. He was unknown in Alex. The Alex people called that time the six-day war. It would not have been hard to persuade them that a stranger was a spy. Dladla would have wormed his way into the community. You heard him tonight: I've known Jews and they were always very liberal. Jesus." Then she was crying again, a soft, plaintive, hopeless sound. "Rhonda was right. She was right to leave this damned country. Why are we here, Yudel?"

Dahlia fell silent and slowly her breathing became more regular until Yudel thought that she might be asleep. He could see only the top of her head, the thick curling hair looking wild and knotted now, and part of her back and shoulders. With a hand in each armpit he made to lift her, but she woke, her head jerking and her eyes startled. "Come to bed," he said. She rose quickly, smoothing the front of her dress, and followed him to the bed where she lay down, her eyes closing immediately as she retreated before a knowledge that was too painful to bear. Just before falling into a deep sleep she sat up and looked at Yudel, as if surprised to see him. "They showed me the place," she said. "You can still see the mark on the road where they burnt him."

In the built-in cupboard Yudel found a blanket with which to cover her. He sat down on the edge of the bed, watching her sleep. She lay curled up, her hands clasping her knees, little inner disturbances flickering quickly across the skin of her face and beneath the lids of her eyes. She was still beautiful to him. He touched her hair and she did not stir. Then he bent forward to kiss her, but stopped before his lips made contact with her skin. He was suddenly aware that he was saying goodbye to this strange, rebellious, fragile victim of life.

He found the woman who had opened the door sitting in the lounge and pretending to read. "May I use your phone?" he asked.

"Go ahead. What's wrong with Dahlia?"

"She had a shock." He looked at his watch and saw that it was past one o'clock. The telephone was on a low table near the window and he dialled his home number. It rang for a while without answer and he tried again. Still there was no answer. He became aware of the woman watching him. "I couldn't get through," he said.

"Is she sleeping?"

"Yes. Tell her I'll phone."

"I'm her sister," she told Yudel. "Who are you?"

"My name is Yudel Gordon."

"Is she having an affair with you?"

Yudel found Blythe Stevens's house after a brief search. By the time he pressed the recessed button that would ring the bell inside the

262

house it was almost two in the morning. While he waited for a reaction he thought about Rosa. Nothing could have happened to her. They had only taken his car number a couple of hours before. They never moved that fast. They wouldn't move before Monday morning, he told himself. But he told it to himself too often for his own peace of mind.

Through a narrow opening in the hedge he saw a light go on in the front of the house. Blythe Stevens's voice reached him from one of the front windows. "Yes, who is it?"

"It's Yudel. Yudel Gordon."

"Who?"

"Yudel Gordon."

"Yudel? What do you want?"

"I want to talk to you."

"Now? What time is it?"

"I don't know. Let me in."

Yudel thought he heard a single curse, uttered deep and disgusted in the back of Blythe Stevens's mouth. "I'm coming."

A light went on in the hall and Stevens came down the front steps, long angular legs protruding from the bottom of a woollen dressing-gown. "It's nearly two o'clock." He slipped the latch on the gate to let Yudel in. "Are you in trouble? Did you get over your injury? You don't look too well."

"I want Robin Du Plessis. I may be in trouble if I don't find him."

He shook his head. "He's in hiding. You won't find him now."

"Where's his brother?"

"He lives near here with his parents, but you can forget about finding Robin. What's going on here, Yudel? Do you know what time it is? Two o'clock. Nearly two o'clock."

"Where can I find him?"

"Actually we've dropped this whole thing. I told you that. We dropped it long ago. We don't have an allocation of funds any more. We're doing other things now."

"Where?"

"Christ, Yudel. They aren't going to be glad to see you."

A black security guard answered his ringing. Only when it became clear that Yudel was not going to go away or stop ringing the bell did he let him through a high steel gate in an even higher stone wall. Yudel followed him up an immaculately paved driveway, overhung by shrubs and trees, to a house of such magnificence as he thought existed only in magazine photographs. As a breeding ground for university radicalism it was a source of astonishment.

The elder Du Plessis, dishevelled, red-eyed and ill-tempered in flannel pyjamas, silk dressing-gown and karakul slippers, answered the door to shout at the guard and argue with Yudel before calling his son.

It was past three by the time Yudel followed him into a house on the far side of town that fifty years before had belonged to one of the city's wealthiest men, but was now a students' commune. It had been surprisingly easy to convince Ralph Du Plessis to lead him to his brother. The name, Wheelwright, had convinced him. "Yes," he had said, "Robin was picked up by him the first time he was detained."

Yudel stopped him just inside the heavy, glass-panelled front door. "I want to speak to him alone."

The younger man's face bore the marks of a liver that did not function well. It was lit unevenly by a street lamp through the ripple glass panels in the door, making it look more puffy than it actually was. "I'll go in with you, then I'll leave. Tell me one thing though: is this going to lead anywhere?"

"I don't know. Maybe . . . " He started framing a reply that would explain some of the possibilities and also the doubts, but the effort was too great. "I really don't know."

The house was only intermittently furnished, an occasional loose floor carpet, hat rack or unframed print punctuating the emptiness of walls and floor. The smell of slowly decaying wood was dense in the air.

Robin Du Plessis was asleep on a camp stretcher in a room that had once been a part of the veranda at the back of the house. A thin pale arm was visible against the dark material of the sleeping-bag he was using. His brother switched on a reading-lamp that stood on the floor next to the stretcher. "Robin."

The figure on the stretcher twisted away from the light, an arm coming up to cover his eyes. Suddenly he sat up, his eyes wide

264

now and fixed on Yudel. Then he looked at his brother, seeking an explanation. "Ralph? What's happening?"

"It's all right. Relax."

"What's he doing here?" The sleeping-bag had slipped down to his waist. His almost unnaturally thin body was leaning forward slightly, the hands grasping the stretcher's frame on either side, readied for flight. His cheeks were even more hollow and the area around his eyes darker than Yudel remembered them.

"It's all right. There's no problem. He's following up something. He's getting somewhere."

"I can't believe this." The hostility Yudel remembered in his face at Zonderwater prison was as clear as it had been then, but now added to it he saw an element of panic that was new. "How can you bring this man here?"

"Talk to him. Just talk to him." Ralph Du Plessis was already backing towards the door. "I'll wait outside. This is not a trap, Robin. Just talk to him." He left the room, closing the door behind him.

Robin Du Plessis sank slowly back on to his elbows. "You can get fucked, Gordon. We've got nothing to say to each other."

Yudel drew the only seating in the room, a folding canvas chair, close to the stretcher and sat down. "You're wrong about me, you know."

"Oh yes. Who pays your salary? If you aren't one of them, what are you doing there? Don't give me a lot of shit about being wrong about you."

"If this had been a trap, there would have been police all over the place by this time. You would have been in handcuffs."

"Oh sure. For all I know the house is surrounded."

"If it was a trap . . . " Yudel was speaking very softly and evenly. It was the voice he used for hypnosis. " . . . then I would accept your rejection at this moment and go. It would make no difference."

Robin Du Plessis was looking closely at him, weighing the logic of what Yudel had said. "Fuck you, Gordon," he answered at last. "I've got nothing to tell you." But Yudel could see a weakening in his resolve and hear that some of the determination had left his voice. "Thanks to that stupid brother of mine I'll have to find another place to hide."

"As you like. Just tell me what I want first." Yudel paused, waiting for a reaction, but this time there was none.

Du Plessis had turned his face away. His mind was occupied by something beyond the room, perhaps something Yudel had wakened that he would rather have left buried. "I don't know anything that is going to help you." It was said guardedly, but this time it was not a rejection.

"Sometime before your arrest you were detained for a month. The officer who took you in was a Colonel Wheelwright." Yudel saw the tightening around Du Plessis's jaw at the name. "Where did he come to get you?"

The young man on the stretcher seemed to be twisting his head even further away from Yudel. "What difference does it make?"

"It's very important."

"Why?"

"Wheelwright is involved."

He seemed to consider this for a while, staring at the floor on the side of the stretcher furthest from Yudel. All Yudel could see of his face was one side from behind, a hollow cheek and an angular jaw line. "How is Wheelwright involved?" He spoke softly, his lips barely moving.

"He may have killed Ray Baker."

"Jesus." The curse was a murmured, repressed sound. "I'm not surprised." Then his thinking took a different course. "I can't testify or even swear out an affidavit. They're looking for me. They've been to all the places they might normally find me."

"Just tell me. It will help."

"I don't know what you want. He came and picked me up at the place where I was working."

"Where's that?"

"The newspaper has a little office across the road from the university. He came there."

"Alone?"

Yudel could still not see Du Plessis's eyes, but he thought he detected a movement of the head and shoulders that came close to wincing. "Yes."

"You were alone in the office?"

"Yes."

"And he was alone?"

"Yes."

"Then what happened?"

"He handcuffed me and took me to the car."

"He did nothing else?"

"He just told me that I was being detained and he handcuffed me and took me to his car. He was parked in a side street, just around the corner from Jorissen street."

"Then where did he take you?"

It was a while before Du Plessis could answer. "He took me to an old house, somewhere near Germiston. I'm not exactly sure. He made me sit on the floor of the car, probably so that I couldn't seen where we were going. He moved back the seat and made me sit there."

"Describe the house."

"It was a big, old wood and iron house, just a shack really. Nobody was living there. At least I didn't see anybody. And it stood all by itself. I saw no other houses nearby. But it was dark. It was evening when he picked me up."

"Were there mine dumps?"

"Maybe." He was speaking slowly, his voice muffled and lifeless. "I'll tell you what I do remember. There were peppercorn trees. I know because we've got one in the backyard at home. They shed these little seeds, millions of them, and all around the steps on this house there were these seeds.

"He took me inside. It was empty and dusty. We went through the entire length of it, I think, to a place in the back. There were stairs in the back, cement stairs going down into a small sort of basement room. He had to move some planks first. It was furnished and you could see it had been in use . . . " He stopped speaking. Yudel leant forward until he could see that Du Plessis had closed his eyes.

"What happened then?" Yudel spoke softly. The other man's pain was a tangible presence in the room.

Without warning Du Plessis threw open the sleeping-bag and leapt to his feet. His thin, almost frail body, naked except for a pair of tartan underpants, was shivering as if seized by a sudden fever. "Why do you ask?" He was looking straight at Yudel and his voice was shrill, the words coming out in a torrent as all restraint was swept away. "If you already know the answer, why do you ask? You know. I can see you know. That's why you keep on digging."

Yudel remained awkwardly in the canvas chair. To rise might have been a challenge or a threat to the younger man. "I don't know," he murmured. "I suspect, but I don't know."

"Fuck you, Gordon," he screamed. "Fuck you. I don't want to talk to you. I don't want to tell you anything." The door opened and Ralph Du Plessis stopped in the open doorway, but his brother turned on him in fury. "Get out of here. What do you want? Get out." Ralph backed away, closing the door. Yudel heard another voice in the passage and Ralph Du Plessis answering. Robin spoke, trying to impose some degree of control on a voice that was teetering on the edge of hysteria. "I can't help you. They want me. You don't know what it's like in detention. You can't do anything. You can't even argue your case. You're helpless."

"Tell me," Yudel said gently. "Tell me what happened."

Du Plessis wrapped his arms around his body, trying to form a shield against Yudel's questioning. His jaw had tightened into a knot of great tension, drawing his mouth into a hard thin line. His voice emerged as a ragged blur of pain. "He raped me. He fucking raped me. And I'm such a fucking coward. He knows I'll never talk." He was making quick dusting movements, starting at his shoulders and ending at his thighs as he tried to rid himself of the contamination of which his confession had reminded him. "He saw me at Zonderwater a few minutes before you visited me there. He came to remind me that he would find me if I talked, that there was no place that I could escape him. Jesus, as if I would talk about it. Look at my fucking body. I look like a woman."

"Robin . . . " Yudel had risen from the chair and was holding out a hand towards him.

"No." He backed away, still dusting himself. "You know. You wanted to know and now you do. So go. Just go and leave me alone." Without warning he made for the door, leaving it open as he burst into the passage. Yudel followed, reaching the door in time to see Du Plessis entering another room. He closed himself in and Yudel heard the sound of a latch being slid into place, followed immediately by the running of water. He wondered how many times Robin Du Plessis had tried to wash away the traces of that memory.

His brother was waiting on the front veranda, his hands deep in his pockets and his collar turned up against the early morning cold. "Well?" he said.

"He's bathing," Yudel said. "Do you think you could stay until he comes out?"

"Bathing? Why's he bathing?"

"Just stay until he comes out."

As Yudel arrived home the first sign of day, a broad softening of the darkness in the eastern sky, was appearing through the tracery of thin autumn jacaranda leaves. He saw the coming of daylight as a warning that time might not be his friend. The hippo's headlights would have shown the crew that the driver of the car was white and their officers would want to know what a white man had been doing in Alexandra after dark and why he had fled from them. As soon as his identity was established they would hand the matter to their Pretoria section and that would mean Wheelwright.

The house was empty. On the previous evening Rosa had left a note in the kitchen. "I am with Josie Kramer. Come and fetch me when you get in."

He left the note where he had found it and went into the bedroom. He sat down on the bed and thought about Dahlia and the circumstances under which he had left her, curled up in an almost foetal position on the bed in her sister's spare room. And he thought again about Robin Du Plessis and the dirtiness from which he could not free himself. But more than anything else he thought about the wooden steps leading up to the old house that Markus Mbelo had called the Attic and the layer of peppercorn seeds that had covered them the only time he had been there. He was still thinking about it when he lay back, intending to rest for just a few minutes, and plunged suddenly, deep below the surface of his waking thoughts into the silence of a welcome, but temporary oblivion.

Twenty-Six

Yudel woke with a tightness around his chest. His watch told him that it was two o'clock. He had slept for close to eight hours. He washed hurriedly and put on a new shirt. From the study he dialled the number of Dahlia's sister and listened to her hostile tones telling him that Dahlia had changed her plans and was already on her way to the airport to go home on an earlier flight.

He started dialling Josie Kramer's number to speak to Rosa, if she was still there, but hung up as soon as he heard the ringing from the other side. She had not rung during the morning and an emotional confrontation over the telephone was something he would rather have avoided.

Yudel switched on the coffee percolator and went to the front of the house where, except for one window, the curtains were drawn. Through the narrow opening the street looked as lethargic as on any other Saturday afternoon. The sharp clear highveld sun cast deep black shadows and even inside the house the air was warm with the gentle temperature of a summer that had continued beyond its apportioned time. Across the road a young woman in red shorts and a yellow sweater was moving along a flower bed, bending to do something with a trowel every few paces. You're being a fool, he told himself. You were in Alex sixteen hours ago. They never react this fast.

He returned to the phone to start dialling Freek, but did not complete the number, remembering that the recorder used on telephones had a device that registered the number dialled.

It took an effort of will for Yudel to leave the house and stand in the sunshine at the garden gate. The woman in the red shorts was down on her knees, the trowel plunging into the soft earth in neat little strokes. Further down the road a teenage boy on a racing cycle with low-slung handle-bars and a high saddle swayed from side to side as he pedalled up the gentle slope. From the yard of a neighbour he heard the sound of a lawn-mower's two-stroke engine. No afternoon could have been more ordinary.

He remembered the coffee percolator. Its gurgling reached his ears before he got there. He poured himself a cup, cut a few slices of bread from the previous day's loaf and sat down to a lunch of bread, polony and coffee. The afternoon newspaper, twenty-four hours old now, lay folded on the table. Yudel spread it open and turned absently from one page to the next, his eyes barely focusing on the contents. A colour photograph on page five seized his attention. The red, white and black banner of the Afrikaner Revival Movement was being held aloft by members of the organization. Directly below the dark arrog-ance of the swastika stood Gys Muller, both arms raised, his face set in an expression that seemed to contain a mystical foreknowledge of his destiny.

Across the top of the page the headline read, "Rural fury" and below that "Cabinet minister prevented from speaking." The story told how Gys Muller and his uniformed followers had taken over a meeting of the government party and prevented their most popular speaker from addressing the gathering. The meeting was notable in that it was the first time the police had ever used teargas on a white gathering. For all their efforts the small police contingent had been brushed aside and Muller had entered the hall at the head of his supporters and taken over the microphone.

Yudel read the report carefully, then pushed the paper aside. He finished his still warm coffee and went to his car where he had left it standing in the driveway.

Seven or eight cars were parked on the verge of the street in front of the house. From the far side of a single-storey mansion that would normally be beyond the resources of a police officer, a thin curl of smoke and the smell of meat cooking over a fire reached Yudel.

Freek's eleven-year-old daughter, Bapsie, answered the door bell. She was wearing a pink and white dress, adorned with frills and ribbons, and a pink ribbon in her hair. "Uncle Yudel," she said, blushing at the thought of how beautiful she looked.

Yudel had never understood Bapsie's admiration for him, but he was very proud of it. He did not have to bend very far to bring his face level with hers. "Listen, Bapsie," he said. "I want you to do something very important for me."

Immediately the young face became serious and a certain difficulty of breathing became evident. She was still ready to die before saying. "What must I do, Uncle Yudel?"

"Go and get your father and bring him to me, but . . . " He paused for effect. " . . . don't let the other guests know. I'll wait in his study."

Bapsie turned and dashed away without further discussion. Yudel crossed the hall from which he could see through the glass wall on the other side of the house. The guests were gathered in loudly talking, wine-drinking groups while Freek, a glass of wine in one hand and a pair of tongs in the other, tended simultaneously to barbecuing the meat and leading the socializing. Yudel watched Bapsie weaving between the adults, stop next to her father and lean against him to draw his attention without alerting the others just as Yudel had instructed. Determination was a strong Jordaan characteristic and Bapsie had her full share.

He had scarcely sat down in one of Freek's glowing, leather-upholstered chairs when his friend came storming through the door to establish the accuracy of what his daughter had just told him. Bapsie was only a stride behind. He stopped abruptly in front of Yudel and stared at him in a way that suggested that something about him had changed. "Where the hell were you last night?" Bapsie took hold of one of her father's hands and in so doing gave her presence away. "Away with you, Bapsie."

"Uncle Yudel doesn't mind if I stay."

"I mind if you stay. Away with you. Go and help your mother." He closed the door behind the retreating child.

"What do you mean, where was I?"

"I tried to call you right after I took you home last night and you were gone already. There was something about you that suggested that you weren't finished for the night. I phoned a couple of hours ago and you still weren't there. Christ, Yudel, why can't you be like other people?"

"I was asleep when you phoned this morning."

"You must have been pretty deep for me not to wake you."

He told Freek how he had spent the night. By the time he had finished Freek's eyes were holding his as if joined by a medium that neither would be able to break.

"According to him Wheelwright screwed him and you think it happened in this place, the Attic?" There was a stillness in Freek that Yudel had rarely seen. "That's what he told you?"

"It was true. He was not lying."

"Come with me." Freek led him down a flight of stairs to the house's lower level and into the pantry that opened off the kitchen. Bapsie, who had not gone far, trailed them from a distance. Freek closed the door and removed a vacuum flask from the freezer. He unscrewed the lid and removed a glass vial containing a tiny globule of a frozen colourless liquid. "The three black kids, there was semen up the arse of one of them. I decided to keep my own sample, right here, in liquid nitrogen. It'll keep for as long as we need it." Freek slipped the vial back into the flask and replaced the cap.

"If you've got liquid nitrogen there, you don't need the freezer," Yudel said.

"Can't do any harm to wear belt and braces."

"My God, Freek, do you realize . . . "

"Do you realize what sort of game we have here?" Freek finished the sentence for him.

The sharp clatter of high-heeled shoes reached them from the tiled floor of the kitchen and Magda Jordaan, a tall handsome woman in her early forties, opened the door and took one step into the room. "I should have known it was you," she said to Yudel. She pointed a resolute finger at her husband. "You, Freek Jordaan. If you slip away today, leaving me with the guests, you will sleep outside tonight. Not on the sofa in the sitting room. Outside. I hope you understand." She lowered the finger and gave

Yudel her attention. "Naturally, you are welcome to stay and join us, Yudel, but you take my husband away today and you and I will have business to attend to." Without waiting for the men to react she stepped out of the room and closed the door firmly but gently behind her.

"She has an admirable forthright way," Yudel said.

"You've noticed that, have you?" He replaced the flask in the freezer and put a fraternal arm around Yudel's shoulders. "Come down and join the party."

The top of Yudel's shoulder made contact with Freek below his armpit. Physical contact with Freek was of an overpowering nature and left Yudel feeling more than usually inadequate. He pulled away, more out of a need to reestablish his identity than to free himself. "There's something else," he said and told Freek how he had only just avoided the armoured car in Alexandra and how they had probably taken his licence number.

"Boetie," Freek said, "how is it you always complicate things so?"

"It's a gift," Yudel said.

"Now you want to get him before he gets you."

"Something like that."

"It's not going to be simple. This is not going to be a clear-cut thing, at least not by Monday."

"I know, but the more I can get, the more I have to fight with."

Freek looked thoughtfully at Yudel and shook his head slowly. "As soon as they get the report from Alex they can take you in and hold you for as long as they like. They only have to justify it to the minister and what does he know? Whatever they tell him, he believes."

"Maybe there won't be a report."

"Maybe not."

"Those kids in the hippo may have slipped and not taken down the number."

"It's possible." They looked at each other in silence. Neither was impressed by the degree of possibility. "So what now?" Freek said eventually.

"I'm going back to the Attic. It looks like Wheelwright has been using it. The first time I was there the caretaker kept asking if I was the police."

"Remember what happened that time."

"I do, every day."

The first sight of the house had the appearance of a dream. It was dark brown, overhung by the peppercorn trees in front, a sombre presence against the yellow clay of the mine dump. Yudel parked the car and walked the remaining distance on the footpath. He could see the place on the edge of the mine dump where he had been standing when they shot him. He stopped for a moment, reluctant to approach the house or the mine dump beyond. The feeling that gripped him brought back the recollection of an incident when as a child he had come upon a pair of puff adders lying in the middle of a path he sometimes used. From that day onward he had always approached that section of the path with a certain amount of horror, despite never seeing the snakes again. In the same way the Attic was the place where he had almost been killed and he could not return to it without experiencing some vestige of the fear and failure he had felt then.

For the first time he took special note of the big old peppercorn trees, their widely spreading branches overhanging the veranda and the ground in front of the house. The seeds, brown and shrivelled with summer's end, were scattered everywhere.

The front door was locked as it had been on his first visit. All the windows that opened on to the veranda were intact as he remembered them. The worn lace curtains in the windows were hanging closed while in his memory there was an image of them tied back on either side to let in the light. He followed the stoep round to the back, as he had the first time, hoping that he would not meet his friend, the caretaker.

He found no broken panes at the back of the house either, but the putty of one small pane was so dried and cracked that, using the screwdriver he kept in his car, it was easy to break it free, remove the pane and release the latch. The window resisted for only a moment before yielding and rolling upwards with a scratching of rollers that had not been used for years.

276

The room he stepped into was large. It had few windows and these were covered by yellow mine dust on the outside and screened by ancient lace curtains on the inside and allowed only a vague, greyish light into the building. In one corner a few wooden benches without backrests leaned against the wall. He recalled that two years before they had been in neat rows. There had also been a blackboard which had since disappeared.

The room's only entrance was into a wide passage that had no windows except for the narrow coloured-glass panels in the front door. The passage turned at right angles to go deeper into the house. Yudel followed it, stopping to look into each room in turn. The first one was small, completely empty and showing no sign of the purpose it may once have served. The next was larger, but not as large as the big room in the front of the house. A few bookshelves, still bolted to the walls were thick with dust. Some sections of planking had come loose and in a corner a pile of religious leaflets indicated that the room had not been used since the Reformed Action Christian Conference had gone out of business.

Most of the remaining rooms were also empty, showing no trace of past activities. The dusty floors, faded and torn wall-paper and barely translucent windows held no clues to the events that made up the house's more recent history.

In one room a cheap plastic foam mattress lay in a corner. A large pane in the only window was broken, letting in more light than there was in most of the other rooms. A high wall, enclosing a drain, hid it from the outside. The broken window also let in the dead leaves of a bluegum that grew nearby, forming a narrow pile against the wall below the broken glass. Stuck to the wall with brittle and yellowed celluloid tape, a printed sign in the shape of a scroll announced that "It is impossible to reconcile Christian values with the practice of Apartheid."

He looked carefully around the room, but there was nothing else. A gust of wind blew in at the window and scudded lightly along the walls, ruffling the leaves. He wondered if this might have been Miller's bedroom. He recalled Markus Mbelo saying that Miller had lived in the house. It made no difference now.

277

Nothing of any real significance remained. Robin Du Plessis had spoken about steps leading to a basement room, but he saw no sign of them. Perhaps this was not the place to which Wheelwright had brought him.

Yudel returned to the window through which he had entered. Almost glowing in the light that came in under the front door, a thin coating of dust covered the wooden flooring. The same fine dust that lay in deep drifts on the mine dump was evenly spread over the floor through much of the house. Yudel went down on one knee and ran a finger over the floor. There was far too little dust for it to have been gathering over the eight years since Bernie Miller and his friends had last made use of the house. The dust only lay thick in the room where the window was broken.

He went back down the passage to the room with the broken window. As in the rest of the house the floor was made of wood planking, but it looked altogether secure. The passage ended against a door that he had assumed led outside, but now he tried the handle and found himself on a narrow stoep that had been enclosed by windows to be used as a kitchen. The sink had been removed and was standing, cracked and discoloured against a partition, on a low pile of loose planks. He had to move some planks first, Robin Du Plessis had told him. Yudel had imagined that whatever planks had been moved would have been floorboards. He dragged the sink and a few cement building blocks off the planks and started sliding them out of the way. As they came clear, one by one, the top of a narrow stairwell was revealed.

The stairs were made of stone and were just wide enough to take one person. At the bottom he could make out the shape of a door, darker than the unpainted walls on either side. Yudel had no doubt that this was it, Bernie Miller's den that he had called the Hole, where he had been attacked and to which Wheelwright had brought Robin Du Plessis to sodomize him. The need to find evidence against Wheelwright was important, but it was not all. As in Durban two years before, he had been driven, since seeing the bodies of the three young comrades, both by a growing excitement, the insidious stimulation the hunt always held for him, and his curiosity, an unslakable need to explore the tangled avenues of human violence. In the semi-darkness at the foot of the stairs his hands searched for the latch. The heavy wooden door was padlocked. It took five minutes and the loss of some skin on his hands to break the latch with one of the cement building blocks. The door held for a moment against his weight, before swinging open.

The room was lit by a small dirt-encrusted window just below the ceiling at ground level. It was furnished by a narrow bed from which the mattress had been removed and a small desk without a chair. A few rows of wooden shelves were fixed to one of the walls and an upright cabinet, its door hanging open, leant heavily against the wall behind the door. A soot-blackened fireplace with cast-iron grate and base had been cleared of ash and coal. At a glance it was clear that, if apart from that one act Wheelwright had ever made use of the room, it had been months since he or anyone else had last been there.

Yudel pulled out the desk drawers one at a time, but they were all completely empty and nothing had been fastened to their undersides. The cabinet held an empty Post Toasties carton and a lidless tin of milk powder, the last remnants of which had formed a yellow-brown crust in the bottom.

He got down on his hands and knees to look under the bed. Apart from wedges of dust along the wall and a few chunks of broken plaster, there was nothing. The space under the wooden cabinet was low and dark, but a narrow shaft of reflected light fell on the wall behind, and he could see that nothing had been hidden there either. Without changing position he looked round the room again. He was within an arm's length of the fireplace. The massive cast-iron base stood on low ball-and-claw feet, lifting it off the cement, probably to allow an air current from below. For a moment it enjoyed Yudel's vague admiration. It was heavy, rugged and built to last.

He sat down on the bare springs of the bed. The room was empty. Whatever secrets it had held, had disappeared with the people who had once made use of it.

His eyes rested on the cast-iron base. It was only a thought, but Yudel found that he had crossed the room in a stride. He had to position a foot on either side of the opening and employ all his weight to lift it just a few centimetres. He held it in position with one hand while with the other he reached underneath. A bundle of newspapers came away in his hand. With great care not to tear them he drew them out and took them over to the desk.

The bundle was not made up of complete newspapers. Pages had been torn out and they were yellowed by the time they had spent there, chewed by mice in places and occasionally streaked by dirty water, but the text on all was completely legible and the pictures clear. The photograph on the top sheet was of the dignified features of Elizabeth Ngcube. The headline above it read, "Ngcube's killing finds an echo."

Yudel paged through the sheaf of old and frayed pages. He recognized most of them: Bensch, Subramoney, Elizabeth Ngcube, the black trade unionist who had died in a motor accident and the liberal professor of law who had been defamed by pamphlet, together with many others: a Durban lecturer whose home had been sprayed by shotgun fire, the sister-in-law of a convicted guerrilla who had been murdered in her bathroom, the three activists who had disappeared without a trace and the four others whose burnt bodies had been found in the scrub fringing a main road. The reports started the year before Baker had died. The most recent was less than a year old.

He had paged quickly through them, comparing the reports to those in Stevens's file. Many of the reports had notes made in ballpoint pen in the margins and now he stopped to read them. Next to one of the articles on the Morris Subramoney case were the words in a cramped, emotionally suppressed handwriting, "Must make contact. Try Durban office." Across the edge of a photograph of Lionel Bensch he read, "Method different. Long range. Amateurs. Use local contacts." The handwriting was that of the same restricted, tormented soul. Yudel glanced at some of the other pages. The writing was the same on every one and every case had at least one such note.

It was only when Yudel read an item on the harassment of William van Ryneveld with a note saying, "Well done, Milan," that he understood what the newspaper pages meant. Someone who was in sympathy with the terrorists had been noting each separate incident and had been trying to make contact with those responsible. A note next to an article on the death of Elizabeth Ngcube said, "Blacks employed. Talk to Milan. He might have information." Yudel went through them all a second time, his immense powers of concentration drawing him again deeper and deeper into the nightmare from which he had fled two years before. The further he read and the more his mind worked on the material it became clear that the one who had made the notes did not know who had committed most of the crimes. Also, the Milan mentioned, could only be Milan Varrevich. There was certainly no other Milan in the republic, but the notes connected Varrevich only to one relatively minor incident.

Eventually, his thoughts still flooding with the possibilities the find had opened, he pushed the papers aside and sat staring at the floor. It was hopeless, as he had always feared it would be. At most, and even that was unlikely, he might get a view into some tiny corner of the whole sordid affair. It was clear that even the man who had collected the newspapers did not know who was responsible for most of the crimes. The man? he asked himself. Without looking again at the notes he could see the script in his mind, the letters cramped tightly against each other, the loops inhibited and ending in jagged points. Superimposed on the restricted tortured hand, he saw a face, its hard and bitter lines, its uncompromising leanness blending it somehow with the characteristics revealed by the pen.

There was something else though. Yudel could feel it, scratching away in the recesses of his thinking. He had to go through the pages again before he realized what it was. There were no clippings related to the killings of Fellows Ngcube and Ray Baker. The death of Elizabeth Ngcube was covered by a number of clippings. Her husband's had been ignored. If the purpose of these pages had been to try to make contact with others of like mind perhaps those were the cases that were superfluous. Baker's clean unworldly features and Robin Du Plessis's pale effeminate ones hung in his mind like the ghosts of past crimes. He was so deep in thought that it was some time before the sound of a door unlocking registered clearly in his mind. He was slow to react even to the footsteps as they came across the old sprung wooden floors, unhurried and purposeful.

Twenty-Seven

By the time Wheelwright and two other men, all wearing suits and all very much bigger and more powerful than Yudel, burst into the room, he was wedged into the narrow space between the door and the cabinet. He was holding the newspaper pages in both hands. His hiding place worked for as long as it took them to get used to the light.

One of Wheelwright's associates, a broad deep-chested man of about thirty, but with hair that had turned white prematurely, dragged him out from behind the door by his shirt front. "Here's the little Jew," he told the others, "hiding behind the door".

"And this?" Wheelwright took the newspapers from him and Yudel saw the recognition they brought to his eyes. The security policeman handed the newspapers to the white-haired man. The eyes that found Yudel's were too filled with anger and hatred for the sense of victory to show itself. "Take them outside," he said, "and burn them."

For Yudel the pages were too precious to let them go without resistance. He threw himself at the white-haired man, driving him backwards. For a moment he had the pages in his hands and was within a stride of the door. A hand had hold of one of his arms. He wrenched himself free with the strength of desperation, swung round and back, feeling his fist make contact with a fleshy cheek. Then he was on the ground with the pages scattered round him. "Get him up," he heard Wheelwright say.

The third man pulled him to his feet. He was fair-skinned, his face covered by large freckles the same colour as his ginger hair.

Yudel felt a twinge of satisfaction to see that the white-haired man's right cheek was bleeding. The man wiped a hand across the cut. He looked surprised to find blood on his finger tips. "Your mother's cunt," he told Yudel. He stepped quickly forward and the power of the blow, thrown with the weight of shoulder and torso, brushed aside Yudel's hands, upraised to deflect it. The punch landed just below his heart and he went down hard, hitting the back of his head against the wall.

Through the sudden confusion of his senses he heard Wheelwright's voice. "Lower, you must hit lower." His head cleared, leaving a glowing ache at the point where his skull had made contact with the wall. The white-haired man was bending over to take hold of him, not expecting resistance. Yudel pushed aside the two fleshy hands and got to his feet under his own power.

"Yissis," the man cursed. "He doesn't learn fast."

Yudel saw the fist that had knocked him down, drawn back again, but Wheelwright raised a hand. "Slowly," he said. "Slowly."

The broad hand was lowered reluctantly. "The little bliksem is looking for me."

"Maybe he'll still find you." The newspaper pages were scattered on the floor, some of them crumpled and torn in the struggle.

Wheelwright inclined his head toward them in a small, restrained gesture. He spoke to Yudel. "Pick them up."

Yudel still wanted the newspapers. The door was open and he knew that, unless he acted decisively, his life expectancy had taken a turn for the worse. He knelt down and gathered the sheets of paper, shuffling them into a neat pile while kneeling on the cement floor. As he rose he swung his right fist in a wide arc in the direction of his captors, missing all three and hurling himself at the door.

This time they were expecting it. The punch landed in the solar plexus and he went down harder than before, the pain bursting upward through his chest and into his head. He stayed on his hands and knees until he felt that he would be able to stand. As before the pages lay scattered on the floor. "Pick them up," he heard Wheelwright say again, his voice low and controlled. Yudel could hear the satisfaction in it.

But now he had accepted that, in the face of the difference between their physical endowments and his, escape was not going to be possible. It was now a time for dignity. He got slowly to his feet without the pages. "You pick them up," he said.

The white-haired man took one small step forward to balance himself as he punched and Yudel saw it coming. He twisted away and the fist glanced off his shoulder to make heavy contact with the wall. The man grunted with pain. "You fucking moffie," he shouted, wringing his right hand.

Yudel almost retorted that it was not he who was the moffie, but he restrained the impulse. Goading Wheelwright with his sexual inclinations did not seem likely to serve any purpose. The white-haired man had regained his balance and was massaging his fist. Wheelwright had a hand on his shoulder to restrain him. "I told you to pick them up," he said to Yudel.

"You pick them up," Yudel said. "I'm busy."

He was looking for a way to distract Wheelwright and for a moment it seemed to work. "You're busy?"

"I'm busy memorizing the faces of everyone present."

But Wheelwright was beyond joining Yudel in one of his games of the mind. The distraction was not going to extend as far as Yudel had hoped. "You listen to me, you little Jew bastard. You're not going to use anything you saw here today."

"You don't know what I've found or what I've seen."

Wheelwright gestured to the freckled man with little more than an inclination of his head. Yudel was roughly searched and the contents of his pockets laid out on the desk. Wheelwright fingered the key ring, identity book, an invoice from a service station, Yudel's departmental security card, two ball pens and a notebook that contained nothing more than a few innocuous names and telephone numbers. Without commenting on any of it, Wheelwright scooped up the items and dropped them into the side pocket of his own jacket.

Yudel held out a hand. "I'll have them," he said.

The white-haired man had lifted both hands to waist level, the fingers outstretched and the palms facing downwards, patting the air as a bull paws the ground before charging. Yudel was trying, out of the corner of his eyes, to keep a watch on the large blunt-fingered hands without taking the focus of his attention away from Wheelwright.

"Yissis, colonel. The colonel said he must pick up the papers . . . "

Wheelwright's eyebrows lifted slightly as he looked at Yudel, his expression asking, Well, what about it?

Yudel's hand was still outstretched, a mute demand for his belongings to be returned. It was possible that, if he could turn this into a simple struggle of wills, he could keep their attention away from more fundamental matters.

"Pick them up," Wheelwright said softly. The white-haired man was still pawing the air.

There was an opportunity Yudel had missed and it rested on the floor among the sheets of newspaper. He needed to take the matter just a little further. "You do it."

"This is enough," the white-haired man said.

"Now," Wheelwright added, his voice barely a whisper through lips that hardly moved at all.

Yudel stared at Wheelwright and swallowed visibly, then he allowed his eyes to flick nervously in the direction of the white-haired man. He could still feel the effect of the blow to his solar plexus, but he had recovered his wind and the pain in the pit of his stomach was not unmanageable. Without arguing further he sank slowly to his knees and started gathering the papers together. The feet of his captors were all around him, but there was still a small opening in the direction of the door if he could use it well.

Yudel's right arm shot upwards, throwing the old and torn sheets of newspaper into the air. Staying low, he rushed for the door. He felt his left shoulder make hard contact with a leg, then he brushed against the wooden doorframe and a moment later he was scrambling up the stairs. At the top, the old stoneware kitchen sink was balancing precariously against the wall where he had left it. He paused long enough to hurl it down the stairs and see it crash against the chest of the white-haired man, knocking him off his feet and into his friends who were following close behind.

Yudel ran for the front door, sliding as he turned out of the passage into the hall and using both hands to stop himself from crashing into the wall. The door was ajar as he expected it would be. His hands, the palms facing outwards, struck its wooden frame next to the glass panelling. At that moment Yudel's foot caught against something and his momentum threw him forward, his stomach making hard contact with the veranda rail. He somersaulted over the rail to land heavily on his right shoulder, tried to rise, but failed at the first attempt. All sensation had left his arm and shoulder. He did better the second time, struggling determinedly upright, only to be faced with the reality of his failure. The door of the house was still empty, Wheelwright and his colleagues possibly still struggling to extricate themselves from the mess on the stairs, but he was looking into the unblinking eyes of Milan Varrevich, and the even barrel of the automatic pistol Varrevich was pointing at him.

The white-haired man was first through the door, a broad black smear down the front of his jacket showing where he had made contact with the underside of the sink, his hair standing awry. Wheelwright and the other man followed close behind. All three looked as if they had been involved in a brief unsatisfactory wrestling match. The level of anger in them, the chagrin and humiliation that anyone had dared treat them this way, was clear on every face. The preliminaries were over. Now they would be getting down to business.

Without waiting for a command from Wheelwright the white-haired man moved towards Yudel. The first punch was short and aimed at his stomach. He tried to step aside, raising his left arm to deflect the blow, but his reflexes were too slow and his arm too light. He took the punch in his side. The second landed against his right kidney and he slipped to one knee. He tried to rise, but the point of a shoe found his solar plexus and he fell back, struggling against a pain that made breathing impossible.

The newspaper pages landed in a pile on the dust next to him and he watched as the freckled man set them alight, the dry and tattered pages quickly flaring into a point of brightness in a slowly darkening afternoon.

At length Yudel rolled on to his left side and, using that arm, managed to manoeuvre himself on to one knee. Wheelwright had come close to him. Now he bent forward until he was near enough to touch Yudel. "You thought you could defy me, Gordon. You are going to pay for your mistake. You're a nothing, an amateur. We deal with your sort every day. You would never have found what you're looking for and now you aren't going to live long enough to try." The lean angular face was almost expressionless, the lips barely moving as he spoke, the eye with the drooping eyelid completely closed and the other little more than a slit as they hid whatever might be revealed by opening them wide. "We have men everywhere. Any time we want to provoke another Langa or another Mamelodi we have men in the right places to start the shooting. Any time our so-called leaders become too soft and the people forget the dangers we face, we know how to unite them."

Yudel struggled to his feet. He looked at Wheelwright with a kind of repelled wonder. The other man's easy reference to massacres that formed a shameful part of the country's recent history was a source of more than just repulsion to Yudel. It was an avenue to an understanding of Wheelwright and those like him. "The people?" Yudel asked. "Who are the people?" He did not wait for the other man to reply. "Your closed circle, complete and perfect, you said . . . it's broken now. Not everyone wants to be part of your nightmare."

Wheelwright moved still closer, the violence within him a restless force seeking release. "You liberals are all cowards, every one of you. We are men . . . "

This time Yudel could not help himself. "Men?" he chuckled mirthlessly. "I thought men preferred women."

His words had stripped Wheelwright naked. The policeman looked quickly at his friends, from one face to the next. Yudel saw an almost convulsive movement in his fingers. His mouth too was working, quickly and soundlessly. He turned back to Yudel. There were no secrets now and no defences behind which either could shield.

What remained of the pages was blackened, no more than a fragile burnt-out wafer. A slight movement of the air was further destroying them, breaking them up and driving them in tiny fragments over the dusty earth.

Wheelwright seemed to move towards Yudel, his one good eye widening as Yudel had never seen it before. For an instant the security policeman's pain and fear were revealed to him. In retrospect Yudel was never sure if Wheelwright had actually moved or what the next moment might have brought. He was stopped by an explosion from the direction in which the cars were parked.

A ball of flame curled skyward, its movement strangely languid. It had barely registered in Yudel's senses when he knew what it was. Wheelwright, Varrevich and the others were all looking in the same direction, frozen by surprise. The peppercorn trees were only a few paces away and, behind them, the unkempt tangle of light bluegum scrub. Despite the pain in his stomach and kidney, Yudel ran. He ran with the desperation of his fear and the knowledge that there would be no other chances.

As he entered the scrub, he glanced back. Only the white-haired one was looking in his direction and, seeing the confusion on the man's face, action from that quarter seemed unlikely. In that moment even he looked back at the flames coming from the burning car.

Yudel stopped to rest against the broad trunk of an old willow that stood on the edge of an overgrown drainage ditch. The sensation, a broad heavy ache, was returning to his right shoulder. The kick to the solar plexus had been the worst and he swallowed down lungfuls of air painfully as if there was an obstruction to its flow.

He had waited only a few seconds when he saw the large figure moving smoothly and carefully through the scrub, his shoulders slightly hunched in characteristic fashion. Yudel stepped away from the tree and waved to draw his attention. Freek came up to him, stopping to look back at the smoke that was being driven off by a light breeze to form a lop-sided column above the trees. "At least you ran in the right direction and waited in a sensible place." He took hold firmly of Yudel's left arm and, with him in tow, hurried down a narrow footpath in the straggling kikuyu grass that grew along the ditch and under the trees. "Come on."

Yudel struggled to free himself. "Let me go."

"Just keep moving."

"I am moving. Let me go."

Freek released Yudel's arm as they came in sight of his Jaguar through the trees, parked in the shadow of the gaunt remains of the old mine headgear. He drove unhurriedly down a track that emptied on to the same road as the Attic's entrance, turning in the opposite direction. They could no longer see the flames. The wind had subsided and the smoke was forming a dense cloud above the peppercorns.

"They'll follow us," Yudel said. "Won't they follow us?"

"Not today." Freek felt in his jacket pocket and brought out eight small chromium-plated metal objects. "Here." He dropped them into one of Yudel's hands. "The valves from their tyres, all their tyres."

"Can't you get into trouble?"

"For taking their valves?"

"No. For burning one of their cars."

"Are you crazy? I'm a police officer. I can't destroy property. For all I know Wheelwright is using a government car. I burnt your car."

"My car?" Yudel's anguish was naked.

"I'm sorry, Yudel. It was all I could think of."

"But my car . . . "

Freek patted the glowing walnut dashboard of the Jaguar lovingly. "You don't think I should have burnt mine?"

He considered the matter in mournful silence. "No, no . . . I suppose not."

Twenty-Eight

The evening twilight had deepened into the bright semi-darkness of the night-time city. The street, like almost every other in white suburbs throughout the country, was completely still. From the corner of the city block in which Freek lived they could see a single car parked under the trees that lined one side of the road. In the driver's seat the shape of a man's head and shoulders could be seen against a patch of light thrown by a street lamp.

Freek moved the car into the street without any hesitation. Then he was driving, smoothly and unhurriedly, the engine only slightly above idling speed in second gear, his decision made by the anger inside him. "I don't fucking believe it," he muttered. "They could at least have sent a professional."

To Yudel there was nothing unusual in the scene. "What are you talking about?" he asked.

But Freek's attention was held too strongly for him to hear Yudel's question. The speed, little more than jogging pace, at which he was holding the car neither increased nor decreased. Yudel was surprised to see the tension in his hands and at the hinges of his jaw.

Except for the car the street was still empty. The angle had changed and, if he had been looking for it, Yudel would have seen that it was now in shadow, the windows dark and the occupant invisible.

They had not quite drawn level with the parked car when Freek braked hard. Almost before they were stationary he was out and moving unreasonably fast for a man of his age and size. The occupant of the other car had barely moved, his eyes widening in the moment of alarm, when Freek had the door open and was dragging him from the driver's seat. Yudel saw the man's right hand reaching towards his shoulder holster, then he was on his back in the road, the hand pinioned by one of Freek's knees. Somehow Freek had a hand free. He removed the other man's gun, lay it on the road and slid it towards Yudel.

Reasoning that this was a good time to demonstrate his interest in proceedings, Yudel opened the door of the car and got out. He picked up the gun in both hands. It was heavy and felt awkward. Being careful not to touch the trigger, he placed in on the floor of the car and closed the door. It seemed unlikely that Freek would need his assistance in any other way.

The man Freek had pinned to the ground was young and, at that moment, very frightened. Freek's revolver was pressing hard against his chest. "Say goodbye to the world," Freek suggested.

"Wait, colonel, wait." The response was that of a policeman.

"What are you doing, watching my house?" The question was accompanied by a sudden increased pressure of the gun against the man's ribs.

"It was an order. It's not my fault. It was just an order."

"Talk, talk, talk." Each word carried with it a powerful short arm jab with the barrel of the revolver, Freek's entire weight riding on the point of the weapon.

"Oh God, oh God." He tried to hunch forward, but was unable to move. "They said I must watch the colonel . . . "

"Who?" Again the barrel of the revolver drove mercilessly into his chest.

"Wait, colonel . . . " His protest was a cry of pain.

"Who?"

"My lieutenant. Lieutenant Grobler."

"Who else?" There was no respite from the barrel of Freek's gun.

"Colonel Wheelwright."

"Are you tapping my phone?" Yudel saw Freek's elbow jerk back to drive forward more powerfully than before. Yudel moved forward to restrain him, but stopped almost immediately.

"In God's name, colonel. Yes." His voice had become shrill with panic.

"Since when?"

"Today, today."

"And Mister Gordon's." There was no sign of Freek's anger easing. Again the heavy right arm plunged forward, the small steel circle of the revolver's barrel taking its entire weight.

"Please." The word was a scream of fear. "Yes."

"What else? What else?" Again and again the short blows worked their destruction on the young policeman's flesh. Behind Freek the exterior lights of more than one house had come on. In one of them the figure of a man in his dressing-gown, fire-arm in hand, was outlined against the light from the front door. "What else?"

"Mister Gordon, Mister Gordon." He was sobbing with the pain of the wound Freek had opened. "We're going to take him in."

"Detention?"

"Yes. Oh God." The movement of Freek's arm stopped, the barrel of the revolver coming to rest a few centimetres from the young security policeman's chest. "If the minister signs on Monday, we'll take him in."

Freek got slowly to his feet and returned the revolver to its holster. From a nearby garden a reedy uncertain voice enquired. "What's happening out there?"

"Police," Freek said. "Go back inside." The sounds made by two doors closing was followed by the switching out of the exterior lights. The security police constable rolled on to his stomach before getting painfully to his feet. Yudel heard his groan of pain as he came erect. The front of his shirt was bloodied in a small area just below his heart. "Get in your car and drive," Freek told him. "Next time I'll shoot you."

"My gun?" The question was tentative. The gun was police issue and had to be accounted for.

"Drive," Freek said. "Get out of here."

They watched him get in his car and direct it slowly down the street, stopping a few blocks beyond as he looked for traffic in a side street before turning. The car moved unevenly out of their range of vision and was gone.

Freek's guests had long since left and Magda met them in the hall. "Was that you outside?" she asked her husband, then answered the question before he could. "Who else would it have been?" She looked closely at them and the expression on her face changed from exasperation to concern. "What's happened?"

"Get the girls," Freek said quietly. "We're sleeping at Attie's tonight."

For a few seconds, the time it took her to read the expression on her husband's face, Magda stood altogether still in front of him, then, without questioning him further, she turned and went towards the bedrooms. "Bettie, Bapsie, come, come." She sounded businesslike and unconcerned. "We're going on a picnic." One of the girls responded vaguely, her voice sleepy, the words blurring into each other. "Uncle Attie," their mother explained. "Come. Hurry up. We can't wait."

"What about Rosa?" Freek asked.

"I don't think she's at home. I'll phone."

"If she answers, say nothing. We'll go get her."

The phone in Yudel's home rang for a few minutes. He tried again and again there was no answer. After that he phoned Josie Kramer. "She's very cross with you, Yudel," Rosa's friend told him. "She went to Irena this morning."

The thought of phoning Irena warranted only brief consideration. Yudel rejected it as unduly oppressive. He found Freek in the kitchen, packing groceries into a box. "Did you get her?"

"She's with Irena," Yudel said. It did not exactly answer the question, but it satisfied Freek.

"Attie is my cousin," Freek said. "He's got a small-holding outside town. We'd better stay away from your place. I don't want to assault another member of the special branch." He smiled, but the expression was uncertain. "I can't believe what happened outside. First that I find myself under surveillance and second that I treated that constable the way I did. Christ, Yudel, I almost pulled the trigger."

The cupboards in Attie's kitchen were enamelled steel, the cement floor covered in places by coarse rope mats and the walls made of prefabricated asbestos. Yudel, Freek and Magda sat round the small kitchen table, drinking coffee.

The farm was to the north of the city, at the closer edge of the broad sandy plain known as Springbok flats. Attie had met them at the front door, wearing a towelling dressing-gown from which naked hairy legs protruded. To Freek's request he had asked only one question: "Do you owe money?"

After Attie had returned to bed, Yudel and Freek had left Magda to settle the girls into strange beds and gone back to town to get a very reluctant General Scholtz, head of the detective branch in the Transvaal, out of bed. He had listened without comment for ten minutes when he interrupted Yudel. "So far as I am concerned, Mister Gordon, the special branch don't detain people without reason. If they want to detain you, I'm sure you know why." A few minutes later the interview had dissolved into a cold resentful silence with him saying, "Now yes, if you go scratching in their salad, you mustn't think they will like it."

Freek held one of Attie's large coffee mugs in both hands, drinking slowly, the steam from the hot liquid rising around his face, a few droplets condensing on skin, eyebrows and overhanging locks of hair. "There's a line I've crossed here," he said. "I can feel it. I think that's why I went for that constable. Nothing is going to be the same after this. Maybe I can save my job and rank, but they're all going to see me differently. The Lord knows, I see myself differently."

"It'll work out . . . " Magda tried to say.

"Do you know what it means for an officer to assault a constable?" Yudel had never seen him this unsure of the soundness of his own actions. Magda's eyes, that reflected her concern, never left her husband's face. "It wasn't that constable I was angry with. He didn't ask to be there. He's just another fool, following orders."

"If it helps," Yudel said, "I was with you all the time and I saw no one assault a constable."

There was no merriment in Freek's brief chuckle. "We'll see if you are still thought to be a credible witness after all this."

"What can I say?" Yudel was talking to Magda. When dealing with her he often felt like a child with an adult. Like Freek she always seemed so sure of herself and so acceptable wherever she went. Yudel had never been able to imagine a set of circumstances with which Magda would not be able to cope. "I'm sorry I got your man into this."

She was shaking her head to stop him. "It's not you, Yudel. It's everything. At other times we've come close to such crises. Some time or other it was going to happen."

Freek folded his hands around the mug he was holding, seeming to draw warmth from it. "The detective branch does not seek prosecutions against members of the special branch," he said. "When we come across something strange we stop looking or we go in some other direction. On occasions we've prosecuted an innocent party, knowing damn well that we had no case. Then when he gets off it gives the impression that justice has been done. You heard the general tonight, Yudel. If the special branch detains you, you must know the reason . . . "

For someone like Freek the security police and the radicals, black unionists, activists and guerillas were locked in their own private war. He would attend to the business of ordinary law enforcement while they conducted hostilities of which he chose to know nothing. In the past he had refused promotions that were attached to special branch postings.

Yudel knew all this and he knew what it was that made this time different. For Freek the difference lay only partly in the fact that his own house was being watched. The intention to detain Yudel was the major issue. Unspoken by any of them was the possibility, the barely acknowledged reality, that if he was taken in he might not come out alive.

"I want to tell you about something that happened to me as a young policeman, about the time we got married," Freek was saying. "It must be years since I last thought about it, but this whole business has brought it back.

"On my way home one night, walking from the bus stop in the days before we had our own transport, I saw a car cut in front of another and force it to a stop. The driver jumped out, pulled the other man from his car and started hitting him. It was late and dark and I couldn't see clearly, but the man who was being beaten didn't seem to be defending himself.

"I started running, shouting at them as I ran, but I was a long way down the road. By the time I got there the one who had been doing the punching was back in his car and the other one was on the ground with his arms wrapped round his head. It looked as if he had been pretty badly beaten. I stopped for a moment to help him to his feet, then I ran after his assailant. He already had his car started and was driving away with the lights switched off. I was young then and I ran like hell after him and actually got close enough to see the licence number.

"I made a note of it and started back to see what I could do for the victim. Naturally I thought he'd lay a charge. But he was gone too. He must have left as soon as I started chasing the other car because I didn't even see him go.

"Young constables don't open investigations on their own initiative, so the next morning I made a report in writing, giving the registration number of the assailant's car. After a month I had heard nothing so I put in a letter requesting to be informed of the matter's progress. A few days later a major phoned me and told me that if anything came of it they would let me know. I pointed out that we had the car's registration number and he told me that my seniors knew their work and, if anything came to light, they would let me know.

"Again I waited a month or so, then sent in a new letter. A week or two after that I was called up before a preliminary disciplinary hearing. There were three officers present and one, he was also a major, started by asking me to explain this complaint I had made against an officer.

"That I'd made a complaint against an officer was news to me and I said so. He had a lot of papers in front of him. He immediately started shuffling them around and grunted something about having the wrong case. I was young and innocent. It was only that night in bed that I realized what had happened.

"Well, he asked me to tell the whole story again and he pretended to make notes. When I finished they shook hands with me and said it would be investigated and I needn't worry any further. It was in their hands. That was the last I ever heard of it. They never came back to me and I never enquired again.

"It was the beginning of the end of my innocence and it taught me something about my country. You don't act against the members of your group. And no one was my group more than my fellow policemen."

Freek stopped speaking. With a large swallow, his cheeks flexing, he finished the last of his coffee. "And that's the problem we have on Monday. We've chosen both our friends and our enemies poorly."

Later, after everything had been said more than once, every possibility considered, every avenue pursued, there was nothing left to do, but try to sleep. Yudel went to the room Attie had invited him to use. For a while he sat at the open window with the light off, looking out at the invisible landscape of a moonless night.

As Freek had said, everything was going to be different now. All that either of them had accepted as being safe and secure had become uncertain. Status, respect, rank, pension, life itself: none of them could be taken for granted. All might be sacrificed to a society that could not afford to recognize the crimes of its special branch policemen.

Yudel wondered if Wheelwright and his friends were also having difficulty sleeping. Or were they confident that they would be able to deal with the small problem that Yudel and Freek represented? Were they safe in the knowledge of their power, the absolute certainty that no one would be able to touch them?

Twenty-Nine

The attorney-general of the Transvaal was a stern-faced man, nearing retirement, who showed no enthusiasm for convening an urgent meeting at the insistence of a police colonel. He had refused to start until both General Scholtz of the CID and Brigadier Momberg of the special branch arrived. "You are after all on Scholtz's staff," he told Freek. "And you want to talk about Momberg's people."

Scholtz arrived first. It was clear that for him Freek's insisting on meeting the attorney-general had compounded his error of Saturday night beyond any likelihood of rehabilitation. He had started apologizing to the attorney-general, explaining that Freek had no authority for this action, when Momberg came in. The special branch brigadier was tall, heavily built and had a tanned, fleshy face. It was the first time Yudel had seen him since his promotion party.

"Yes, mister," Momberg said to the attorney-general, "what's this I hear?" His tone of voice was designed to create an expansive effect. The question did not require an answer. He was smiling broadly and shook the hands of Scholtz and the attorney-general warmly. By now he would know how Freek had dealt with the constable set to watch his house. Yudel wondered how much else he knew about Wheelwright's activities and whether the special branch presence at the Attic and the detention order, at this moment waiting the minister's attention, had been directed by this man. Momberg did not offer Freek his hand. Stopping close, without looking directly at him, he muttered. "I must say that I'm disappointed, old friend, bitterly disappointed." He was unable even to acknowledge Yudel's presence.

"I think the floor belongs to you, Mister Gordon," the attorney-general said in English.

Scholtz made one last attempt to abort proceedings. "Mister attorney-general, this staff member of mine had no authority ... "

"We are here now. Let's hear what Mister Gordon has to say."

Yudel was the only person in the room whose home language was English, he responded in Afrikaans, talking directly to the department of Justice man and looking only at him. Had he turned his head he would have seen the scepticism and disapproval on Scholtz's still-chagrined face, the studied ease, one leg outstretched, of Freek's posture, and Momberg's complete disgust, the full lips twisted downwards at the corners of his mouth.

He had been speaking for less than a minute, picking his way carefully through the mass of material, when he mentioned the name Wheelwright for the first time. Immediately Momberg sat forward in his chair, waving both arms as if he was the referee in a contest and a foul had been committed. "Wait a bit, wait just a little bit. If one of my men is going to be slandered, I want him here to listen for himself."

Yudel stopped speaking. He could see that Momberg was trying to treat the matter as a staff problem that could be handled by getting the affected parties together and discussing it. The attorney-general nodded as if what Momberg was asking, was altogether normal. He glanced at his watch. "All right, gentlemen, I have very much to do this morning. Why don't you all come back at eleven? That should give you time to find Colonel Wheelwright, brigadier."

Scholtz and Momberg led the way into the corridor, Momberg contriving to stop in the doorway of the waiting room with a hand on one of Scholtz's shoulders, compelling Yudel and Freek to wait for him to move. "This is going to help nothing," Scholtz was saying. "This thing can have serious repercussions . . . " It was a term old man Williamson often used. To many senior civil servants avoiding repercussions was their primary function. "There's a way to do these things . . . "

Momberg's brotherly hand on Scholtz's shoulder seemed to be steadying him. "It's nothing, old friend, we'll handle it . . . " He half-turned towards Freek without looking directly at him. "You strayed off the path this time, little brother," he said. "I must tell you I'm very surprised."

Yudel could see the tightening of muscles in Freek's face. He was not a man who readily forgave humiliation. "Excuse me." Freek's voice sounded forced and under strain.

Momberg had not changed position, still blocking the door and not allowing his eyes to meet Freek's. "What's that, old friend? What are you asking now?"

"I said excuse me. You're in my way."

"You want to come past?" The idea appeared to surprise the brigadier. "This man wants to come past," he told Scholtz who had been listening to the conversation. "Let's go and find coffee. I'll send someone to fetch Colonel Wheelwright."

They moved out of the doorway, Momberg lingering a moment longer to demonstrate unequivocally where seniority and power lay. Freek strode past them and down the corridor to the lifts with Yudel trying to keep up. In the lift, Freek spoke to him. "You've got to handle this thing, Yudel." His face was white with anger. "We've got to show that bastard that he can play whatever games he likes, but it's not going to help him."

"Where are we going?"

"I've got a friend in this building. I want to make a call to Cape Town. I've got a man standing by there."

Freek's friend was out, but his office was open and Freek made the call. The conversation was brief, Freek nodding in acknowledgement, his face serious. After he had hung up he looked at Yudel. "The minister signed it without looking at the names. I told you he does that. What they put in front of him gets signed. It'll come back in the bag tonight and tomorrow they'll have it in black and white." It was not necessary for him to tell Yudel how important the morning was going to be for both of them or how strong a case he would have to make. For almost forty-eight hours it had been the only matter occupying their minds. "Now let's go to the canteen. If they're there I don't want them to think we're afraid of them."

"Aren't we?" Yudel asked.

"No. We do have a realistic appreciation of the odds though."

They entered the canteen fifteen minutes before they were due back in the attorney-general's office. Wheelwright had been found and was sitting at a table with Momberg and Scholtz. Only Scholtz looked up as they entered. Yudel saw him say something to the other two and Momberg incline his head in their direction in a vague dismissive gesture. Like his boss Wheelwright was careful not to look at them.

To Yudel it seemed that it was the very ordinariness of the surroundings, the office staff moving around the building, cups of coffee being dispensed, a sour-faced cleaning woman rubbing down a counter, that protected him. Sitting next to Scholtz and Momberg, Wheelwright's arrogant, bitter face offered no clue to what he was thinking. In this setting he did not easily fit into the events at the Attic. There had been no restraining normality on Saturday afternoon. All inhibition had been pruned away by the place's isolation, all attitudes revealed.

Yudel started slowly. He described the background to his involvement and his first meeting with Blythe Stevens, not sparing himself in any detail. He had already decided that once an official investigation got under way it would be impossible to hide anything.

At the mention of the money he had hoped to earn Momberg muttered, "There you have it, ignoring regulations." But the brigadier's interruption did nothing to stop the flow of Yudel's words. He had gone over what he needed to say many times on the day before and his near perfect memory kept fresh the details of each case. Now he was listening to his own voice, playing little conscious part in the direction the words were taking as his powerful ability to recall facts and details took control.

Yudel's fingers were pressing into his thighs and the muscles of his shoulders and back were drawn taut by the tension inside him. His breathing was quick and shallow and he could feel the

pressure in his forehead and jaw, caused by the almost unconscious effort he was making. He was aware that the tightly-
strung state of his nervous system was making everything much
easier. Nothing was lost through a lack of urgency or through
any part of him being too relaxed. Some inner part of his mind
was talking, tracing the events as he knew them, missing no
important detail and directing it all to the stern face of the
attorney-general.

He spoke about the background to his investigation, the
comprehensive detail in the pamphlet defaming the liberal law
professor, the small coincidences when acts of terrorism were
aimed at people in whom the security police were currently
showing an interest, and the larger coincidences, the events at
the Attic, how the attempt on his life had been made there and
how he had been trapped there by Wheelwright and his friends,
the crossbow bolt that had wounded him and the similar one
that had been fired into Professor van Deventer's study, the man
with the sagging eyelid like Wheelwright's who had held back
Elizabeth Ngcube's daughter at the Lesotho border on the night
the girl's father had been murdered, William van Ryneveld's
accusing of Milan Varrevich and that security policeman's
presence with Wheelwright at the Attic, the old newspapers with
the notes in the margins and the surprising omissions . . .

Suddenly Momberg was no longer able to contain himself.
"Where are these newspapers?" It was the angry confident
interjection of a man who knew the answer to his question. "All
I hear is circumstantial shit. Now I want to know where are
these newspaper clippings?"

The attorney-general, whose expression had grown gradually
more worried as Yudel was speaking, put the question. "Do you
have them, Mister Gordon?"

"No," Yudel said. "They were destroyed by Colonel Wheelwright and his friends."

Momberg threw up both arms in a gesture that was intended
to dismiss the entire matter finally and beyond all chance of
reopening it. "I've heard enough." He was on his feet. "All this
man has is slander with no real evidence." On the far side of
Momberg, Wheelwright had allowed himself the smallest of

smiles. "I don't think there's any reason for me or my colonel to stay."

"Is there more?" the attorney-general asked Yudel.

"Yes, there is."

"Then, General, I can't stop you from leaving, but I must hear everything Mister Gordon has to say."

Momberg had already taken a step towards the door and Wheelwright was on his feet. Before either could get back to the chairs they had been sitting in, Yudel was speaking, going on to other aspects of his investigation and what it had revealed. Without looking he was aware of them again taking their seats. It was a victory, but a very small one.

The case he was building relied on too many guesses and coincidences and was weakened by too many empty spaces. He knew that he was conducting a kind of dance, moving around the edges of the ballroom without ever reaching its centre. The core of it all was in his hands and, even if it was not conclusive, it would destroy Wheelwright. Yet the decision to use the material was not uncomplicated. The night before he had told himself that it was necessary and that he would have to do it, but despite this there was a part of him that held back.

Yudel needed time to think, but thinking was impossible under these conditions and, if he let this moment pass, there would be no further chances. He listened to his own voice, the words forming a delicate, fearful pattern now, as he retreated from the one thing that could protect him.

The attorney-general provided the relief he needed. "It's one o'clock," he said. Yudel looked at his watch. It seemed impossible that he could have been talking for two hours. "We'll meet back here after lunch. Two o'clock."

This time Yudel and Freek avoided the canteen. They found a sandwich bar in one of the many nearby arcades and sat down to a lunch to which neither gave much attention. "You have to do it," Freek said.

"Won't we be pillorying him for the wrong thing?"

"How many options do you have?" The list of detainees will

be on the way back from Cape Town this evening. You can't afford to be generous."

"I'm not even sure that it's entirely accurate . . . "

Freek was losing patience. "Come again. What have you been telling me? What about Du Plessis?"

"What we have here are two separate matters." Yudel was trying to explain it to Freek, but he was still struggling with his own understanding of the matter. "Going by what Neels Uys said, we are dealing with ordinary sexuality. If we look at the killing of Ray Baker and those three young activists and the rape of Robin Du Plessis, we are seeing the ugliest possible form of the need to exercise power over others."

"So what are you saying? Are you telling me at this late stage that they can't exist in the same personality?"

"No. Given the nature of Wheelwright's sexuality, that his distorted drive for power should show itself this way is logical."

"For Christ's sake, what is the problem then?"

"The problem is that to the attorney-general my evidence that Wheelwright raped Baker and the others before killing them will be as thin as the entire case so far."

"There's the sperm we took from that body."

"Can they force him to supply a sample?"

"The question is, will they, not can they?"

"If they don't all we'll prove is his homosexuality. And we'll destroy him for that, not because he's a murderer."

Freek, who had been leaning over the table, trying to get closer to Yudel, perhaps as a preliminary to shaking him, sank back in his chair. Yudel could see that he understood the problem and it was not without difficulties for him also. He shook his head to throw off all doubts. "It makes no difference. You have no choice in this. He's an evil bastard. Nothing else comes into it."

"Before this little man continues," Momberg was saying as Yudel entered the attorney-general's office, "I want my protest noted. As far as I am concerned he is just trying to defame my branch. I have heard nothing that could be used as evidence . . . "

305

The attorney-general was nodding in apparent agreement. Yudel knew that it would be best to save him the need to answer. "I haven't got much more," he said from the doorway.

Momberg's broad mouth twisted in distaste, he again contrived to avoid looking directly at Yudel. "You've got nothing. I've heard nothing, only gossip."

Yudel went directly to the chair he had occupied before lunch and sat down. The attorney-general and Freek followed. For the second time both security policemen were still on their feet when he started speaking. "We now come to the matter of the unnatural sexual acts performed on the detainee, Robin Du Plessis, who is willing to testify, and on the bodies of one white and three black activists before they were murdered. I have in my possession a sperm sample, obtained by the district surgeon of Pretoria . . . "

Yudel got no further. Wheelwright seemed to fly headlong across the room and Yudel was on the floor, his head and shoulders under part of the attorney-general's desk. Chairs crashed against the wall and someone was on his knees next to him. Momentarily he saw Wheelwright in profile, the normally immaculately positioned hair flying wild around his head, then he was gone, disappearing in a single spasmodic movement, his leather-soled shoes clattering across the floor. Another chair crashed over and slid heavily before coming to a stop and the room was still.

Looking cautiously from beneath the desk before emerging, Yudel rejoined the company. Wheelwright was pinned to a far wall by Freek's forearm pressed against his throat. "I've got evidence." His voice, gurgling with the constriction and higher-pitched than usual, shook with anger. "I've got evidence in my office." His chest was heaving with effort and emotion. The seemingly immovable control, the supreme arrogance that went with special branch inviolability, the unquestioned power: all were gone, lost in the fury and panic that went with the exposure of something far more shameful than the killing of a few activists. "You fucking moaf." The muscles on one side of his face were twitching independently of their owner's wishes. "You'll pay for this, moaf." It came from the word hermaphrodite and to many like Wheelwright it was the ultimate insult.

Freek released him, backing slowly away. Wheelwright turned the panic-stricken workings of his face towards his boss. "I've got evidence in my office. I've got plenty of evidence."

"Yes, then go fetch it." Momberg was gesturing with both hands, his head shaking from side to side, his big voice booming as he tried to regain the control his colonel had just lost. The moment had come upon him too quickly and the damage was as yet beyond assessing. "Go fetch it then."

Wheelwright was gone, leaving the door open. The girl from the waiting room, her tongue protruding between her lips at the unusual excitement, appeared briefly in the open door, then closed it. Yudel spoke. "Do you want me to continue?"

"You wait for my man." Momberg's voice held the tone of command.

"He's not coming back," Yudel told him.

Momberg was looking directly at Yudel for the first time now. His mouth opened as he tried to reply, but closed again without saying anything.

"He knows the truth. He can't come back."

"You'd better continue, Mister Gordon," the attorney-general said. "I'll tell you this though. This whole thing is going to need a ministerial decision."

"Wait." Momberg was talking to Yudel. In the same way that he had not been able to look at Yudel, now he was unable to look anywhere else. "You wait. First I'm going to phone. I'm going to phone Colonel Wheelwright's office."

"Phone security," Yudel said. "He's had enough time to reach the main entrance . . . " He left the thought unfinished.

It took a moment before Momberg moved to the phone. The attorney-general had leant back in his chair, offering him access to it. The brigadier dialled the number of the main entrance security. "Security. This is Brigadier Momberg. Has Colonel Wheelwright left this building in the last minute or two?" Yudel was watching his face and he saw the barely perceptible change, the slight pinching together of his lips, the hardness entering his eyes.

Momberg hung up and started towards the door. "I want him back here." It was a deep angry growl, but to Yudel it was

307

nothing more than a performance for the benefit of those in the room. It was the sort of reaction Momberg would want them to remember. "I want him back here now." Then he was gone. Like his colonel he did not close the door behind him.

Thirty

"I don't think he meant us," Yudel told Freek.

"You heard what he said. He said, I want him back here. I am a police officer. Momberg is my senior. I took that as an order." Freek smiled, a wry, sardonic expression. "I always do my duty."

Freek drove quickly, slipping red lights if he saw no traffic in the side streets, watching the speedometer rise above the speed limit. "By this time Momberg's own staff will be reacting," Freek said. "I want to bring him in myself."

The address was on Waterkloof Ridge, overlooking Pretoria's spreading, tree-filled suburbs. The area was home to the owners of large companies, cabinet ministers, a few heads of government departments, managing directors of the South African branches of international conglomerates and others who possessed the particular skills needed to accumulate large sums of money. It was not the sort of place where police officers lived. The house stood high above sloping lawns that were dotted by a network of stone-sided ponds. Substantial wings ranged to either side of a gabled façade in which a heavy wooden door was surrounded by stained glass windows that imitated the style of earlier centuries.

Freek parked in the drive, then led the way up the broad, curving stairs in the centre of the house. The door was standing open and he went in without knocking. He barely paused in the hall before moving through an arch into the passage that led to the wing on the right-hand side. Yudel had not seen Freek take out his revolver, but now he was carrying it in his right hand, holding it at shoulder level and pointing it at the ceiling.

They found Wheelwright in his study. This time he had closed the door behind him. Freek pushed it open, waited a moment for it to swing wide, then stepped into the opening. The security policeman was sitting at his desk, his elbows resting on the polished surface, his forehead supported by the points of his fingers. Next to one of his elbows was a half-empty bottle of brandy and a broad glass containing a little of the same liquid.

The room was large, with broad bay windows opening into the garden. On two sides the walls were decorated with the symbols of Afrikaner history. The yoke from a team of oxen, an old muzzle-loader rifle, the wheel of an ox wagon, its wooden spokes gleaming with fresh varnish: all were reminders of heroic deeds in other ages. The wall behind the desk was almost completely hidden by two large flags, one from the old Afrikaner republic and the other bearing the swastika of Gys Muller's Afrikaner Revival Movement.

Wheelwright looked up as they came in. The movement was slow and preoccupied until the shock of seeing them jerked his head back. Yudel saw his right hand make for the drawer on that side of the desk. Before it had travelled more than a few centimetres Freek's voice froze its movement with the certainty of a physical obstruction. "I'll easily kill you," he said. "I won't lose a single night's sleep over it."

The hand that had been moving to the drawer hung suspended above the desk, then sank slowly to its surface. A brief shudder passed through Wheelwright's head and shoulders and was gone. He averted his eyes and reached for the bottle of brandy. His hand shook as he poured a little of the liquid into the glass and brought it to his lips. His greying hair that, until an hour ago, Yudel had only seen carefully slicked back in immaculate order now hung over his forehead in tangled disarray. His tie had been removed and, with his jacket, occupied the front of the desk. The drooping eyelid was heavier than ever, almost closing over its eye. But it was the loss of control, the unsteadiness of his hands and the shudder, that again passed quickly through him that surprised Yudel. "This is my house. What are you doing in my house?" He had found his power of speech, but the sound of his voice was ragged and uneven.

"You're coming in with us."

"Let me see your warrant." Wheelwright managed a smile, a bitter extending of his features.

"I don't need one," Freek said. "You're a police officer and so am I and I'm acting under orders from your superior. I don't need a warrant." There was no gloating, no enjoyment of any sort in Freek's voice, nothing that suggested this was anything more than business. "Yudel, get the gun out of his desk drawer."

Yudel came out from behind Freek, passed round the desk, carefully staying out of any possible line of fire. He found the automatic under stationery in the top drawer. "Little Jew, this means nothing," Wheelwright said. "Your day will . . . " He lost the direction into which his threat was developing. Instead he raised the brandy glass to his mouth, spilling a few large drops on the desk as he drank it down.

"Get on your feet." Freek's voice offered no possibility of an argument. "This is a direct order from your superior officer."

"Who's my superior officer?" Wheelwright leaned slowly forward and drew a sheet of paper from beneath his jacket, leaving it where Freek could see it. "I have no superior officer."

Freek took the paper from him and Wheelwright chuckled, a coarse croaking sound. Yudel was watching Freek and saw the surprise come into his face. "The bastard has resigned," he said.

Wheelwright's ravaged laughter subsided into a few final disjointed chuckles. He spoke to Freek: "You have chosen sides against your own people. You could have been with us. You were one of us. You were a man we could have used. Instead you chose this Jew above your own kind. We have a list of names, old friend. And we won't forget you. You will have to pay for your foolishness.

"These people who are running the country now, they are not true Afrikaners. Where do you think all these reforms are leading? Do you want to see Afrikaner women and children in concentration camps again? Do you want to see your family ruled by the kaffirs? Do you want your wife and daughters raped and murdered? You want the genocide of your own people? You and your type, Jordaan, you've learnt none of the lessons of Africa." Something of its usual control had returned to his voice. "You're a fool. You could have been with us."

Yudel reached out a hand as if to restrain Freek. "Don't answer. There's nothing to say."

"Listen to the little Jew. This time he's right. For once he's right."

Freek took the automatic from Yudel and went to an open window. With a long sweep of his arm he threw the gun, its high looping trajectory ending in one of the fish ponds. "Let's go and report, Yudel." He slipped Wheelwright's resignation into one of his inside pockets. "This belongs on file."

In the doorway Yudel paused to look back. The former security policeman seemed to have forgotten about them. He was staring at the point on his desk where his letter of resignation had lain. The hard, dissolute face looked curiously pensive. For the moment the violence that was part of his personality was hidden.

By the time Yudel reached the broad stairs in front of the house Freek was already at the car and a second vehicle was stopping in the drive. Two men, in plain clothes, whom Yudel recognized as being special branch operatives, got out. They took a few suspicious, bewildered steps towards Freek and stopped. "Jordaan," one said, "what are you doing here?"

"My job," Freek said. He gestured towards the house. "You can forget about him. He's not coming back."

Epilogue

After leaving the house on Waterkloof Ridge, Freek drove directly to the building in which Brigadier Momberg had his office. The Pretoria head of the special branch received Wheelwright's resignation without comment and without looking at Freek.

On the next day, Tuesday 29th April, a further meeting was held with the attorney-general of the Transvaal who said that, while Yudel's story gave grounds for concern, he doubted that it would stand up in court. He agreed to accept the charge of common assault for the incident at the Attic, to treat the rest as a priority and to make a decision before the week was over.

On the Thursday the attorney-general's office opened a murder docket against the former security policeman. By that time Wheelwright had been appointed to a leadership position in the Afrikaner Revival Movement in the northern Transvaal and himself became the subject of a security police file.

Friday saw the deputy minister, a tall square-faced man with a friendly and self-deprecating manner, fly in from Cape Town, where parliament was in session, to deal with the matter personally. After reviewing the evidence he instructed the attorney-general to halt proceedings. "Consider the position he now holds," he told a small meeting to which Yudel was invited. "Suppose we compel him to undergo testing and we find that it was not his sperm in the black youth, do we want to give these people that sort of propaganda weapon? The case, in any event, hangs on the semen. The rest is speculation. And, if he is found guilty, think how our enemies overseas will use it."

The men who had been with Wheelwright at the Attic turned out all to be security policemen and all filed affidavits disputing Yudel's version of events. After further consideration the attorney-general declined to prosecute the assault charge either. The authorization to detain Yudel that the minister had signed on the Monday was never put into effect.

Milan Varrevich's presence with Wheelwright at the Attic, six hundred kilometres from his own sphere of jurisdiction, was the subject of a separate departmental investigation. He was warned for acting without the knowledge of his seniors and a report entered in his personal file.

The Du Plessis brothers slipped across the border into Botswana shortly after Yudel had last questioned Robin. Ralph went on to London where he joined the staff of a famous university. Robin crossed into Zambia and made his way to the offices of the ANC in Lusaka. He was given a clerical job and contracted AIDS from a typist.

Reverend Dladla was elected a community councillor, a government-sponsored position. The authorities, not realizing that Fred One-night Tuwani had been an activist, decided to employ his death for propaganda purposes. On the morning when they asked the security police to check on Tuwani the computer was down and a junior operator told them that they had nothing on a man by that name. As a result the name of the library where Dladla works was changed to the Frederick Tuwani Public Library. Dladla's wife, Flora, divorced him and became a Jehovah's Witness.

Blythe Stevens also left the country to settle in London where he is an active member of the Anti-Apartheid Movement. He is currently working on a thesis entitled, "The Myth of Terrorism".

The Reverend Markus Mbelo was elected to the executive of the National Forum, a political body that excludes whites. During the winter of 1987 he suffered a stroke while having intercourse with his sullen, obese receptionist, leaving the left side of his face paralysed. On a visit to London he was given a standing ovation at a meeting of expatriate South Africans. Blythe Stevens, who had introduced him, told them the damage had been caused by a police baton.

Phineas, the cleaner, did not get his house. He died of tuberculosis the same year.

Lionel Bensch and his family slowly gained control of the fear that had been thrust into their lives. Bensch found a special peace of his own on many trips with his son, Willie, among the great ramparts of the Drakensberg mountains. He did not long remain the only former member of the ANC's military wing to be living freely in the country. In 1989 a new State President released many of Bensch's former colleagues who had been serving jail sentences for their activities.

As the years passed, Professor Marius van Deventer discovered that he was not a leper among all Afrikaners and Afrikaner organizations. He has responded to many invitations to address gatherings, but it took his prestige some time to recover from the humiliation of being tarred and feathered by good Afrikaner boys.

Poena van der Merwe, head clerk in the transport section, received a commendation for vigilance, a special increment to his salary and the use of his own departmental car on weekdays.

Dahlia left South Africa a year after the last time she saw Yudel. She phoned him and gave him the time when she would be passing through Jan Smuts Airport. He had intended to go, but was distracted by an emergency in Pretoria Central. By the time he was free he had forgotten about her flight. That evening in his study he remembered and felt guilty intermittently for a week. She settled in Manchester and became secretary to the local branch of a large trade union, where she played a role in the dissolution of the branch chairman's marriage.

Freek had been wrong about the killings ending. The assassinations continued. In the years that followed, black activists disappeared off the street never to be seen again, while others died in shootings, stabbings and beatings. In some cases the bodies of the victims were burnt. Black political figures who favoured cooperation with the government also died in assassinations and mob killings, the pendulum of violence continuing to swing back and forth between the extremes of left and right, leaving few immune from its depredations.

Freek's part in Yudel's investigation was rewarded by his being passed over for promotion for the fifth time. The reason given to him was that he had assaulted a member of the force. He dismissed the lost promotion by telling Yudel, "It's all right. Colonel is not a bad rank."

Rosa was fetched by Irena when Yudel failed to come home on the Saturday night. She stayed for two months. Towards the end of the period she filed for divorce, but withdrew it the next day. After a two-hour lecture from Magda Jordaan she returned to Yudel on condition that he would never again become involved in political crimes.

After Wheelwright's resignation Brigadier De Beer called Yudel into his office and told him that as far as he was concerned Yudel was vindicated in every possible way, but if he drew even the slightest attention to himself during the six years before De Beer's retirement he would personally kick his arse all the way down the stairs and out of the building.

Yudel never doubted that Wheelwright and Varrevich had been involved in some of the crimes. He would have wagered anything he possessed on the proposition that a sperm sample taken from Wheelwright would have matched that found in the young activist. Freek acquired a sample of Wheelwright's handwriting and Yudel compared it, employing only his excellent memory as a reference, to the script of the newspaper pages in the Attic and believed that they were the same, but this too was of no more than curiosity value.

Whether Baker had died by the same hand as the three comrades, and as for the killings of Fellows and Elizabeth Ngcube, the attempts on the lives of Bensch, Subramoney and himself, or whether the older man at the Lesotho border the night Ngcube had died, had been Wheelwright, Yudel turned away from it all to immerse himself in problems that offered a better prospect of solution.

In 1990, four years after Wheelwright's resignation, a small, uncertain spot of light was shed on the matter when a judicial commission of inquiry into the death squads was brought into being. Before it began its work Brigadier Momberg sought and was granted early retirement. The evidence presented to the commission indicated that a branch of military intelligence might have been responsible for some of the killings and the security police for some others, but the majority of the cases remained in complete darkness with no evidence led and none available.

For a long time Yudel was made aware by newspaper reports of the activities of Gys Muller and his movement. Occasional casual remarks by fellow civil servants showed him that Muller was not without support. Every day, degree by gradual degree, the inevitability of majority rule grew. Many white South Africans felt that the new State President's government had gone soft and perhaps a strong man was the answer. Perhaps then the inevitable might no longer be inevitable. Yudel tried to close his mind to it, but there were times when for weeks he was haunted by the image of the Afrikaner Revival Movement's swastika. He could not rid himself of the fear that the single-minded self-assurance that was so much a part of Muller might eventually be a deciding factor. On more than one occasion he saw Wheelwright's unsmiling face in the background of press photographs at Muller's rallies. In all of them he was dressed in the uniform of the movement and never far from his leader's side.

Arnoldus Du Toit of Sandown Private Investigations had a brief respite from the anxiety that caused him to sleep with a loaded revolver under his pillow when Milan Varrevich was recruited for an armed adventure in a neighbouring state. Varrevich and the rest of the party were taken prisoner by the police of that country. In court he wept, begged for mercy and denounced the South African government. While in prison he was visited by Maureen Baker who was still searching for her son's killer when she died of cancer in 1988. The diplomatic service arranged Varrevich's release less than a year after he was imprisoned and he returned to South Africa to take up an executive position in a private security company.

It was shortly after this that Yudel passed him crossing Church Square in the centre of Pretoria. He was wearing dark glasses, but the recognition was immediate and mutual. Yudel stopped and Varrevich slowed his stride, both involuntary reactions. Then the former security policeman averted his face and hurried on.

The flask with the frozen semen is still at the bottom of Magda Jordaan's freezer, among the meat, fish and vegetables. Occasionally, when searching for something or rearranging its contents, she has been tempted to throw it out, knowing that her husband will never be able to use it. So far she has resisted the temptation.